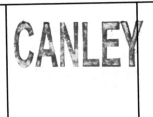

Jane Elmor has lived most of her life in London, where her occupations have included playing in bands, dealing in vintage clothes, co-writing/producing a comedy musical in fringe theatre and composing for short films and TV . . . amongst other things. *My Vintage Summer* is her first novel.

MY VINTAGE SUMMER

It all began in the summer of '76. The year the sun scorched the grass the colour of sand and no one could sprinkle their lawns or take a bath, and the year Lizzie could no longer run around without her top on . . . Schoolgirl friends Lizzie and Kim grow from small-town adolescents to women on the hedonistic stage of London in the early eighties. There they join Kim's older sister, Vonnie, an untameable force of nature who is everything they'd like to be . . . or is she?

JANE ELMOR

MY VINTAGE SUMMER

Complete and Unabridged

CHARNWOOD
Leicester

First published in Great Britain in 2008 by
Pan Books
an imprint of Pan Macmillan Ltd.
London

First Charnwood Edition
published 2009
by arrangement with Pan Macmillan Ltd.
London

British Library CIP Data

Elmor, Jane
My vintage summer.—Large print ed.—
Charnwood library series
1. Teenage girls—England—London—Fiction
2. Female friendship—Fiction 3. Sisters—Fiction
4. London (England)—Social life and customs—
Fiction 5. Bildungsromans 6. Large type books
I. Title
823.9'2 [F]

ISBN 978-1-84782-573-5

Published by
F. A. Thorpe (Publishing)
Anstey, Leicestershire

Set by Words & Graphics Ltd.
Anstey, Leicestershire
Printed and bound in Great Britain by
T. J. International Ltd., Padstow, Cornwall

This book is printed on acid-free paper

Acknowledgements

Thank you to Rebecca Saunders, Julia Churchill, Lucie Whitehouse, Elizabeth Wright, Joanne King, Jill Harris, Tessa Hadley, Simon London, my family and friends — without whom, etc.

Prologue

The locks on the door to the top flat are smashed and broken but it still takes several fumbling attempts to open it. When it is finally pushed ajar, a stench flees through the crack, as though desperate to escape. It is the worst smell you could ever imagine, like sour milk, old sweat, fish, eggs and hair-removing cream liquidizing into a rotten soup. We shrink back for a moment before forcing the door wider against the open rubbish bags lining the dark corridor, leaking brown discharge into the bare floorboards. The opening door disturbs a hum of lazy, overfed flies, which rise and resettle. Roaches scuttle into the walls. Hand over mouth, I follow Kim as she rushes to the kitchen to open the glass door onto the tiny roof terrace. There is only just enough room for us to step out and stand without touching more piles of decaying waste, oozing like an acid trip with parasitic life. We both retch.

'*Oh my God . . .* '

We share a look, grimace; I hear myself laugh nervously.

'Let's try and open all the windows — get a breeze flowing through.'

Holding our breath we return inside to prise open the kitchen window, held shut with nails

1

and masking tape. We find tools — a dirty knife and spoon from the sink — to try to bend the nails away from the frame, returning to the terrace for gulps of air. We can't shift it. Kim leads me back down the corridor to the bedsitting room at the front of the flat. Two sash windows behind pinned-up blankets give more easily thanks to rotted frames, letting in street noise and heavy dub bass. We hang thankfully out of a window each.

Kim pulls down the blanket at her window and turns back inside, so I do the same, beginning to view the room through the dust motes careering in the shafts of sunlight. A Marshall amp and speaker dominate the space. A battered bass guitar in a sunburst finish leans against it, plugged in with a curly lead. A stained, burnt mattress with a sleeping bag takes up a corner of the bare floor. The only other furniture is a heaped clothing rail and shelving made from boxes turned onto their sides. Crumpled clothing spills across the floor. Thigh-length boots and odd stiletto shoes, a pair of worn-out ballet pumps. An old record player and ghetto blaster are surrounded by piles of albums and cassettes. Bottles and cans everywhere. Dozens of candles sit in hardened pools of wax around the fireplace. Above them, Tarot cards, silk scarves, smears of something decorate the walls, all arranged in the shape of crosses. I move closer and jump. An intricate pyre of cigarette ends and rotting fruit in the grate crawls with maggots.

'*Shit* . . . ' Kim is back in the corridor at the

bathroom door, peering in. I go to look. I can hear the drone of bluebottles before I see anything. My eyes grow accustomed enough to see that the toilet is filled up to its rim and that dried blood and puke splatter the floor and sink and smear the mirror. We shut the door.

We need rubber gloves and newspaper and bags and bleach and disinfectant. A welcome excuse to leave and steel ourselves better for our return.

A woman in flip-flops opens the door of the flat below as she hears us on the stairs. She yells in Spanish, pointing angrily at her ceiling.

'Yes, we know. We're sorry. We're coming back to clean. Five minutes. Cinco minutos.'

'You've remembered your Spanish!' We giggle as we run down the stairs.

Out on the street I light a cigarette, hands shaking. 'Oh my God,' I say again.

Kim shakes her head, stunned. 'I had no idea it'd got that bad. She wouldn't let me in any more.'

We walk towards the shops in freaked-out silence. The flat is in the only shabby building left in the row. Looking through the windows as we go by reveals open-plan conversions with polished wood floors sweeping through to backs with chrome fitted kitchen areas and French windows opening out onto decked courtyards. The housing association is sitting on a gold mine. I'm not surprised they've been trying to get rid of their sitting tenant for so long.

I struggle to find something a friend should say.

'Are you sure you can handle doing this, Kim? Maybe we should get, like, a professional cleaning company in or something.'

'Wimping out?' She's half joking, eyeing me sardonically.

'I didn't mean that. I can cope if you can.' I almost wish she couldn't, though. 'It's just. It must be awful for you.'

'Yeah, but. I just thought. There might be some sort of clue or . . . something that would help us understand. I don't know. Probably not.' Kim's voice struggles through her tightening throat. 'I just wanted to do something for her.'

'How're Patti and Jeff?' I say.

'Well,' she shrugs awkwardly. 'They're staying with their friends in Shepherd's Bush so they're not too far from the hospital. Dad's been drinking too much; his blood pressure's up. He's a state, really. Mum's more practical. It's her that went to see the housing trust to try and deal with all the problems. She says in a way maybe it'll all be for the best, in the long run. Vonnie couldn't have gone on, living like that. Of course, that upsets Dad even more. But maybe she's right. Maybe this could be a turning point.'

'Yeah,' I agree, in as hopeful a tone as I can muster. I don't ask how she is. We have formed over the years a way of skirting over the difficult things. It's never seemed a problem in our friendship. If anything, it's been one of its strengths. Kim is the one person I'm as sure as you can ever be that I'll know when I am really old.

We get the cleaning stuff from a pound shop

and buy a couple of takeaway milky coffees from the only proper caff left. Calmer now, more ready.

Inside, we put on gloves and make head holes in the top of black bin bags, wearing them, the way squares used to do for fancy dress parties when they went as punks. We start by putting the rubbish into new sacks and taking them out to the street. The flip-flop lady looks out again, tutting as we clump up and down. The main room is the easiest after that. The pyre is scooped onto newspaper and put in two bags. We don't know how to kill maggots. We just shiver and gag and throw disinfectant over the ruddy stain.

'I think I should take the bass and amp,' says Kim. 'Just in case. You never know who could get into this place. I'll get Paolo to bring the van tomorrow.' Drummers. Useless father figures, but they do have vans. Kim flicks the switch to test it. The speaker crackles as it warms up and I thrum the strings of the bass.

'Seems to be working.'

It's a Fender Jazz, circa 1976, really nice. I want to sling the strap round my shoulder and play it, but it doesn't seem right. I switch it off.

Kim is starting to pick cautiously through things. 'Hey, remember this?' She holds up a cracked old leather jacket with *Loose* painted on the back in white nail varnish. 'Remember her having to pick off the letters the first time she wrote it 'cos she spelt it *Lose*?'

We laugh then, really laugh, until Kim puts her arm in front of her face as her laughter contorts into crying, the jacket hanging limp from her other hand as she stands there in the middle of the room. She tries to control her features. She has her mother's lucky genes and could still pass for thirty, except for the creases around her eyes and mouth that hang about for a beat after her expressions, like sustain. I don't know how to comfort her. There seems to be too much space between us. I approach but she turns away from me, embarrassed, and says, 'I'm OK.'

I tear off a black bag and hold it open for the jacket. 'That's got to be one to keep, I think.'

Kim sniffs it and wrinkles her nose. 'I'm not so sure.'

She holds it out for me and my nostrils flinch at the sharp, acrid stink. Sweat, alcohol, fags, something else. I poke my rubbered fingers gingerly into the inside pocket and they come out with a briny mulch on the tips.

'Yeah, maybe not.'

Kim turns away with her eyes shut. I don't know what to say. I take the jacket and dump it in the bin bag and go to wash my gloves in the kitchen.

'Maybe you really shouldn't do this,' I try again on my return.

'I'm all right now, really. Anyway, what can we find now that's worse?'

It's hard to imagine.

Kim goes through a pile of ragged clothes.

'I'm scared to look.'

Everything is rank and mottled with mildew. Several Fifties cotton blouses in greying pastels, stained and torn. A cocktail dress with limp bows

6

and fringes and a broken zip held with safety pins. Those ski pants we all used to wear with the stirrups under the feet; how funny they look now. Sixties suit skirts taken in tight with terrible hand-stitching. She hadn't even cut off the excess material, just left it bunched at the seams. It hadn't seemed odd, at the time, on her. A silk kimono that crumbles at a touch, devoured by moths. Hardly anything that can be saved by a wash.

And, oh my God, my white dress. The one I got from Camden market at the start of it all, the one she wanted. 'It's a Vonnie dress,' she'd said, but it was mine because I saw it first. I loved it, I really did. Straight, simple, with spaghetti straps and a scoop neck, made from some sort of bubbly silk that you never see any more. I felt like one of the Vandellas in it. I wore it with black kitten heels and bare legs and my black three-quarter-length leather coat, with the big matching buttons left undone. I was in my Moddy phase: hair dyed blackest black, shaved up the back and back-combed high, curving down into points around my cheeks. I remember feeling beautiful when I looked like that. Everyone said the look suited me. I wore it like an identity. It was like being somebody else.

She must have rescued it years later when it didn't fit me any more. I'd put on weight and the seam taken in around the bum had finally given out. I think about keeping it, but it looks beyond saving.

Eventually, Kim needs to pick Franklin up from school. Franklin wants to visit Vonnie, but

Kim doesn't think it's a good idea just now. She plans to distract her by shopping for new trainers. Franklin wants Converse ones, like Kim's. Imagine, being a teenager and wanting the same shoes as your mother. Times have changed.

We pour bleach wherever we can. Relief and disinfectant begin to overpower the smell. We wash our gloves in the kitchen and I go to put the new cleaning things in the cupboard under the sink, but Kim suddenly lurches forward to stop me.

'Don't look in there,' she says quickly, her hand tightly gripping my arm. Her urgency makes my heart race. Whatever she knows is in there, I don't want to see.

'When does this have to be cleared up by?' I ask as we leave.

'As soon as. The fumigators are coming on Wednesday. I'll come back tomorrow for the bass and the amp and anything else I should look after.'

'Do you want me to come?'

'No, I'll be fine. I'll have Paolo with me. Thanks for coming today.'

'It's OK. Call me if I can help. I don't mind.'

'All right.'

But I hope she doesn't. I hear excuses running through my head already, the way they did when Kim first called.

The tube station is in the opposite direction from Franklin's school, but I stroll along with Kim. Toby is away working, as usual, securing a deal for his hot new band in Japan. I don't feel

8

like going back to an empty house.

I haven't walked around these streets for years. Funny really, considering it was the only place I ever thought I really belonged. Saying you lived in West Eleven was better than saying your name. It said so much more about you, and made you so much more. Made you someone. You were In with the In Crowd. It was the only place I'd lived in London where I'd known several people in the same street, people I wanted to know. We'd drop in on each other, whenever, and just hang out. It's all we ever seemed to do, although 'doing' didn't really come into it. I can't remember what it involved. I wouldn't know how to hang out now.

'Wasn't this Ruby's place for a while?' asks Kim, as we pass a basement room that could possibly be the one she rented for a time from a Portuguese couple who didn't mind her practising trumpet. Neither of us can remember the number, although at the time we were round there every other day. If it is the one it's unrecognizable now, with a patio and pots of expensive plants, where it used just to be the place you passed the bins to get in and out. I ask Kim if she's heard from Ruby, but she hasn't. How could even friends like Ruby drift out of your life so easily? Soulmates that shared your wild dreams. Last Kim heard she'd gone into social work and was buying a flat with her boyfriend.

We pass the flea markets where we bought all our clothes and records. I can't help but look out for the guy with the quiff who pressed rare

9

rockabilly records and always gave me a freebie. Of course he's long gone, unless he went into importing oriental furniture in the shop that's there now. And there's the house where the rock star lived, who you coolly treated like anybody else, just saying, 'All right?' as you passed him in the street. He smiled at you more when you were blonde. I saw on the news that he'd died. Kim says someone we knew went to the funeral. It was 'great', apparently. They were re-releasing his back catalogue on CD.

The old men's pub on the corner. Where's the old Rasta who was always sitting on the pavement outside grinning, swaying his mossy locks to the reggae? I glance in. It's become a bar with cool blue neon strips and modern art on the walls to replace the old maroon flock wallpaper. It is filled with young white men with salon haircuts and designer jeans talking on mobiles. Loud music blares out, chart music.

'Chirst, when did it become OK to listen to this stuff?' I try to joke, but neither of us laughs. We fall quiet as our shared past seeps into us like fine rain. We pass the corner where we used to busk and the wall we graffitied with the name of our band, to make it look as though we had a following. There's a billboard up there now, rotating advertisements for Orange, United Colors of Benetton and a TV show putting together a brand-new girl band.

But we are seeing Vonnie posing in her stilettos, slapping the double bass she managed to nick for a time off Billy, as she sucked in her cheeks for the photos. Hearing the echoes of

Kim and Ruby's horns, and their laughter as they were introduced as the *Bra Section*. Feeling the rhythms that Nick bashed out on bongos and congas and toy marimbas and anything else she could find, while I strummed the bust-up old flamenco guitar I found in a skip. And Ava's wild voice, dancing around the racket while she danced around the crowd gathered about us as though we were the very centre of everything.

The excitement flickers from its embers once again, before dying back into a wistful ash.

As we turn into my old road I am haunted by my own ghost. It is as if a drop of the essence of me lingered on when I left, infusing the atmosphere like patchouli. My ether, forever padding up and down in winklepicker shoes, tiny steps from too-tight skirts, arm swinging the snakeskin vanity case. I copied that from her, apparently. I was stealing her identity, she said, when she had it out with me. I'd said I didn't know what she was talking about, and I'd thought, how can anyone's identity rest so precariously on the swing of a handbag?

But it had, obviously.

I suddenly hope I don't see anyone I used to know. I don't want them to see me now, without my Sixties eyes. I don't want to see them now, either. But I recognize no one and no one recognizes me. The people have changed. I don't know why I'm surprised by that.

Franklin strolls out of the school gates with her friends. She is so at ease, so urban, leggy and narrow-hipped in flared burgundy school trousers. Who would have thought the Seventies

11

would've ever come back in? Nobody who'd seen them the first time round, that's for sure.

'Aren't those your old trousers?' I joke with Kim, to chase away the shadows as Franklin spots us and wanders over.

'I never had anything that gross.'

'You did! They weren't gross at the time; they were really cool. Your family were always so trendy.'

'But you hated trendy things.'

'I didn't. I was jealous as hell.'

'Were you? I'm sure you said you hated trendy things. I remember thinking you were really cool like that.'

'Did you?'

It is news to me. How funny, to find out Kim had thought me cool. I'd always been so desperate to impress her, and never thought I had.

'I probably only said I hated anything trendy because I could never compete. Remember those awful boys' shoes I made my mum get me when you got your wedges, and everyone teased me mercilessly because they looked like brothel creepers? Or when I was desperate for a denim dress like yours and my mum got me one from Littlewoods with puffed sleeves and a floral S-belt? God, you laughed at me.'

'Did I? What a horrible friend! Why did you ever put up with me?'

'No one else would, remember. We weren't exactly popular.'

Franklin is here. She is unembarrassed by her mum, just kisses us on the cheek like we are friends and rolls her eyes good-humouredly when I say how much she's grown. When did I

12

become the kind of parents' friend that says that kind of thing? She is going to be beautiful. She has her mum's bones and her dad's skin, and hair a cross between the two, tamed into a knot for school. I'd have given anything to look like that when I was her age. She is fourteen — the age Vonnie was when I first met her. It is astounding. To me now, Franklin seems so young and innocent. To me then, Vonnie was so grown up and already filled with all the knowledge you'd need to go out in the world. Even when, with my adult eyes, I try to picture her at fourteen, I can't see her for the kid she must have been. However much time has warped me into this other age and place and time, Vonnie will always be one step ahead of me.

We imagined we would have kids at the same time, Kim and I, the way best friends often do. But Franklin was an accident and Kim couldn't face an abortion, even if she didn't feel ready to be a mum. I'd thought she was too young. There was still so much we wanted to do with our lives. I remember thinking it like it was yesterday. Being excited about all the things I wanted to achieve. There was still time. Becoming mothers just didn't come into it — kids would have got in the way. I'd felt sorry for Kim.

If I'd had a daughter then too, would she and Franklin be best friends? I half wish I had. I have a sudden understanding, for the first time, of why people have kids. It's like living it all again without having to actually go through it.

You could be glad they have it all in front of them, for their sake and your own.

1

Lizzie

For us it all began in the summer of '76, the year the sun scorched the grass the colour of sand and no one could sprinkle their lawns or take a bath, and the year I could no longer run around without my top on. According to my best friend Kimberley, my boobs were already as big as her sister Yvonne's, even though I was only eleven and she was nearly fifteen. It wasn't saying much. Kimberley called Vonnie's gnat bites, they were so small. If mine kept on growing I would have to ask my mum if she would buy me a bra and I couldn't think of anything more embarrassing. Getting boobs was even worse than starting your periods because they were harder to hide from boys. Before I'd ever met Vonnie I wanted to be like her, just because it didn't sound as though she'd ever need a bra. She'd got away with something and to me that made her seem free.

That summer was the first time I was allowed to go and stay with Kimberley for the weekend.

'You'll probably think Vonnie's pretty,' Kim had said. 'She certainly thinks so. But I don't. If you ask me, she's pretty ugly.'

Kimberley wasn't speaking to Vonnie when we became best friends. She couldn't remember what they had fallen out over in the first place, but whatever it was, their fight lasted for months. It made me scared to meet her; she seemed so mean. The first night I was there she was out, but we heard her let herself in way after we'd gone to bed. Her dad hadn't gone to pick her up or anything. I was on a zed bed, as close to Kim's as it could possibly be, and we were still awake, giggling in the dark at the thought of Miss Hodge and Miss Miller being lesbians.

Kim's house wasn't like other people's. She said it was because her dad was an architect and he'd designed it himself and had it built on a bit of land on the outskirts of a posh village. It was big and white and modern with huge windows and no wallpaper and instead of an upstairs it sprawled about, with arches and walkways through to other bits. Her mum and dad had their bedroom in an annexe with their own TV and en-suite bathroom with a shower. When they went to watch TV after dinner it was almost like being alone in the house with no grown-ups. From Kim's bedroom we could hear the front door open and close and someone banging around in the kitchen.

'She's probably drunk,' Kim said. 'And I bet she's been *snogging*.'

I went, 'Urgh.' We thought about snogging for a while.

'Has she got a boyfriend, then?' I asked.

'Oh lots,' said Kim. 'One of them gives her lovebites and Mum calls him the Vampire.'

I tried to imagine my mum joking about my boyfriend. Not even my only boyfriend, *one* of my boyfriends. She always invited my new friends round for tea to check they were suitable, but I didn't know if she'd do that if it was the kind of person who'd bitten my neck. I thought I'd rather die than sit up at the table at my house eating lettuce and Marmite sandwiches with my mum and Mr Grundy and my *boyfriend*. I really couldn't think of anything worse. And then I tried to imagine having a boy attached to my neck by his mouth. Was it something boys liked, or were you supposed to like it? And what were you supposed to be doing while he was stuck there? I didn't think I wanted a boyfriend.

After a while Kim leant over and whispered, 'Vonnie says she's Done It, but I don't believe her.' We thought about that for a while too.

Eventually I said, 'Did it hurt?'

'She said it was agony and she bled pints of blood all over the sheets. She had to wash them herself before Mum saw.' Of course I'd imagined Doing It before, but not where. I certainly couldn't imagine doing it in my mum's house.

I was thinking up the right questions to ask without looking too stupid when a shadow loomed into the light that was breaking through the crack in the bedroom door from the hallway. I looked up as the door was pushed wide and a silhouette leant against the door frame. An orange outline of wild, corkscrew hair flared out over a big, upturned collar. A glow moved from hip height to mouth level, where it brightened for a moment before an exhalation of smoke drifted up towards the huge moon of a paper lantern behind.

16

'Wonders will never cease,' Vonnie slurred, taking another drag of her cigarette. 'Kimmie's actually found a friend.' She blew the smoke into the room at us and her breath smelt of something else strong and sharp and fiery. It made her seem like a dragon.

'Go away, you stupid old witch,' Kim spat.

Vonnie cackled and went, 'Ooooooh!'

'I mean it! Get out! Get out!' Kim was going crazy. 'I hate you!'

The shadow kicked the door wide and slunk towards us cackling, stretching out its spindly fingers towards our beds and grabbing at our feet. Even though I knew it was Kim's sister it spooked me and we both started screaming and scrabbling to the heads of our beds.

'Shut up. Mum and Dad'll hear you, you baby,' Vonnie suddenly snapped and stopped laughing. She took a final swipe at Kim before putting her thumb to her teeth and flicking it towards us as she turned to flounce away.

'That's an Italian rude word,' said Kim when she had gone. 'It's like doing a V-sign.'

But it was way cooler than doing a V-sign. I could imagine doing it to the boys when we went to the big school next year. They wouldn't know what it meant, but they'd have to pretend they did.

*   *   *

The next morning I put on the clothes my mum had packed for me. She'd made me a dirndl skirt in a flowery print and bought a new smocked top

17

with puffed sleeves to go with it. I put them on with ankle socks and my brown Clarks sandals. I was about to put my pigtails in when I saw how Kim was dressed and then I changed my mind about the pigtails. Kim was wearing maroon cords with purple denim pockets and a purple V stitched at the knee above the bellbottom. And she had a matching stripy tank top. We'd only ever seen each other in school uniform before and now she suddenly looked like a trendy teenager and I was still a silly little kid.

'Is that what you're wearing?' she asked, which was a stupid question really.

I still replied, 'No,' though. I felt myself go red so I started brushing my hair. 'My mum forgot to pack my jeans and stuff. I don't know what she put these things in for.'

Kim said, 'Oh,' but I don't think she believed me.

We went out into the garden. It was enormous, with a lawn with a Swingball in the middle, and a fish pond and a tree house. Kim shinned up into it with the ease of a boy and I followed, making sure not to care about getting dirty. I forgot about my clothes until Yvonne emerged at midday. All she had on was a tiny string bikini, big round sunglasses and a straw cowboy hat. She sat on a lounger on the patio and smeared herself all over with suntan oil. Then she lay back and took her top off, just like that, without caring who was looking, and covered her face with her hat.

Her boobs were practically nothing. She didn't have any hips either, or a tummy, or any fat at the tops of her legs. They were straight and long and bony and shiny and I couldn't stop sneaking looks at her. Their mum and dad brought lunch out on a hostess trolley and sat on loungers next to Vonnie, and she still didn't bother covering herself up. Kim's mum called us over. Vonnie sat up, pushing her hat back, and I knew she was looking me over behind her glasses. Why did my mum make me wear such stupid clothes?

Their mum and dad asked me lots of questions about where I lived and what my mum and dad did and stuff. I never knew what to say about my dad so I just told them my mum worked at a hospital and hoped people would think she was a nurse and stop asking about my dad. Vonnie just kept staring in my direction. She drank wine with her parents and lit up a cigarette after she'd finished eating. She stubbed it out again after a couple of puffs and took her sunglasses off, swinging them from her fingers while she looked me up and down. It was the first time I'd seen her eyes. They were huge and round and luminous green, like a cat's.

'You're quite pretty,' she finally declared. 'And you've got nice hair. We should plait it all over for you later and make it go frizzy.'

I went red and I didn't know what to say. They were all looking at me. Kim rolled her eyes at me with her back to Vonnie so she couldn't see. I giggled back to show I thought it was a stupid idea. But I didn't really. I'd never been allowed to have my hair curled or cut into a style or feathered or anything. I wasn't even allowed flicks at the side.

Kim said, 'Come on, let's go to the rec.' She didn't even ask her mum and dad if we could, and she got down from lunch without asking, too. Her parents didn't even say behave or be careful crossing the road or don't talk to any strangers. So we went to the play park in the village and sang Abba songs as we swung on the swings standing up. I was the blonde one and Kim was the dark one.

'Maybe we should crinkle my hair. Agnetha does do hers curly sometimes,' I suggested. 'Then we could dress up as them properly later.' But Kim said she didn't feel like doing Abba any more.

I didn't know if she meant just then or ever, but I didn't want to ask.

★ ★ ★

When we got back to Kim's there was loud, crashy music coming from Vonnie's room.

'Let's spy on her,' said Kim, so I followed her out through the sliding glass doors in the dining room and round to Vonnie's window, the other side of the house to Kim's. She had a crooked bamboo blind that was still down even though it was daytime, and we crouched down to peer through the slit at the bottom. When our eyes got used to looking in I could see her room was a tip. She had a big Coca-Cola lampshade that gave the room a red light and there were records and clothes all over the floor. Yvonne had cleared a space and was exercising in a dancey sort of way in bare feet and a pair of silver hotpants and a

20

boob tube. She had her hair tied up with bobbles in high, puffy bunches that stuck out at the sides of her head. She was bouncing up and down in a jerky motion with her arms swinging out, but she was a lot better than Pan's People. She started singing along to the chorus of 'Rebel Rebel', pouting at herself in the mirror.

She twirled round with her arms above her head and then danced over to her cigarettes on the bed, stopping for a moment to light one. She threw the packet down, shaking the match out and tossing it at her bin as she started to move again, sucking at the cigarette in her other hand. I'd stolen a cigarette once from Mr Grundy's packet and taken it to school in my pencil case, and Kim and I had smoked it at the bottom of the playing field, but we hadn't liked it. Vonnie made smoking look brilliant though, and I thought maybe I should have another go sometime. And then Vonnie turned and saw us and shouted, 'What the fuck do you think you're doing? Fuck off! You little perverts!'

I didn't know what perverts were, but it didn't sound good. I ran away quickly, but Kim was shouting back, 'You can't stop me. And anyway, you're the pervert!'

I could hear Vonnie's sarcastic laugh. 'How can I be the pervert, you dummy? You're the one spying on people like a peeping Tom.'

'Well, you think you look great, but you don't: you look stupid,' Kim said back. 'Doesn't she, Liz?'

I didn't want to say anything so I shrugged and said, 'Come on,' and backed away.

My mum didn't like me being called Liz. She didn't mind Beth, if I had to be shortened to anything at all, but she preferred me to be my whole proper name, Elizabeth.

But I didn't like Elizabeth. It was old-fashioned and boring, and I didn't stop people calling me Liz or Lizzie any more.

I hoped Vonnie wouldn't tell on us. My mum had said if I was any trouble she wouldn't let me stay again. And I really wanted to. Being at their house was like being on holiday the whole time. Mum had told me to be helpful to Kim's mum, but it was difficult to find anything to help with. They had a dishwasher instead of washing up and Kim's mum never seemed to be in the kitchen or doing the housework.

We went into the sitting room, only they called it the lounge, and Kim put the telly on, which was a really big one, and colour. They didn't have flowery armchairs and a matching sofa or a fireplace. They had an orange leather chair that you could spin round on and a huge brown velvet couch that was more like a bed, with shaggy cream cushions that matched the carpet. They didn't even have curtains, just some macramé thing hanging in the window with beads on. There was a coffee table with chrome legs and a smoky brown glass top and a pile of Vogues and other fashion magazines on it.

'Can I look at them?' I asked Kim.

''Course,' she said. 'Why do you even ask?'

'Are you allowed to? My mum doesn't let me,' I said.

'You mum's a weirdo,' she laughed.

22

'No, she isn't, she's normal,' I said. 'You mum's the one who's weird.'

'No, she's not. She keeps up with the fashions 'cos she was a model in the olden days when she was young,' Kim replied.

'No, she never,' I said, but Kim said that yes she was and she could prove it, and she went and got some photo albums off a shelf in the alcove.

I've seen pictures of my mum when she was young, and she was pretty and slim, in those dresses with a little waist and a big full skirt. But she still looked like my mum. Kim's mum didn't look like anyone's mum in photos. She was thin as a stick, in tight skirts and high stilettos, and she didn't smile but stood posed like a statue. She was very glamorous. I didn't know whether to believe it really was Kim's mum or not, but there were also pictures of her getting married to Kim's dad, and with Vonnie and then Kim when they were little. They were often in nice places, like hot countries with beaches and palm trees.

They didn't seem to have their tea at a certain time at night. It was late, though. We were allowed to help ourselves and eat where we liked. I'd never eaten Italian food before, not counting Alphabetti Spaghetti. Kim's mum and dad and Vonnie had theirs in the dining room, which had a really long table and chairs' with high backs like thrones, and they drank wine in big purple glasses like goblets. We had fizzy grape juice in goblets too, so it looked like wine. Vonnie sat at one end in a floaty turquoise top that was see-through. Her hair was newly washed and curled into ringlets that cascaded over one

23

shoulder. She sat with her back straight and her legs crossed to the side, and ate really small mouthfuls only using her fork. She was like a real-life princess.

We were allowed to eat in front of the TV and watch anything we wanted; they didn't even check. We saw *Starsky and Hutch*. We both liked Starsky best. I liked Hutch too really, but I never said. There was a horror film on afterwards which Vonnie came and watched with us, about teenagers being chased by devil people who could move objects with the power of their evil thoughts. It was really scary and I thought I'd have nightmares, but Vonnie just laughed at it.

Kim was sitting in the swivel chair and after the film finished Vonnie winked at me and did a shush sign and slid silently across the couch. She suddenly grabbed Kim's ankle, like one of the devil people did to a girl in the film. You've never heard anyone scream so loud. Vonnie and I laughed together. Kim joined in in the end. Their dad came in to see what all the racket was about and I thought we were going to get into trouble, but Vonnie told him what she'd done to Kim and he grinned too, a fuzzy sort of grin with out-of-focus eyes. He didn't even seem to realize we were up past bedtime or watching things we shouldn't.

There was jazz music coming from the dining room and Vonnie went back with him to have more wine. Kim and I tried to move objects with our minds for a while, but neither of us could. Kim tried to cheat by sneakily raising the table with her knee to make her glass slide across, but

I caught her. We got sleepy and lay end to end on the couch. We thought the boy who saved the girl in the film was quite nice and wondered if any of the boys at the big school would look like that. We made a pact we wouldn't have a boyfriend unless the other one got one at the same time.

We must have fallen asleep because next thing I knew was Kim's mum throwing quilts over us and turning out the light, and the sound of her Scholls slapping as she walked back down the corridor.

2
Beth

I travel back to mine and Toby's on the tube, but my mind doesn't want to come with me. It is as though I have time-travelled back to my past, my old life, my old self, and got stuck there. I can't bring my soul back to the present. At Hampstead station my body carries me down the High Street and into our road, through our wrought-iron gate and up to our front door, but it's as though I am seeing it all for the first time, through the eyes of my young self, the eyes of Lizzie. Somewhere in the time-travelling process things seem to have switched around and actually I'm still in the past, but travelling into the future and seeing a glimpse of what becomes of me. I am amazed. This future me lives in a fuck-off posh house in Hampstead. *How do I get here?* Lizzie asks. I feel I should know, but when I try to tell her, the answer slips away from me like a dream in the morning.

My body pulls me urgently inside the house. It's got the heebie jeebies after Vonnie's flat. It kicks the front door shut behind me and strips off my clothes as it heads for the washing machine, bunging them straight in and washing my hands before I touch anything else. It runs upstairs and immerses me under the shower, scrubbing my head and body until my skin is sore, to get rid of any invisible eggs that may have been laid on me. I was like a junkie on the tube. I scratched my head so much the guy next to me moved away.

When I'm as convinced as I can be I'm clean, I go back downstairs and smoke another unofficial cigarette out the French window. Officially I've given up. Nobody smokes any more. It's become the disgusting habit squares always said it was, even at gigs and parties, for Christ's sake. In my heart of hearts I still think it's cool, though. I can't help it. It's Vonnie's fault. She always looked amazing the way she smoked a cigarette.

Vonnie. I flick the butt away from me with the exaggerated gesture she used to use, into a bush where Toby will never look, and turn back into the room. The shower has made me feel more normal in my surroundings, but still it gives me a shock to see my reflection in the vast gilt-edged mirror above the Georgian fireplace. A grown woman looks back at me, standing in a luxurious hotel bathrobe in magazine-beautiful surroundings, like an advert for some lifestyle-inducing product or other. Not Lizzie at all. How did I become the woman with the sleek hair and expensively maintained skin?

The house is unusually still and quiet. I don't know what to do with myself now my cigarette's over.

'Fucking bastard,' I say, out loud to Toby, for being away. At least if he were around I could lose myself in his stories about the hassles of his work — the lead singer who'd walked off stage in a huff halfway through an American tour; the day spent cajoling him over the phone. The poor album sales of an ex-boy band member who'd gone solo. The massive deal he'd finally secured for his next big thing. I love all that stuff, usually. I drink it in like a tonic. Or, even better, there'd be people coming over that I could get ready for: industry types Tobes has to entertain: Japanese execs, wannabe rockstars, actual rockstars. I am cool in these situations — the hostess with the mostest, Toby calls me. I am an asset to him. 'You were so great tonight,' he always says afterwards. 'You did me proud.' And it makes me feel I have slipped into the right life for myself, the one that fits me.

I flop onto the perfectly distressed leather couch and try and acclimatize, adjust myself back into the woman that lives here, the woman I've been for the last however many years it is since the Vonnie days. It's hard. Somewhere along the line the years have melded into decades, but suddenly I can't get beyond being twenty-two. I've got the feeling I've gatecrashed some music biz type's party the way we used to do. Any second now Vonnie and Kim and the girls will suddenly come bursting in from the kitchen, laughing hysterically with all the booze and drugs they've managed to filch. I never thought in a million years it'd be the sort of house I'd one day have. But then, nice houses weren't something I ever dreamt about. Saying goodbye to my youth wasn't something I ever thought about, either.

It just wasn't going to happen, not to us.

I play the messages on the answerphone. Most are for Toby. One invites us to a private party at Soho House later. I get a sudden guilty flash of Kim back at her place on the White City estate. Maybe she'd like to go. Just get out and fucking forget it all. I reach for the phone and call her.

'*Pronto?*' Paolo shouts into the phone, over loud music — a frenetic mixture of jazz and drum 'n' bass — blaring from his home studio.

'Hi, Paolo — it's Beth. How's things?'

'Ahh, bella Betty! Bella Betty Boop!' He says this every time. '*Come sta?*'

'*Bene, bene.* And you?'

'I am very well thank you very much for the asking.'

'Good. Is Kim there?'

'*Si, si, momento . . .* ' He drops the phone and bashes through the flat yelling for Kim. He must tickle Franklin or something as I hear her breaking into giggling squeals and Kim's laughter as she approaches the phone.

'Hi, Beth.' She is breathless.

'Sorry, am I interrupting something?' I laugh. At least she's got some life going on at hers.

'No, we were just dancing to Paolo's latest tune. It's great — can you hear it?' She doesn't hear me saying 'YES!' as the music suddenly deafens me while she holds the phone to the speaker. Paolo and Franklin start rapping in Italian and laughing maniacally in the background.

'He knows some guy who might use it on this porn film he's making for cable.'

'Cool! It's great.'

Paolo is always just a moment away from his big break. He plays drums for about six different bands at a time, all just on the brink of being discovered. He plays every recording session he's offered, just in case it's that final connection on the circuit that will conduct him to success. Any cash that comes his way goes on the one missing vital piece of equipment that will mean he can finally produce next summer's dance hit. He never gives up on his dreams. It always embarrasses me that Toby never gets round to listening to any of his demos, or coming to any of his gigs.

'I haven't got time to do any more favours for losers,' is how he puts it to me, which I translate for Paolo into, 'Toby's company isn't taking on any new stuff at the moment,' or 'Toby's in New York,' or even, 'Toby loves it; he'll see what he can do.'

Paolo is never deterred. 'Music is my life,' he slurs without fail every time he is drunk, which is most nights. 'Music is my blood.' At which point he'll insist on a spontaneous jam, wherever he is, with whatever he can find to play. This will either charm whoever's in the room, or make them leave it. He doesn't care which. He doesn't even notice. He is in his own world, which he extends, when he remembers, lovingly around Kim and Franklin. But it doesn't look like a loser's world to me. It's a world where magic can happen. I understand why Kim is so in love, and I am glad for her. Franklin's dad — now there was a real loser.

'I was just calling to check you're OK,' I say, but I already know my concern is redundant, for now. She has obviously been drowning her sorrows.

'Yeah, I'm kind of all right, thanks. I was a mess when I got in. I really wanted a bath but I didn't have any money to top the key up for the meter, and when Paolo got back we had a huge row 'cos he'd blown all his dole already, and he only got it this morning. Stupid bastard went to Waitrose to do the shopping, can you believe him?!'

'Oh no!'

Paolo realizes she's talking about him and starts ranting in the background. I can't make out what's he's saying, but Kim swears at him good-naturedly in Italian.

'Still, at least he spent it on food for a change. And he had a couple of quid for the hot water and ran me a bath while he made a ginormous pizza the size of our table, and we're on our third bottle of vino, so I've forgiven him. He was trying to cheer us up, I guess.'

She shrieks as Paolo (I imagine) grabs her round the waist from behind and swirls her around.

'Dance with me, *balli, balli!*' he shouts, and Kim drops the phone. It is usual for me to be on the end of the phone hearing about Kim's life, whether it's happening there and then, like now, or she's recounting her hassles at the housing office, or embarrassing fights in the street with Paolo when he's pissed, or being hauled in to talk to teachers about her difficult home life to

31

excuse the trouble Franklin's in at school. Over the years Vonnie has often been one of many traumas Kim has had to cope with. Her life is so full of stress that I often don't know what to say. We were in it together forever; at least we were to begin with. But we somehow ended up in different worlds, or rather at different ends of the same world.

Usually I feel guilty. My life seems so easy in comparison. But tonight there is something else that is making it hard to listen. I realize with some surprise that it's envy. However hard her life is, it is still somehow emphatically hers. Kim picks up the phone again.

'Sorry, Beth — what were you saying?'

'Nothing. Look, I know this sounds a bit . . . I dunno — inappropriate — but you don't feel like going out, do you? There's a party in Soho and I just thought . . . you might just want to get out or something.'

'Oh, thanks, Beth. It's a nice idea but I'm too done in now, I think. Plus Paolo's cooked and everything. And Franklin's a bit hyper. I should stay in with her really. I think she's pretty freaked out about Vonnie, you know. Thanks, though.'

'I didn't think you would, really. I just thought, you know. If you didn't have anything going on you might need to take your mind off things.'

'Yeah, thanks. I would've done, but . . . I'll be all right.'

'OK. Just give me a call if there's anything I can do, all right?'

'Yeah, I will.'

'I'll call you tomorrow.' I pause for a second. I don't know what to say about Vonnie, but I can't just not mention her as if nothing's happened.

'I'm sure everything'll be all right, you know? Vonnie, I mean. I'm sure Vonnie'll be all right.'

'Yeah, well. Been here before.' Kim tries to laugh. 'Anyhow. Ciao for now.'

'Bye.'

I keep holding the phone not wanting to put it down and be on my own. I try to think of who else I could call up and take with me to the party. Out of the dozens of people I know there's no one right. I need it to be someone who knows about Vonnie and Kim's the only one now. It used to be that everyone around me knew Vonnie. I guess everyone still does in the world I used to inhabit with her. After all, it was me that moved on.

I have a sudden, real gut-wrenching stab of yearning for the old days when we all used to be together all the time. No one had separate lives or other things they had to do. When we heard about a party we'd just stack a load of forty-fives on the Dansette spindle and take turns in the bath and in front of the mirror with the hairspray can and the crimpers, trying clothes on and throwing them off again, borrowing someone else's, doing each other's make-up. Getting ready to go out was sometimes better than the party itself.

Even the first time Vonnie went into hospital, however awful it was, at least home wasn't some place else entirely where I had to go and get through it alone.

I dial Toby's mobile. I can usually catch him at this time, early tomorrow morning where he is. But it goes to his voicemail.

'Hi, babes, it's only me. Thought I might catch you, but maybe you're asleep.' Being asleep isn't usually a reason for him turning his phone off. 'Nothing urgent, just checking in. Give us a call if you get a chance, but don't worry if you're too busy.' It comes out more sarcastically than I mean it to. 'Miss you,' I add sweetly. 'Lots of love . . . '

Fuck it. I'll go to the party on my own. But the thought of leaving the house suddenly makes my stomach lurch, as a big swooping feeling comes over me like a flapping black crow. I feel like I'm about to throw up so I lie back on the couch in a sweat waiting for it to pass. Maybe the shower was too hot or I scrubbed too hard. I try to block out thoughts of Vonnie's flat.

Anyway, I might want some company, but not the kind I'll get there. The guy who's giving the party is a wanker.

I need a drink. I pad through to the kitchen to pour myself a vodka tonic. The kitchen is ludicrously big with state-of-the-art equipment — Aga, Smeg, the works, tastefully mixed in with antique bits and pieces and the de rigueur original features. In fact the whole house is ludicrously big with state-of-the-art everything, tastefully mixed in with, etc., etc. The sort of place you feel a sense of your own importance in. It's always made me feel relieved, like I'd made it, somehow. I thought of it as the height of good taste, but suddenly it seems to me smug and vulgar, owned by the kind of people we would have scoffed at back then. Vonnie had already slipped out of reach by the time we moved here and she's never been round, but if she had she would have called it *fucking bourgeois*, probably.

I feel out of place, suddenly, the way I did when I first stayed in a fancy hotel or flew first class. Like it's not really meant for the likes of me.

3

Lizzie

The arsehole of the universe was how Vonnie unaffectionately referred to Bridgwater. I'd never noticed anything wrong with it before. It was just where I lived, the extent of my world. But Vonnie changed the way I looked at everything, as though she had transmitted her knowledge to me through her radioactive-green stare.

After she said it I could see what she meant. It even smelt like an arsehole, with the emissions from the cellophane factory wafting over our side of town. Vonnie always had an air of being deeply offended that she had been dumped into the world anywhere near it and never forgave her parents for living anywhere but London. She was always going to get the hell out and go up to *town*, as she called it, as soon as she could.

When I saw my home again after my weekend away, my mum's old terraced house seemed even smaller and darker than ever, and so quiet you noticed the clocks tick. After the good time I'd had at Kim's I felt too alive to be inside it. I couldn't settle down to my homework straight away like I usually did, and buzzed around the place getting under my mum's feet.

'Are you coming down with something?' my

36

mum asked, and checked my forehead for signs of a temperature.

'I feel fine,' I said. She said my eyes were shining like they did when I was little and about to get ill. We were in the kitchen at the back, where my mum always was when I came home from school, with a pinny over her blouse and skirt. With her grey hair shampooed and set once a fortnight she looked like a granny compared to Kim's mum. The kitchen was a small extension tacked on to the back of the house where the outside loo had been. My dad was going to put up proper fitted cupboards and everything, but had never got round to it before he died, back when I was eight.

'Well, you may as well make yourself useful if there's nothing wrong with you and you're not doing your school-work.' Mum gave me potatoes to peel while she sliced cold meat onto a serving plate. She turned back to the sink and I could see the varicose veins on her calves making blue lumps in her tights.

'Did you get your homework done at Kimberley's house?' she asked. I thought back over the weekend and realized we hadn't done any at all. There hadn't seemed time for boring things like homework.

'Uhuh,' I said, raising the intonation on the 'huh' so it sounded like a yes, even though it wasn't.

'And did you say thank you for having me to Kimberley's mother and father?'

Kim's mum and dad hadn't been up when we left for school so I hadn't done that, either. We got up and dressed and out to the bus stop all by ourselves. My school skirt was crumpled from lying on the floor where I'd left it on Friday night. We could help ourselves to anything we liked for breakfast. They had Sugar Puffs *and* Coco Pops and I had both mixed together, and Kim opened two bottles of milk at once so we could both have the cream off it. Kim had to take Vonnie a cup of coffee in bed before she could get up for school.

Kim had been sent to a different school from Vonnie because their mum and dad thought it might be the school's fault that Vonnie was so bad at it. Kim said Vonnie was bad at it because she was stupid. Vonnie wore a red pleated skirt that she hitched up really short by folding over the waistband. She wound her red and black stripy tie round loads of times so it was really fat and short, and she didn't do it up tight round the collar but let it hang with her top button undone. She pinned her crazy hair back at the sides with sparkly heart-shaped hair clips. I liked the way the red of her hair clashed with the red of her blazer. There were badges on the lapel, with names of bands I hadn't heard of. She must have had pierced ears because she had gold studs in. She had a cigarette with a grapefruit for breakfast, leaning against the bar they had in the kitchen like the ones they have on American TV shows, yawning sulkily.

Eventually she said in a gravelly voice, 'I feel like shit. Fucking bad hangover, man. School's a drag; I might bunk off after register,' and she stubbed out her fag on the grapefruit peel and began to clear away the wine glasses from the night before. Then she washed the floor with a mop. Her skirt swished from side to side as she moved and she didn't care that anyone could look up it and see her pants. I hadn't thought doing chores could make anyone look sexy before. Vonnie didn't seem the type of girl who would agree to doing chores either, but when she was rinsing out the mop in the sink she said, 'That's a fiver Mum and Dad owe me,' and I realized they got paid for doing the housework. It wasn't fair.

I set the table for three on the tablecloth in the breakfast room.

'Did you have a nice time?' Mum asked, finally. I was bursting with it and it all came out in a scrambled rush, the funny sprawling house with everything modern, the big garden with the tree house, the colour telly, the loud music, the teenage sister who had henna in her hair and danced around and changed her clothes all day.

'Why doesn't she just wear what she's put on in the morning?' Mum asked. 'She sounds like rather a silly girl to me.'

'No she isn't,' I said, but I couldn't think of a good reason why she wasn't.

I was careful not to tell on Kim's mum and dad. I didn't mention the wine and the late nights and the bad things on TV and the not getting us breakfast or seeing us off on the bus.

We had tea at six when Mr Grundy, the lodger, came in from work — cold meat and mashed potato as it was Monday, with my mum's home-made chutney. He always said,

'*How*,' to me like a Red Indian because of my pigtails, and I had to look like I thought it was funny every time. He thought it was funny every time, and he had this big open laugh that let you see all his nose hair and fillings. He was very tall and had to fold himself in to sit at the table. His knee often touched mine underneath and I had to squeeze myself against the wall to avoid it. His nose whistled while he ate and he talked with his mouth full. Mum would chat to him about his day at the council or the news or some such boring thing and he would always insist on talking to me, too.

'So, who's a big girl now then, eh? Away from Mummy for a whole weekend?! What did you little ladies get up to? All sorts of naughty things, I bet.'

Mum said I had to be nice and polite to Mr Grundy, but I hated him. She said we should be grateful to him because he made our life easier, but I didn't see how. Mum was always doing his washing and making sure he had his breakfast and tea on the table at the right time, and she made his sandwiches for work. And he didn't even go up to his room after tea but came and watched TV in the sitting room like we were a family.

I went and did my homework in my room.

I'd had to move into the boxroom the year before, when Mum said we were going to take in a lodger because Dad hadn't left us any money. To make up for it she'd said we could do it up how I wanted and I could choose the wallpaper myself. I'd chosen a pink flowery print that now

40

made me want to puke, so I'd started covering it up with anything I could find: a map of the world, which was nice and big and nearly covered a whole wall; pictures from comics like Josie and the Pussycats and Scooby Doo, posters of the Rubettes and David Essex, unfolded from the middle of pop magazines. You could only have the furniture one way round; it was the only way it fitted. It was all old furniture like everything else in our house, but at least I'd been allowed to paint it white. My room was next to the toilet so I had to listen to Mr Grundy having his poo in the morning.

★   ★   ★

We only had another week of school before the summer holidays. On the last day we had a lecture from Podge, our headmistress, about what it would be like up at the new school. It was much bigger than ours, so we might feel small or insignificant at first, she said. Also teenage boys tended to be very naughty, but we shouldn't let them distract us from our education. She tried to be all modern and trendy too, saying how she knew all too well how attractive boys could be, but we couldn't believe she knew that well at all. We must remember to behave properly, the way we'd been taught. She got all teary-eyed and embarrassing because she'd been a teacher for a hundred years and now she was retiring. Afterwards me and Kim burnt our exercise books in a ceremony behind the prefab.

I saw Kim loads when we first broke up. She was the first best friend I'd had, and the last too, as it turned out. She was allowed to come into town on the bus on her own and we went swimming down the baths and had Fanta and crisps out of the machine after. We played Charlie's Angels down the park and went to the fair when it came. She came to tea once, but we got the giggles because of Mr Grundy, and Mum told us off afterwards. It wasn't fair because Mr Grundy hadn't minded; in fact he seemed to quite enjoy it.

But then in August Kim went on holiday with her family to the Canary Islands for three whole weeks, so I wouldn't see her until we were back at the new school. Mum wouldn't let me stay home by myself all day, so I had to drag along to work with her, cleaning up after mad old people and letting them pat my head. She liked me coming with her; she said it cheered the poor things up, but it didn't do much to cheer me up. I got a postcard from Kim that was a picture of a long golden beach with sun umbrellas made of straw and a bright blue sea with people swimming. She wrote, *Having a lovely time, it's very hot and I got burnt and am peeling. Vonnie's going out with a Spanish waiter called Pedro and they took me to a disco, wish you were here, love Kim, xxx,* and she'd done a circle over the 'i' in her name instead of a dot. I decided I would do that with my name too.

I tried to sunbathe next to the vegetable plot at the back of our house, but I was embarrassed to put my swimming costume on so I only got my face, neck, arms and legs up to my knees in the sun. I got a line round where my T-shirt was, but my legs didn't seem to change colour at all, even though I smeared them with Trex. I thought maybe it was because they were too hairy. They did seem terribly hairy to me and I wondered if there was something wrong with me. It was all right for Kim; her hairs wouldn't show so much when she had a tan, and anyway, she always had Vonnie to lend her razors and show her how to do stuff like that properly. Vonnie didn't seem to have any hair on her body at all. She had skin like frankfurters; it was beautiful. My mum didn't have all the things Kim and Vonnie and their mum had in their bathroom. She had a pink Yardley lipstick and that was it — I know because she said it was what she wanted for her birthday every two years or so.

I didn't want to ask my mum because I knew she'd say, 'Don't be silly, there's nothing wrong with you — everyone has hairs on their legs. And anyway,' she'd go on, 'you're too young to worry about your appearance. You should be worrying about your schoolwork so you can go to university.' I couldn't go into a shop and buy anything as embarrassing as razors. So I decided to borrow Mr Grundy's. He had his own sink in his room, so I snuck in when my mum was at the shops to pinch it. His room smelt of BO and my mum's furniture polish. His yesterday's vest and Y-fronts were still hanging over a chair. They were horrifying. The pants especially. That awful pouch bit at the front with the gap for his thing to poke through. Gross.

I got his razor off the sink, and his Hi Karate shaving foam. On the way back out I thought I'd take a quick look in his bedside cabinet, just in case. You never knew what you'd find out that you might need to know one day. Inside were a loo roll and a stack of magazines of nude ladies with their bits out. I'd seen these things before, of course, but not in connection with anybody I knew looking at them and certainly not Mr Grundy. I hadn't had the chance to really study them before either, just a quick glance at the top shelf at the newsagent's. So I borrowed one of those too, to read while I was locked in the bathroom.

The razor was really sharp, so sharp you didn't notice it cut you until you saw a thin line of red begin to ooze through the foam. It happened quite a few times, especially round any knobbly bits like my ankles and knees. The trouble was, when I'd done up to my knees and washed away the blood and foam, the bareness of the leg below my knees made the tiny hairs above my knee show up when I hadn't even noticed them before. I studied the ladies in the pictures but they didn't seem to have any hair at all, except for on their you-know-whats. Some of them didn't even have that. I didn't know which looked worse. The hair gave me the creeps, but at least it covered things up a bit. Without it, it all just looked like giblets to me.

In the end I shaved my legs right to the top. I also shaved my arms, the back of my neck, and anywhere I could reach. Once I'd washed all the mess off with a flannel my skin felt lovely. I'd have some good scabs to pick soon too, from all the cuts. I tried on some of my mum's nylon tights and her evening shoes that almost fit me now, with heels and strappy backs that she used to wear when she went out with my dad when I was little. She had a sparkly dress back then that made a swishy sound when she moved and she smelt of peardrops when she kissed me goodnight.

I made a minidress out of a towel and walked up and down in front of the mirror on my mum's wardrobe door. I was still a bit knock-kneed but if I walked right, with my feet turned out, and let my hips sink into each step, you couldn't tell. I sat on the edge of the bed and crossed my legs. If I ignored my face in the mirror the rest of me looked almost like a woman. It was incredible.

After that whenever Mr Grundy looked at me I felt as though he knew that I knew about his magazines. I always blushed, as though it was me that was the rude one.

★ ★ ★

Mum wanted to take me to school on the first day, but I managed to stop her. Instead she just took me as far as the bus stop to meet Kim and then let me walk in with her. Kim was the brownest person I'd ever seen. We pulled our socks down and put our legs next to each other for a laugh. Mine were white as snow with dark stubble and scratch marks where I'd been

45

itching. Kim dared us to leave our socks hanging down like that when we walked in through the school gates, but I knew she just wanted everyone to see how nice her legs were next to mine, so I didn't.

4

Beth

I wake up with the horrible feeling you get when you don't know where or even who you are. I eventually recognize the bedroom I've shared with my husband for ten years, but the horrible feeling doesn't leave. It's as though I have broken in while the occupants who really live here are away. My nerves are on edge and my heart is thumping, as though they might come back any minute and find me here in their bed and say, *Who the fuck are you?*

The thought of a cup of tea with another illicit cigarette pulls me downstairs into the kitchen. I try Toby's mobile again while I boil the kettle, but it's still voicemail. For a second or two I wonder if he's all right, but it passes. Toby is not the sort of person you have to worry about.

I reach under the sink for my secret stash of Marlboro Lights. Toby would never look under there. Mind you, I could put them anywhere and he wouldn't find them. Sometimes it seems as though our home is just another hotel to him. He doesn't know where anything is or how anything works, only where to find his pressed shirts and how to order takeaway or a movie on cable. If anything breaks down he never tries to fix it. Often when something stops working he just buys another newer, better version of the same gadget. Toby has no complaints about built-in obsolescence. He can keep up, beat it even. It's a sign of his success, you could say. I've rescued CD players and personal organizers from bins before now, when they've only needed new batteries.

I light up and take a proper smoker's drag on my cigarette before forcing myself to check in with Kim. There is no news. No change. Vonnie has been unconscious since she was found, thanks to an anonymous call, and rushed to hospital. She is still lying there, somewhere between life and death, attached to tubes that pump her with the life force to keep her on this side, just. I can't imagine it. Vonnie always had enough life force of her own to keep her going through ten lifetimes over.

'Is there anything I can do?' I ask.

'No, it's OK. Me and Paolo are driving over when he's up and collecting her stuff and I'll clean up some more.' I am about to interrupt and insist on helping when Kim adds, 'Then I'll head over to the hospital to see her.'

'Oh. Right. OK.' There is an awkward pause I should fill with an offer to go too, but it remains an awkward pause. *Please don't ask me to go.* I pray in my head, and Kim kindly cooperates.

'Are you sure you don't need me?' I say instead.

'Yes, really. Thanks though.'

'All right. I'll call you later then. Take care.'

I am relieved, and also not. I know it's shitty, but I can't face seeing Vonnie. I feel as guilty as if

48

it was me that put her there. I try to stop remembering the last times I saw her, when I pretended I hadn't, suddenly changing direction on Portobello Road to avoid her, or ducking and turning to sift blindly through a heap of clothes on a market stall until she passed.

The day stretches before me with nothing to fill it but worry and memories. The past won't let me go, tugging me backwards, strong as temptation, and the day begins to progress without me. I decide to take a shower — I'll never get clean enough. It's all the micro-organisms, the bacteria too small for the human eye, that bother me. How do you ever know if you've got rid of those?

After my scrub I take clean clothes out of the wardrobe, but something makes me inspect them before I put them on. They seem clean but the thought of them next to my skin makes me shudder. I can't quite bring myself to pull the T-shirt on, even though it looks pristine and smells washing-powder fresh. I drop it in the laundry basket with the jeans and look for something else, pulling more things from the shelves that all end up in the washing. Even though they are clean. I finally find a pair of M&S pyjamas still in the polythene they came in, a birthday present from my mum who has no concept that some people just don't wear pyjamas or nightdresses. I'm grateful for them now, anyway.

I take the basket downstairs and refill the washing machine. I begin to fold the clothes from yesterday, the ones I wore to Vonnie's, but then something makes me throw them in the bin. I don't think I can wear them again.

I make coffee and take it into the sitting room and stare out through the French windows. There is something relieving about being in the soft new jersey pyjamas Mum got me. They are so *not me*, adding to the feeling that everything I have is borrowed, like someone who has been through a trauma in which they have lost everything. I suddenly want to speak to my mum, although I never usually call her on a weekday morning. I sit on the couch and press memory eight.

'Four six one six one eight?' Who answers the phone like that any more? My mum lives in a black and white British movie from the 1940s. She'd still have an old Bakelite phone with a dial if it weren't for the touchtone already installed when she moved in. She doesn't live in the house I grew up in now, and it's a relief to me. I dreaded going back there once I'd left home. When I did, I felt myself overwhelmed by the shadows of our former selves, to the point that the shadows were the solid things, like statues set in stone, and we were the intangible shade they cast. She has a bungalow now, in Devon, not far from the sea. The house is full of light.

'Hi, Mum. It's just me.' My voice is only slightly too high.

'Oh, hello, Elizabeth. What a nice surprise.' Now that I have finally become Beth to everyone else around me, the one abbreviation she ɔves of, she still always calls me by my full . I no longer mind, and sometimes even quite like it; times like these. I find some reassurance in it, as though it's the one thread that has connected me from beginning to end without snapping. She is in a nice mood — her voice is relaxed and without the tinge of anxiety that sometimes colours it if I call in between the regular Sunday slot. I love her voice when it is like this; it tinkles in a singsong way, soothing like stream water over pebbles. A sudden gush of self pity pools in my throat so that I can't speak without my words drowning. I cough to try to clear it. I want to tell her everything that's happened with Vonnie. It is a shock to be in such shock. I don't know why I'm so affected by it all. She has been out of my life for so long.

'How are you, dear?' Mum asks. I breathe in again.

'I'm fine. Fine. I just thought I'd give you a call. Have you been having this wonderful weather down there?'

'Yes, it's lovely, isn't it? I've been out in the garden all week. The nasturtiums have gone crazy, so I've been cutting them back a bit. They're beautiful but they're taking over everything. I only wanted a splash of red in the bottom corner, but they've spread along the whole back fence and they're clashing with my delphiniums.'

It's great when she's chatty like this. I have no idea what nasturtiums and delphiniums are, but I try. 'It's quite nice when things are a little wild though, isn't it? I expect it looks quite pretty.'

'Well, yes, I don't like gardens to be too neat and tidy, but I had my colours all planned out

51

and it's not quite how I envisaged. Still, it looks a bit better now. It's been murder on my arthritis though; my hands are practically seized up.'

I make a sympathetic noise, sucking in air between my teeth. 'Have you got anything that helps that? Any creams or anything?'

'Well, not really. I'll have a nice soak in the bath later. But there's nothing I can really do about it. It's just old age.'

I don't want to hear about my mum's old age.

'Yeah, I've been out in our garden lots too,' I lie. 'The honeysuckle smells gorgeous.'

'I bet it does. You're lucky to have that little haven right in the middle of London. I was amazed how little I heard the traffic when I came up.' She's said this every time since. She hates London, and has hardly ever been except to visit me and Toby, once we were properly married. She must have imagined everywhere in London was like Oxford Street, and was shocked to find residential tree-lined streets with no tower blocks and screeching police cars.

'Did Toby fall asleep on the lounger again?' It's what he did when she stayed last. He wasn't best pleased at having to forgo a launch party at Abbey Road studios for my mum's visit, and the effort of making unsophisticated conversation, along with the wine, had finally taken its toll.

'Not this time, no,' I laugh. 'He's still away, actually.'

'Still? Gosh. When's he coming home?'

'Oh, not till Sunday.'

'That's a long trip this time. Couldn't you have gone along?' Mum never understands why I don't go with Toby on his business trips.

'It's not like that, really. Toby gets everything arranged by the record company — it's not the sort of thing where wives go along. It's all business.' Verbatim from Toby.

'Well, it seems a shame. It'd be nice for you. You could sightsee while he was working and then he could take you out for dinner in the evenings.'

'Yes, but his kind of job often involves working in the evenings. Honestly, Mum, I'd be on my own and at a loose end. It's fine. Anyway, we'll have a holiday together soon; he's going to look at his schedule and take some time off when he gets back.'

'That's nice.' She senses that I'm trying to bundle up the conversation. 'So what have you been up to?'

'Oh, nothing much.' The flies of Vonnie's flat buzz around in my head again. 'I met up with Kim yesterday.'

'Oh, did you? How is she?'

'She's fine. Fine.' I'm still reluctant to admit anything that puts her in a bad light, any reference to drawing benefits or being an unmarried mother, or having a boyfriend who isn't the father. Or a junkie for a sister. I pause, not knowing where to start about Vonnie.

'I had a visit from Beverley at the weekend,' Mum interjects. 'Do you remember her?'

Do I ever. Beverley was the lodger after Mr Grundy. She became more my mother's daughter than I was at the time.

'Vaguely,' I say, as interestedly as possible.

53

'She brought her children with her. Gorgeous little things, they are. A girl and a boy. Chloe's six and Joseph's two and a half. He's a real little handful, but I must say, Beverley copes with him very well. She is such a wonderful mother.'

'Really.'

'Yes! She was always so under-confident as a young woman — it's marvellous to see how much she's blossomed since she got married and had children.'

I don't reply. My rising fury won't let me.

'Anyway,' I continue, rather too forcefully, 'as I was saying, about Kim. Remember her big sister, Yvonne?'

'Yes, of course I do.'

'Well, she's . . . been having problems for a while now and — '

'It doesn't surprise me,' Mum interrupts. 'I always thought she was rather an unstable girl.'

I am not in the mood to prove her right, however much I want to talk about it.

'Well, it's not her fault really.' My defences are up. 'She's been ill.'

'Yes, well I doubt her lifestyle helps her much. Her parents should have taken her in hand much earlier on. I always thought they let her run wild. It doesn't help to spoil a child. If they'd instilled a bit of discipline she might have been able to cope a bit better once she had to lead her own life.'

My efforts at connecting snap back as though they are on a spring. There is another silence as I curl my feet into myself.

'So, what's happened?' Mum continues.

'Oh. Nothing,' I say, like a sulking teenager. 'I don't know why I mentioned it. I haven't really got any interesting news since last time we spoke.'

'Oh well. I'm sure you'll have lots to talk about once Toby's back.'

'Yes. I'm sure I will.'

'I can't say I've done anything exciting either. Just been enjoying the sunshine while we've got it.'

'Me too.'

'Well, if you don't mind I'll skip off now. I promised I'd pop round to Mrs Harris with a pot of my strawberry jam, and I want to catch her before she goes off to her club.'

'Oh, OK. I didn't mean to keep you. Just save a jar for me, all right? I'll come and visit soon.'

'Don't you worry about me, dear. You just look after that husband of yours when he gets back. His work must wear him out.'

'I will. If he gets the chance I know he'd love to come down to see you too.'

'Well, I'm sure he'd rather spend the time with his wife than his mother-in-law. You just enjoy being together and come down to me when he's away again.'

'Well, like I said, that'll be soon.' There is a bitter ring to the words, but my mother either misses or ignores it.

'That'll be nice. Take care, dear. Cheerio.'

'Bye.'

★ ★ ★

There isn't even any housework to do as Lucia has just been. I wish there was some ironing, or the stairs needed vacuuming, something rhythmic and soothing, with a sense of satisfaction at the end. I pace around the room, stopping finally in front of the white baby grand in the corner. I stroke the lid, remembering its arrival at the new house, and ours. We had one of those tense moving-in rows about my battered old suitcases of band memorabilia that I'd taken immediately to the attic.

'If that old junk's going straight up there what the fuck are you hanging onto it for?' Toby said, as I tried to smuggle my things past him. 'You can't need it — just chuck the crap out, for fuck's sake.'

He doesn't have the temperament for moving house. As his patience with domestic hassle reached its limit, I began to feel ashamed of the last of my belongings, my collection of instruments, as they unloaded into sad little huddles at the edges of enormous rooms. Our living space had suddenly outgrown them, and they looked lost and out of their depth, where before they had stood proud, stamping their eccentric identities on my rented rooms. They had been so much a part of the furniture, the crucial elements I had decorated my transient spaces around, amongst Fifties fabrics splashed with colour and jazzy impressions of guitars and trumpets. But now they looked like silly, discarded toys. Gourd rattles, chimes, penny whistles, African drums, washboards, harmonicas, a vibraslap, a theramin. I had obsessed over anything with keys — melodicas, xylophones and glockenspiels. I had a squeezebox, a harmonium, a broken Farfisa organ and pedals for a Vox Continental, in case I ever managed to pick up a Vox Continental. They had been interesting, had made me feel interesting. But now they somehow seemed surplus. You could get all those sounds on samples now. It was ridiculous to hang on to them when you were a woman and a wife. It was time for me to grow up. I moved them into the loft too.

'Hey, what are you doing with those?' Toby exclaimed, when he caught me.

'I thought you were tired of my junk,' I snapped, the tensions of moving house tightening the invisible tethers between us as though we were caught in an increasingly intricate cat's cradle.

'Your junk, yeah,' Toby retorted. 'When did I ever say that was your junk?'

'You didn't have to say it. What of my stuff would you not call junk?'

'Oh come on, don't be stupid. Obviously I don't think musical instruments are junk. They get played all the time when people come round. For fuck's sake! Why would I think they were junk? Bring them back down, Beth. What's wrong with you?'

But I don't bring them back down. 'Forget about it, they're not important,' I sulk when he persists, winding him up to the point of climbing into the loft himself and practically throwing them down.

'Yeah, breaking them really helps,' I shouted up.

'Not as much as if they're stuck up here,' he replied, and I sighed and flounced down the stairs.

*　★　★*

'Babes, I love that you collect these crazy things,' Toby said later, skinning up after an Indonesian takeaway. 'I feel really proud when you're the only one in the room who knows how to get a sound out of them.' He was giving me a neck rub, in advance of us christening our new sofa from Heal's. 'I really like you having music as a hobby. Why d'you think I bought a baby grand? For me to play 'Chopsticks' on with two fingers?'

The house seemed so vast after Toby's basement flat. When he tried to describe it to me after he'd first seen it, he said, 'I'm not joking, you could fit a fucking grand piano in there and you wouldn't notice.' And, as a whim, and no doubt one of the little in-jokes he has with himself, he bought one to prove it. It's a white baby grand, and he was right: I don't notice it. I've hardly touched it, except to dust. I always shyly declined to play when we first had dinner parties, and nobody asks me any more, not even Toby. He is silently outraged that I have never really accepted it, this gift he has come to believe absolutely was truly, altruistically, for me. Other musician friends sit at it instead, and everyone shouts requests for tunes as the evening wears on and we get drunk on vintage wine and high on hash.

I open the lid and sit down. Maybe I'll be able

58

to remember how to play it. Maybe it'll take my mind off Vonnie. The keys seem a vast territory I don't know how to begin to explore. After a long while, my fingers tentatively trace *Für Elise*, the only thing they remember how to play, as though everything that followed never happened.

5

Lizzie

The promise of learning the piano had been the thing that finally made me relent over a lodger coming to stay at our house. We'd got Nana's old one when she died and it was out of tune with a few notes missing, but I loved how you could make thunder roll out of the bottom and angels' bells ting from the top, just by touching different keys with your fingertips. It was like making magic.

'If we get a lodger we'll be able to afford your piano lessons,' Mum had said, after I'd gone on and on about it. It was a deal. Mr Grundy had moved in and I'd practised every day since. The teacher at the new school said I was a natural. I could play *Für Elise* already.

At big school there was a whole music block and you could go in whenever you wanted. Kim and I were in there all the time. We had been put in different forms and it was a good place to meet up. It was also a good way of hiding from boys.

At primary school they had seemed just like us, only stupider. Now we were around boys in the fifth and sixth forms who were really big with deep voices and hairy as gorillas, and they were a lot more scary. Other girls seemed to take in their stride having older boys around, as if it was the most natural thing in the world, and they blossomed suddenly, losing their National Health glasses and the braces on their teeth. Some of them even got boyfriends who were in the years above us, and started parading around the school with them at lunchtime or sitting in the mixed common room acting all grown-up with their legs crossed, smiling and flicking their blow-dried hair about.

But boys made Kim and me awkward and tongue-tied and red in the face. We giggled too much and got silly and the other girls called us *jooovenile* and stayed away from us as though it was catching. Pretty soon we became known as *You Two*, said in a way that made it sound like an insult. But we didn't mind. We didn't see what was wrong with being Us Two and anyway, we had each other. It's how we found out about music. What music really was, when it wasn't stuffy old sheet music and scales and trying to stretch an octave.

We were mucking about in the band room one lunchtime when Marie Bunyan kicked the door open. Marie Bunyan was a hard nut and hung out with these other two thickos that we called Mungo and Midge, though not to their faces. She was in the fourth form and went out with lots of blokes who'd left school already, and went all the way with them. Other girls called her the Martini Girl. Any time, any place, anywhere. Marie had short, straight, burgundy hair with flicks hairsprayed hard and sharp as knives. She drew blue eyeliner around the insides of her eyelids, which made her look even more spiteful.

She always had big blobs of it in the corners. You didn't want to get on the wrong side of Marie Bunyan.

I stopped playing the theme from *Love Story*. Kim stopped doing her ballet dancing. She didn't really do ballet, but she was making up a joke dance to go with the music. Marie came into the room smirking, Mungo and Midge on either side of her like dogs. They seemed much bigger than us, with proper bosoms and fatty knees beneath their American Tan tights. I got up from the piano.

'Was that *Love Story* you were playing?' asked Marie, and I squirmed and said, 'Sort of.'

She laughed in a sneery sort of way. 'Go on then. Play the whole thing.'

I didn't want to but I was scared to say no. I glanced at Kim and she nodded at me, so I sat down again and played it, a bit too fast, sensing them closing in around my back. I could hear Mungo tittering but Marie went, 'Shush.'

At the end I waited for her to give me a Chinese burn. But instead she just said, 'I love that film. Ryan O'Neal's really hunky.' Mungo and Midge agreed. 'What else can you play?'

Kim and I had worked out the *Pink Panther* theme together so we played that, Kim doing the ba dum ba dum at the bottom and me picking out the tune at the top. We were relieved to hear Marie joining in singing and clicking her fingers, which meant Mungo and Midge did too.

At the end Marie stopped smiling and brought her face up really close to mine. 'I bet you think you're really clever, playing that,' she snarled. We shook our heads and prepared for the torture. 'Well, I bet you can't play this. Budge up, squirt.' I gratefully gave up the piano stool. 'It's called boogie woogie.'

I watched her fingers as they crashed up and down the keys. She was terrible at piano. She banged the keys as though she wanted to break them and often hit two notes at the same time, but it didn't matter. Boogie woogie was so cool. All she played in the right hand was the chord over and over again on the off-beat against the rolling bass line in the left. It was a delicious racket and made you want to jump around. I watched her fingers really hard so I wouldn't forget what to do.

'You're really good,' I said after, and she said, 'I know.' She punched me hard in the arm to show how tough she was and tied my plaits together under my chin.

'See you around, suckers,' she said as she swaggered out with her hounds to heel. She thought she was it, but she wasn't.

We waited at the window until we'd seen her streamlined head pointing off into the distance. Then we scrambled back to the piano to learn it ourselves. It was so much fun. It was as close to skipping as you could get sitting down. Kim said she thought her dad had some records that sounded a bit like it. Next time we were round her house we got them out and played them all and sat round looking at the covers. They had pictures of black men in hats and suits, grinning and squinting through the smoke from the cigarettes dangling at the corners of their mouths as they played. The music drew Vonnie out of her room and she bounced into the lounge, doing a step she called the Pony. She knew loads of steps because she did dance at school. She was brilliant.

'If I wasn't going to be a popstar or an actress, I'd be a dancer,' she said, stopping to flick the ash off her cigarette. She studied one of the record covers for a moment. 'He's really cool, that guy on the bass. That's what I'm gonna play when I'm in a band, only an electric one.'

'You can't play bass,' Kim scoffed.

'How do you know, smartarse?' She hit Kim over the head with the album cover. 'For your information, Steve's in a reggae band and he's teaching me. I'm saving up to get my own.'

Steve was her latest boyfriend. He was a decorator she'd met when he was working at her school. He'd asked her out after seeing her practising her dance routine in a leotard through the hall window, while he was painting the outside of the building on a scaffold.

'You hardly ever see any girl bass players. I'll be so cool.'

She flicked through the pile of their dad's records and chose a Louis Jordan one to put on. She started doing a shuffly dance to 'Choo Choo Ch' Boogie'. Kim tried to copy Vonnie's steps, but she kept getting her feet tangled up.

'I'll teach you properly if you like,' said Vonnie. 'I'll work out a routine and you can be my chorus girls.'

She showed us a basic jive step and how to shimmy. She told us to practise for a bit and bunny-hopped out of the room, and when she came back she was all dressed up like one of the Tympany Five, in her dad's old suit from the fifties, her thumbs tucked into a pair of braces and her hair up under a trilby, pulled down low and wonky over her eyes. Even in baggy old men's clothes she looked amazing. Kim and I eventually got the hang of a couple of moves, but in the end we drifted back to the couch just to sit and watch her. When a slow, sexy song came on she sang along in a husky voice and even started doing a jokey striptease. She whirled her tie round in the air, and then hooked it round my neck like I was a gentleman customer. She stripped all the way down to her pants, which were no more than little scraps of red lace, and sat on Kim's lap.

'If I wasn't going to be a popstar or an actress or a dancer,' she said, when the song was finished, 'I'd be a stripper.'

The only thing she put back on that night was her dad's shirt, which she left unbuttoned so you could still see everything. All her mum did when she saw her was raise her eyes to the ceiling and say to their dad, 'Where did you get that daughter of yours from?'

★ ★ ★

Kim and I learnt how to play boogie woogie together, with both of us at the piano at the same time. Kim played the bottom bit and I would mess around at the top with whatever I liked; anything seemed to fit, the crazier the better. I learnt how to whizz down the whole keyboard with my thumbnail. We tried to play with our backs to the piano, or with our feet. We were in the music block any chance we had.

Music became our refuge, a real place where we could go to escape for a while. Our bodies were beginning to betray us, just when we least needed it, just when there were male eyes everywhere to see every new bump and curve taking us over. I started my periods earlier than Kim and hid them from her until she started hers. I only told my mum because I thought there was something wrong when it didn't stop after one wee. She gave me things that made me feel I was sick and should be in hospital; pads and belts and loops and pants with plastic liners. They weren't easy to hide, especially when we had to change for swimming. Girls that admitted it got off swimming, but I don't know how they could say just like that, 'Miss, I've got my period,' like they didn't care who knew it.

Kim was the same as they were; she just came in to school one day and boasted, 'I came on all over the sheets last night.' *Came on*, she said, casual as anything, as though it was her own expression and not one she'd got off Vonnie. Vonnie and her mum had shared womanly smiles with her and said, 'Join the club,' as though it was a good thing to happen.

We discreetly checked each other's skirts for lumps and stains as we got up from our desks. Boys hung on the fencing around the netball courts as we dropped passes, trying to conceal the horrors going on beneath the grey PE pants we called passion killers.

6

Beth

I try to lose myself in my playing the way I used to. Just let my fingers travel where they like and root out melodies and chords to follow. But it's no good. The corners of my eyes are working overtime. I keep seeing things moving out of them, and I'll jerk my head around to catch spiders and roaches and maggots and flies that disappear when I really look. It's making me jumpy. Lucia keeps the house spotless, but I'm suddenly too aware of the undersides of sofas and chairs, or the insides of the piano or the backs of the cabinets behind me, and I find myself interrupting my playing to peer and scratch and tuck my feet up from the floor.

It disturbs me that I never see them. If I can't see them, where are they? They must be somewhere. I don't know how I have managed to live here all these years without ever noticing the dark places that now loom at me everywhere I turn. I was only ever aware of the space in the house before, but now it is the edges of the space that I notice. I feel as though any minute my eyes will become microscopic, able to see the woodworm gnawing the skirting boards and the bacteria multiplying on the damp dishcloth, and the germs hurtling towards my mouth whenever I take a breath.

I soon give up. I hate how useless I am at piano now anyway, when it used to come so fluently. I bang the lid shut. It makes our wedding photo on top of it rattle, as though it is clamouring for my attention. I pick it up and examine it while I wipe the dust from the crevices around the frame. It's such a great picture: my hair in a towering peroxide beehive, under which eyeliner draws my eyes into paisley shapes that match the pattern on Toby's purple shirt. Toby is in wraparound shades, which he had kept on throughout the ceremony. I look like a girl who's making up half the world's coolest rock and roll couple, not someone giving up on their dreams. I look happy.

My wedding dress was my pièce de résistance. A white lace Foale and Tuffin minidress suit, the matching bolero jacket with buttons the size of saucers. Toby's mum got it for me, through a friend of a friend who actually was Tuffin or Foale, and still had their finest one-offs. It made me feel getting married was something that suited my idea of myself after all.

The me that had been reborn under Vonnie's moon had decided I would never get married, just like Vonnie had said. The me that had lain in my room as a teenager dreaming about the life I was going to have, and the girl I was going to be. After meeting Vonnie I had different dreams from those I'd had before about what I'd do when I grew up. I didn't want to be a nurse or a teacher any more, or the best day of my life to be my wedding day, the best thing that ever happened to me getting married. I was going to do something else, something different, although I didn't know quite what. But I was sure that whatever it was, Vonnie would lead the way.

In the end though, it wasn't somewhere I could follow. In the end I fell in love. That was all. Was there anything so wrong in that? So why do I feel as though I've committed a great crime against her?

My stomach suddenly twists as an image of my wedding outfit now appears in my mind, hanging in polythene in a separate wardrobe from my current clothes, on a rail with all my old stage gear, vintage cocktail dresses and mohair suits. I break out in a sweat. I never washed them from gig to gig. I used to like the musty smell of them, stage sweat, perfume and alcohol, taking me instantly back to the moments I felt most alive. I realize I can't remember how long it's been since I even slid open the door of that closet. It wasn't nostalgia that made me keep them, but a vague expectation I would wear them again, some day. I used to flick through them the same way I did my other clothes when I looked for something to wear, and tried them on sometimes, for parties or when I fantasized about playing again. Then they became unflattering, or maybe they always had been and I'd finally noticed, or maybe I just couldn't get away with them anymore. Anyway, I could afford to buy what I liked, things that fitted properly without taking in side seams or letting out waists. The rail has become a museum of retro clothes, a museum of my past.

God knows what has happened to them since I

last looked. A flash of the silvery wriggling of moths making Vonnie's stained, disintegrating clothes appear to move in my hands lets me know I won't be able to sleep with my old clothes right there in the adjoining room. I don't think I can even eat, or do anything, now I've thought about what might be in there.

I can't open the wardrobe door for fear of what might fly out at me, so at first I slide it open a crack to spray in enough moth killer to at least mean the moths will be still when I come across them. I find a plastic apron and new rubber gloves and cover my hair with a plastic bag before finally pushing the door wide.

One by one I take my outfits off their hangers and place them into black bin bags. Some of them would be worth something, if I needed the money. The top with *Biba* written across it in dulled gold glitter, which I wore with a miniskirt and gold tights and knee-length black plastic crocodile boots the time I gogo danced at Alice in Wonderland. The full-skirted taffeta dress, printed with red roses, I wore the day we dropped acid at a free GLC gig in Victoria Park, still with the tears and dirt stains from crawling around in scrubland when I thought I really was a rose bush. The velvet psychedelic hipsters I wore with the black turtleneck and Cuban-heeled Chelsea boots the day I was photographed for a Japanese youth magazine called *Dig the Scene*. The Frank Usher grey silk evening frock with the bow I wore when I was being Holly Golightly the night Toby took me to dinner at Sheekey's to discuss our future. His and my future, it turned out, rather than the band's. The Mary Quant op art dress I wore the day Billy Diamond finally noticed me.

''Ullo, Little Miss Sixties,' he winked at me, and I knew I could get him if I wanted.

Even my mum's black nylon petticoat, the one I wore to see the Clash.

I am so sentimental. I have clung on to these for dear life, as though they represent me, hanging shapeless and hollow in a forgotten cupboard, far better than my own living flesh.

Finally, I take my wedding outfit off the rail and inspect it through the polythene with a magnifying glass. When I am satisfied there are no holes in the plastic wrapper, I take the dress out of its sheath, lie it on top of the plastic, and examine it thoroughly. I see no signs of life. I put it back in its wrapper and after disinfecting and debugging the entire inside of the wardrobe, hang it back on its own on the empty rail.

The rest I take to the back garden and tip out of the bin bags onto the middle of the lawn with screwed up pieces of newspaper. I splash lighter fluid over the pile and light it, changing my mind suddenly at the last minute and shouting, 'No!' as the blue flames begin to lick at my clothes, my memories. I grab the sleeve of a corduroy jacket — it busked all around London and had a nod of acknowledgement from Ray Davies — Ray Davies of the Kinks! Nodding to me as though I was one of his kind! — and drag it free. As I turn it to inspect for burns I find a white cobwebby mesh of eggs in the worn,

71

yellowing armpit. I heave and chuck it quickly back on the emboldened flames now taking possession, and stand back to watch it all go up in smoke.

I feel lightheaded, weightless as ash.

7

Lizzie

My obsession with clothes began with Vonnie. She showed me you could build a whole new identity for yourself, just through what you wore. Vonnie was a punk rocker before I even knew what one was. It was when she was in her last year at school and we were turning into real teenagers. Whenever it was the school holidays Kim's family went to visit their friends in London to go shopping. I'd never been to London and neither had my mum, and it sounded like the most exciting place ever. I listened to all Kim's stories when we were back at school, wishing I could have gone too, instead of mooching round the house or going as far as W.H. Smith's whenever Mum was feeling rash enough to let me.

Kim showed me her photos of Vonnie down the King's Road in Chelsea, where there were people with blue and pink spiky hair, wearing ripped clothes held together with safety pins. Vonnie had her hair in loads of little knots all over her head, gripped in place with clothes pegs, and had made holes in her tights. She bought black lipstick and a dog collar and a pair of thigh-length PVC boots. Kim bought some new jeans that were drainpipe, and she laughed at my flares when we next met to go down town together. I took them in on my mum's old Singer, so I could only just get them over my ankles. Kim had her hair cut like a boy's, and I laughed with her about long hair, even though I still had long hair.

To me Vonnie was as amazing as a species from another planet. I had no idea that even ordinary girls like me could grow up to be that way. I hung on to Kim's every word, waiting to catch the bits of Vonnie that she sprinkled like fairy dust, as though they could somehow magic me too into something so exotic. Vonnie went to a punk gig and pogoed and got off with a mohican. Vonnie got a rose tattoo on her bum. Vonnie grew the hair in her armpits and dyed it emerald green. Vonnie got drunk at school and told her teacher to fuck herself. Vonnie got expelled weeks before her O-levels. Vonnie didn't care about her O-levels.

'What do I need stupid exams for?' she said to their mum and dad. 'I'm going up to London to get a job in a shop on the King's Road, and I'll be in a band and be discovered and become a filmstar. You don't need O-levels for that.'

Vonnie made me think about life. It seemed as though the word had two opposite meanings, and Vonnie was going after the second kind, the kind I hadn't known existed before. One that meant really living, not just getting by while the clocks ticked in quiet houses and you worried about the bills and how things would be when you were old. For Vonnie life was an adventure to go out and experience, not something you should protect yourself from until you shrivelled up and died. It made me braver. It made me realize you didn't have to follow the rules about the way you were meant to be.

Kim and I hated having to go to lessons without each other. Once, we decided to stay in a music room together instead of going to a class, and nobody noticed. So we did the same again the next week, skiving off different classes by different teachers. It got to be a habit. If it was ever noticed we blamed our periods.

It wasn't long before we got in with the bad older girls like Marie Bunyan, running into them when they were bunking off too. They started egging us on to do naughty things that we could get into trouble for. It made my heart race, but I soon discovered that, however scared I was, however much I dreaded the dare — when it was over and we'd got away with it, it was the best buzz in the world. You felt strong, as though you were above ordinary people and their rules didn't apply. You could do things you weren't meant to and that gave you super powers. Like you could become invisible or fly.

The time I got caught, I did it for Vonnie. She was getting ready to go back up to London to stay with their friends for the summer. After she got expelled her mum and dad thought it might get it all out of her system if they let her do whatever she liked for a while. Not that it seemed any different from the way they had treated her before, to me. But they thought she'd soon find the reality of having to get a waitressing job and somewhere she could afford to live — which wouldn't be a nice flat in Chelsea — would make her realize she was more free living at home and retaking her O-levels at the tech.

The people she would stay with were people her mum and dad had known when they were young. The woman was her mum's best friend from when they were both models and her husband was a television producer and they lived in Shepherd's Bush. I couldn't imagine parents having friends who lived in London. I couldn't imagine parents having friends. They had a spare room and said Vonnie could stay there, but she had to pay rent. Kim had heard her mum chatting to her friend on the phone about it. They were laughing together about how long Vonnie would last before she realized it wasn't so easy and came home.

Vonnie said she was leaving forever. She would meet some really cool people that she could share a flat with, through her job in the Great Gear Market. She told us all about it when she was sorting out her stuff for going. She and Kim had stopped fighting so much. In fact, she was being really nice to Kim, giving her lots of her old records and clothes as she was packing.

She let us go into her room after tea. No one was ever allowed in her room. We entered in hushed reverence and stockinged feet, peering round in wonder as though we were going through the back of a wardrobe into a strange land between worlds. The room was dark but glowing red from the Coca-Cola lampshade and had a smoky haze from the joss-sticks burning. It smelt musky and foreign and you could feel the reggae bass as well as hear it.

There was a big purple beanbag that Kim sat on, and I sat cross-legged where I could find space on the mangy leopardskin rug on the floor. Vonnie was trying on outfits in front of a full-length mirror propped against the wall. She had on fishnet tights and a leotard and her new thigh-length boots, and was putting on different things over the top and flinging them off again — a leather miniskirt, a denim jacket with the sleeves ripped off, a belted rain mac, a grandad coat left undone.

'Everyfink looks shit,' she moaned in a cockney accent, dropping the 't' off the end of 'shit'. She was twisting in front of the mirror, examining herself from all angles. She was going to see the Damned when she got up to London, at the Hammersmith Palais. She wrapped a red kiddie kilt round her waist, which only just covered her bum.

'Hey, that's mine!' said Kim.

'Well, you haven't worn it since you were nine,' Vonnie retorted. 'Anyway, it was mine before it was yours.' It looked a lot better like that, on her, than it was meant to look, down to a little girl's scabby knees with beige socks and brown Supergirls. But she still flung it off and sat instead at her dressing table on a stool that was a bin as well, with a furry top and a picture of Marilyn Monroe on the side. Her table was piled high with make-up, and she started rifling through to find things to paint her face with. Whenever she found things she didn't want any more she chucked them to Kim and me. I got lots of stuff to experiment with at home — some sparkly blue eyeshadow, orange rouge, a pink strawberry-flavour lipgloss.

Vonnie put on her black lipstick and drew dark circles around her eyes with a kohl pencil. It made her eyes look enormous. She put some white powder on her face, drew thick streaks of red lipstick under her cheekbones, and began to comb her hair the wrong way up so it stood out in a big mad bush. She looked like a funny startled creature that had just come out of a cave. And even more beautiful at the same time. She stood in front of the mirror again, and tried on several more jackets.

'I got nuffink to wear,' she said, throwing them on top of massive heaps of clothing all over the floor. 'What I really need is a cloak or somefink. I'm gonna get a whole load of new stuff when I start getting proper dosh.'

Along with the make-up I got some hippy beads, a cheesecloth gypsy skirt, a *Small Ones Are More Juicy* T-shirt and some singles — 'I Love to Boogie' by T-Rex, 'Fox On the Run' by Sweet and 'Play that Funky Music' by Wild Cherry. I stuffed my treasure into the bottom of my gym bag to smuggle it home.

I could imagine Vonnie in a cloak over that outfit. She was right, it was just what she needed. She'd look like a bat, or rather a vampire, with the cloak flapping at her sides flashing her compact little body in the leotard.

When I had to go into Miss Pollard's office with my excuse for why I hadn't given in my homework I saw the perfect thing hanging up on the back of her door. The teachers all wore their black gowns whenever there was a special do, like a prize-giving ceremony. They always looked really silly, but it wouldn't look silly on Vonnie. I told Kim about it and we worked out a plan for stealing it, but I was going to be the one who did it and no one was going to take my glory away from me.

We hung around Miss Pollard's office as inconspicuously as we could, but whenever she came out she locked the door behind her. We went round the back to where her window was, overlooking the netball courts. The window was quite high up, but one of us could get to it with a leg-up. We stayed back after school, waiting until most people had gone home, pretending we were practising shooting with a netball. When no one was around Kim made her hands into a step and I got up to try and open the window, sliding Kim's penknife in to move the clasp on the inside. But it wouldn't budge. I didn't know how long we had before Vonnie went away, and I had to have the cloak for her before she left; I just had to.

I got down and threw the netball at the window, but it didn't break. I swapped it for a big stone.

The shattering glass made a huge noise and we instinctively started running, but then I stopped, thinking if anyone had heard it they'd be here in a few minutes and I'd have lost my chance. Kim was laughing hysterically, but I pulled her back and made her hoist me up to put my hand through the glass and turn the handle. The frame was quite narrow, but I got in with just a glass cut on my shin. I grabbed the cloak and scrambled back through the window. We legged it through the car park and down the side entrance behind the science block. By the time we got there we were weak from laughing and running, and fear. We stopped down the alleyway outside the school fence to recover and peeked back to see no one was following us. I was so delighted with my booty I put the cloak on and started flapping my arms and jumping about, cawing like a crow for Kim's amusement.

That's when I turned round and saw Greasy Priestly walking grimly towards us from the other direction. Greasy Priestly was one of the teachers you were truly scared of. He had a violent temper and you had to be ready to duck in lessons in case he heard you whispering and threw the blackboard rubber at you. He taught history and we were doing World War Two, which made it all the more unbearable in his classes because he put Brylcreem on his hair and smoothed it over just like Adolf Hitler. All the boys sieg heiled him when he turned his back.

He was too furious to even speak at first, just jutted his bottom jaw, which was always a bad sign. I knew this was really serious, but I could feel the giggle bubbling up inside me. I could tell Kim was having the same problem by the way she was hanging her head. When he finally spoke his voice was quiet and low, as though it was taking all his efforts to control.

'Is this the way you've been taught young

ladies should behave?' he said. 'Hmn?' He
shoved his face into Kim's and began to circle
around her, shouting. He was so horrified by our
loutish behaviour he didn't seem to have noticed
the gown. I put my hands behind my back and
slowly, slowly pulled as much of it as I could up
into my arms to try and hide it. But it was no
use. Once he had finished circling Kim he got to
me and finally registered what I had on. He
grabbed my shoulder and spun me round.

'And WHERE did you get THIS?' His eyes
were doing their Adolf bulge but the giggles had
gone away.

He marched us back to his office and said we
were staying there until he found out the truth. I
was already later than I'd ever been, and worse
than my mum being angry was her being
worried. I took the blame for the whole thing, so
Kim could catch her bus home. Priestly told us
to report to the headmaster's office first thing
next morning.

Kim got away with detentions and a warning.
The headmaster told me I was turning into a
delinquent and my parents would be informed
and made to pay for the damage. I was
suspended for a week. Kim felt bad for me.

'God, I'm really sorry, Lizzie,' she said. 'It
doesn't seem fair. It's a real shame too; Vonnie
would've really loved the cloak.'

It almost made up for it, until my mum was
told what I'd done and grounded me indefi-
nitely, banning me from seeing Kim. She insisted
on picking me up at the main school gates every
afternoon like I was in primary school, in front

of everyone. I tried to say it was nothing to do with Kim, that it was all my idea. But she just replied that I'd never done anything of this sort before I'd met her, and she couldn't think what or who else could have possibly been such a bad influence on me.

I was crying so hard and for so long I was sick, and I think her resolve almost weakened, but she strengthened it again when she finally got out of me exactly why I'd wanted to steal a cloak in the first place.

★ ★ ★

However hard she tried to keep me and Kim apart, my mum couldn't stop us getting together in the music rooms. When I was stuck at home I would shut myself away at the piano and make up moody songs in minor keys. In the music rooms I would bash them out much louder and more angrily, like the ones by the bands on Vonnie's tapes. Kim said they were brilliant and persuaded her mum and dad to give her saxophone lessons so that we could play together. I taught myself how to strum the chords on one of the school's classical guitars. Sometimes we were told to keep the noise down by people who were trying to practise serious pieces for exams. Sometimes we told them to fuck off, depending on who it was and how carried away we'd got with our new punk personas. We developed a superior sneer for anyone who was into disco music or Dean Friedman, which was everyone else at school. We weren't even intimidated any more by the older boys who had scribbled Led Zeppelin on their school bags in biro and never washed their hair. It was as though Vonnie was our antenna, receiving all the information we needed and channelling it to us, so we had the secret of cool while the rest of the school went about in ignorance. She tuned out the interference when we got it wrong, like the time we thought it was OK to like the Boomtown Rats.

8

Beth

I get a call from Kim early Wednesday morning, but I am already up in a mad frenzy of cleaning. I have been up half the night, unable to remain lying down because of the bed bugs gnawing their way into my skin. I became convinced I could hear them. I finally stripped the bed linen off in the middle of the night and vacuumed the mattress with the Dyson, turning it, vacuuming, turning again and then again to sponge it with Dettox. I've pulled the furniture away from the walls, sprinkling flea powder into the carpet before shampooing it and hoovering. I'm on to washing the walls down when she calls.

'She opened her eyes,' Kim says as soon as I pick up. 'She mumbled something. Mum said it sounded like *fuck's sake!*'

We laugh, the fluttery laugh of relief as if nerves have wings and come flying out on your breath when it's over.

'She's getting better, then!'

'Dad was with her at the time while Mum got some sleep. He'd just put 'Big Noise from Winnetka' on the CD. He's sure that's what did it. Vonnie loved it when she was little. He says he used to sing the bass line to her, bouncing her on his knee. She used to ask for it all the time. He thinks that's why she was always so mad keen to be a bass player.'

Kim's words tumble over each other while I automatically clean the phone and let her rattle on.

'Mum asked if we could bring more music to play her — they don't really know what her favourite songs are. They remember punk of course, from before she left home, but they don't know what the tracks were. And not much since. I've got her record collection here and I'm going through . . . '

'Something by the Damned?' I suggest. 'That was one of the first big punk bands she went to see, wasn't it?'

'Oh God, yeah. 'New Rose' is the obvious one — it's the first one I remember her blasting out of her room. It's got to be here somewhere.'

'And the Clash, of course. She hung round with them a bit, didn't she?'

'Yeah — I've got 'Guns of Brixton'. It was one of the first bass lines she learnt to play.'

'Oh — and what about 'Oh Bondage Up Yours'? D'you remember her going round doing that intro?' Kim joins in with me, reciting the opening lines, building up until we're shrieking. It feels good and we laugh.

'Let's face it, it's kind of her theme tune!' I say.

'Yeah, it scared the shit out of my dad when she snuck up behind him doing it and then leapt in front of him in her full war paint shouting right in his face. I think she even got told off for that.'

Kim goes through Vonnie's records while I take her voice downstairs on the handset to see which of the tracks Toby and I might have on CD to play on the portable player Jeff has installed in Vonnie's hospital room. Kim finds as much as she can on Vonnie's cassettes but there are several crucial tracks that only I have.

'Do you want to come by and pick them up?' I ask, before I realize how ridiculous that is. I am miles out of Kim's way. Vonnie is lying in hospital between Kim's place and mine. But far nearer Kim's. 'Or actually I should bring them round to yours,' I add quickly.

'Um . . . isn't that a hassle for you?' Kim asks.

'No. No. Not at all. It's fine,' I say, but I can tell Kim is thinking about the route.

'Wouldn't it be better if I met you at the hospital?' She finally says the thing I've been dreading. 'You can get the tube to Paddington. It'd be a lot easier for you.'

'I really don't mind,' I interrupt. But she carries on her train of thought.

'Plus we could get there a bit quicker. She might be coming round and I'd like to be there when she does.'

I can't argue with that, however much my heart and stomach thrash about as my courage shrinks and begins to crush them. 'Of course,' I say. 'I wasn't thinking.'

We arrange to meet in an hour and a half outside St Mary's. I haven't got time to think about it or change my mind, even though my brain is racing with good reasons. I rush to pack up the CDs and get ready to go out. I don't

86

know why I'm in such a state. *Get a grip*, I keep saying to myself. *Kim needs you.*

It doesn't work. I am shaking and sweating as I sit on the tube and have to get out at King's Cross for air. It is a heavy, overcast day, like a manifestation of my mood. I head for the taxi rank to go home again, but hear myself saying, 'Praed Street, please,' to the driver. I sit squashed as far as I can to the left, hoping the driver can't see my face, pinched with panic, in his rear-view mirror.

I stand on the street by the main gate waiting for Kim, trying to calm myself with a cigarette.

'Are you all right?' she asks as she approaches, as though it's her that should be the strong one, for me.

'Sure,' I say brightly. 'How about you?'

'Yeah, OK.' She is smiling with hope and begins to head for the reception. I follow, taking deep breaths. Just before the entrance Kim stops and turns to me.

'I guess this might be a shock to you, Beth. Just to warn you. Vonnie . . . You haven't seen her for a while and . . . Well, she looks pretty bad. You know?'

'I know,' I say, but I realize I don't, really. Any time images of her lying ashen and unconscious on a stretcher or in a hospital bed have tried to enter my mind they have been replaced by the old pictures of her in my memory. I keep subconsciously touching them up and airbrushing as though I've got Photoshop in my head, altering the hue and saturation, turning up the brightness.

87

I'm glad Kim has thought to tell me so I can prepare myself, but it doesn't help me much as I follow her to the lifts. In fact, it has the opposite effect, as I become more resistant to the situation rather than more accepting. It is too real. I don't know how Kim is doing it, moving to meet the horror ahead of us in strong strides. The hospital smell of disinfectant and sickness begins to infiltrate and I find myself holding my breath to stop it getting inside. I can't let this in, I just can't. My legs turn to treacle with the effort of trying to move forward, as though I am tied to the end of a huge elasticated rope pulling me backwards, and then I can't feel them. They can't go any further. As the lift arrives the edges of my vision begin to blacken the way they do when you're about to faint. I am shutting down. My insides are about to spill and I cover my mouth with my hand and look wildly around for a toilet. I can't see one so I stumble back the way we came to get outside before I'm sick.

It takes Kim a while to realize I'm not in the lift with her, and she catches up with me just after I've splattered coffee-coloured liquid against the wall outside the hospital entrance.

'Christ, Beth, are you OK?' I hear her ask and she brushes my hair out of my face as I lean over. She finds a tissue in her bag for me to mop my mouth with.

'I feel better now, thanks,' I gasp. I don't tell her why, though. 'Sorry. I haven't been feeling right all morning.'

'You should've said,' Kim tuts. 'You shouldn't have come all this way. I've got enough of

Vonnie's music to be going on with. God, I'm sorry, Beth, I didn't mean to force you to come.'

'You didn't,' I say. 'Really. I was glad to.' Kim has a bottle of water which she lets me have. I see her glance inside.

'Look, you go on in,' I say, handing her my CDs for Vonnie, adding slyly, 'I better not come. In case I've got a bug or something.'

'Are you sure you're all right?' says Kim. Bless her, I think, guiltily. She doesn't want to leave me while I'm like this but she's desperate to see Vonnie.

'Totally,' I say, patting her arm to make her go. 'I'm just going to fall into a cab home. You go on in. Say hello to Von for me.'

Kim grins. 'I will.'

'I'll call you later.'

She practically runs back into the hospital and I shakily reach for another smoke before I head home. For once I am glad my body is rebelling against me. I don't know what's up with it but it seems to be fighting whatever I try to do, as though I'm a foreign body in my own flesh that my immune system thinks it needs to attack. I'm not usually so pathetic. It's probably just as well Toby is away. He can't bear sickly people.

Just as I think it, my mobile begins to buzz in my bag. It's Toby.

'Hey, hon,' I say, excited to hear from him at last. It seems like an age since we spoke, as if a whole era has come and gone while he's been away. I sit on a bench to talk.

'Hi. How ya doing?'

I laugh. 'Well — could be better.'

89

'What's up?' he asks. 'Where are you?'

'Outside a hospital. I was meant to be visiting Vonnie but I was just sick,' I say cheerily.

'What's wrong with you? What's wrong with her?' he asks. He is already stroppy at the mention of illness and hospitals.

'I don't know what's wrong with me. Nothing, really. But Vonnie took an overdose.'

'What, another one?' he says. He has no empathy for mental anguish. I usually like it about him. Life is simple in Toby's book. You just get on with it. Sometimes things go well, if you work hard. Sometimes you get pissed off when they don't. If you're ill you take medicine to cure it. You don't make yourself ill of your own accord. What's the point of that?

But this time his impatient tone annoys me. It feels heartless and out of place, while I'm sitting outside the hospital too freaked out to see her as she struggles to pull through inside, maybe only feet away from me.

'It was really serious this time,' I say. 'It's been touch and go. Everyone's worried sick.'

'Who's everyone? Why've you got so involved?' Toby asks. I'm surprised by his irritation.

'Who do you think?' I retort. 'Her family. Kim. You remember — my best friend? I have known Vonnie since I was a kid, you know.'

'Yeah, but you hardly see her any more.'

'So? That doesn't mean she doesn't mean anything to me.'

I don't know why we've started bickering so suddenly. A couple passing by glance at me as my voice rises. 'Christ! What's the matter with you? Did you just phone me to pick a fight? And where've you been lately anyway? I've left you loads of messages.'

'Look, I'm really busy, all right? Where d'you think I've been, in the fucking jacuzzi all day long? It's never-ending here. You should know that by now. I've got meeting after meeting, and then I have to do the social shit all night; I'm knackered. And now I'm trying to call you before I have to go out *again*, when all I want to do is get some sleep, and you have a go at me!'

'It was *you* having a go at *me*!' I shout back. 'I'm not having an easy time of it myself, you know. You're always away when I need you,' I blurt.

There's a silence and I know I've gone too far. I retract.

'You're not *always* away when I need you,' I say. 'I just wish you weren't away now. It's really . . . I'm finding it really hard.'

My voice wavers. I hear Toby let out a sigh. He doesn't like people feeling sorry for themselves either.

'Well, that's why I asked why you got involved. It's not your battle, is it? For God's sake. You've had the sense to move on in your life. Be there for Kim, sure, but don't get *involved*. What good is that to anyone?'

'Well, you'll be glad to hear I'm not being much good anyway,' I snap, suddenly realizing that, under the relief, I despise myself for being so useless. 'I tried to be here for Kim but I can't do it. I couldn't go in with her. I came running out like an idiot and threw up. There, are you happy now?'

'God, calm down, Beth, for fuck's sake. Are you all right now? Can you get home?'

'Yes, I'm all right now,' I answer, stroppily. 'Of course I can get home. I'm not a baby.'

'I didn't say you were, I was only worried about you being ill.' He has had enough of my petulance. 'Look. I've got to go. I just wanted to check in with you. Go home and chill out and call me tonight when you're feeling better and I've had some sleep. OK?'

After a sulky pause I say, 'OK. Bye.'

'I love you, all right?' says Toby.

'Yeah, me too,' I say and flip the phone off abruptly so that I've had the last word. Not much of a last word, but a last word nonetheless. I don't know why the row blew up out of nowhere but I'm still angry with him as well as myself. How can he think I'm not involved, whether I like it or not? Does he really think my life with him means I've completely separated from the person I used to be, like a snake shedding its old skin and slithering away?

I think about it. Perhaps that is what I tried to do, when I set about my marriage. Shed my old self, and all the Vonnie that went along with who that was. Maybe that's why my body is having such a violent reaction. Maybe it is just not possible to get someone like Vonnie out of your system once she's been there, like a viral infection that you never completely get rid of but survives inside you, dormant until something causes it to flare up and break out again.

How can the person I share my life with not know what she was to me? I suddenly feel completely bereft and alone. There is nobody who knows.

Vonnie is as much a part of my make-up as the very DNA that strings me together.

★ ★ ★

When I finish my cigarette I wander back out along Praed Street towards the station. I watch two hookers heading for the Special Clinic. *Honey and Trixie* I think automatically, and wish Kim was still with me so we could share the joke. She's the only other person in the world who would know why that was funny, apart from Vonnie herself. Though I doubt Vonnie would even remember giving us those names. It wasn't Vonnie who was the impressionable one, after all.

Only Vonnie could have ever made me think that being a prostitute was as glamorous as being a filmstar. I reach the girls just as they turn into the clinic entrance, one in a dirty white miniskirt with thin, bruised legs, one with rashy, sallow skin who meets my eyes with a heroin-glazed stare. I look away. It is painful. I could be looking into Vonnie's eyes at that exact moment, inside the hospital, and they could be staring back at me like that, accusingly, emptied of everything she ever was.

I walk towards the black hole of Paddington station and the clouds finally begin to spill, great fat drops like tears. The colour drains out of the world around me and blurs to a background of grey. I feel reality setting in like an inevitable

93

condition you just have to accept as you get older, like arthritis or lumbago.

But I am not ready for the things that set in when you're old. Sadness saturates my heart until it feels too heavy to carry. Something about the hookers — as if they really were Honey and Trixie and this is what happened to them — and finding out they are not wild and beautiful and free after all, but sorry and desperate, trips a switch inside me, like the electric going out.

I head down into the black hole as though it's the future, praying for something, anything, to find the switch in the dark and flip it back on.

9

Lizzie

I finally managed to convince my mum that I had learnt my lesson. When I wasn't at the piano I was always in my room scribbling furiously in my exercise books. She even tried to encourage me to take a break, suggesting we went to the Odeon to see the *Pink Panther* film.

'It's not healthy to work all the time, Elizabeth,' she said. 'Everything in moderation. We should have some fun too.'

I got out of it by saying I had a tummy ache, although really it was just one of those awful pangs I got when my mum tried to do a nice thing and got it totally wrong. Like I would want to see a *Pink Panther* film with my mum, when Kim and Vonnie were planning how they'd get in to see *Pretty Baby*! All I knew about it was that you had to be eighteen to be let in. Vonnie said she saw X certificates all the time and had been doing it for years.

'Why don't you sneak out and come too, Lizzie?' Kim asked.

I shrugged. 'I'm not bothered. It's only a stupid movie,' I said, but inside my heart had started thumping with the hope of it. And the dread of it too, mixed in.

'Surely you can slip out? You only live down

the road from the Odeon.' And she left it there like a challenge, like someone else's chocolate on the sideboard.

All of Saturday I was like a cat that had been caught stalking a bird in the garden and been locked inside. I couldn't forget the bird was still out there. I paced the house and sniffed around doors and windows, incapable of thinking about anything else.

'Elizabeth, for goodness' sake, will you please settle down and do something? You're giving me a headache,' my mum said. She sent me to the butcher's in the end to get some pork chipolatas.

'You wouldn't mind making sausage and mash for you and Mr Grundy later on, would you, dear? I can't face cooking; I've got one of my migraines coming on.'

It was such a relief to get outside. I had to pass the Odeon to get to the shops on the high street and I saw the poster for *Pretty Baby*. Brooke Shields was beautiful. I found myself looking on the board to see what times it was on. Seven forty-five must be the one they were going to.

When I got back Mum was looking deathly pale. She really was getting one of her migraines. She took a tablet with a glass of water.

'Will you be all right if I go and lie down for a while?' she asked me. 'I think the only thing I can do now is try and sleep it off.' I wondered if it was one of her really bad ones. When those set in, she had to stay in bed all day with the curtains drawn, and sometimes even the day after that. I tried really hard not to hope it was, but I couldn't help it.

I got through tea as quickly as I could, with one eye on the clock. Mr Grundy tried to do his good-with-children routine.

'So, just the two of us this evening, Bizzie Lizzie.' He made his voice all jolly, as though it would fool me into thinking he was good fun to be with. 'How shall we entertain each other, eh? How about a game of Scrabble?'

It was quarter to seven. Kim would be in Vonnie's room trying on her clothes while she applied blusher the way she said would give her cheekbones. They would be listening to records and singing along and laughing excitedly at the prospect of their night ahead. I thought about my night ahead, playing Scrabble with Mr Grundy on the coffee table, with the *Generation Game* on TV in the background, and I felt the sorriest I'd ever felt for myself. My life was awful. I burst into tears.

At first I forgot Mr Grundy was even there; I just threw my face into my arms on the table and wept great fat rolling tears and snot onto the tablecloth.

'Lizzie! What on earth's the matter?' I was so overflowing with sympathy for myself, I even spared a bit for Mr Grundy. He sounded so ludicrous, trying to talk to a crying girl. I couldn't say anything at all, until he came and sat in the chair next to me and stuffed a rumpled grey handkerchief up through the gap between me and the table.

'Thank you,' I sniffed, and blew my nose and wiped my soggy face.

'Let me get you a drink and you can tell me all

about it,' Mr Grundy soothed. 'Orange squash? Or perhaps a nice hot cup of cocoa would make you feel better.'

'It'll take a whole lot more to make me feel better than a cup of fucking cocoa,' I blurted, and the shock made us both jump and stare open-mouthed at each other's faces. I don't know who it was whose mouth twitched first, but whichever, it set the other off like a spark, and we both started giggling. The more we thought about it the funnier it got until we were practically hysterical. We couldn't stop.

'Shhh — you don't want to wake your mother,' said Mr Grundy, as I snorted into his hanky. I'd never seen a grown man giggle uncontrollably before. His giggle was different from his big boomy laugh. He hunched himself in as if he was trying to stop himself, but his shoulders shuddered with it and his nostrils flared in and out as it escaped. His screwed-up watery eyes kept staring at my face, which was dreadful, because the second I looked up or opened my eyes there he was, and that would start me off again, and that would get him going. It was weird to giggle in this intimate way with Mr Grundy, like you only ever normally did with your best friend. But it was good to laugh, whoever it was with. I dried my eyes and blew my nose again, and smoothed my hair back away from my sticky, puffy face.

'That's better,' said Mr Grundy. He got up and went into the kitchen, stooping back under the door frame to say, 'I take it that was a 'no' to cocoa, then?' I giggled again. He looked so pleased with himself about his funny remark, and it was quite witty for him — I had to give him that.

He made us both a cup of tea instead and came and sat back down again. I apologized for swearing.

'I've never sworn properly at anyone before,' I said.

'So, your first time, eh?' he replied. 'Congratulations.' And he raised his teacup in a toast to me. He really was being very good about it. I felt grateful, and it made me want to explain. So I told him everything — how my friends were going to the cinema but I couldn't go because I was grounded and how it wasn't fair because I'd taken the whole blame for something Kim and I had both done for her sister. And as I was telling it I really didn't sound as bad as all that, or as though I deserved quite such a harsh punishment. I began to feel quite innocent, sitting there pouring my sob story into Mr Grundy's sympathetic, hairy ears.

When I'd finished I glanced at the clock again. Mr Grundy saw me, and turned his head to look himself. It was twenty past seven.

'So what time did you say the *Pink Panther* was starting?' he asked.

'Quarter to eight,' I said, praying there was a showing of the *Pink Panther* that evening too, just in case he checked.

'If you promise to be very good and to come home the minute it's over,' he said, 'I'll turn a blind eye to you slipping out the front door now. You have to promise you'll be really good and make sure your friends see you home. I'd come and fetch you, but if your mother wakes up while we're both out the game will be up. If I'm here I can let her assume you've gone to bed. If she finds out different, I'll take the blame and say I didn't know you weren't allowed out and encouraged you to go to the cinema as a treat.'

'I don't know if I should,' I said, although I did know really. 'I don't want to get into more trouble, or get you into trouble either.'

I knew it was the right thing to say. Mr Grundy was the sort of man who liked to think of himself as the head of a household.

'Don't you worry about that, Lizzie. To be honest, I can't see anything wrong in you going down the road to the picture house just once on a Saturday night with some people your own age. You can't be cooped up here all day with old fuddy duddies for company.'

I felt a sad stab at the thought of Mr Grundy recognizing what he was.

'You're not an old fuddy duddy,' I said, and kissed him on his scratchy cheek. He seemed to sit up a fraction straighter in his chair.

'Go on, off you go.'

He patted my bum lightly as I brushed past him out of my seat.

* * *

I ran to my room and flung my clothes out of my drawers to find something grown up to wear. I pulled on a little cotton camisole Mum had brought me to go under blouses that were too

100

see-through, with my drainpipe jeans. I threw some make-up in a bag as I shoved my feet into my plimsolls. I was too short in them, though. I needed something to make me taller. My mum didn't wear high heels either, only spongy court shoes and sandals that wouldn't hurt her corns. There were only her old evening shoes, in the bottom of her wardrobe. I had to risk sneaking into her room to get them. Mum shifted and sighed when the wardrobe door creaked, but I couldn't stop myself now if I tried. When I had them I practically fell down the stairs, so I could get my mum's white rain mac on before Mr Grundy saw me in a camisole. Mr Grundy opened the sitting room door and tiptoed exaggeratedly to the front door to help me open it quietly.

'Have a nice time and be good,' he whispered. 'If your mother gets up I'll put my bedroom light on with the curtains open, so you'll know.'

I didn't know what I'd do if she was up when I got back, but I was past caring. As soon as I got into the street I ran as fast as I could. It was like being in a thriller, and I imagined I was running for my life from some evil horror. It made it more exciting than ever.

I changed my shoes and put on my make-up and brushed my hair in the public toilets. Heels made you stick your bum and chest out to balance yourself, front and back. The shoes made a clackety noise as I walked, with lots of scraping in between as I dragged a heel across the concrete before I learnt how to pick my feet up properly. I got a heel stuck in a grating and had to hop a couple of steps. They were still slightly too big and I had to clutch my toes like crazy to keep them on. It really was hard work being a woman, just getting a hundred yards.

I lurked self-consciously outside the cinema waiting for Kim and Vonnie. I recognized them before they recognized me. Vonnie had a tight black dress on, the sort of thing I'd only ever seen on stars in films before. She strode along swinging her hips in high, high stilettos as though she'd been born in them. Her hair wasn't just hennaed any more, it was bright orange, and she'd crimped the curls out and tied it up with a scarf on top of her head. The sprouts of hair coming out of the top seemed to lick upwards like flames, making her look as though she was on fire. Kim was having the same trouble walking as I'd had. Next to Vonnie she looked like a clown. She kept tugging her miniskirt down where it was riding up her gawky thighs.

When I said, 'Hi,' and stood by them in the queue they stared at me in disbelief.

'You made it!' Kim laughed, and we jiggled up and down excitedly together. We stood behind Vonnie while she got our tickets and tried to still our nerves and act like older girls. The man in the ticket booth cast a disgusted eye over us, but didn't say anything. Vonnie bought us each a Coke and a big bag of Revels to share and headed upstairs so she could smoke. We got the row at the front, so we could lean forward on our elbows, or sit back with our legs dangling over. We threw Revels into each other's mouths and Vonnie offered us cigarettes. When the lights went down Vonnie started taking swigs out of a bottle she had under her coat.

Pretty Baby was cool. It was about a girl younger than me who was going to lose her virginity and become a prostitute. I felt so happy, lost in a world where I was beautiful Brooke Shields and everybody wanted me. Even when I was nudged from my fantasy by Kim to giggle about something rude, I would remember I was out on a Saturday night with my girlfriends, and even my reality seemed fantastic.

At the end of the film, some grown men slunk into the row behind us. One of them asked Vonnie for a cigarette, and she turned and offered them round. When they asked our names she said in a husky voice,

'I'm Emmanuelle. And this is Honey and Trixie.'

When the lights went up they got a good look at us, and Kim and I managed to sneak a peek at them too, when we bravely turned round. At first all three men crowded around Vonnie, but the one called Dazza was the one Vonnie directed her answers to. He was the best looking, a bit like John Travolta, with black hair and a cute dimple when he flirted. When Vonnie started chatting to him, the other two tried to talk to me and Kim, but we just sniggered together. Dazza asked Vonnie if we wanted to come to a party and Vonnie said, 'OK,' before we had a chance to think up some excuse. I just smiled to hide being scared and wondered how I would get away.

When we stood up the men seemed really big, even though we were in heels. They surrounded us, trying to separate us off into pairs with them, and we left the cinema wrapped in their foreign, musky presence. It was a totally new smell to me, men on a Saturday night, a mixture of cigarettes, Denim aftershave and something that made you feel in danger. I felt naked and vulnerable and I put my coat on as soon as I could. Dazza said he would bring his car round and we could all squeeze in to go to the party.

When he was gone, Kim and I managed to get together behind Vonnie again. Dazza's mates started larking about with each other, showing off.

'Are you up for it?' Vonnie asked us. We must've looked worried, because she smiled.

'It's only a party; it might be a laugh,' she said, but Kim and I looked at each other. Neither of us wanted to go because of everything we'd been told about getting into cars with strange men. We didn't want to say so, though, and look stupid in front of Vonnie. In the end I said, 'I better get back else my mum'll kill me.'

Vonnie looked at Kim, but she shook her head, embarrassed.

'You go if you want,' said Kim.

'Nah — I'm not bovvered,' said Vonnie, kindly. 'It'll be a duff party round here anyway. You've got to be in London to find the good parties. Shall we blow them out?'

We nodded, gratefully.

'Hey, guys,' Vonnie called, stalking up to them as Dazza pulled the car to the kerb. 'We're gonna give it a miss. Have a good night.'

Dazza kept trying to get her to go with them,

calling her 'baby' and stroking her bare arm to coax her into the car. But Vonnie wasn't having any of it. They didn't scare or intimidate her. She was the one with the power. His mates soon gave up on me and Kim as we huddled dimly together like sheep. They were drawn back to Vonnie's luminescence like moths. I watched her, mesmerized. She even made turning guys down seem like a come on. I could understand why she made Dazza act like such an idiot. When she laughed her face shone. Every way she stood was like a pose in a magazine, without even trying. She just seemed to really own her body, not like us two, having to pull and push our limbs about as though we were operating puppets.

Eventually she got bored of playing with them.

'OK, guys. The truth of it is we have to start work now, so if you want to stand around taking up any more of our time you'll have to pay for it.' They didn't get her at first, but she went on. 'Seriously, I make fifty quid a trick and you boys are wasting my valuable time.' The looks on their faces went from adoring to bewildered.

'You're no fucking prozzie,' said Dazza. 'You're having me on, right?'

'Look, do you want to pay for my time or not? If not, fuck off and let me earn my living.'

The looks went from bewildered to disgusted.

'Shit, Jesus!' Vonnie suddenly hissed, making them jump. 'It's our pimp!'

She pointed to a huge biker coming along on the other side of the road eating a bag of chips. Vonnie got hysterical.

'Fuck! I mean it! Get out of here before he

cuts your fucking balls off! Go on, fuck off!'

She ran along the kerb a bit, away from their car, and began acting as though she was touting for business. Dazza and his mates called us bitches, slags and cunts and screeched away in their Ford Cortina.

'Vonnie, you're supposed to be looking after us, not getting us called terrible names in the street,' Kim scolded as we skulked shamefaced after her.

Vonnie roared with laughter.

'Who cares what tossers think of you? It's what you think about yourself that matters.'

I'd never considered what I thought about myself before. Only what my mum thought of me, and what other girls thought, and my teachers, and boys, and I always tried to be the way they wanted. It was getting more and more difficult because the different ways they wanted me to be were going further away from each other in opposite directions, like roads from a junction.

We tottered to the taxi ramp after Vonnie, who had started dancing down the middle of the road singing 'Sweet Transvestite' at the top of her gravelly voice. My mum hated anyone making a show of themselves in public. But I couldn't see anything bad about it. She looked so funny and sweet, like a scene from a film. She really didn't care what anybody thought. I would have been flattered and grateful if someone good looking had chatted me up, and would have been really upset if he ended up thinking I was a bitch or a slag or the C word. But it didn't bother Vonnie.

106

When we caught her up and hung around waiting for a taxi, I asked, 'Didn't you like Dazza, then?'

'He was all right for round here, I suppose,' she said. 'But he'd be nothing up town. You get guys to die for up there.'

'What's it like, then?' I asked, shyly. 'Having a boyfriend?'

'It's cool,' she said. 'They can treat you nice and make you feel pretty good. But you should never fall in love with them. Then they think they own you and want you to settle down and get married or some dumb thing. No man's ever gonna tie me down. I've got my own life to live. I'm always gonna be free.'

A silence fell as we stood, with smiles of wonder on our faces as her magical words drifted around us and melted into our skins like snowflakes.

★   ★   ★

I wiped off any remains of lipstick and poked my head round the sitting room door as I sneaked back into the house to say thank you to Mr Grundy.

'My pleasure,' he said, and when I glanced at him through my hair he really looked as if it was.

★   ★   ★

At first I thought it was going to be easy from then on, giving my mum the slip. But I never got another chance like that again. She didn't get any more migraines for ages. I had to listen to Kim going on and on about all the things Vonnie was letting her do with her before she left home.

I drank in the stories and grinned along, like I was enjoying them. But it was too painful to know what I was missing out on. I couldn't bear it. I started looking forward to getting home and shutting my bedroom door. What my mum didn't know was that when I was scribbling away in there I wasn't being good and doing my homework at all. I was writing lyrics about not being understood and running away and never settling down and being free forever.

Sometimes I would only pretend to go to sleep when my mum and Mr Grundy did. When the house fell silent I would turn my bedside light back on, throwing an orange scarf over it so it wasn't too bright. I would try my hair in different styles, or do something with my awful clothes to make them more cool, hitching skirts up with belts, or tying shirt ends in a knot. I dug out clothes I thought I'd grown out of so they were dead tight, or short.

One night I tried on all the things that I'd got off Vonnie. They were my favourites, even though she'd thrown them out because they were out of fashion. They were so unfamiliar it was easy to imagine being another, older girl in them. The *Small Ones Are More Juicy* T-shirt was really tiny and the words went fatter where they stretched out across my swelling bosoms. I didn't wear my bra underneath. I tied her old gypsy skirt loosely, so it hung at my hip bones, and the T-shirt was so short my tummy button showed.

The material of the skirt was soft and pale and see-through, like petticoats. Pants showed under it, and I wondered what Vonnie used to do. I took my pants off. Standing in front of the bedside light, you could see the shape of my legs and a shadow at the top of them. I wound the necklaces around my wrists and ankles, and the beads and shells rustled against each other.

I mussed up my hair and watched my face transform in the mirror as I practised doing my make-up. I didn't just look different, everything about me was different. The exotic smell from the T-shirt of coconut oil and Vonnie's hot body, the sound of the tinkling jewellery, the feel of breathy fabrics on my naked skin. It made me move differently. I wished I wasn't confined by my little boxroom, so I thought I'd go to the bathroom just to see how it felt to be able to swing my hips for a few steps.

I tiptoed onto the landing and reached out to push open the bathroom door, just as it was pulled from the inside. It made me jump, and the bathroom light came flooding out to catch me, exposing and blinding me. I instinctively drew my hands over my chest and mouth, and then saw with relief that it was not my mum but Mr Grundy who appeared around the door.

I made him jump, too, when he saw me. Then he smiled. Then he looked at me again. Instead of moving past me, he stood and opened the door wider so the light shone on me even more. He really looked at me then, first at my face, then down, slowly, over my body. I realized I was trembling, and could feel it making my skirt flutter and beads chink. I felt the goose bumps exploding over my skin and my nipples pushing out into the soft cotton film. And still I lowered my arms to my sides so that Mr Grundy could see, and I watched him read the words across my breasts before his eyes stroked their way back up my neck and lipsticked mouth to share a flicker of amused knowledge with mine.

10

Beth

A vast enlargement of a photograph of a face hangs in a matt black frame in the stairwell. It is an arty close-up in semi-profile, the contrasts enhanced and shaded in blues, catching a perfect moment as a shining stroke of white-blonde hair swings across pouting lips, singing fervently into a silver microphone. A passionate crease sets off black arching brows over smoulderingly kohled eyes, which glance sideways into the camera, burning an eternal connection through the lens into whoever studies the picture from the other side.

It hangs amongst gig posters, publicity shots of popstars, and gold records on what Toby calls his Wall of Fame. The other pictures are of stars that Toby has made; the girl is me. Was me. I used to think of it as my favourite image of myself, but now it doesn't even feel like an image of myself. When guests peruse the collection they exclaim, 'Wow! Who's that?!' and are amazed when they find out. 'It's incredible!' they enthuse. 'You were really something!'

'Thanks,' I say, as though I am flattered. As though it is a compliment that it's utterly unbelievable that it's me. I suddenly hate the picture. I can't bear to look at it. I feel as though

I am standing accused, jeered by a past self who thought I would become so much more than I have. Face to face with unfulfilled potential, tormenting me with glimpses of what was, and what could have been. '*How could you do this to me?*' the girl seems to shriek into the mic as I pass, her voice reverberating around the stairwell as though it's an empty venue.

★ ★ ★

My purge of the house continues. I have scrubbed my way from the top rooms to the halfway mark, this picture in the stairwell. I am leaning, balanced precariously on tiptoe at the bend of the stairs, struggling to release it from its hook to take it down. A sudden ring of the doorbell makes me jump and I drop it. The picture catches the edge of a step and shatters, the frame and shards of glass crashing down the remaining stairs. On reflex I shrink back around the stairwell away from the front door, but after that explosion there's no way I can pretend there's nobody home. I tip my head and peek down to see the flap of the letterbox lift as somebody peers in.

'Hello? Are you all right? Hello? Can you hear me?'

It is a boy's voice, full of concern, and I realize he might think I've had an accident and call the police or an ambulance or something. I have no choice but to answer.

'I'm fine,' I call lightly. I pick my way down the stairs, laughing. 'It sounded a lot worse than it

112

was,' as I reach and open the door.

A skinny kid with brown eyes smiles at me anxiously.

'Sorry,' he says. 'I hope that wasn't my fault.' He is softly spoken, too new to have yet dropped the middle-class politeness of his upbringing in favour of the usual streetwise cool. He looks beyond me, to the picture on the floor at the foot of the stairs surrounded by smithereens of glass.

'Don't worry.' I wave away his concern. 'It's an old one. I was taking it down, not putting it up.'

'Do you want help clearing it up?'

'No, it's fine, honestly. It really wasn't your fault. Are you looking for Toby?' I have already guessed he is another hopeful young thing.

'Yeah. I met a guy called Jack at a gig. Told me to send him a demo. I was in the area so I thought I'd drop it by in person. I hope you don't mind.'

Jack works for Toby in A&R. He pretty much never gives out Tobe's home address. Only if the artist is really worth bothering Toby with directly and he doesn't want the demo to get lost in the pile at the office.

The boy shyly holds out a brown envelope. He has less of the pose and attitude of most. He has dark spiky hair, badly cut, and it gives me a pang for my youth. It reminds me of the awful cut I gave myself as a teenager, the way it stands up on one side and falls flat on the other, as though he is standing in a strong wind. He doesn't look as though he's been to a hairdresser or made any attempt to style it in spite of the array of *product* available these days. It makes me warm to him.

113

He isn't dressed in the usual rock boy uniform either, the way most of them are — currently skinny drainpipes and baseball boots. He has a loose T-shirt with no brand name on the front and baggy workmen's trousers, not even the scruffy surfer/skater style. He looks as though he's bunged on some older brother's cast-offs, as though he really doesn't care about clothes and isn't just trying really hard to look as though he doesn't.

'He's away right now. But I'll make sure he gets it.' I take the package from him. 'You play guitar, right?' He has perfect hands for a guitar player, slim but with incredibly long fingers. I like looking at people's hands. You can tell a lot about the kind of person they are. His are quite feminine, soft. They make me want to hear his music. He clocks me looking at them and he smiles and nods as he realizes how I know.

He shifts to go. 'When will he be back? It's just I've got a couple of gigs coming up and I could put him on the guest list if he's around.'

'Not till Sunday, I'm afraid.'

'Oh. Well, the first's this Friday at the Capo. But I'm playing again on Sunday at the Twelve Bar if he's back in time. There's a flyer in there anyway, but if you could just say I'll get him in.'

'Oh, it's OK. Toby knows them down there. Save your precious guest list places for your mates or your chick or something.'

'Oh, right. Of course.' He smiles, pushes his hand through his hair and blushes. I realize I've made him feel foolish and naive, and for some reason I blush too. What's wrong with me? I usually enjoy my easy banter with these youngsters. I know they find me cool, the older woman-of-the-world type — a role that is fun to play, far removed from their young, jealous girlfriends and clueless mums. Toby enjoys the crushes they get on me. Although I deny that they do have crushes I know what he means, and I'll miss it as I grow older and the boys that come round stay nineteen, and the feeling stops.

'Listen, do you want to leave a note or something?' I say to cover up. 'Just to say Jack sent you?'

'Oh, yeah, if that's OK. That'd be good.'

I open the door wide for him and he lopes in, attempting to tread around the glass on the tiles until he's in the middle of the hall, awkwardly looking about.

'I'll just get you a pen.'

When I come back I see he's crouching, looking at the photo on the floor. He glances sidelong up at me.

'Why are you taking this down?'

'Oh . . . ' I gesture at the stairs, 'it's old. And we've run out of room on Toby's Wall of Fame. I'm sure he'll be bringing back some shots of Eye Candy to put up.'

'Eye Candy?'

'The band he's signing up — it's why he's in Japan. Brand-new girl band — five Japanese schoolgirl lesbians.' I raise my eyebrows at him.

'They'll go a long way.' He nods sagely.

We share a look and a grin. He has the deepest, darkest eyes I've looked into for a long time. I have a secret thing for brown eyes. Not that Toby doesn't have great eyes — he does, the piercing blue I imagine they mean in Mills & Boon romances, and I know they are attractive, in a dazzling sort of way. But I find I can never really look into them for long. I can't sink into them the way you can with dark eyes. They seem to reflect me off their surface, somehow, like sun on glass.

The boy ducks his head and goes back to studying the photo.

'Whatever image they come up with to sell them won't be as sexy as this.'

He seems too shy to make such a remark and it takes me by surprise. Eventually I say, 'Yeah, it's a good photo.'

'I don't mean the photo,' he replies quietly, thankfully still staring at it. I realize I'm glad nobody knows it's me, and distance myself further from it by trying to joke, 'Yeah well — where is she now?' But my aim of witty and cynical misses, and it comes out sad and mean. I force a laugh, to show I meant to be funny, but he doesn't smile.

Instead he says, 'What do you mean?' and looks up at me, quizzically. 'You're still here.'

I laugh again, to try to cover the moment when I just don't know what else to do with myself, half of me, the autopilot half, acting as though it hasn't happened, this moment of connection, of truth. I wait for the good hostess to take over, the one that is used to always smoothing out wrinkles and creases in social gatherings with drunks and coke heads when egos and the worst of emotions run high. But I can't seem to summon her up under his gaze. I wish I'd had time to do something with my hair before I'd opened the door. God knows what I look like. My eyes are nothing without the definition of eyeliner and mascara, insipid and small. I release my hair from my ear so it falls across my face and shrink back a little, to hide in the shadow of the half-open door, out of the glare of the sun pouring over every crease and liverspot and facial hair.

Eventually I say, 'People don't usually recognize me.'

He seems genuinely surprised. 'Really? *Really*?! How can they not? You look exactly the same!'

I tut and sigh. 'I do not and you know it. Don't be kind.'

'I'm not being kind.' We're suddenly comfortable, easy with each other. He takes his envelope back, and the pen, and sits on a stair to scribble a note to Toby on the back. As he writes he says, 'You look older, of course you do. Not plastered in make-up and hair gunk. But you.' He passes them back to me and stands up. 'Your whatever you call it. Your spirit. Your soul.' He pulls a face to show he knows he's sounding wanky. He looks cute when he's being funny. 'Whatever you call it. It's the same.' I put on a studious face and look from the picture to the hall mirror and back again.

'D'you think?' I say. 'Is that a good thing?'

'Don't fish,' he teases. He has a self-assurance lurking underneath his shyness that unnerves me. It is the thing that undoubtedly gives him his stage presence, taking over from the unassuming

117

boy that came to the door and making him able to get up there and do the rockstar thing. The confidence that comes from being responded to in the way you hope. He must be talented, then. With his sweetness it is an exciting mix.

He starts to go, turning to smile, 'You know you're beautiful.' Only he says it *bewdiful*, like a Sixties groover, and makes a jokey peace sign as he goes through the door. I go to close it behind him and watch him swaggering a little down the path, pulling a cigarette from a pack in his backside pocket and hunching over to light it. I shouldn't be so pleased by that.

I'm grinning as I close the door. A boy like that has every right to swagger. I feel glad that he isn't too shy to know what he has. I'll bet he gets some groupies. My heartbeat has stepped up a few bpms and I feel revitalized, the way a track is when you up the tempo, even just a notch, and it suddenly comes to life. Sometimes it's all it needs. I feel silly too, falling for the charm of a young muso after all these years of knowing all about them, having them sussed. He must be laughing inside at how he can wrap women round his little finger.

Yet still I find myself looking myself over when I pass a mirror, checking how I appeared to him, for signs of my *spirit*, my *soul*, hoping for the best.

Although the Jiffy bag is sealed, I can't resist opening it to have a look at his demo CD. I am secretly hoping for a photograph of him on the cover, but it is plain white with a simple wobbly line drawing of a guitar being played by a half-finished man. The wording is handwritten in capitals that slope away at the end of the line. It makes a refreshing change from most demos, so glossy now that they look like record company releases. The look of it is kind of like naive art, amateurish and totally unpretentious, but with a unique style. It is so him, somehow. He must have drawn it himself.

His name is Jesse.

Jesse Porter: 3 songs, is all it says.

Why I am nervous about hearing his music I don't know. I have to prepare myself before putting the CD on. I desperately don't want him to be disappointing. I try to imagine the worst it could be so that I'm pleasantly surprised whatever he sounds like. I decide that anything will be OK as long as he's not thrashing about with his mates trying to be next in the Busted / McFly line.

The recording sounds live. Just an electro-acoustic guitar and his voice, closely mic'd, intimate, so you can hear his fingers sliding along the strings to reach notes, and his breaths between phrases. It is heartbreakingly beautiful. His playing swerves from delicate fingering to wild distorted strumming on choruses, with his voice diving and soaring above it. He has a vast range, deep and rich at the bass, a man's voice, yet still able to reach a boy's falsetto at the top. It has a quality to it, a timbre, that soaks in, like oil.

When the three songs end the silence is bare. All I can do is play them again. I listen this time in headphones so I can lose myself utterly in his music. As I do, his words begin to speak to me. 'Last Chance', the first song is called. *When*

119

life's near misses are all starting to show, When your dreams are all fading, where do you go? It's your last chance, and your last chance is slipping away. He is too young to know about dreams fading and last chances. How can he write this at his age? It disturbs me that he can see this in other people. I feel as though I opened the door to him naked.

The second song is an angrily strummed protest song called 'I Don't Believe'. I haven't heard such heartfelt passion for an age and as he spits a list of the things he despises I feel as thrilled as the first time I ever strung three chords together and spilled my guts.

The third song is called 'Out There Somewhere', his fingers as soft on the strings as a breeze. *If you got lost along the way,* he whispers into my ear, *you know I will come looking. I won't give up till I find you. I will make it OK. I know you're out there somewhere.*

I don't know how many times I play Jesse's songs, but when I finally stop I feel we have known each other forever, this boy and me, and I have forgotten everything else. Everything. When I take the headphones off my actual life seems the unreal one that just fills the gaps between songs. That's how it used to be when I made music myself. The songs were what living was for, and the rest of the time was to be engineered around them, just so they could exist. They needed space to be born and to grow until they matured and told exactly the right story. A perfect song has a life all of its own. I'd forgotten I used to feel that.

I eventually sweep up the broken glass and wonder what to do with the photo. It was nice of him to say it, and he seemed to mean it, but he is too young to really know. I am not the same any more. However much I search for it in the mirror, I can't find that spirit-soul. I bear a vague resemblance to me, only older. I am empty, only filled temporarily with his. For now I put the picture in the cupboard under the stairs, too unsure of myself to throw it away. It is, after all, the only proof I was ever there.

* * *

I lie awake all night like a teenager, thinking of Jesse. It is not a crush, exactly. I am too old and wise for that, surely? He is the sort of boy I wish I'd had as a first boyfriend. It makes me feel sad that I didn't. Imagine how differently you would turn out if your blossoming years were nurtured by a tender, lovely boy like that?

I try to shut out memories of the passing of my innocence by listening to his music, flowing through me like air. A spore of him has drifted in on it and settled. His voice echoes around my caverns, saying, *You're still here. You're still here.*

The idea of going to see him play on Friday on my own has crept into my head. Although I try to banish it, any time I drift off to sleep I wake with a start, drenched in sweat after nightmares of being buried alive in the dirt on the Euston Road.

11

Lizzie

At the time I didn't think about the thing with Mr Grundy as anything other than one of those life experiences you went through as a teenager. *I want to experience everything*, I remember thinking — or was it Vonnie who'd said that, before she went away? For me Mr Grundy was a means to an end. I got to the age when I really needed my own pocket money and all I had to get it was me.

Vonnie did go to London, like she said she would, and as the weeks turned into months and the months rolled on towards a year we all discovered she really meant what she said and was never coming back. She had signed on at the parents' friends' house, and got the DHSS to pay her rent. It wasn't quite the lesson Patti and Jeff intended her to learn. She found plenty of jobs too, cash in hand, at record shops in Camden and stalls selling bondage gear in Kensington Market. She soon winkled out the people she was looking for and belonged with, with green hair and safety pins in their cheeks, and she moved in with her friend Sam, only she spelt it *Psyam*, from the record shop, who had tattoos all up her arms and a ring through her nose.

Vonnie could buy anything she wanted. Every week she bought albums and tickets to gigs, and studded belts, and a leather jacket. The first thing she saved up for was a bass guitar and an amp, and she began to play along to her Cramps and Siouxsie and the Banshees and Stranglers singles. She painted the walls and ceiling of her room shiny black.

And Kim began to buy things, too. We would stand leafing through the records in the New Wave section, next to boys from college wearing black eyeliner and hairspray. The hippy shop began selling Elvis Costello badges and X-Ray Spex T-shirts amongst the incense and cheese-cloth shirts, and Rock On Records next door put *Never Mind the Bollocks* in their window between Little Feat and Joan Armatrading. A cluster of punks began to collect on Saturdays, growing like a tumour on the benches in the shopping precinct. Kim earned more money doing housework now that Vonnie didn't have the monopoly on it. She could buy the things that would make her fit in. I was getting left behind.

Mum wouldn't let me get a job like a paper round or handing out leaflets like other kids, even though I was fourteen and it was a long time since I'd been grounded.

'I don't want you roaming the streets and me not knowing where you are. There are areas you don't know about that are very rough and dangerous for a young girl. I can take you shopping if there's anything you need, Elizabeth.'

She wouldn't understand the things I needed,

or that I really did *need* and not just *want* them. I couldn't be who I wanted to be without them. The things were keys to the doors of who you really were. But I couldn't explain this to my mum. She thought I just was who I was, with no notion of this real me locked away inside. Mr Grundy didn't either, but at least he seemed to realize that I needed pocket money to go out with my friends.

'I'm meeting up with Kim for a milkshake in the Wimpy,' is all I had to say, and he would fish around in his trousers for a pound note.

'That sounds like fun,' he would say, as he handed it over. 'Have a nice time.'

Or, 'I'm just taking a break from my homework — I think I'll go down town.'

'Good idea. It's very stuffy indoors; some fresh air will do you good. Here, why don't you treat yourself to something?'

It was never in front of my mum. The money was our secret. It was never very much. Just enough to buy a couple of singles I could play on our old record player that I had reinstated in my room. Or some joss-sticks I could light when Mum was out, or a Hint of a Tint, or some black nail varnish to put on my toenails. Or a pair of little stringy knickers instead of the full navy-blue cotton briefs Mum always got for me. Just enough to keep up.

When Kim got a new school skirt that was straight instead of A-line, I took mine in a touch, and turned up the hem another fold.

'Gosh, you've grown,' my mum said, looking at my knees. Mr Grundy looked too, and smiled at me from behind my mother.

To show my appreciation of Mr Grundy's kindness, I would sit in the armchair opposite his, and let my newly shortened skirt ride up my thighs as we watched telly in the evenings. I would stare at the television and cross my legs, and re-cross them, and never adjust my skirt as it rose, innocently, as though I didn't know Mr Grundy could see.

He began to make sure he would catch me before I went out to the shops.

'Buy yourself something nice.'

A pair of black nylon tights. White pants with a pink loveheart. Tampons. Hair-removing cream.

When I changed back into my uniform after netball I left my camisole off so that my bra showed through under my shirt. I left an extra button undone.

Next time I had taken my bra off too.

Mr Grundy gave me an extra pound.

All I felt was pretty and wanted. It was nice to have someone interested in me. He asked me what I had bought, and why I wanted it. I found I could talk to him without feeling silly, in a way I'd never done with any grown-ups before. I could just say that the records made me want to jump around, or cry, or scream and shout, or just lie on my bed and dream, and he didn't make me feel foolish. He would just nod, as though he was really listening, and understood.

As months went by I was able to buy more expensive things. I saved and bought a proper grown-up bra that was underwired and lacy and pushed my boobs up together, making them look like a bottom on my chest. I put it on with my little white pants, and when I heard him come upstairs I opened my bedroom door so that he could see. Mum was at a meeting at the care home. She had taken on a higher-up job, now I was old enough to be left and could be trusted to be sensible.

He stopped at the top of the stairs and looked. He swallowed.

'My God, Lizzie,' he said. 'You're beautiful.'

I felt it too.

★ ★ ★

The decade fell away with my childhood, like the place you've just been through on a moving train. I found out from Kim that the Clash were playing in Bristol and that her mum and dad thought she was grown-up enough now to let her go if a friend went with her. They would get the tickets and even take us there in the car.

'You have to get the money to me tomorrow, Lizzie, if you want to come. We have to buy them quickly before they sell out.'

I suddenly needed more than the odd pound note.

I only got a brief moment alone with Mr Grundy that evening. Just long enough to tell him that my friend was going to a concert and I didn't have the money to go, but if I missed out I would die.

'Die!' said Mr Grundy. 'Well, we can't have that, can we?'

We heard my mum coming back down the

passage from the kitchen.

'Come to my room later, and I'll see what I can do,' he whispered.

When we'd all said goodnight and gone to our rooms I wondered what would make Mr Grundy understand that I had to have a ticket. I dug around in my drawers for something that would make me look worth more than a pound, and found a white broderie anglaise nightie my mum had bought me years ago. I hated it, but when I tried it on and looked in the mirror I thought Mr Grundy might like it. It was too small now to do the buttons up the front so I left it open. I crept along to Mr Grundy's room. He was sitting up in bed reading a magazine, which he closed as I came in and put under his bed.

'Mr Grundy,' I whispered. I never learnt his first name. I came up close to the side of his bed, in touching distance. He looked me over.

'That's a very pretty nightdress,' he said. 'Give us a twirl.'

I turned round slowly, holding the material out so he would be able to see my naked body moving as the light shone through the holey cotton. When I faced him again we smiled at each other.

'Lovely,' he said. I knew I was. 'So why don't you tell me what's so important about this concert?'

I sat on the edge of the bed, and tried to explain what the Clash meant to us, without hurting his feelings by saying we were in love with the bass player. Instead I told him about the energy of the music, about what it would feel like

127

to hear it live, to actually be there as they played, how excited we would be if we were part of it too. He stared at my body as I talked and I felt the sleeves slipping down my arms and the front opening widen across my chest.

'It means everything to me, Mr Grundy,' I said. 'It really does.'

'Sorry?' he wheezed.

'I'd be really grateful if you'd lend me the money to go. It's four pounds fifty. I'll pay you back somehow, I promise.'

'Oh yes, of course.'

He reached for his wallet on the bedside table. He was shaking as he searched through it, as though I was emanating an invisible force that was making him crumble from the inside out. He found a fiver and handed it to me.

'Thank you,' I said, leaning forwards and kissing him on his forehead. My hair swooped and brushed across his face and my boob fell out of the nightie. I started to stand up, but his hand fell on my arm and pulled me nearer.

'Don't go yet, Lizzie,' he breathed, urgently. He was holding on to me with an anguished look on his face, so I stood there. 'If you stay a bit longer you'll be paying me back. Then we'll be quits. Does that sound fair to you?'

I nodded. Part of me didn't really want to stay any longer, now I had what I'd come for, but another part did. My ability to put Mr Grundy under my command hypnotized me, too. And it did seem like a terribly easy way to pay him back.

'You look very pretty,' he said. 'You've got

beautiful hair.' He reached up and stroked my hair, tucking it behind my ear and shoulder, away from where it was falling over my breasts.

Out of the corner of my eye I saw his other hand begin to move in his lap under the bedclothes. He pulled me closer to him. When I was near enough he put his hand on the inside of my knee. He stroked my leg, moving higher with each stroke. He was breathing hard and his other hand began to move faster and faster until it made the bed shake. It made my boobs jiggle, as I sat there, fascinated, and he practically went cross-eyed from staring at them. He clutched my leg tighter as he began to grunt and the bed began to squeak, and I started to worry that Mum would hear, or that I would get the giggles. Especially when he screwed his face up and groaned loudly. He doubled up as though he was in pain and I hoped he wasn't having a heart attack. I knew from the boys at school that men did this all the time, but I'd never imagined it took such an effort.

'Are you all right?' I whispered, but he just panted. At least he didn't stop breathing. His breaths gradually slowed down to normal, and he undid his face from its knot and lay his head back against the pillow. He took his hand from up my nightie, smoothing the skirt back down.

'There you go,' he said.

'Thank you,' I said, suddenly feeling a bit silly sitting there like that with my boobs still sticking out. I drew the nightie back over them and felt my face start to go red. The part of me that had wanted to go as soon as I got my five pounds took over again, but it seemed rude to leave him like this.

'Go on, off you go,' Mr Grundy waved me off with his face turned away.

'Are you sure you're all right now?' I said, hoping he was. He seemed all limp and exhausted, like a week-old balloon. He managed a tired chuckle, as if I'd said something funny.

'I'm fine,' he said.

'All right. Goodnight then.'

'Goodnight.'

'Thanks again, Mr Grundy.'

I slunk out of the door and back to my room, and went to study myself in the mirror. I opened my nightie again and tried to see myself through Mr Grundy's eyes instead of my own. My boobs really were starting to look like nice ladies' breasts, instead of just a couple more lumps of puppy fat stuck on. In fact, my puppy fat seemed to have disappeared altogether, and I even had a waist instead of a tummy. When I looked at my face, I saw I was smiling. But it no longer pushed my cheeks out as though they were over-stuffed pies. I had cheekbones, without even painting them on. Looking through Mr Grundy's eyes, I could see that I was growing up pretty. I threw myself on my bed, giggling, and thanked God. It was such a relief. It was what it must feel like if you were put in the top set, or picked for the netball team. Only better.

As I lay there I went over what I'd just done with Mr Grundy. I became aware of the sherbet pumping through my veins. I tried to ignore it, as it started to make me feel a bit disgusted, when it was caused by Mr Grundy. It was going to be embarrassing at breakfast time. I was glad I'd got my fiver there and then and didn't have to ask him for it in the morning. I didn't think I'd have the nerve. I was back to feeling good again, though, when I thought about my fiver, still clutched in my right hand. I drifted off into dreams of the fantastic new world I could now afford.

★   ★   ★

The Clash were amazing. It was worth doing much worse things than watch Mr Grundy having a spasm. Luckily my mum had no idea what sort of band they were — they'd never been on *Top of the Pops* or anything — else she'd never have let me go. But she did, after I had worn her down for long enough, and she'd called Kim's mum and been reassured by her posh, unworried voice saying they would take us there, and be there to pick us up right outside afterwards too. I was even allowed to stay the night, as part of Mum's new trusting me thing. I had paid for the trouble I'd got into before, and proved I could be good whoever tried to lead me astray, so she thought.

We got ready together at Kim's house so my mum didn't see her old lacy black petticoat that I was borrowing from her, hitched up with a belt to make a miniskirt. It had splits up the sides and I wore it with black ribbed tights that I made holes in and Kim's baseball boots with pink fluorescent socks. Kim spiked her hair up with glue. I wished I was allowed to cut my hair short. All I could do was tie mine in two bunches on top of my head and back-comb them so they went all messy. We used Kim's old face paints to give ourselves purple lips and black shadows on our cheekbones.

Kim's mum giggled at us as she swung her fur coat around her evening dress and put her lipstick on. They were having dinner at a posh restaurant while we went to the gig.

'We'll have to drop you off in a dark alleyway so no one sees you're with us,' she said, as if we were the embarrassing ones.

★   ★   ★

As the Clash came on, everyone surged to the front. We pushed our way to Paul Simenon's side of the stage and got near enough to see his hollowed-out face, shining beneath his backlit spiky halo, his sinewy muscles straining in his cut-off sleeves while he thrashed away on the bass held way down low, his long, skinny legs planted wide. You could see the spit spraying over the microphone when he came to the front of the stage to shout into it.

I'd never felt so immersed in sensation. The only thing it was anything like was when I was little and had swum in the sea underwater with goggles and a snorkel when we went to Cornwall for a holiday. It was like being in another world. The sound seemed to pour right through your eardrums into you, so there was no difference between inside you and outside. The crowd

132

moved you like a rolling tide you couldn't fight, so you didn't really exist as a separate thing, but were swept along as a part of something much, much bigger. At first I was frightened and thought I would drown, the way I had when I had looked up from snorkelling to find I had been sucked much further out than I thought I was, and couldn't see my dad.

I clung on to Kim to stop panicking and had no choice but to let myself be taken. Afterwards, I felt as though I'd been baptized. We spilled out of the hall in a stream of other drenched, dazed worshippers, flopping out onto the street like fish gasping for our water, which still thundered in our ears like receding surf.

The land we were thrown back onto seemed too dry and quiet. We did our best to contain our rapture as we clambered into Kim's dad's car. But I felt as though I had been washed right through, entered and taken over by some new spirit that gave me faith, although I didn't know what in.

We lay on Kim's bed until the world tilted on its axis to let the future spill into the room, looking at Clash photos and reading their lyrics and wondering what it would be like to be Paul Simenon's girlfriend. Kim planned how we could get to other towns to see them play again, or any other bands we could follow. I knew I had to go too, whatever it took. I didn't care what I had to do to get there.

12

Beth

When we were in a band ourselves we would scoff at the 'old' people who still went to gigs, thought them sad weirdos to not have moved on after the age of twenty-five. I don't know where we thought they should have moved on to, but gigs and clubs were for the young — us. We thought being the young generation was set in stone. It was our birthright, our identity.

Now there is a young generation, and we're not it.

It is so shocking, as unbelievable as waking up to find you have changed sex overnight.

And Kim and I have become the sad old weirdos that still go to gigs. Often it's to see the bands that Paolo is playing with; sometimes it's just because we suddenly feel as though something is missing and we realize we haven't immersed ourselves in live music for too long. Because of Toby's job I am saturated in highly produced pop or rock, everything cooked to death on computers in studios, and sometimes I need a taste of something raw. Something a little bitter, slightly off key, with bum notes or fluffed words, out of time, speeding up towards the end. Human imperfections are the ingredients I crave. So we'll go along to the Twelve Bar or Cassady's or the pub venues in Camden, and sit through sometimes the direst of performers, just to have the real thing running through our veins again as though it's serotonin, just to be thankful that there are still people up there doing it for real, however bad it is.

It's the ones that are good I wonder about. Sometimes you see someone you know is destined for big things — there is a buzz about them, the venue is packed for once, and industry people actually have turned up like they said they would. And they may get a blurb in *Time Out* or somewhere calling them the one to watch out for. Six months later, a year later, you remember them and wonder what happened.

I've still got our *Time Out* blurb, somewhere.

When I call Kim to check in on Vonnie I hope she'll come to the Capo Bar with me. But Paolo tells me she and Franklin are at the hospital for the night. Kim has sent her exhausted parents back to their friends to get some sleep, now the immediate crisis is over.

'OK, *bene*,' I say, and just manage to prevent my terror of going out alone from inviting him. Paolo is really not the right person to go with to see Jesse play. He would be shouting into my ear the whole time and I wouldn't be able to zone him out and slip away into myself for my own private audience with Jesse.

I don't know if I've ever gone out anywhere on my own. For years I've been able to get into anything, as an addendum to Toby. Before then, when we were in the band, our life was the going out at night, whether to our own gigs or other bands', or parties or clubs. It was as though we were living in our own time zone, as if our own line of longitude had superimposed itself over the Greenwich Meridian, so that morning was our dead of night, afternoons were for breakfast and evening was when our sun would climb the sky.

I spend the entire day getting ready. Putting on clothes, taking them off, pinning my hair up, taking it down. I want to look right, but I don't know what the right look is. I only know I have to look as though I haven't spent the day trying. I settle in the end for an expensive Chinese silk shirt, dressed down by crumpled linen loons and glittery Flojos. I paint my toenails a clashing silvery green. The fact that I've had difficulty eating since being at Vonnie's bedsit means that my stomach is unusually flat where it is bared in a triangle between the last two shirt buttons left undone. I have a sudden desire to have my belly button pierced. A glint there would be the perfect finishing touch. I choose in the end to pin up my hair messily at the back, leaving the front to hang down in case I need the cover.

The only going out make-up I know is blackly drawn out eyes. I apply the liquid liner across my lids in the magnifying mirror, watching it squiggle across the fine lines that are appearing at the corners. Am I too old for this make-up now? How do you know when you've become one of these ridiculous older women with bleeding lipstick and doll-black hair? Do they look in mirrors and still see their younger selves looking back?

By the time I am ready the silk shirt is darkened with circles of sweat spreading under my arms, and drying them with the hairdryer leaves a white tide mark. I am already late and in my fluster my fear of going wins out at last. I tear everything off, get into my sweats and burst into tears. I try to calm myself with the T'ai Chi I've been attempting to learn in the garden, trying hard to ignore the disappointment dragging at my limbs. But I feel like a complete arse. If I saw some stupid woman like me doing T'ai Chi on Hampstead Heath or something I'd fucking laugh.

It is this self-loathing in the end that makes me pull on my jeans and an old T-shirt and trainers and wipe the smears of make-up from my cheeks as I flee the house. I can't stay home with myself like this. I let my body take over, carrying me to the tube station and down into the bowels of London. *Don't think about it, just don't think.* The Northern line rumbles me along to King's Cross, where I am squeezed onto the Hammersmith and City line and farted out at Baker Street. *Don't look, don't breathe.* As I walk to the Capo I keep my eyes focused on the pavement ahead to avoid treading in anything. I'm glad I'm not in flipflops.

Heading down again — wishing so much of London life wasn't lived below ground, as though you're being eaten alive — into the club. The stairwell is filled with groups of people checking mobiles or coming up for air. The basement is packed. Friday night is audition night, and a gaggle of musicians hover by the stage with guitars ready-slung across their shoulders. It's an unnerving place to play. No sound check, or space between acts. You have to be ready to slip on the minute the act before finishes and just slot into your thing. You get only two songs in each half to grab the audience. The memory of stage fright gives me palpitations, but I hold it together. Sweating is not out of place here. I survey the crowd as though I'm looking for someone I'm meeting. I always feel stared at even when I'm not. I check my watch as though they're late and head back to the bar. As I'm queuing the guy that runs the club passes.

'Hey Beth! How you doing?' We kiss on the cheek. 'Toby down?'

'No, he's still in Japan. I — a kid we know's playing tonight. Jesse Porter?'

'Oh, you know him? Yeah, he's good. You've missed his first time round, but the second half's only just started. Got quite a following here tonight. You'll spot them.' I know by his expression he means girls. 'Is he one of Toby's?'

'Not yet. I'm . . . checking him out for him while he's away.'

'Wise. I'd snap him up if I were him. Could be his retirement plan, I reckon.'

We laugh and he shouts to the barman to get me a drink before he moves on.

'Cheers, Barry.' I head back inside with a Beck's and my new-found purpose for being here. I'm checking out acts for Toby. It makes me feel less stupid to be here on my own. I'm A&R, and I know the owner.

I stand by the arches along the edge of the

room where I can see the audience and the players. I spot Jesse in the corridor to the toilets, crouched over his guitar case with his plectrum in his mouth, retuning. Near the front of the stage is a table of young girls talking animatedly through the current act, a trio of cello, piano and a female singer with a great voice and no stage presence. I feel for her as she struggles to master the crowd. They get a pleasant round of applause at the end, the kind that makes you want to give up and die.

Barry introduces the next up, a hyper-trendy guy with an electric guitar and shades, who believes his own press before it's even been written. He sings soulish songs in a light voice that doesn't quite live up to his look and overuses his wahwah. I peer round and see that Jesse is standing watching him on the other side of my pillar. Before I can stop myself I reach out and touch his shoulder. When he looks round he doesn't recognize me. Oh God.

'Hi — it's Beth.' I try to stop my smile from faltering. 'You came round for Toby yesterday?'

'Oh, right! Of course. Sorry, it's just your hair's different — it threw me for a minute.'

We stand smiling awkwardly.

'What are you doing here?' he asks. Why did I do this?

'I just thought I'd come and check you out, you know.'

'You came to see me?' He seems amazed.

'Well, you know, as Toby's away . . . ' I swallow my voice, preparing for his disappointment that it's only me. A poor substitute for the one with the power to make his dreams happen. But he hides it well, nodding appreciatively.

'Wow. Thanks,' he says instead, as though he's really touched.

I offer him a swig from my bottle and he takes it. I watch his mouth close around the bottle and blink away thoughts of the bacteria in his saliva from food, kisses, his fingers on the plectrum. Our hands touch as he gives it back. I hope the girls are watching. I quickly drink from the bottle before I wipe the top. I prepare to gulp back the upsurge of disgust at someone else's contamination spreading around my body. But the only feeling that comes is one of being special, to have something of Jesse inside me, as though I have been touched by a healer.

Then I am distracted by Barry calling Jesse up to the stage.

'Good luck,' I say, and he walks on stage, plugging in his semi-acoustic and drawing the stool up to the microphone, getting whistles and cheers from his fans, at which he grins modestly. He doesn't make much impact at first, checking his tuning and volume and arranging his shirt sleeves. He pushes a hand through his hair and introduces himself and his first song over the chatter, one he's just written, he says, called 'I Met Someone'. He looks my way as he says it. I'm sure he does.

However much Barry begs the audience to respect the musicians, they never usually shut up for long. Until the second verse of Jesse's song. His music insists itself quietly, stealing through the room, creeping up on people and altering the atmosphere like a new season. They stop ordering drinks and leaning over tables to speak to each other. Those still shouting on the steps get shushed by people at the door.

It isn't just me, then.

By his second song, 'Out There Somewhere', I am completely submerged in him. Everything around me has fallen away and there's just him and me. His voice reaches to me like a lifeline and begins to pull me up and out. I know the song as well as if it were Bob Dylan's, and that is who he is to me: Bob Dylan, or Jesus, maybe. Some sort of saviour, with me his disciple or craziest fan. Something like that. I can't remember ever having been so moved by someone just sitting, playing and singing. I am filled with longing for something, although I'm not sure what. For him, for passion, for life, for my youth back ... I don't know. But it overwhelms me.

I am aware if anyone is watching me I look ridiculous, but I don't care. I can feel an expression on my face halfway between joy and pain. I know my forehead is crinkling in the way that has over the years dug grooves between my brows. But my heart is filling up as though it is being refuelled and becomes full, too full, and I can't change my face. Tears spill out. As he comes off stage I shrink into the shadows to wipe my eyes.

He pushes through to the backstage area, the soundman and other musicians slapping his back and congratulating him. When he's put his guitar in its case in the tiny room at the side that passes

141

for backstage he comes through to the audience, waiting politely for the spaces between songs before he squeezes through to join his table of friends, not far from the group of girls. It's not long before they are reaching over to say, 'You were great!'

Because of my lack of food my head is already swimming from just one beer. I don't know what to do now. I wouldn't know what to say to him if I managed to get as far as his table. If I caught his eye I would at least wave goodbye, or more probably do something naff like give him a thumbs-up. But he is surrounded by a swarm of people wanting to know him, so I decide to leave.

On the way out I bump into Barry again, and as I'm on my own he insists I wait until he's closed the show, which he always does with one of his own tunes on piano — it's the perk of running your own club, I guess, somewhere you can always get a gig — and have a drink with him and his mates afterwards. Not quick enough with an excuse, I am propelled to a table of people I am introduced to as Toby's wife and bought another drink. Luckily the last act are a guitar and fiddle duo playing wild East European gypsy tunes, too loud to try to speak over, so I accept a cigarette from one of Barry's friends and look as though I am listening to the music. Although really I am watching the back of Jesse's head, bobbing as he listens, distracted regularly by people around him trying to get his attention.

Barry wraps up the night and I try to join in with the chat around the table about the acts, and answer polite questions about what Toby's doing in Japan. Barry gets caught up by a queue of people wanting to speak to him and handing him demos, so it is easy to make my escape from his table of friends. I am too desperate to pee to hang on until I get home, although I've really tried. I have to go to the ladies'. As I come back from the loo Jesse is standing in the arches being handed a card by some guy, who then leaves. Suddenly the crowd seems to clear around us. Everything and everyone else fades to black, as though a spotlight has searched out just him and me. I have a moment when I can make a choice. Either summon up my courage and speak to him, or chicken out and slip past, invisible. It turns out to be one of those split-second, life-altering moments. My fear paralyses me and prevents me doing either. And then, as if he knows, he turns and looks right at me.

He smiles.

13

Lizzie

The thing that helped me through it all was the Vonnie voice, playing over and over in my head. It made the prospect of being out in the world on your own exciting, not scary, in the same way it made being skint and living in a squat and working in a shop exciting not scary. Vonnie made me rethink everything I'd grown up learning. She was the opposite of fairy tales. She didn't get taught any lessons when she did bad things, she didn't need any rescuing, she didn't have to wait around for a prince to make her life any good. Just being her looked like a happy ending to me.

The Vonnie voice talked to me when I lay in my room alone. It stuck up for me and answered back when other voices in my head crowded in, calling me bad names for what I was doing with Mr Grundy. Vonnie was the only one I imagined would understand, when I worried about people finding out. '*Why not?*' she'd shrug. '*You may as well use him — he's going to be perving on you anyway; you may as well get something out of it too.*'

The Vonnie voice was always on my side. It would just laugh at the voices that told me off, voices that usually sounded like my mother's, and answer back, 'Look where being good got you!' I had to agree with the Vonnie voice. What was the point of being such a goody-two-shoes anyway? It didn't seem to make my mum's life any better. She was practically a servant, in her job and to Mr Grundy, to make ends meet. My way of making money was a lot easier than housework, and didn't take as long. And men seemed to admire me a lot more than her. 'You be as good as you like,' said the Vonnie voice. 'Your reward will be in Heaven.' It was one of Vonnie's favourite things to say. She said it when she got Kim to do something for her, as her cheeky way of getting out of owing her back, as well as about people who did nice things and got nothing out of it themselves. 'I'll take my rewards here on Earf, ta very much.'

The Vonnie voice made me feel good about myself when no one else's did.

I practised Vonnie's inflections and expressions as though I was learning another language. She had her own exotic foreign ways, and you couldn't help but copy them when you spoke in her tongue, the way when you were doing French conversation your voice went singsong and you developed a pouty shrug. In the language of Vonnie you answered most things with a world-weary, unbothered, 'Yeah right,' or 'Fuck off', and referred to anything you didn't like, which was pretty much everything, as 'bollox' or 'shit' (without the 't'). It was like being another person, when you had the speaking right.

I learnt not to animate my face too much, and

145

wore a knowing expression as though I found everything ironic and droll. Except when I found something highly amusing, and then I'd throw my head back and burst into a throaty guffaw, only I didn't open my mouth as wide as Vonnie did, because I had lots of fillings and she didn't. Her gestures and mannerisms were like nobody else's I had ever seen. They weren't even like movie stars', who tried to be sexy the whole time. She was sexy, but it wasn't like she was having to please men with everything she did. Although she did.

She just had a way about her. The way she held her cigarette up high, and flicked the ash off instead of tapping it. The way she wound her legs around each other when she crossed them, as though they were made of stretchy rubber. The way she rolled her eyes and snorted when she was drunk. The way she could arch one eyebrow without the other, or wink sexily, without screwing up her face. The way she stood in her high heels with her hands on her hips and her bum sticking out, and the way she swung her hips as she walked. When she finished a cigarette in the street she didn't just drop the butt, but threw it ahead of her, so that when she caught up she would walk over it in her stiletto, squashing it within a stride.

I took up smoking and practised, only I stomped mine out with my new Doctor Martens. I'd found a boys' pair in Oxfam, so they were already good and scuffed and worn in. Although I'd tried I just couldn't get the walking right in heels. The me that wasn't Vonnie felt vulnerable and stupid in them, as though I couldn't run away if I had to. But I felt good in my Docs. They were a size too big and too clumsy to scurry along the edges of walkways. You had no choice but to stride out in them, as though you had a right to be there.

I liked them best with short skirts, like I'd seen girls wearing in pictures in *NME* and *Melody Maker*, which I had started to buy every week without fail. They made even my legs look spindly thin. I developed a long, louche stride in them, which involved squared-up shoulders and clenched fists. Kim did the same, and we went around like that, two abreast on a pavement or in a corridor at school, not making way for anyone coming towards us.

When we had to be in our school uniforms we tied our ties the wrong way round, so that they were pencil-thin like the Jam's. We wore Clash and Ruts and Rock Against Racism badges down our blazer lapels so that even in our uniforms we would still be visible to the people we needed to see us. We bought more every time they were confiscated by the teachers, as though we'd disappear into nothing without them to mark us out. Kim put more and more gel in her hair for school, seeing what elevation she could get away with before a teacher made her brush it flat. I wore mine in scruffy pigtails and bunches, trying to make it a bit like the punky girls in bands that dressed like naughty schoolgirls, but Kim still sneered at me for having long hair like a hippy.

'You're not aufentic unless you got spikes,' she said.

The only time I had ever had my hair cut was when my mum trimmed it, in a straight line across the bottom every six months or so when it was getting raggedy. I don't know why I always had to have it long, but I did. I know she was a bit older than most mums, but sometimes it was as though she was from a whole century ago. I was getting braver at home, but I knew I'd never be allowed to cut my hair.

Or not braver, exactly. Maybe just more careless about hiding the new me, this other creature I was turning into, imposing itself upon my mother's house like a cuckoo in the nest. I was growing bit by bit into a species of woman my mother didn't recognize.

At first I always wore my long gabardine school coat to smuggle myself out of the house, and changed into my Docs and make-up in the loos before heading up the high street. But then I would forget to change back into my pumps again, or remove my eyeliner before sitting at the table at home for tea. Mum never said anything even if she looked, so I began to let other things slip, too. Little knickers I'd bought myself went into the household wash instead of being rinsed out by me in the sink and hidden inside the lagging around the boiler to dry. Records were played loud in my room at homework time without headphones.

And the coat eventually was left flapping open, showing my miniskirts and boots and legs. It wasn't a look my mum appreciated. She squawked indignantly and helplessly, and I took no notice. She seemed to shrink back against the walls as I spread, lurking baffled in the shadows, wondering what had happened to the timid little thing she'd given birth to. It was as though I had tricked her all this time into thinking I was the same species, and now as I gathered strength I took over. I was trying out my feathers until I was able to fly.

I was cruel to her, although at the time I thought it was her that was cruel to me, of course. I left her standing powerless in doorways as I strutted out, and often came home to find her waiting, pink-eyed and ruffled with worry. She tried to talk to me about my appearance.

'Why do you deliberately make yourself so ugly? You just look cheap and trashy. And you're not that sort of girl, Elizabeth. Where did you get these rags, anyway?'

I threw it back at her. 'These *rags* come from Oxfam, which is the only place I can afford, *actually*.'

'Well, if that's the only problem, Elizabeth, you should have told me. You're old enough to have a clothing allowance now. Why don't I take you shopping on Saturday? Debenhams is good value, or if that's not fashionable enough, Dorothy Perkins seems to have some nice things for girls your age.'

'I'd ravver die than wear anyfink from there,' I sneered in reply. I made a mental note though, of Dorothy Perkins and Debbie Nams, for my list of good names for girls in punk bands. My mum had no comprehension why anyone would choose death over a skirt from a chainstore. She tried to make me see sense.

149

'They're only clothes, Elizabeth. Do you really think clothes are so important?'

But I had a smart-alec reply for everything. 'If clothes don't matter, why do you care so much what I look like? You're such a *snob*.'

The more I pushed her the more I realized she couldn't do anything about it, not any more. And off I would stride into town, boot after boot, fists clenched, stud belt slung across my hips, old leather jacket creaking as though I was Lee Van Cleef.

We were finally accepted by the gang of punks hanging around in the town centre and they let us join in, drinking cider from tins and sniffing glue. There weren't many girls who were punks and we impressed them with the records we bought and how much we knew about the bands. They started inviting us out and Kim would stay over with me and we'd climb out of my bedroom window at night to go to gigs.

They were usually in pubs with rooms out the back, where boys on Art Foundations at Taunton Tech played in bands called Inertia and Poke It With A Stick. Drinks would appear for us from somewhere — plastic pints of snakebite — sloshing onto a beer-keg table that we perched round on stools, rolling cigarettes on torn-jeaned knees from packets of baccy. We put in hours and hours of cigarette-rolling practice whenever we were huddled together in one of our bedrooms.

With the help of *Vonnish* I managed not to smile at these kinds of boy. They were more into you if you stayed cool, with a blank expression on your face. However thrilled we were that we were sat round a table with skinny bad boys with safety pins through their cheeks, we never showed it. We maintained an air of being totally unimpressed. The only excuse for being animated instead of zombie-like was if you were 'out of it'. Sometimes when we caught each other's eyes and couldn't hide our excitement, we had to pretend to be out of it, so we could have a freak out, jump around and shriek and laugh wildly. You had to pretend you'd forgotten what you did the night before if you messed about. '*Fuck, what did I do? I was so out of it.*'

When a band played you all crushed together and pogoed. We were always covered in bruises. You'd hopefully end up snogging. Usually whoever was nearest you when the pogoing stopped. Punk boys didn't ask you out or pay you any compliments. They were just suddenly there, face leering into you, and then a beery tongue shoved into your mouth and a hand squeezed your tit. Punk boys didn't have to be polite to get what they wanted from you at all; they just grabbed it. And we acted like that's all we wanted too, and kept to ourselves the agonizing crushes we got on the less revolting ones, along with our fantasies of coupledom and love and good names for punk babies. I got pretty close to going out with Arry, as close as you could get without being 'possessive', which was the worst thing you could possibly be. I regularly ended up with his hands inside my clothes outside on the cellar steps, or in the bus shelter if we'd managed to stumble that far. He often scratched me inside with his rough nails and made me bleed, but it was a good hurt. The other marks, lovebites and teeth marks, I had to cover up with spot concealer and dog collars. I liked having them on me though, especially when only I knew about them. I could feel possessed and possessing without anyone accusing me of being possessive.

Punk was a godsend for ugly, stupid boys. It was a good excuse to be as moronic as possible. You had to pretend to be really thick to keep up. Being ugly only seemed to work one way, though. The ugly girls still weren't as popular as the pretty ones. When I think about it, the thing I liked best about boys wasn't really the boys themselves, although we thought it was. It was the talking about them afterwards, or the getting ready for them beforehand — looking each other over, knowing we were what they wanted. It was being the girls that was the exciting thing.

The boys confirmed what I'd begun to suspect through Mr Grundy; that I was getting good at being a girl. Mr Grundy didn't approve of my new look, but it didn't stop him. In fact, the disapproval seemed to give him licence to go further. He tutted and frowned at my holey black tights, but he was very fond of poking his fingers through them to touch the bare skin on my inner thighs while he fiddled with himself. He was disgusted with me for going out wearing a petticoat for a dress, but when I came home he would be at me the first chance he had, stroking the staticclingy fabric around my bottom as he pulled me onto his knee to tell me off. And then looking down the lacy top as he placed my hand in his trousers and taught me what to do.

Mr Grundy began to repulse me. At the same time, I needed to know the things he was teaching me.

'Where d'you learn to do that?' Arry would groan as we groped drunkenly in a shadowy doorway, and I reached in through the zip of his leather trousers under cover of his grandad coat, wrapped around us both. I was proud of my achievement. I knew he told his friends I was good by the way they grinned at me appreciatively. When they did I knew I had guilty eyes, thanks to Mr Grundy. Boys and men could look into them, in that hungry, searching way they had, and I knew they found what they were looking for as I met their gaze. I knew my eyes were telling them I could give them what they wanted. Sometimes Arry made way for one of his mates to find out for himself.

I supposed this made me a slag.

But for some reason, I couldn't quite care. It made me a lot freer than being good made me. It made me unafraid.

14

Beth

'Hey! Thanks so much for coming down,' Jesse grins, saving me from myself.

For want of something better I say, 'You were *great*!'

He scratches his head and smiles.

I can't do small talk. And I'm drunk.

'No really. You weren't just *greeeat*,' I say it in a pisstakey, music biz way, waggling my hands, which only goes to demonstrate how drunk I am. 'I mean. You have something. Something very special. The indefinable . . . thing. You have The Thing. Whatever happens, never forget that. You're meant to do this.'

He looks at me as though he is listening, so I go on. 'You should never stop doing what you do. You have a gift and you should cherish it. Don't throw it away carelessly like it's nothing. Promise yourself that whatever life throws at you, never lose faith that you have this thing.'

I should be embarrassing him, but he doesn't look embarrassed. I've embarrassed myself though, so I smile. 'I'm sorry. It's just . . . I've seen an awful lot of guys with guitars in my time, but I can't think when I've ever seen someone who has . . . It before.' I pause and think. 'Except maybe Jeff Buckley.'

'You saw Jeff Buckley?!' His eyes are wide with excitement and awe, and we lean against the pillar simultaneously and sink deep into conversation about, I don't know what. Music we love, musicians who make it, the indescribable Thing.

I don't know how long we talk for, but it feels like a millionth of a second and forever at the same time. We are finally rounded up by the bar staff and nudged towards the exit. Jesse's mates find him at last; 'Where were you, man? Let's go eat.' And I bob up into the street with a group of them, turning to head towards Soho. I hang back to go the other way, to catch a taxi on the Marylebone Road, and call out goodbye.

Jesse turns and says, 'Aren't you coming?'

It hadn't occurred to me to include myself in his plans, but he says it in such a simple way as to make it seem silly that I would leave now. He makes me feel accepted. It is a warm night and the air, even this polluted, over-breathed city air, feels good on the skin.

'Come on!' he insists, smiling. In the end he reaches out and takes me by the hand and pulls me. I was never very good at saying no when people are expecting yes. 'Aren't you hungry?'

I am suddenly starving. As we all meander diagonally down towards Oxford Street he keeps my hand loosely in his. It's an experience I'd forgotten all about, wandering the city late at night as though it's yours, with a group of strangers you've only just met but who are somehow yours too. It's what made me fall in love with London, and with life. A girl asks Jesse

155

for cigarette papers and he drops my hand to delve in his pockets. He stops to readjust the gigbag on his back and I fall in with a guy with a mohican of dreads tied up in an elastic band. Jesse's friends are not trendy and designer clad. They seem more like traveller types or buskers.

'Who are you, then?' he says in a friendly way.

'I'm Lizzie,' I reply.

'All right, Liz? I'm Mickey,' he says, and offers me a toke on his spliff.

★   ★   ★

We get to an all-night greasy spoon on Old Compton Street, losing a few people on the way who run for a number seven heading west. We take up two tables. I get to sit opposite Jesse, and the girl slides in next to him. She's one of those pretty pixie girls with wide-apart eyes in a tiny face and a stud in her button nose. Mickey is high and loud and talks as though there's no tomorrow. I'm so lightheaded it makes me giggly, as though I'm breathing in too much helium and could any minute float away. I already feel I have reached a different altitude, being here like this. I'm not used to it and I should seem out of place, but no one else appears to notice. I don't feel as though I can eat, but I know I must to weigh myself down, so I add an order for tea and chips to their fry-ups. As they talk I work out that most of them seem to live together in east London. Mickey is a sampling freak, and has the bug-eyed, pallid intensity of someone who spends too long communicating with computers, as though he too is running on an electrical charge.

'So what do you do that I can sample then?' Mickey asks me. 'What do you play, or are you vocals?'

I am ashamed that I am neither of Mickey's options for being.

'I don't play,' I admit. 'Not any more.'

'Why not?'

I laugh. 'I don't know. It didn't work out. I got old.'

'You daft fucking cow!' Mickey is outraged. 'When does music ever not work out? When do you get too old for it? Fuck's sake, what are you like?'

And then he's off on one, into a tirade about the state of the music business and the arseholes that run it. I catch Jesse's eye and he mouths, 'Sorry,' probably wishing he'd told Mickey I was Toby's wife. Mickey gets distracted by the arrival of his bacon sandwich and a mate shouting across to him from the other table.

'What did you play, then?' asks Jesse, adding with a smile, 'before you got old.'

'Oh. Nothing properly. Guitar mostly. Keyboards, badly, when I had to. Percussion sometimes when we went busking. It was a long time ago.'

'Come on, you're not that ancient. When?'

'It was in those post-punk times, you know. When you could just get up there and do it and it didn't really matter how badly you played as long as you had . . . I don't know. Balls. Something to say.'

'You're so lucky,' he says. 'I would have loved to've been making music then. That whole era was such a breath of fresh air.'

We talk about some of his heroes from that time. He loves Patrick Fitzgerald and has heard of obscure bands like Clive Pig and the Hopeful Chinamen. He's impressed I've been on the same bill as the Happening. Something about him glows when he talks about music. It is his passion. I somehow seem able to light him up with the things I say. I haven't excited someone like that for a very long time. The girl — Amie — is bored by us and dozes off against Jesse's shoulder. They look right together and I wonder with a pang if she's his girlfriend. If I were her, I would be in love.

'Come on, let's get her home,' says Mickey when it's the right time for a night bus. He shakes her awake and pulls her from her seat as everyone chucks their pound coins and fivers into the saucer and leaves. He eventually hoists her up and gives her a piggyback up Charing Cross Road.

At the junction with Oxford Street I prepare to say goodbye, again.

'Hang on a minute,' Jesse says, and stands with Mickey arranging something or other. He then surprises me by kissing the girl goodbye and slapping hands with the others as they cross to catch a fifty-five on New Oxford Street. He begins to walk with me up Tottenham Court Road.

'I need a 134,' he says, 'What goes your way?'

I haven't caught a night bus for so long I have no idea.

'A taxi?' I suggest, and he stands with me just ahead of the bus stop while I try to hail one. Even this late all the cabs that go by are taken. Twenty minutes pass and a 134 arrives. He makes no move to get on the bus.

'I can't just leave you here in the middle of the night,' he says. I try and push him on, but he won't go. 'Unless you come too?' he suggests. The doors are about to close so I jump on with him without thinking. 'It's not that long till the trains start running,' he says. 'Just hang out at mine for a bit, then you can get the overground to yours.'

⋆ ⋆ ⋆

Jesse lives in the attic of a shared house in Kentish Town. It's a self-contained space, the kitchen area under one sloping eave with a bar separating it from the rest of the room. Apart from a low sofabed, left out, the room seems to contain only guitars, recording equipment and CDs. He has a keyboard but no computer, recording instead live onto a multi-track recorder.

'Can you quantize and edit OK on it?' I ask as he puts the kettle on for tea.

'You can but I don't,' he replies, coming over and switching it on. 'I just try and play it right all the way through. Chopping it about and shunting it into place seems to lose something more than just the mistakes. I mean, there's nothing worse than bad timing. But you shouldn't have bad timing. You should be striving to play it right. That's what it's about, isn't it? The little fluctuations in rhythm, the slowing down or speeding up to build it; they should be there. It's what makes a song happen. And chopping it together — it might make it more perfect, but. It's kind of like cosmetic surgery, I guess. It takes away the interesting bits, as far as I'm concerned. Removes the essence of what makes that person them.' He stops himself in his flow. 'Sorry, I'm rambling.'

'No, you're not.' Listening to him speak is like listening to him play, for me. His unashamed idealism is a relief, like a cool cloth on a headache. 'You're making perfect sense to me.'

The way he is, unposing and spontaneous, somehow releases me from the way I am, trapped in my prison of inhibition. I find myself picking up his twelve-string despite myself, although it's an age since I played, and watching my fingers quietly remembering chord sequences and rhythms.

'What are you working on then?' I ask, and he brings up the track on the desk.

'I've only put down the guitar and a guide vocal so far,' he says, adjusting the sliders. 'I haven't finished the lyrics.'

A fragile, half-hummed melody weaves its way around a simple C Major verse beautifully picked on an acoustic, before plunging into a dark chorus in E minor. I can hear the counter melody on piano before it is there, and slide over to the keyboard to pick it out with one finger. Jesse stands halfway between his speakers. Something about the way he listens rather than watches loosens my fingers towards the right keys. I find a harmony on the chorus that he loves.

'You have to sing that!' he urges, hurrying to set up the microphone. 'Don't lose it; it's great!'

'I can't sing,' I protest, but despite myself I am already humming it and picking up the words. He scribbles down the lyrics of the chorus for me on a piece of paper from his stack of notes; *Like the North Star, I'll steer my boat by you.*

He puts me in headphones and adjusts the recording levels as I sing along. My voice sounds alien in my ears, but I am high enough from the beer and spliff — and just Jesse himself — to be able to hear what he can in the harmony I've found. He is right, it really does work. When the levels are right and my voice sits behind his in the mix my outer walls fall away and I'm just music. He records a few takes until he captures the One, and we sit on the floor like teenagers and listen, grinning.

He puts the track on a loop and opens the window in the roof above the sofabed. We lie back looking up at the stars.

'Who's it about?' I ask, the question that has been playing on my mind, trying to work it out and fill in the missing lyrics. I want to know who this person is that he steers his boat by, and I don't want to know, too.

'I guess it's kind of about a muse,' he answers. My heart flaps and sinks. I can't compete with a muse.

'I nicked it, actually.' Jesse turns his head to look at me and quotes, '*He's like the North Star — you can guide your boat by him.*' He grins.

161

'Bob Dylan said it about Johnny Cash.'

I remember his smile and I remember smiling back. We must have drifted into sleep, while our voices swirled together, shimmering into the night sky like heat.

15

Lizzie

My mother did her best to keep me under control, but it was like trying to stop the spread of a fire with her bare hands. She tried to ground me again when she discovered her dirty, broken high-heeled shoe.

'Do you know how my shoe got broken?' she had asked, and I had shrugged sarcastically and said, 'Don't ask me. Maybe Mr Grundy borrowed them.' I refused to tell her anything, however obvious it was that I knew. 'Why d'you care anyway? It's not as if you ever wear them.'

Maybe that was the reason she was so upset.

'That's not the point, young lady. I don't mind about the shoe. If you wanted to wear them for an appropriate occasion and asked to borrow them I wouldn't hesitate to lend them to you. What worries me . . . ' She took a breath and smoothed her hair, the way she did when she was about to broach subjects that embarrassed her. 'You're too young to know, Elizabeth — but if you go out dressed in . . . in a certain way you'll get into trouble. People — men — will think you're ready for . . . something you're not ready for yet. And you'll get yourself into a situation you won't be able to handle.'

I eyed her in a sneering, disdainful way. It was

laughable, her trying to protect me from some wild, unknown maleness out there, when it was going on right under her very nose, with a man who was paying her for the privilege. I am ashamed, now, when I think what a fool I made of her. But then I just saw a fool.

This time she enlisted the help of Mr Grundy, telling him I was under no circumstance allowed out of the house when she wasn't at home. She said she would be grateful if he would keep an eye on me when she had to work a late shift.

'Of course. I'd be only too glad to help.'

We shared a cold laugh when he told me, him at the irony, and me at her stupidity. I called Kim as soon as she'd gone out and arranged to meet in a pub. As I turned to run up the stairs to get ready, I bumped straight into Mr Grundy, who was suddenly looming over me.

'Where are you going?' he said in a hurt voice.

I was taken aback. 'I'm going to meet me mates. Why?'

'Did I just hear you say you were meeting in a pub?'

'Yeah. What of it?'

'I just don't think that's a very good idea.'

'Yeah, well, no one asked you.' I tried to step forward but he didn't budge.

'But you're too young to go into a pub.'

'Y'what?!' I said, curling up my lip in punky contempt. 'I'm too young to do a lot of things.' I smeared the sarcasm on really thick. 'It hasn't bothered you before.'

A look of utter fury blazed across his face at my daring but I didn't flinch. It was the

164

cheekiest smart-alec response I had ever come up with and I was high with it. Mr Grundy stared at me while he battled to control his temper.

'What have I ever done to you that you didn't want?' he finally said. He was right; there was nothing I'd ever said no to. Nothing I hadn't initiated, actually. Satisfied that I couldn't reply, he went on in his most patronizing voice, 'Pubs and bars can be very dangerous places for young girls.'

I smirked to show he hadn't got the better of me.

'Especially when they look like *that*!' he snapped, casting his disgusted eyes over me. I had on an army vest that was long and thin, worn as a dress. I'd cut slits all over it and had no bra on.

'Well, you don't seem to mind it,' I finally retorted, and tried to storm past him. But he put his arm out across the stair blocking my way. I stared at him in outrage.

'Lizzie, it's different with us,' he hissed. 'You like being with me, you know you do. And you know you're safe. You know I won't hurt you. Other men will take one look at you out there in a bar and think you're just loose and worthless, to be used and thrown away like rubbish.'

I laughed in his face. 'I don't give a fuck what they or you or anyone else thinks! It's my life and I'll do what I want. It's not up to you to tell me what I can and can't do! Just let me past!'

I was shouting and it felt good. I tried to shove him out of the way but he grabbed me by the tops of my arms and shook me. It made my hair fall sideways, revealing a huge maroon bruise of a lovebite on my neck. Mr Grundy stared at it in shock.

'You're hurting me!' I tried to struggle free but his grip dug into my flesh and pinned me there, like some sort of specimen under inspection.

'Well, I see it's already too late,' he finally said. I could tell he was enjoying me wriggling because his nostrils were starting to flare. 'You're already quite the little tart.'

'Let me *go*, you stupid old man!' I shouted and pushed him. He overbalanced and fell onto the stairs, but he still managed to keep hold of me. I was shocked and scared by Mr Grundy's strength. He seemed such a weedy man, so easy to push aside, but the more I tried to worm my way free, the more caught up I became in his quicksand of limbs. My army vest was riding around my waist as I kicked out. He got me on my back against the stairs, his heavy thigh weighing down my legs, one hand clamping my arms above my head while the other worked its way over my writhing body. He groaned and started swearing a lot; *you want it, you dirty little girl, you slutty bitch*. He was trying to snog me, which he'd never done before. I tried to twist my face away, but my hair had got tangled up in something and I could feel it ripping out as I fought. His slobber was all over my face. He had me utterly trapped. As he unzipped his trousers I thought, *This is it. It's happening to me. I'm being raped. I'm losing my virginity to Mr Grundy*. The last thought was even worse than the one before. He got his knees between my legs and I braced myself as he positioned himself over me. The only things I could move without breaking were my eyes and mouth. So I looked right at him, defiantly, to disguise my terror.

'Go on then,' I whispered. 'I know you won't hurt me, after all.'

I watched as the fever left his eyes and they clouded with anguish. A string of saliva dangling from his lips began to wobble as his mouth contorted. He tried to stop but he was too far gone. Instead he shut his eyes against me while he held my arms with one hand and finished himself off with the other. I tried to flinch away from his stuff but I couldn't. My hair was like a web I'd woven to trap myself. It was caught in everything, his watch strap, his shirt buttons, his cufflinks. I felt it land over the side of my face.

'Oh God,' he whimpered as it did, and then repeated like an echo in a cave, *oh God, oh God, oh God*. When he finished panting he coughed and put himself away. He weakly attempted to get up, but my hair went with him. He tried to untangle it from his arm and chest but got nowhere. In the end I grabbed my hair and ripped it from wherever it was stuck, leaving clumps behind. I sat up, dazed, pulling my pants up and my dress down. I began to shake violently with the aftershock, the way you do after coming flying off a bike and picking yourself up and realizing you're still in one piece. I thought I might be sick. Mr Grundy was sitting on the bottom stair with his back to me and his head in his hands. I turned and crawled up the

167

stairs to the bathroom.

'*Dirty old bastard*,' yelled the Vonnie voice in my head as I ran a bath. '*Filthy fucking pervert.*' It helped, but not much. I wiped the slime from my hair and scrubbed the side of my neck before I got in the bath, and put my head right under when I was in too, and scrubbed again, but when I got out I could still feel it clinging there, the way you can feel a paper party hat even when you've taken it off.

I wrapped myself in a towel and stood in front of the mirror. I always liked how my hair looked when it was wet. It twisted and turned in sexy, glistening tendrils that snaked and dripped onto my shoulders. As I looked, my hair went out of focus and my eyes zoomed in behind it in the mirror, to my mum's sewing box, which she kept by the laundry basket. It was suddenly all so inevitable, somehow, as though I was watching a film I'd already seen and knew what was going to happen. I went over to it and took out her pinking shears and stood again at the mirror. Tendril by glossy tendril I chopped my hair off, leaving a scattering of lifeless rats' tails on the lino.

★ ★ ★

People reacted to my new hairstyle as though they were witnessing a car accident. My mum dropped her cup back onto its saucer on the table and cracked it, bringing her hands up to her mouth in an instinctive attempt to control the cry that escaped her. She actually looked

168

truly scared of me. I'd been pretty scared myself, when I'd woken up in the morning and suddenly seen myself in the mirror before I'd remembered what I'd done. My heart had started beating as though I had a band with two drummers playing inside my ribcage. My head looked as though moths had got to it in the night. With shaking hands I'd scooped out some hair gel and tried to get my tufts of hair into some sort of shape before I faced going downstairs.

As she looked at me my mother winced, as though flesh had been sliced from my bones.

'It's only hair,' I attempted to shrug, to comfort myself as much as anyone else. Tears spilled down her cheeks and over her hands, still clutching her reaction in as though it was vomit. She kept gulping it back. When she finally let go of her mouth she blurted out, 'What have you done? You stupid, STUPID GIRL!'

I tried to shrug again, but my shoulders were still up by my ears from the shrug I'd tried before.

'Cut my hair?' I suggested, trying to smother my own horror with sarcasm. It didn't help my mum's much. She flew at me and slapped me hard across the face.

'Wipe that smirk off your face. You look ugly enough as it is,' she shouted. 'You've gone too far this time, you horrible child,' she choked. 'What have I done wrong? What are you trying to do to me?'

I tried to stand my ground, but it was hard to be defiant to someone who was blaming themselves for what I'd done. I stood there awkwardly while she broke down into loud sobs. It had been so liberating at the time, chopping it all off, but now I felt naked. There was nothing to hide behind any more. My true self was exposed and my mum had finally seen me for how I really was. How ugly I really was. In the end she shoved me towards the door.

'Get out of my sight,' she said, averting her eyes, 'I can't bear to look at you any more.'

She really couldn't. I don't think she looked at me properly again until my wedding day. Even then I was hardly the picture of the daughter she wanted, but it was as close as I ever got.

I kept to my room whenever I was at home, only coming out for silent, cutlery-chinking meals. When Mr Grundy first saw me, peeking out from where he was cowering in the sitting room, he put his hand on his chest as though he was having a heart attack. I smiled at him with as much saccharine sweetness as I could muster. He was horrified by what I'd done, and I saw his mouth open to make some shocked remark, and then the events of the night before replayed across his face, and his jaw clamped shut again. He knew he was to blame and he had the decency to skulk about guiltily, terrified I'd tell on him if he didn't play by my rules. It was incredible how much power cutting my hair off gave me. I was like Samson in reverse.

As I walked in to school everyone that passed me seemed to slow down and steer round me, not wanting to gawp, but gawping still. I did my best Johnny Rotten face back at them but inside I felt humiliated, a freak. When Kim saw me though, it began to turn around. Things had been so awful at home at the weekend I hadn't called her about what had happened. I braced myself for her scorn and laughter, but after her initial open mouth her face broke into an admiring grin.

'Fucking hell! You did it!' She ran her hand over the crusty tops of my spikes. 'You look fucking *great!*'

We broke into manic laughter and she grilled me about the trouble I was in. It was a relief to see the light side of it as I retold the horror of my weekend. I took the piss out of my mum crying and hitting me and she killed herself laughing at my impression of her. For once I was her hero. I'd proved I was the real thing. My hair was more punky than hers as I hadn't even had it done by a proper hairdresser. She took me on a lap of honour around the school.

Now I had the hair right, the punky boys were drawn to me like flies round a shit. And Kim got a lot more attention too. I was starting to see how it all worked.

I was the first to lose my virginity. We were desperate to lose it while it was still illegal, of course, and I managed to get rid of mine just before I turned sixteen. It was at a party, in a field behind the house of someone whose parents were away, on magic mushrooms and a cowpat. Arry and I had already done everything but, so it was really just a technicality. But I wanted it to be official. I wanted the bit of paper, the seal of blood. The red stain was like a stamp on my passport that proved I had been there. It wasn't the pints and pints of blood that we were expecting from Vonnie's stories, and it didn't hurt all that much either. But when Kim asked I said it did, to carry on the tradition.

I felt closer to Vonnie than I'd ever been, more of a sister than her real sister was.

Arry didn't even know I was a virgin, and never found out that terrible secret. It was over very quickly, and he blamed the cold.

'My balls have fucking disappeared,' he complained, rummaging around in his trousers as he lay above me. 'You'll have to make do with a lazy lob.'

I tried to make him think I'd enjoyed it more than I really had by being all over him when we went back into the party. He was stupid enough to believe he must have been so good it had made me fall in love with him.

'Don't fink it means anyfing,' he said gruffly, removing my arm from round his neck when he was back with his mates. 'It don't mean we're togevver or nuffink.'

16

Beth

I open my eyes to the sun streaming in onto Jesse's sleeping face. His sweet features waylay the discord about to strike in my head at finding myself in this strange situation, instead sending a melodious thump to my chest.

He is beautiful.

His skin is uncrumpled, flawless with youth, with the quality of both china and fruit, fine and smooth and juicy. His beard growth is sporadic and soft, not yet speckling his cheeks with the rough grey of shaving, but lying in cute wispy tufts around the outline of his face. Fine hairs from his eyebrows stray towards his hairline and each other and there is natural shadow on his lids, which fluctuate while he sleeps. The fringes of his eyelashes curl over his cheeks in perfect crescents, long and dark. He has full red lips. When he becomes a man he will be what they call chiselled, but now he still has that childlike lack of form to his cheekbones and nose, as though the clay is still wet, before life has sculpted its marks.

I can understand why ageing men yearn still for young girls with perfect skin. It is the outer signifier of that inner hope blooming, the lack of bitterness and damage.

173

He lies in an open way, on his back but angled towards me, with one bare arm curled around his head, revealing the downy hair of his armpit. I am hunched in towards him, stiff around the hips from sleeping in jeans, with my arms across my chest and my face squashed into the pillow. I realize we are in the bed, not still on top, and the song has stopped playing. Some time in the night he must have turned it off, undressed and pulled the duvet over us, but I have no memory of it.

The thought of his eyes suddenly opening onto my face as the sun's rays interrogate it so unforgivingly makes me slip quickly and as quietly as possible out of bed. I can still get away with my face at nighttime, but daylight is too exposing. I need to clean my stale mouth before I breathe on him.

I creep down to the bathroom at the bottom of his flight of stairs and take a shower. When I put my clothes back on, they smell of dried sweat and cigarette smoke. I scrub my teeth with a squeeze of toothpaste on my finger and study my face. I splash it with cold water to shock away the puffs and creases and find a cotton bud to poke the kohled sleep from the corners of my eyes. There's no sign of a girl in the house, no make-up to borrow. I can feel my skin stretching dry across my face and open the cabinet, finding a man's aftershave moisturizer to use on the worst of it, my cheeks and forehead. I towel-dry my hair and comb it through. A snail trail of silver weaves its way through it. It needs a redye. I pull out the worst offenders glinting on the parting. I find somebody's spot concealer to

174

blend in the shadows under my eyes and broken thread veins around my nose. I consider sneaking away now, just carrying on down the stairs, before a real day ruins the perfection of the night before. But I have left my trainers in Jesse's room.

I tiptoe back upstairs but Jesse has already sat up and is scratching his head, yawning and blinking in the sun.

'Hello,' he says, smiling up through squinting eyes. I feel ludicrously shy for a grown woman.

'Hi,' I reply, letting my hair fall across my face as I bend down for my shoes. I sit on the floor to put them on.

'Have you got to be somewhere?' he asks. His first-thing voice is gravelly sweet, like a purr. I should probably say yes.

'Not especially,' I say instead.

'Then at least let me make you a coffee.' He stumbles out of bed in white boxers, and I concentrate on tying up my laces as he passes me to the kitchen. He yawns some more, and stretches. He has a boy's physique, bare chested with a slight line of hair descending from his belly button. I'm not sure how I notice this while I'm so studiously not looking.

'I don't remember falling asleep,' I say. 'Or you turning the music off.'

'No. You were out,' he smiles, and I hope I wasn't snoring or catching flies, with my jaw hanging slack in an unflattering, middle-aged pose.

'You looked so angelic, I tried really hard not to wake you.'

175

I grimace, unconvinced, and he laughs, shaking his head.

'What?!' I say.

'It's just . . . you. I'll show you.'

He is far more relaxed than me, obviously more used to this situation. He must wake up with strange women a lot. Or girls, at least. I feel like a girl myself, as though our ages have interchanged somehow over the course of the night. It has all been so surreal and otherworldly it wouldn't surprise me if they had, the way things like that can happen so normally in children's stories.

He brings two cups of coffee and sits on the edge of the bed, leaning over for a notebook lying where he slept. He passes it to me, open on a page with a line drawing of a sleeping profile. I recognize the tilt of my nose. The mouth is curving into a slight smile.

'That's very kind of you, but I do not look like that when I'm sleeping!' I laugh to hide being touched that he drew me in my sleep at all, let alone in such a pretty way. He tells me he is at art college. He is practising drawing with a continuous line, like Cocteau.

It pleases me that he is an art student, fits my idea of him and how musicians should start out, the way they did when rock music was young. I had jadedly supposed he was probably on one of these after-my-time courses that have sprung up all over the place — degrees in pop music or how to make it in the music business, or at least studio engineering.

'Why not music?' I ask.

176

'I can't read it, for a start,' he answers. 'I taught myself to play. I've only just got my head round this gear. I'm doing extra shifts to pay it off.'

He works in a cafe-bar in Covent Garden. I digest all my new information slowly, worried that it might somehow dilute my idea of him, as some sort of essence of music. Once I've adjusted I become more curious about this new, real person.

'So what do you want to do with your life, Jesse Porter?' I ask.

I forget to be self-conscious as he answers and we sink once more into this other, deeper place. I wonder if he is like this with everyone, if I've just forgotten that this is how people are when they're young, or if it is a special place he just goes with me. He talks unashamedly about his dreams. He talks about music in terms of art instead of Making It — he wants to be a proper well-rounded artist, not a popstar.

'I don't give a fuck if I don't get a big record deal. I don't wanna be rich and famous. That's not the point.'

'You might change your mind about that later,' I laugh. I'm prone to snigger cynically inside at such naivety but somehow find myself believing him utterly, with a fool's faith, like a born-again.

'Why? Did you?' He asks, not sharply, to get the better of me, but as though he wants to know.

I deflect his question. It's a skill I've developed well over the years.

'Success is a lot about luck and fashion and

being in the right place at the right time,' I say. 'What about when you're thirty, or forty, when other younger people are making it who are far less talented than you and you're washing dishes, too exhausted to play when you get to the minuscule amount of free time you have left over? Too broke to take time out. How do you think you'll feel then? Don't you think you might wonder what's the point of it all?'

'I can't possibly know,' he answers. 'All I can hope for is that I've been as good as I can be. Created something that I'm proud of. Not sold out.'

I am amazed to hear someone young talk about selling out. It seemed to me as though selling out became buying in, and everybody has. Where has he come from? He must have hippy parents, or maybe the winds of change are blowing again and he's just a product of his time and I'm out of touch. Maybe I really did get old. He is so self-possessed. I was never like that at nineteen. I was the opposite, possessing nothing of myself, as though the pieces of me fluttered around outside and I had to chase around trying to catch them. I sometimes wonder if I ever did.

Sometime later — twenty minutes? an hour? two? — he gets up and pulls on some clothes and sets up his studio to play the song again. I put my face in my hands, preparing for the disappointment that so often comes the morning after, when you have separated out from the music and come down, and can judge it the way you can see faults in other people but not yourself. But the disappointment doesn't come.

My over-critical faculties can only weed out one iffy moment when I hold a note too long and it wavers. I peek out at Jesse, who is nodding to the track, smiling at me.

'Not bad for someone too old who can't sing,' he says, and I agree.

While he makes us some toast I tentatively fiddle around on his keyboard. I can hear a descending bass line and repetitive piano notes at the top, rippling over it like water. I find them, finally.

'That's it! It's so perfect!' Jesse enthuses, '*Pleease* record it for me.' I protest, of course, saying my fingers are too unrehearsed to be able to carry it all the way through without fluffing.

'If you'd use your bloody edit and quantize tools I would.'

'Don't be such a drip!' he goads. 'Do you think I'd ask you if I thought you were going to ruin it?'

I give in to his insistence, making him give me time to practise and get my fingers used to it first. Something about music makes time have no meaning, and it disappears as we drift away again. We are finally satisfied with a take in the late afternoon. At least, Jesse is. I am too aware of the lack of fluidity in my playing, but it is nothing that can be perfected without weeks of practice.

'It serves you right for giving up,' he says. And then after a beat, he asks again, 'Why did you give up?'

'What is it with you lot?' I say. 'To most people getting old and past it is a perfectly good reason.'

'Not to you,' he replies. 'I don't believe it of you.'

'Well, it's true. I got married. Other things took over.'

He doesn't buy it. 'Why did you give up?' he asks again.

I can't tell him.

'I can't tell you,' I say. 'It hurts too much.'

I can feel the ache at the back of my throat and lower my filling eyes. I have never voiced the pain I feel about what happened. He puts his hand on the back of my head and pulls me to him, holding me there like a friend. I stop breathing so as not to cry. He is the right height for me to lie my head on his shoulder. I can smell the salt on his skin. He strokes my hair at the nape of my neck.

'Whatever it is shouldn't have stopped you forever,' he says quietly. 'Will you play some more for me? My songs need you.'

We are interrupted by his phone ringing. I break away so he can answer it. He picks up and makes arrangements for something on that evening. I can hear a girl's voice and wonder if it's Amie.

'I have to get ready,' he apologizes. 'Mickey's done a soundtrack for an installation in Brick Lane. D'you wanna come?' I shake my head. I am suddenly struggling to hold on to myself.

'I'd better get back,' I say, and look around for my stuff. I realize I don't have any, apart from my hair clips scattered on the floor by the bed. He lends me a jumper to get home in. I hadn't realized I was shivering. He takes me downstairs to show me out, saying hi to a housemate who peers out of a first-floor door. On the front steps we stop and I put my hands in the back pockets of my jeans, where I always put them when I don't know what else to do with them. It is difficult to say goodbye.

I remember it was Toby Jesse really came to the house to see.

'If he's back in time tomorrow Toby'll try and make your gig.'

Jesse frowns minutely for a moment. 'It doesn't matter,' he says, shrugging. I feel he is trying to say something, but doesn't know how. Or maybe I am reading too much into nothing.

'It does,' I say. 'It should.'

'Just promise me you'll come back and put some piano and backing vocals on my other tracks,' he says.

'I will,' I say, and try to grasp onto the thought of it as a definite thing that will happen. But it is like trying to shape something with dry sand. The more I clutch it the more shapeless it becomes, sifting through my fingers and blowing away.

'Thank you for having me,' I add. 'I . . . '

I can't find the words.

'I had a really good time,' he says for me, and then he adds, ' . . . with you.'

We hug then, and he kisses me close to my mouth.

It is hard to let go but I do, and I leave, turning to smile goodbye. Standing there he looks like the kind of boy I loved when I was a kid, all vanilla skin and melty chocolate eyes, before my sexuality matured and developed an acquired taste for something far less sweet.

I force myself to walk away, until I suddenly hear him call, 'Lizzie.'

I turn back again. He has come into the street in his bare feet.

'You've got my number. Call me. Any time.'

I giggle and kiss him quickly again and say goodbye. It lifts my spirits somehow, this last gesture, him running into the street barefoot to say one more thing to me. There is something hopeful about it.

I am too restless for stations and bus stops. I don't know where I'm walking but I let my legs carry me onwards down street after street, while my heart stays with Jesse.

I feel I could walk all night, but familiar surroundings jog my mind into catching up with my body and I realize I'm nearly in my own road. I consider walking round the block some more but something tells me it's time to go home. I need to calm down, have a long soak in the bath, let my layers settle down again inside to where they were before, flat and heavy like wet, fallen leaves. Sort myself out before Toby comes home.

I open the front door to the sight of Toby's luggage in the hallway. I see the reflection of the TV in the gloss of the sitting room door. Then a shadow crossing the reflection, then Toby's frame itself, standing in front of it.

'Where have you been?' he asks, simply, as I tug my hands up into the sleeves of Jesse's jumper.

17

Lizzie

All the same, I shacked up with Arry. It wasn't a decision; I just ended up at his bedsit like a bit of litter stuck in an eddy. He had a room above the Sue Ryder shop where everyone used to go when all the pubs shut, to smoke and take drugs. I wound up there when I was meant to be at school more often than not, while proper kids were swotting for their O-levels. Mr Grundy wasn't the only one who liked me in my school uniform, however much Arry called me *middle class* for attempting to go to school at all. It was one of his favourite insults. Anything I did that he didn't like was middle class.

'Wot — you're going to be an anarchist, but you just thought you'd get your O-levels first, yeah?' he sneered at me.

I imagined he must have left school before he was sixteen because he was a true rebel and refused to join the rat race. I imagined him as a sort of James Dean of our times. I didn't find out until later on that he didn't have any O-levels because he was thick and had failed them.

My mum had given me up for a lost cause. Every now and again she would try and parent me, scattering some words of wisdom in the hope that they would take root and grow, but she knew by now they were falling on stony ground.

'You don't know how much you need your qualifications in life, Elizabeth,' she would say. 'I know you don't realize it now, but until you're sixteen I'm your guardian and while I am I'll put you through your exams whether you like it or not. I've tried to teach you this as best I can but ... ' She was just going through the motions, really. 'When you're sixteen you can do what you like.'

I realized I made her ashamed. I was her failing personified, walking about for all to see. I realized she might actually want me to turn sixteen and leave home. I was too painful to look at any more. When I found out that you could get twelve pounds a week off the dole and your rent paid for doing nothing, I had to agree with Arry. It all seemed pointless. I didn't turn sixteen until after O-levels, so I sat them anyway, however middle class it was, kind of a last deal between me and Mum. At first I thought I'd just sit there and hand in blank pages, as my punk protest, but I soon got bored, so I read the questions. When I got bored of doing that, I had a go at answering them. Sitting for O-levels and not answering the questions seemed more pointless than not taking them at all.

After the last one, the rest of our year went to a wine and cheese party the nerdy prefects had arranged for them in the sixth-form common room. They tried to make us join in too, but we were already cutting up our ties in the changing rooms, downing bottles of cough medicine and hauling ourselves into our drainpipes to head down town.

I never really left home. I just gradually went back there less and less, taking more and more of my belongings each time I went from there to Arry's, until the scales tipped and I was officially more there than anywhere, if you judged on weight of my stuff alone.

At first I let Mum think I was staying with Kim, but she saw me hanging out in town with Arry and the other punks enough times to know. She always pretended she hadn't seen me. Even when I was back home she seemed not to see me. She let me come and go, which I only ever did when Mr Grundy was at work. But it was as though she wasn't all there, or thought I wasn't. One of the two. She carried on doing the housework and peeling potatoes, and if I was there at a meal time she automatically set the table for me too, and we ate and strung sentences together into a conversation that hung between us over the table like darning, hiding the hole.

At first we still hung round together, me and Kim, just like when we were at school, only without the school part. The only bad thing was that we didn't have anywhere to play music any more. We started practising at my mum's when she was out, but the stupid old cow next door complained about the noise. Kim still played her saxophone at home, but they didn't have a piano or a guitar at their house. I spent more and more time lying about the bedsit with Arry, and Kim came into town less and less. She started earning money helping her dad do up an old barn he'd just converted into a modern house for one of his clients. At the end of the season she'd saved enough to go up to London to stay with Vonnie.

★ ★ ★

The same thing happened to her that had happened to her sister. She only went to London to visit but ended up staying there, sucked in, as though London was an incessantly whirling tornado that held people in it by its own centripetal force. Kim asked me to come too, but I stayed on with Arry. It seemed the thing to do when he was my boyfriend.

At first I always told him I'd be moving to London, but when it came to it I couldn't, as though I was stuck in my own vortex, only somehow mine felt more like I was being sucked downwards, like dirty bathwater going down a plughole. Getting a boyfriend had seemed to be my goal, but when I got one I couldn't for the life of me remember why. I didn't know what you were meant to do once you'd arrived at *Having a Boyfriend*. It was like getting off the train at the station you'd been heading for and finding once you'd walked across the platform to the exit that there was nothing else there. The station was all there was. By the time you'd found out and turned round to go back, the train had already gone.

When I got letters from Kim telling me about her crazy life hanging out with Vonnie's crazy friends I didn't feel like the lucky one any more. I felt left behind.

I hadn't realized that if I was shacking up with Arry I couldn't get my own dole. They considered me his dependant and said they'd add an extra few quid onto his. Arry came up with a plan to get round it, which involved me getting a job as a waitress in the Golden Egg and saying I lived at my mum's so that he could still sign on and keep his dole to himself.

I'd come home after the lunchtime rush to give him a fried-egg sandwich and his first shag of the day. He was always still in bed. Anarchists didn't seem to do much. It got boring after a while. But whenever I wanted to do something other than hang around with him he'd get really pissed off.

For someone who didn't believe in possessive love, he was very possessive. If he ever got to the post before me he'd tear up my letters from Kim. If I talked to his mates when they came round he'd accuse me of fancying them afterwards, or sometimes even before they'd gone, which was really embarrassing. They mostly stopped coming by.

We stopped going round to other mates' places, too, after I made the mistake of picking up Robbo's guitar when we were at his and picking out the chords of 'Ever Fallen in Love with Someone You Shouldn't Have'. Robbo was impressed and said I was pretty good, for a girl. He plugged his bass in and we started jamming. When I looked up Arry was staring at me in a fury. He got up suddenly and somehow as he passed me his arm flailed out wildly and knocked his cider off the amp I was sitting next to. The glass whacked me on the side of the head. The cider went all over me and Robbo's guitar.

'You fucking wanker, watch my guitar,' shouted Robbo, leaping to its rescue as Arry stomped out and I wiped myself down with the sleeve of my oversized holey mohair jumper.

I didn't pick up a guitar again the whole time we were together, just in case. In fact, I didn't do a great deal of anything, just in case. It seemed that the less I did, the less I annoyed him, so I did less and less. It was a matter of trial and error, to get the way of being right. Anything could set him off. He was hard to work out and it was exhausting to try. Without my mates, with the Vonnie voice fading away, I found it hard to put up a fight. I was just ugly, unlovable me, after all.

Arry seemed to see me as something to rebel against as well as everything else, like I was tying him down and a threat to his freedom. It wasn't fair. I wanted to be just as bad, just as rebellious as he was. But it was as if being a girl I was the antithesis to his punk lifestyle, even though I was a punk too. Arry didn't seem to want me when I was around him, but I would have hell to pay if I stayed out of his way for too long. He was suspicious about anything I did when I wasn't with him. He'd come into the caff sometimes and just watch me work, watch how I was with the customers. At the same time he hated me going out with him to gigs and parties, saying I was cramping his style. He would often split up with me, only to get in a fury because I agreed we probably should break up, paranoid about why I wanted to. He'd insist on getting back together a few hours later, just because he couldn't bear not knowing what I was doing, which was always nothing.

His final solution was to keep me as his girlfriend but just to lock me in while he went out. This arrangement seemed to suit him well, and to be honest, I'm ashamed to say, it didn't bother me much either. I guess I'd been worn smooth as a pebble by the constant pounding of Arry's moods.

I enjoyed the relief of being left alone. I could listen to the music I was into that Arry couldn't stand, which was basically everything that wasn't pure thrashing punk and had a tune. Arry hated the Two Tone thing but privately I adored it. Before I was living with Arry, before Kim had gone to London, we'd gone to see the Two Tone Tour, the Selecter, Madness and the Specials all at once for one pound fifty. We'd fallen head over heels. We danced all night, in amongst a great heave of sweating bodies bobbing up and down. We were so jealous of Pauline Black, jumping about in her suit and pork-pie hat, on tour with all those cool, cool blokes.

When I brought over my record collection to the bedsit and first played my Specials album, Arry had flung it out the window and it had landed in the road and gone under the wheels of a van. But I'd got Kim to tape it for me, along with lots of other stuff, records that Vonnie had, originals of all the Prince Buster songs. I got her to send them to my mum's house so they'd get through to me, and I hid them at Arry's where we kept the cleaning stuff.

We were also allowed to play music in the kitchen at the Golden Egg. The other girl that worked there, Julie, was a modette. She wore ski pants and a little suede jacket and her boyfriend dropped her off at work on his Lambretta. She looked cool on it, leaning back against the backrest instead of putting her arms around him, looking out nonchalantly through her cat shades, with her little boxy handbag on her knees. She brought in tapes of old soul music, stuff she danced to in the all-nighters at scooter runs at Bournemouth and Weston-Super-Mare. That's when I first heard the originals of 'Heatwave' and 'Tears of a Clown'. She played me all the girl groups and I learnt the words of 'Wild One' and 'He's A Rebel' by heart. They made me feel better about being with Arry, although I didn't see why a girl's way of rebelling had to be going out with someone rebellious. Somehow blokes, they just rebelled.

Me and Julie became friends. I adapted my make-up a little bit so it was more like hers, making the eyeliner a little more refined and sharply drawn, and trying on her pale, pale lipstick. Not so Arry would notice. Just so I would. She had peroxided hair, quite short, parted on the side, with her sideburns coming down into points on her cheeks. I wasn't allowed mine spiky for work anyway, so I did the same with mine, brushing it forward around my face.

'You look right smart,' said Julie. 'You've got

such a Sixties face, you lucky bitch. You're *gameen*. Like Mia Farrow.' At our break times we'd pore over pictures she collected of the Sixties, from her mum's old fashion magazines and books about mods the first time round.

When I think of the first time I fell in love, I think of this time. Not because of Arry, but because of the music I discovered on the side, soul, my secret affair.

★ ★ ★

In the summer of 1982, Arry's granddad died and I took my chance. Arry had to go down to Cornwall with his family for the funeral and he was going to be gone a whole weekend. As soon as I heard the news I secretly scribbled a letter to Kim, giving her the number of the phone box at the end of my street and a time to call me there.

'I can come up to London this weekend,' I said. 'Can I stay with you?'

Kim sounded really chuffed. She would come and meet me off the coach on Saturday morning. We arranged to speak to each other, same time, same place, the Friday before, just to be sure it was happening. I prayed Arry would go to the funeral. He wasn't happy about it, especially as it meant leaving me for an entire weekend. He tried to make me go too, but luckily his mum put her foot down and said I wasn't allowed to. She thought I was a tramp for the way I dressed and for living in sin with her son. The last thing she needed was her son showing up with his trashy girlfriend. I was very grateful to her.

'I'll probably just go up town, and then I'll go round and see my mum,' I said to Arry.

'Who are you going to meet up town?' he asked. We had variations on this conversation for the next three days, until finally his straight brother Darren came round to pick him up on Friday afternoon, with a spare grey suit he had for his job at Comet to lend Arry.

'You can't turn up looking like that,' said Darren, casting an eye over Arry's greasy spikes and swastikas. But Arry was determined to be an anarchist at least until the funeral itself, and they left, bickering down the stairs. As they clambered into Darren's Nissan Cherry, Arry yelled up to the window, 'I'll find out if you get off with anyone. I've got me sources.'

He slammed the door and I watched them drive away, Arry still with his head bent to one side because his spikes were too tall for the roof of the car.

I gave them enough time to be sure they'd left town, and then I went round to Julie's. She was lending me some clothes. I didn't tell her where I was going, just that I wanted to try out a new look while Arry wasn't around. She was pleased to be my stylist. She made up my face first, and moussed my hair over so it swooped forward from a side parting.

'You should grow it into a bob,' she said. 'You're lucky, you could do anything with your hair; it's so dead straight. I can't wear mine longer than this; it's too blimmin curly.' She showed me pictures of the Supremes on her records, and I studied the wigs they wore.

'You'd be able to do summit like that with your hair.'

She put the record on and started going through her wardrobe as she danced about, pulling out miniskirts and little jackets and black and white checked tops.

'Why don't you become a modette?' said Julie. 'You're going to look ace in this stuff. You'd get a new boyfriend no trouble. You get some lush boys on the scooter runs. You and me could go round together. Go on, we'd have a right laugh.'

She put me in a minidress that was one half black, one half white, with a shiny patent white belt through the belt loops on the hips. She got me some white tights to put on and some pointy black winklepicker shoes.

She hung bright plastic hoop earrings on me, and added bangles for my arms and a white plastic cap, and propelled me to the mirror. The image that looked back at me was of a pretty girl, not just a girl who might be pretty underneath all the war paint if she stopped scowling. I laughed, and I still looked pretty, not gruesome the way I did when I laughed with black or green lipstick on. I started dancing too, trying to copy Julie's moves. Julie was thrilled.

'You look like the Beat Girl!' she exclaimed, and then she got dressed up too so we could dance together in front of the mirror. She taught me some Sixties dances — the Hitchhike, the Monkey and the Mashed Potato — and then some cooler shuffly steps they did at all-nighters.

'You're not a bad dancer for a punk,' she said,

as we grinned breathlessly. I could feel she was right. Dancing to soul music was like being released from a prison. The rhythm section became your heartbeat and pumped the blood round your veins and the brass riffs soared in and lifted you up and out and over the walls. I felt I could dance forever.

I only had to stop because it got to the time I'd arranged for Kim to call me at the phone box. Julie let me borrow an outfit for the weekend — a pair of her ski-pants and a turtleneck sleeveless top under a little Beatles jacket with no collar — and I rushed as fast as my kitten heels would let me to the phone box.

Kim hadn't forgotten me. She said we'd have a great time. Vonnie's boyfriend had a gig in a club on Saturday night that we could go to. I went home and shaved my legs and my armpits and put a blue-black semi-permanent on my hair to make myself look more like the Supremes. I went to bed early so I'd get up in time for the coach at seven o'clock, but I spent most of the night awake. I felt too good to waste it on sleep.

18

Beth

'Toby! You're back early!' I leap into the exclamation and propel myself forward with arms outstretched to smother the shocked pause that's hung between us for a fraction of a second.

'I thought you weren't back till tomorrow?' I lean up to kiss the sharp stubble around his mouth and hug him.

'Yeah, I got it wrong because of the time difference.' He kisses the top of my head. 'I'm all over the fucking place with jet lag. I tried to get some kip but I couldn't.'

'I would've had some dinner ready if I'd known. Are you hungry?' I head for the kitchen, my eyes darting around to check how I left the place. I remember the mess of going-out clothes I left all over the bedroom and wonder if he's been upstairs yet. 'What time did you get back?'

'I dunno — a few hours ago? Where were you, anyway?'

'Tea?' I'm filling the kettle, getting the cups out.

'Yeah, go on, I'll have a cup. Proper strong English tea, milk and two shugs.'

'I know how you take your tea, Tobes!' I joke. 'How was your trip? Did you have a good time?'

'Well, it wasn't a holiday, Beth. It was work,

195

you know? The usual shit. Showcases, VIP lounges, tours of the night spots, endless head nodding and gift swapping with the Japs.'

Toby is blasé about his job. He gets mad if I refer to it as in any way enjoyable. To me and most people it sounds like a cool and glamorous career, but Toby says he hates it. He seems to have forgotten how much he wanted it in the early days, how hard he worked to get where he is now.

'Did you get the deal you were after, though?'

'Yeah, I did. We had to go higher but it'll pay off. Single's a guaranteed number one. We're on the UK tour and merchandising already.' He yawns wide and loudly and pulls out a stool to prop himself against the bar while he blabs on for a while as he tends to do about his work. He just needs a prod in the right direction to get him started and he's off. I need the time to get my story sorted in my head.

'Talking of talent, this boy came round with a demo for you,' I say, before Toby can ask again where I've been. 'Because you weren't here I played it. It was pretty good so I went to see him perform at Barry's last night. He's worth you checking out, I reckon. I mean, he's raw, but he has something. He's playing again tomorrow night at the Twelve Bar.'

Toby is irritable. 'Look, Beth, I'm really knackered, all right? It'd be nice if I could have a day off for once.'

'OK,' I placate. 'It doesn't matter; he'll be playing again.'

'Yeah, well, it's not like I need another act to

deal with right now.'

'I know. I wouldn't bother you with it if I didn't think you'd be interested. I'm just passing on stuff that's happened while you were away.'

'Yeah, well. Anything else I have to deal with before I can chill out? How's the studio?'

I've forgotten about the studio. I was meant to keep a check on it. Toby owns it, or owns the mortgage on it, or technically I do, as he put it in my name. It is in a converted chapel that the label uses for first recordings of its new signings. We get paid for the use of it. It's kind of my job, I suppose, to oversee it, although I'm vague about what that entails. There's a studio manager who pretty much does everything, though he calls me when there's money needed for new equipment or some kind of problem. I'm hoping because I haven't had any messages from Ady that everything's OK. Toby got it in the first place to record acts he believed in, to give them a head start. He dreamed of being a producer in those days, but never got the time out from A&R, especially when Giant broke big and he was head-hunted by the major labels. An up and coming 'punk' band have been booked in there all week, supposedly recording a five-song demo. I was meant to make sure that the promise of a rock and roll lifestyle hadn't gone to their heads via their noses and that they did actually get it together to put some tracks down in between swaggering around in their shades taking drugs and pulling girls.

'Fine,' I reply, hoping for the best. 'I mean, I haven't been down there or anything 'cos Kim phoned about Vonnie the day after you left. I went and helped her clean up Vonnie's flat afterwards — '

Toby tuts. 'Christ, why did you have to do that?'

'I didn't *have* to, Tobes. Kim's my friend. She asked if I would so 'course I said yes. What's wrong with that?'

'Nothing, I didn't say there was. Fine, if you wanted to. But surely you could have got to the studio once while I was away?'

'I've had a lot on my mind, all right? It hasn't been that easy to just carry on as normal when something like this has happened. You don't know what it was like at Vonnie's. You didn't see what her life has been like. It was awful, Toby. And we didn't know if she was going to pull through. It was really serious. Why are you acting like it was nothing?'

'I just don't see what it is to you. And why it's meant you've dropped everything you're supposed to be doing — '

'I haven't *dropped* everything,' I say sarcastically. 'Anyway, I don't see why you can't understand. And you know Ady is perfectly capable of running the studio. Don't make such a big deal out of nothing.'

'Nothing?! So the studio's nothing now is it? Have you any idea — ?'

'Toby! That's not what I meant and you know it!'

'Well, why you put some fucked-up old junkie before everything we're trying to build here I don't know,' Toby shouts back. It shuts me up. It

198

shocks me like a slap to hear Vonnie — *Vonnie!* — referred to as a fucked-up old junkie. How can Toby see her like that? Surely he can remember her the way she was, in the glory days? I realize that was all a very long time ago. By the time Toby came on the scene her shine had already begun to fade. She has been a junkie far longer than she hasn't. In fact, was she ever not a junkie of one sort or another?

I am not grateful to Toby for pointing this out to me. I can't even remember Vonnie thinking junkies were cool, although I'm sure she did when we were young. It just doesn't sound so exciting with *fucked-up* and *old*. The force of these thoughts stings and Toby thinks I am about to cry.

'Look, I'm sorry,' he says, putting his hands on my shoulders. 'I didn't mean it. Let's stop this. It's blown up out of nowhere. I'm just tired and strung out. All right?'

'OK,' I agree, removing Toby's hands. 'Why don't you go and crash on the sofa? I'll do us an omelette and bring it through.'

'Can we have chips?' Toby asks as he obediently takes his tea through to the lounge.

★　★　★

We eat in front of the telly, watching MTV2 until the starchy food settles on Toby's stomach and takes its effect, stupefying his wired nerves. I nip upstairs and quickly shove my scattering of clothes into drawers and run Toby a bath with relaxing oils. I pull him up off the couch, hoping

199

the bath will make him sleepy enough to crash out so I can have some time to myself. I get in the bath after him and take deep breaths while he collapses on the bed next door.

I seem to have got away with my night out.

Thinking about Jesse stops the horrors about Vonnie scuttling around in my head like mice. I wish I had talked to him about it all when he asked me. I wish I was with him now, to tell him everything. I wouldn't use the phrase *fucked-up old junkie* when I told him about her. I would say how beautiful she was, in her own crazy way, and how she let me see that life was there for the taking and I could do anything I wanted. Jesse would listen and understand. He has the purity of youth, like untrodden snow, untainted by the things life throws at you later. The wrong turns that you take, the mistakes you make, the chances you miss that don't come round again. I'd give anything to have that back. I'd undo the thing I did that made Vonnie fall. I'd hang on to what we had as though our lives depended on it.

As it turns out, they really did.

It is too unbearable to think about. I am too exhausted to reason it away, but too wide awake to sleep, as though I too have been on a long-haul flight. I go downstairs in my towel and load up the dishwasher. I hate thinking about tomorrow, knowing Jesse will be at the Twelve Bar and I won't because I have to have a day off with Toby. Will Jesse be disappointed I'm not there? Will he even notice? I'm close to tears at the thought of either. Of having to let him go.

I hear the toilet flush and try to snap out of it.

Toby stumbles down the stairs.

'I'm fucking wide awake again,' he says. 'What are you doing still up?'

'I couldn't sleep,' I say, getting a glass of water. 'Thought I'd clear up.'

He looks at me in my towel for a moment.

'Hey, I forgot,' he says. 'I got you a present.'

He leads me into the lounge where his bags are still scattered around the floor and rummages about until he finds a plastic bag. He pulls out a box, beautifully wrapped as ever, courtesy of Japanese shop assistants.

'Toby, where did you find the time to get something for me?' I gush, ignoring the airport logo on the carrier bag that Toby stuffs back in his luggage.

It is, as expected, expensive lingerie, only this time in white. There is a silk mini slip with a lace trim and a white string for underneath. There are also hold-up stockings with a white lace band around the top. Toby has conventional tastes.

'They're beautiful,' I say. 'You shouldn't have spent so much on me.'

'You're worth it,' he says, leaning in for a snog. I can see where this is headed. 'Why don't you put them on?'

I smile and he takes my hand and leads me up the stairs, past the empty space where my picture was.

There is nothing wrong with my sex life with Toby. It's just . . . predictable. I put the outfit on in the bathroom and check my vague reflection in the steamy mirror tiles. There's something in the colour of it, the swing of the skirt over my thighs, that makes me think of summer gym kits and that maybe Toby's been around teenage girls too much while he's been away. But still, the drift of the silk makes me feel quite sexy and as though I'll be able to get into it. Toby is waiting for me, lying on his back on the bed with an erection. It promptly stands to attention when I walk towards him. '*Oh God, yes!*' he says, and I crawl up the bed for his favourite position. Toby is what you'd call a bum man. It makes me feel slightly foolish, sitting there with him saying *I love you* to my bum while I'm trying hard not to get thrown off, like someone the wrong way round on a horse.

19

Lizzie

When the bus first hit the outskirts of London I checked my make-up in a little mirror and put my pinching shoes back on ready to get off. But it was another hour and a half before we even got into the centre, inching along in three lanes of honking traffic. At the coach station I panicked that I'd never find Kim, but then this flat top came towards me from the crowd shouting, 'Lizzie!'

'I hardly recognized you!' we both said, and both laughed.

'I like your hair!' we both said again.

A flat top really suited her. She had a little longer bit at the front like a quiff and she had on torn jeans with roll-ups and a *Rebel Without a Cause* T-shirt. She turned and fell in with the torrent of people all heading up a wide road like a gash between the buildings. You could hardly see the sky. I stuck to Kim as closely as I could without holding her hand. At the train station we descended into the underground. Kim headed down one of the tunnels and I held on to the back of her T-shirt so I wouldn't lose her.

'Do I need a ticket?' I asked.

'Nah — we'll chance it,' said Kim and started running towards a platform where a train was screaming in. Sitting on the tube we were both giggly, for no reason, the way we'd been when we first got to be best friends in school. It's what made us best friends in the first place. We both found something to laugh about when there was nothing funny, until the rest of the girls tutted and went, 'God! You two!' And the name stuck and that's who we were.

It was nice to be us two again. It felt like something to laugh about. Kim asked me if I was a mod and I asked her if she was a rockabilly, but neither of us were. We looked at ourselves in the reflection opposite our seat. Kim showed me how to move up and down to distort your face in the curve of the glass. The best one was when Kim had a really big forehead and my face was squashed like I hadn't put my teeth in. We cried with laughter then.

When we came to Brixton and Kim went to get off the train I was scared. All I knew about Brixton was what I'd seen on the telly about the riots. I didn't feel I was quite dressed for a war zone, but Kim didn't seem bothered about anything but the ticket man waiting at the exit.

'Hang back here a sec,' she said, standing behind a pillar until everyone else had gone through. When they had, the ticket man sauntered back to his office.

'OK,' said Kim, and I scurried after her as she walked quickly out of the station. I tried to act like it was a normal thing I did every day.

I thought I could hear the rumble of bombs and gunfire, but when we got out into the street I realized that the earth was just quaking with loud reggae booming out of cars and flats and shops. It was just the same hot sunny day as it was everywhere else. I had never seen so many black people in one place, but none of them were fighting. Kim led me through a market selling things I didn't recognize that were probably vegetables. I felt people were staring at me as though I was the stranger. I tried to act like Kim, as though I wasn't some bumpkin up from the sticks.

We headed off the main busy street and were suddenly confronted with a massive block of flats that towered over us. It looked as though an alien spaceship from another planet had just landed in the middle of a wasteland. Kim headed into the heart of it and we began to ascend the stairs in the middle, as though we were going on board. It had an air of being abandoned and uninhabited, but as we rounded one of the landings what I thought was a rubbish bag moved as Kim stepped over it. I jumped and let out a little squeak but Kim just said, 'All right, Rats?' and the creature raised its blue furry head and gestured a greeting with its hand tightly gripped around a can.

We finally got to a deck halfway up and I followed Kim along a walkway around the outside that let you see the whole sprawl of London. London had no edges where you could see the land beyond it. It just went on and on as though that's all there was. I felt dizzy and walked as close to the inside wall as I could. Kim went into one of the doors left wide open and shouted up the stairs that we were back.

'They're not up yet,' she said and led me into the kitchen to make some tea. I didn't know who 'they' were. The kitchen had a serving hatch through to a sitting room with nothing to sit on. There was a portable telly on a wooden stool and some cushion sponges on the floor opposite it. There was graffiti all over the walls and the odd band poster. Our voices seemed to echo around the space and my voice sounded peculiar. I tried to act normal.

'So, who lives here?' I asked. Kim shrugged.

'I don't know really,' she said. 'Whoever. It's a squat. Me 'n' Vonnie are staying here so we can say we're homeless and get our names down on the housing list. I don't know about anyone else. Most of our stuff's at Vonnie's boyfriend's.'

I followed her up the stairs with mugs of tea. Kim peered around a bedroom doorway (the door was leaning against the wall by the bathroom) and said, 'Anyone who gets up now gets a cup of tea.' I peered round too. There were no curtains so the sun flooded in over several bodily lumps lying around on mattresses, zipped into nylon cocoons.

'Give me tea,' said a scratchy voice from under a cloudy puff of pink hair, which finally parted to reveal Vonnie's sleepy face. When she could open her eyes she finally grinned at me.

'All right, Lizzie?' she growled and reached out for a packet of fags and lit one. I kicked off Julie's shoes and wobbled over to her across the mattresses to give her a cup of tea.

'Ta,' she said. 'Your reward will be in heaven.' She shifted up onto her elbow to look out the window and yawned. 'Come on, you lazy sods.' She kicked any bodies she could reach. 'It's a really nice day. Let's go up Camden.'

When she finished her fag she leant up and flicked it out of the window, half-losing her sleeping bag in the process. She was totally naked. Her body was still amazing. She seemed skinnier than ever, narrow and compact as though she was never in danger of spreading, and you could see the bones and muscles flex under her smooth skin as she moved. She gathered the sleeping bag around her and got up to bounce to the toilet. Shouts and groans started up as she tried to jump over the other bodies on the mattresses but landed on legs and arms. She cackled maniacally when she tripped and landed on someone.

'Fuck's sake, Vonnie!' growled a man's voice, but I don't think he really minded, as he then grabbed her to hold her down and tickle her.

'Don't! I'll piss meself!' she squawked, and he let her go, turning to watch her bare back. He put his tattooed arms behind his head to look round. He had a really skinny face and big sticky-out ears and tram lines shaved into the sides of his bleached hair.

'So who's your mate?' be asked Kim, leering at me.

'Oi, Stan — leave her alone. She's got a boyfriend,' called Vonnie over the noise of her peeing from the open door of the bathroom.

'What?!' he said, arms up in innocent protest. 'Can't a bloke ask a bird's name?'

'I'm Lizzie,' I said, wishing it was something better.

'Nice to meet you, Lizzie,' he said. 'Any of those teas going begging? I'm gasping, me.'

He was ugly as sin but he had a cute grin. I gave him a cup of tea and squatted on the edge of a mattress while all the caterpillars started to stir and the metamorphosis began. A plump girl called Ruby sat up and began to take giant rollers out of the front of her hair. Kim introduced me to her and her friends, two rocking girls sharing the bed called Terri and June down from Glasgow. They were all wearing Fifties babydoll nighties and rollers in their dyed hair. There was a boy called Nick with a crew cut, only he turned out to be a girl. I realized when they kicked Stan, and not Nick, out of the room so they could get dressed, and Nick got up and had tits. Stan went, scratching his balls through his greying Y-fronts to a chorus of 'Urgh!'s.

Ruby leant across to an old Dansette and put a rockabilly record on really loud, which started off a load of banging on the wall from the flat next door and shouting in what sounded like French. Ruby turned the volume up and they all started singing along. I sat and watched as they all started grabbing clothing from cardboard boxes or nails bashed into the walls, like little girls dressing up. Vonnie put on a pearly pink cocktail dress, skin tight, with nothing underneath. It was made of see-through lacy stuff that you were probably meant to wear a petticoat under, but try telling Vonnie that. She swept her cerise hair up while shoving her feet into the highest, pointiest pair of stilettos I'd ever seen, like she must have cut off her outer toes to get into them. She strutted around the flat, fixing her make-up in whatever bits of mirror she could find.

They were finally ready, all dressed up like they were going to a party. Ruby had on a rocker's skirt, belted in really tight at the waist and a tight little cardigan over a huge conical bra and flat winklepicker shoes. Terri and June were also in Fifties prints with handbags and ponytails and red lipstick and hair all curled and back-combed and coated with extra-super-massive-rock-hard-hold hairspray. Nick still looked like a boy in bondage trousers and DMs and a biker jacket. Stan had bleach-spattered jeans, brothel creepers and a Meteors T-shirt with the sleeves ripped off.

I started to feel dowdy, as though I had wandered out of a black and white movie and into a Technicolor one. But then Vonnie stood back and looked me up and down and said, 'I like your look, Lizzie. You look the best I've ever seen you. You've blossomed. It suits you to be Sixties.' The other girls agreed. They were all so friendly and fun. I felt a smile widen across my face and stay there.

Back in the kitchen, Kim mixed up rum and ginger and put it into Thermos flasks to take with us. Vonnie shook some slimming pills into our palms.

'Puts your depression on a diet,' she grinned. Everything she said was just right.

The French punks were up by the time we clattered past their squat next door, standing at the windows in leather jackets and underpants, wolf whistling and rubbing themselves against the glass.

We laughed and sang our way to the tube. On the platform Stan stood away from us shaking his head. Lots of people were staring. It made me shriek louder still. On the tube everything started to go funny and wobbly as we washed down more Ponderils with the contents of the flasks. At Camden Town station Vonnie stalked ahead, gave the ticket man twenty pence and said, 'One child please,' while his eyes popped out of his head and roamed down her body, following her arse as she wiggled past. The rest of us barged past and ran.

Vonnie started begging in the street for a bit — 'Have you got ten pee, mate? Ten pee for a poor starving orphan,' and we all joined in. Everything seemed to get funnier and funnier and more and more ripply, as though we were in a tank filling up with water. We finally caught a tide drifting into the Electric Ballroom to meet Vonnie's friend Fliss, who was working on a clothes stall. I couldn't feel my legs and started to think I was a mermaid. I just swished my tail to stay upright and floated about smiling, thinking, *What a beautiful aquarium*, while everyone goofed around to cover up their pilfering.

'What's the batter with you?' Kim asked as she swam up beside me, and that was when all the fish jokes started.

'I'm sorry,' I said. 'Did you say something? I'm just a little hard of herring.'

'Oh, for cod steak,' replied Kim, 'I've haddock with you.'

I used my fins to propel myself in and out of the stalls and people as though they were seaweed, touching and feeling cloth and jewels like they were treasure. It was then I saw the white dress. I saw it just before Vonnie did, and Vonnie was mad that I'd spotted it first. She dived towards it, but I was already turning it over in my hands.

'I've been looking for a white dress for ages,' she said. 'It's a Vonnie dress.'

But Kim said, 'I think it's a bit more Lizzie,' as though I had an identity of my own that such a dress would suit. 'Anyway, Lizzie got it first.'

I thought about letting Vonnie have it, but I couldn't. It was so Sixties. And it would have been too big for Vonnie. You had to have tits in it. It was fitted to the body with a really simple scoop neck and little straps. It was the material that was so special, with little raised silky scallops all over it that caught the light like scales. I could imagine Ronnie Spector wearing it, with a white ribbon around her backcombed hair and patent stilettos, probably leaning against a two-tone Cadillac or coming down the steps of a Boeing 707 waving or some such glamorous thing. I held it up to myself with that image in mind, and could just about see it working, almost, if I grew my new black hair like Julie had told me to. I could see my identity more and more clearly, as though it was something coming to the surface.

The stall holder was hovering by us so I couldn't nick it. I asked him how much it was,

211

and when he said, 'Sick squid,' he didn't understand why we fell about laughing.

It was a lot of money on top of what I'd already paid getting here and I was nipped by a worry that Arry would notice. But I brushed it aside. Arry was a hundred fathoms down.

Kim knocked the bloke down to a fiver for me.

'You gotta know how to eel and deal,' she said and passed me the plastic cup off the flask before we darted off.

'D'you wanna come back to my plaice?' drawled Fliss when we got back to her stall, the first time she'd joined in with all the stupidity. She was pretty cool. We all went back to her flat up the road for tea, which consisted of a packet of Bourbons that slipped out of Nick's sleeve after she'd wandered round a corner shop, and something Fliss prepared on an album sleeve that we passed around in a circle and smoked. We hung out until it was time to see Vonnie's boyfriend's band, Rebel Yell, who were playing at the Dublin Castle. When it was time everyone redid their make-up and back-combed their hair again. We were all still laughing. I was in a magical world, like Atlantis. I thought, *I could never feel better than this*.

But that was before I ever laid eyes on Billy Diamond.

★ ★ ★

Billy Diamond was everything you could ever want in a boyfriend. I was desperate for him the second I saw him. The first thing I took in was

212

the whole of him, from across a crowded room, where he was elevated and shrouded in smoky light. His silhouette was wrapped around an upright bass as though they were dancing together, his whole body bopping with the rhythm he was making. The entire room was jumping with his pulse as it reverberated out from him in ripples.

His head was bent forward so that all you could see of him was the gangster hat on the back of his head and the strands of sleek black hair shaken forward. He had huge muscles on his arms, which shone as they flexed to work the bass. It was as though he had the power of an engine, shunting everything into motion as he leaned the bass across his left thigh while his right leg pumped up and down like a piston. The double bass didn't seem so big in his arms, more like a petite woman. I couldn't take my eyes off him. Something about it made me feel rude, as though I was watching him fucking. When the song ended we'd got near the front. He swung the bass out on the last note and brushed his arm across his forehead to wipe the sweat and flick his hair off his face. His deep-set eyes glinted out from his dark face like lightning and he skimmed his electric gaze across the crowd until it finally landed on us, on me. He grinned like the clouds breaking. As the drummer began to pound out the next song he leaned across and grabbed the singer's microphone, still staring my way.

' 'My Gal Is Red Hot'.' He winked. 'This one's for Vonnie,' and he let the mic stand go and threw himself on the bass, whipping it mercilessly until the whole place erupted in a frenzy. I glanced to my left, where Vonnie stood pouting proudly and sucking her cheeks in, for the benefit of me and all the other girls sneaking envious looks in her direction.

20

Beth

The street lighting shines through a crack in the curtains of our bedroom window, falling on Toby's squashed face. He is in deep sleep, lying naked on his front with his face pressed into the mattress, snoring and probably dreaming of schoolgirls. I am propped up on the pillows in lingerie that is too young for me, writing a song in my head for a boy half my age. I eventually peel off the white stockings and slide under the sheet in an attempt to sleep. The light catches the luminous film of the stockings, highlighting the stretched, worn emptiness as they lie discarded on the floor like used condoms.

I had been looking forward to Toby coming home so that I could escape the clutches of the past and get a sense of reality. Toby is usually so good at allaying fears, being practical. He has his feet on the ground. But now he is here I resent it. He seems in the way, stretched across the bed taking up all my space, both literally and in my head, pushing out my memories and coming between me and Jesse. Meeting Jesse had loosened the knots in my chest and let me look forward. I had a glimmer of hope, something I haven't felt for a long time, like the first sunshine on your face after winter. But now that Toby is back, it's like having to turn my face away and go back inside.

I remind myself it is Toby Jesse came to see. He wants Toby to listen to his demo and see him play. He wants Toby to give him a chance at his music career. I just put myself in his path while Toby was gone.

The only way I can carry on seeing Jesse is for Toby to meet him too, but I don't want Toby to. I feel possessive of him. He is mine. Toby will take him away, inevitably. If Toby likes the demo he will make things happen for him. Where do I fit in? How do I even tell him I've been making music with him? I don't know how to say what I was doing last night. I don't suppose I've done anything wrong but I feel as though I have. Hanging out and crashing with a young singer-songwriter hardly fits with the term Wife, but I haven't actually done anything bad. Have I?

And then there is a far worse feeling, of course, than the practicalities of the music making, surfacing from deeper down. I miss Jesse. I want to see him again. I want to be in his room with him, and not just for the music. But now I can't see how I ever can. It doesn't fit with this role I have carved for myself in life. Not even my life, but Toby's.

A panic rises up. I know that what would calm me down would be playing the piano. I'm excited how quickly my fingers remembered how to make melodies and rhythms. But I can't because it will wake Toby however quietly I play on the baby grand. I wish I had my old keyboard that I could plug headphones into and stay up all

216

night playing, the music going round and round, out from my fingers, in through my ears and out through my fingers again, a circuit of sound.

I try to imagine telling Toby I've started collaborating with Jesse, as I would if I were a musician, as I might have done years ago when we first met. But now the notion I would do such a thing seems ridiculous to me, let alone Toby.

It was Toby who gave me permission to give it all up. It made me feel loved.

'Look,' he said, holding me in his arms while I cried again in his old basement flat before we got married. 'Stop beating yourself up. It's not the end of the world. You don't have to try and force something if it makes you feel like this. There are other dreams you can have. I'll love you whoever you are and whatever you do.'

I was so grateful that he still loved me even though I'd fucked up. That he wanted me to be his wife even though I was a nobody. It was a relief at the time to give up, to try to become someone else instead. It was fun to throw myself into a new life, playing my part of a groovy, successful couple, doing up the house, making it a place where Toby could entertain. I worked for Toby for a while when he was starting to get a name for himself as the guy with the eye for new talent, and tried to forget my own dreams to be somebody myself. I didn't really need to be any more.

Our whole married life and before, I have felt as though he has somehow saved me from something. But now suddenly I feel an uncomfortable resentment rising up inside me like heartburn. I think about all the instruments around the house — the baby grand, the guitars, my old keyboard in the loft — none of which I can get out and play right now in case I disturb Toby. I have such limited time slots with him because of his work that I have to somehow weave myself around him, like water round rocks.

I want to be myself, just go down and strum an acoustic quietly, and when he comes in say, 'Actually, I played with Jesse today. He likes what I do. I'm excited about music again, Toby. Isn't it great?' And for Toby to be happy for me, encouraging. I try to imagine how he'd react, but I can't see it. I can't see myself really saying my dialogue, either. That's the problem, I suppose. I want to be myself, but being myself seems hard here, at home with Toby. It wasn't hard with Jesse. Isn't that strange?

After tossing and turning for what seems like hours it occurs to me I have Jesse's phone number. It's too late to speak to him and anyway, I'm too scared, but I could at least text a message. Just something to let him know that . . . I don't know. That he meant something.

I creep downstairs again like an intruder. When I put my phone on it buzzes to let me know there's voicemail. One from Ady to say the band didn't show up at all on Friday, two from Toby earlier when he got home, asking where I was. I grab Jesse's demo for his number and sit on the step of the French window for a long time starting and then deleting texts to him. Nothing seems adequate. I want to say *thank you for the music* but realize it's an Abba lyric. There have been too many pop songs written now. They have rendered even the deepest sentiment trite, made words have no meaning. In the end I write, '*Still filled with your music. Thank you for letting me play, Lizzie x*' and send it before I get too guilty and sensible. Five minutes later the beeps of my mobile receiving a text make me jump out of my skin. I go to the bottom of the stairs and listen in case Toby has woken again. There is silence. I rush back into the sitting room and check Jesse's text with trembling fingers.

'*Am home, playing it now. Still sounds great. Trying new track — no good, needs your touch. When can u come again? Jesse x*'

My heart soars. It does. There's no other way of describing it. I laugh. I didn't particularly ever want a mobile but Toby got me one so he could always get hold of me if something came up. Now I am so glad of it. It is like getting a text from God, the answer to a prayer.

21

Lizzie

The time I was meant to be getting up to catch the coach home on Sunday morning we were only just getting ready for bed. I didn't want my trip to be over. The worst thing was knowing that it wouldn't actually end when I was back in my stupid little life; it would be carrying on for Kim and Vonnie and everyone else. Just without me.

The darkness had started to lift and everyone was flopped down on the mattresses, yawning and giggling quietly. Just as I was about to drift into sleep Kim said, 'Come on, let's go up to the Roof of the World,' and she pulled me up and led us all to the top of the block past the broken lifts, up the graffiti'd stairs. At the top I caught my breath. I'd never been so high in the air. We looked out over the unconscious world, watching the bruised sky develop through black, blue, purple, red and pink as daylight hit and aroused the city from its crash. For some reason being here made me feel like I mattered; I don't know why. It was almost as though we were the pulse that kept the city going as it lay there in its coma, or a nerve twitching at its temple. I felt a part of things. I was happy to be alive.

I ached for the person I could be.

Vonnie had made it sound so easy.

'Come up to London, Lizzie, and join our band,' she'd said, as we sat on the tube after the gig. We were all sitting on the white plastic chairs we'd nicked from outside a pub so there would be something to sit on back at the squat. Kim and Stan had even taken a table too, and a parasol, and we'd set them all up in the standing room bit of the train. Vonnie was sitting in Billy's lap, draped over one knee with her dress riding up her crossed legs and Billy's hand smoothing her bare thigh. I blushed, for two reasons. One, I felt so honoured that Vonnie thought I was cool enough to be in a band with her. And two, it made Billy look up at me from where he was kissing her neck.

'What band?' Billy teased, grinning, and Vonnie kicked back at him with her stiletto.

'I'll fucking show you, Billy Diamond,' she said as he grabbed her wrists while she tried to hit him. 'If you're lucky I'll let you be my bass roadie when we make it.' They fought for a bit until they started snogging, again. They'd already had it off once, in the toilet at the Dublin Castle when Billy's band had finished playing. Vonnie had held back coolly while other girls flirted with him as he made his way to the bar. She sat at a table smoking, waiting for him to come to her. When he did they didn't speak. He just bent over her and kissed her hard on the mouth and then stood beside her playing with the strap of her dress. She leaned into him and put her hand round his leg, like they owned each other. The way they were together filled me with longing. Vonnie stubbed out her cigarette and

221

slid off her seat to go to the loo. He downed his beer and followed her. A bit later Ruby went to the loo, but came back as the queue for the ladies was starting to wind round the stairs.

On the tube their kissing got so heated we had to look away. Vonnie had to break it up when he began to get carried away and she tried to get off his lap, but he wouldn't let her. They shared a throaty chuckle about why she had to stay there.

'You'll get me arrested,' I heard him mutter into her ear. She threw her head back and laughed her laugh.

'So what do you play then, Lizzie?' Billy asked, shifting in his seat.

I couldn't meet his eye when he spoke to me, in case I gave myself away. But Kim saved me.

'Liz can play anything,' she said, as though I was something to boast about. 'And she writes songs.'

I braved a glance up at Billy.

'Well, *all right!*' he said, nodding at me with an amused crooked smile. 'Now we're getting somewhere. What about everybody else?' He had a jivey way of talking, still with a London accent but with an American easiness to it, a musician's lilt. He went round everybody, sorting out who was going to play what in the band, making us all giggle. He became like a band leader, bringing us in on our imaginary instruments. Vonnie came in first on bass, *ba dom dom dom dom ba dom dom dom dom*, then Nick joined in, beating out the drums on the table. Billy took off his pork pie hat and put it on the back of Nick's head, sweeping his greased hair back with his free

222

hand. He wore an old zoot suit with baggy pants and pointed black and white brogues, like a real grown-up man. The knee without Vonnie on it bounced up and down as he pumped out the beat with his foot. The shot material shimmered off the muscles of his thigh. When I dared to look up he brought me in on piano, so I screwed my eyes up and went for it, crashing out the old boogie woogie tunes I'd learnt on my imaginary keys. When I glanced back at Billy I saw that he knew I could really play.

'We're rockin'!' he cried, and brought Kim and Ruby in on brass, *boo pap pap pa dah dah*, getting Terri and June to be the backing singers, standing swinging together beside us in their swooshy skirts. In the end Ruby got so carried away she fell off her chair and we called her the bum note.

At Embankment Billy took his hat back off Nick's head and said, 'Well, goodnight, ladies,' before putting it back on his own, sweeping the double bass case onto his back as though it was nothing and pulling Vonnie off the train. He folded her into his side as she tripped along next to him, swinging her vanity case out wide with her other hand. He raised his hat to us as the train pulled out of the station.

When we'd finally lugged the furniture back to the squat the French punks had just about got up and dressed so they came round to ours. Someone brought the Dansette down and we put on Prince Buster records, and the punks rolled their trousers up to be Rude Boys, skanking round the room. The front door was

223

left wide open and throughout the night other people beamed in and out, and a girl with green dreadlocks emerged from upstairs and everybody cheered because it was the first time she'd got out of bed for five days. I hadn't even known she was there. I'd thought she was a pile of dirty washing in the corner.

'What day is it?' she asked. 'Have I missed anything?'

★ ★ ★

On Sunday afternoon I finally had to catch the only other coach home. As I left with Kim everyone piled up at the window and stuck their heads out, shouting at me to come back soon.

'Get writing some songs for our band, Lizzie!'

When we reached the bottom of the block of flats and started to walk away they were still yelling and singing. We could even hear them at the other end of the street before we turned into the market place and I turned to wave at their heads clustered at the window, as small and bright as a handful of Smarties.

★ ★ ★

Arry was waiting for me at the bus stop. Someone who knew someone who knew Arry had seen me getting on the coach on Saturday morning. It was the sort of small town where the gossip spread like VD. I felt suffocated. No one knew you in London. You could be whoever you wanted.

Arry looked me up and down with narrow eyes, trying to look mean through blobs of mascara. Wordlessly he took hold of my arm and marched me back to the bedsit, his grip tightening like a strap and his nails digging deeper and deeper into my skin. I didn't even bother trying to save myself with some kind of excuse. There was no point. There was no excuse good enough for being me. When we got in he tried to push me around a bit, but I didn't care. The only thing I felt was sorry for him. He thought he had so much power over me, but he didn't. I wasn't even there, not inside. He didn't know that when I was away at the weekend I never really came back. It was as though I'd stayed in London and had to send my body back like a servant to do all the dirty work closing up my winter residence.

I lay awake after Arry had finally worn himself out and slept with his arm across me like a bar, snoring. What on earth was I doing here? How had I let Arry happen to me? My life was out there somewhere, waiting for me to wake up and find it. And I was going to.

I started working out in my head how I was going to get away. I'd be able to get dole in London because I was myself again, not a belonging of Arry's. I calculated how many weeks I would have to work at the Golden Egg to save up enough to last me until my dole came through in London. And to buy a guitar. I made a list of things I would take with me. There wasn't much. Only some clothes and records. I wondered how and when I would manage to pack them and get out without Arry knowing. When was he ever out for long enough? How would I carry my records? I decided to gradually sneak them round to my mum's house one or two at a time so he wouldn't notice and leave them there until I could come and get them at a later date, only taking the ones I couldn't live without to start with. I looked forward to scouting Oxfam for new clothes, Sixties clothes, that I could buy and hide at my mum's until I was ready to go. I felt excited that I'd finally be able to wear them.

I'd leave my stud belt and black nail varnish for Arry.

★ ★ ★

I was back in London within a week. I couldn't wait. When I called Kim with my plans she said, 'Come now! Me and Vonnie have just got on the housing. We've been to see a flat in Ladbroke Grove. It's just off Portobello and everything. You can get the last room if you're quick. You can share my dole till yours comes through and we can make a furniture claim to the DHSS for our instruments. Come *now*, Lizzie.'

It was an offer I couldn't refuse, even though I hadn't saved any money. It was Arry's week for his giro. When I got back from the morning shift on the Friday he'd cashed it and gone to the pub to get smashed and play Space Invaders. It was as good a chance as any. I grabbed what I could and started to write him a note. I couldn't think what to say. In the end I put, *Dear Arry, I'm going to London. Don't try to find me. I'm never coming back.* I laughed out loud as I read it. I didn't even bother signing it. He didn't know who I was anyway, or care. I had to leave town before he found it.

I struggled round to my mum's with my records. She was out at work, so I left another note for her. *Mum, I've gone to London to live with Kim. I'll let you know the address. I'll be fine. Will call, Love, Lizzie. P.S. Don't give my address to anyone.* It was all so easy. I had a quick look in the Marvel tin where Mum put emergency money and took twenty pounds. I added a PPS to the note. *Have borrowed some emergency money. Will pay you back, x.*

I felt a pang of guilt about leaving her. She was always getting left, one way or the other. But it seemed to be the only way I could avoid being left myself. I decided I never wanted to be the sort of woman who was left ever again. She'd be all right, anyway. She had a lodger she really liked now. Mr Grundy had gone as soon after I had as he could without arousing suspicion. He got a transfer to another council and left no forwarding address. The new lodger was a student nurse Mum had met at work called Beverley, who was away from home for the first time and acting like a big baby about it. She was the same age as me, but she wore pastel dresses with sailor collars and had a Lady Di haircut. She was probably the type of girl my mum wished I was. I thought she was retarded. But I was glad my mum had someone to look after. It seemed to be what she liked doing best. The pang of guilt ended as I realized that now my mum had a replacement daughter I was even more free to go.

Then I ran to the station. I spent half my week's waitressing money on a single ticket to Paddington. I had to wait for an hour, getting more and more nervous. As the train pulled out of the station I thought I saw a spiky head bobbing up onto my platform. But I wasn't sure. I might have imagined it to add to the drama of my escape. I felt like I was in a movie. My life lay ahead of me like the kind of open road you see in films and I couldn't wait to go down it. The small towns and countryside flew by as I hurtled forward and I promised myself I was going to live life to the full, and never hang around ever again as though I was stuck in the waiting room.

22

Beth

Doing nothing with Toby is suddenly hard work. The strain of trying to relax together gives us both headaches, which we blame on the muggy heat. I move to and fro through the house as though I'm stuck in a pen, finding things to distract myself with; unpacking Toby's bags, doing his washing. He goes down to the basement to work out. I can feel time passing. I want it to pass, and I don't. This Sunday with Toby I want over, but I'd rather fill it with something else. Toby can't help himself: the minute he sits on the couch with a cup of tea he makes a few calls to check in with anyone else from work who can't switch off on a Sunday. As soon as the calls are made he jumps up.

'Fancy doing brunch?' he asks, already pocketing his phone and shunting his feet into his Birkenstocks. We stroll down to our favourite cafe in the village. The sun breaks through as we take a table outside and Toby puts on some sunglasses.

'New shades?' I enquire, and he looks at me sardonically over the top of them.

'Yeah — guess what? Another gift from the Japs.' He rolls his eyes and I smile. The shades are too young for him, highlighting the spread of grey through his temples.

'What else d'you get?' I ask, to keep the conversation going.

He lists a few things, to do the same. I listen and nod and grin in the right places. I try my hardest to appear as though I'm not having to appear anything, as though I really am chilling out. But inside my head and heart are working like a runaway engine, fuelled by the desperation over seeing Jesse again, or not. I've had feelings for other guys while Toby and I have been together, of course I have, but nothing that has spilt out of my fantasies into my real life with Toby. Nothing that has made spending time with Toby so unbearable. I want to see Jesse playing later, and the only way I can think to do that is to get Toby to come.

But I don't want Toby to be there.

The snatch of life I had with Jesse is out of place in my real life. The two seem unblendable, like oil and water. Actually, the fear is not so much Jesse meeting Toby, as me meeting me. I feel more unreal now than I did yesterday. But I know I am really here by the solid forkfuls of sausage and bubble and squeak that are disappearing into my face and going round and round in my mouth. I thought I was starving but my churned-up insides make it harder and harder to swallow. The egg is undercooked and when I scoop up the phlegmy nodule that can always be found somewhere, not yolk, not white, but something in between, it stretches up from my plate like snot and I retch. I try to swallow by taking a slurp of latte, but I spot a smear of lipstick on the rim of the glass and put it back down again. I excuse myself to go to the loo and puke.

When I sit back down at the table, Toby hasn't noticed.

'Aren't you hungry?' he asks, looking pointedly as I pick over my plateful of food.

'I guess not,' I reply. 'I don't feel that great, actually.'

I can just see the tip of the crease between Toby's brows deepen in annoyance behind his shades.

'Aren't you going to eat that then?'

'I can't manage it all. Go on — you have it.'

Toby reaches over for my plate and places it on top of his. He has a big appetite. For everything. I envy the way he gets stuck in to life, whatever we are doing. On holiday he'll be climbing rocks and diving from the highest point, snorkelling, water-skiing, while I sit back with my face in the shade and dream of smoky bars.

My wasted breakfast has somehow already ruined the day and Toby gulps down his cappuccino quickly, wipes his mouth with the serviette and screws it up, throwing it down onto the plate and finding his wallet in his bum pocket, sifting through it for English notes. He places a twenty under the ketchup and scrapes back his chair. I hasten to make amends, scurrying after him and putting my hand in his.

'Thanks, Tobes. Sorry about that. What do you fancy doing today?'

'I dunno. What do you feel well enough to do?'

231

He is snapping. People feeling unwell gets on his nerves. Toby is never a tad off colour or a little bit nauseous or feeling woozy. He's always either well enough to live life, or properly ill, one or the other. When he's ill you'd think he was dying. Every breath exhaled is like a death rattle.

I watch my feet walking along the pavement, one and a half steps to every stride of Toby's size-eleven sandals. I have little Chinese pumps on which do nothing to dispel the feeling of being a told-off child. He puts his arm round me and slows down so I can keep up.

'Sorry, hon,' he says. 'I'm still really wired. Jet lag's a fucker. I wouldn't mind a kip myself.'

He buys a Sunday paper to check the music reviews and back home he sets out loungers in the back garden while I make smoothies. We manage to while away some of the afternoon pleasantly as I blindly flick through the magazine until Toby eventually nods off.

I creep back inside and check my phone for texts. No new messages. My need to see Jesse outweighs my worry about Toby meeting him. I decide to have one more try at suggesting the Twelve Bar later, making it sound like a fun thing to do rather than work. Maybe after his nap Toby'll be more amenable to it. He doesn't seem to like his own company for long, or mine. If Toby doesn't want to go, maybe I'll say, '*Well, I might just go along anyway — I'm in the mood.*' What would be so bad about that?

When Toby is up again, pacing about at a loose end, I am bright and breezy, upbeat, hoping he'll catch a mood for going out and having fun. I wait for a good moment to casually bring up the evening ahead, and I'm just about to when Toby says, 'What do you fancy doing later?'

'Well,' I reply. 'I was just thinking about that. There's a couple of things we could do. What are you in the mood for?'

'Well, something. But I'm too fucked for a lot of stuff. I was thinking we should catch a movie. What d'you say? We haven't been to the flicks for ages.'

Going to the pictures is our middle ground, not going to acoustic clubs or browsing round flea markets, not diving or water-skiing. We both love the movies equally. Heading down to the big screens in the West End, a jumbo box of salted popcorn and a Coke between us, we sink in pleasure into the seats somewhere in the front few rows and share the escape. It doesn't really matter what we see. If it's crap we slag it off all the way home in the back of the taxi. It seems to bring us closer.

Usually I'd be really pleased with Toby's suggestion.

I hesitate, willing myself to say, '*Or there's that boy playing at the Twelve Bar. I think you'd really like him. Oh, come on, Tobes, it won't be like work. I'd really like to go.*'

But I don't. Toby frowns at my hesitation.

'Well, what would you rather do, then?' he asks, but it feels more like a challenge than a question. My guilt is making me too sensitive, perhaps. But preferring something to our middle ground seems too big a rebellion.

'No, nothing,' I insist. 'I was just trying to remember what's on at the moment. Let me get the *Time Out*.'

I go through to the coffee table and flick through the cinema listings. Shit. I could cry at missing Jesse's gig, but I'm too angry at myself to produce anything but watering eyes and a wince.

We decide on the latest Tarantino at Leicester Square, going for the early evening showing so we don't have to hang around the house any longer. From the cab my eyes scour the streets around Charing Cross Road for the sight of a boy with a gigbag on his back heading for a sound check. For a group of young people with dreadlocks and parkas and their lives ahead of them. There are plenty of those, but not the one I'm looking for.

While Toby queues for the popcorn and Coke I go to the ladies and sit in a cubicle writing a disappointed text. *Sorry, can't make gig. Toby knackered. Next time? Good luck, x.* It won't send in the loos, so when I stand with the huge cartons while Toby goes to pee I wander to the entrance and send it from there. I haven't got time to wait for a reply so I switch my phone off until halfway through the movie, when I excuse myself to take a pee again.

My message signal beeps as it picks up a signal and I read it with trembling hands. *No problem. 1 nxt wknd. More important, when can u come round again? Am in Tues, Thurs, Fri.* He's made a smiley face emoticon at the end. I am sweating. Have I been gone too long for a pee? I have to reply quickly. *Tues good. (& Thurs! & Fri!!) Looking forward, give me a time, will b there, x,* and I switch my phone off and dash back inside, trying not to look too shifty and thrilled.

Toby turns to look at me as I slide into my seat. It's unheard of for me to miss one moment of a film, however much I need the loo. I touch my stomach to remind him I'm not feeling well. He passes me the Coke and I brush his hand as I take it. We share the opinion that Coke is great for an upset stomach. Something about the gas making you burp always seems to relieve it. It's funny how couples write their own private manuals for everything. Coke for sickness, chips for comfort, the gym for stress, films for filling holes. That's all in the one Toby and I have written over the years. I feel my heart make a sudden guilty clutch at the love I have for him and place my hand over his on the armrest. I am amazed at my own duplicity. For I am also running with my arms outstretched towards my Tuesday with Jesse.

I can't remember what the film was about at all. It makes our usual critique on the way home difficult, but I bluff my way through.

'It was great; I really enjoyed it,' I enthuse. Luckily Toby did as well.

★ ★ ★

On Monday morning I can't wait for Toby to leave for work. My fingers twitch around making coffee and helping him get ready and I have to

235

dig them deep into my robe pockets to hide their desire to push him out of the door. The minute he goes they escape and run riot, turning on my phone and placing it on top of the piano, remembering the melodic line I'd put down at Jesse's on the keys while they wait to check his message. It's there. *'Great! Any time. 11 too early 4 rock n roll?'* My fingers spell out my reply. *'No! Yes! I'll b there anyway!'*

I only stop playing for coffee and cigarettes. Music fills the house. Jesse's, and mine. I play his demo and find piano parts for the songs he's recorded already. I work out the chords for the song I have started to write in my head for him. I pursue trails of half-formed melodies until I capture them and shape them into pieces, both hands beginning to run together again as they relearn to take control.

By the time Toby gets home I have managed to slip something on that makes me look dressed and think about supper. I am humming in the kitchen making seafood pie when he comes home. I give him a big hug. The scene pleases him.

'Smells good,' he says, dumping his bag on the floor. 'You look nice.'

My happiness bubbles out like uncorked champagne and spills over in a fizz of chatter. I dish up at the table instead of taking it through to the lounge, where we usually eat in front of the TV. I ask about his day and he tells me. We have a nice dinner together, talking to each other as though we're on a date. I realize I feel connected. Obviously I connected with Jesse, obviously he connected me to music, still obviously the two have connected me to myself. But I am surprised this has allowed me to connect with Toby too, rather than shut him out. That can't be right, surely? It makes me feel like a femme fatale, talking so animatedly, listening so interestedly to Toby, flirting even, sitting sideways on to the table and swinging my fork, wearing the strappy summer dress he loves, knowing he feels this is all for him, and because of him. When it is neither. I wouldn't even mind getting it on with him later, I feel so . . . alive. But that won't happen so soon after the last time, on a Monday night.

'You're in a good mood,' he says as I take his plate and pour him some more wine.

'I know,' I say, ready to venture that I've been playing piano all day and really enjoyed it. But he doesn't ask. I should say it anyway, but the stubborn part of me won't. *OK, I'll keep it to myself then*, I think. *If you're too uninterested to ask.*

It becomes my excuse to have my secret, my way of justifying to myself my actions and my silence about them. If he asks, I'll tell him. Whatever he asks, I'll answer with the truth. But he has to ask. He has to care enough to ask.

It is unfair of me, I know. I have allowed Toby to be in the driving seat the whole way and now that it's me choosing a direction I should at least have the decency to take over at the wheel. But I allow him to steer on blindly into the dark while I sit in the passenger seat keeping my knowledge to myself. It is mean and cowardly, but I do it anyway.

23

Lizzie

I bought an A — Z at the Smith's at Paddington station and made my first attempt at getting around London by myself. I didn't have a clue where I was or how I was meant to get where I was going. Latimer Road seemed to be the nearest tube station to Kim's new street — my new street! — and after working out the tube map I finally found the right platform for the Metropolitan line. I watched out of the window as we rattled past flyovers and tower blocks and rows of houses backing onto the railway line, wondering what kind of house my new room would be in. It didn't matter. Wherever I was heading, I knew I was finally going to find the life that would fit me, like Cinderella slipping her foot into the shoe.

I got lost in Latimer Road, trying to find my way around the maze of concrete blocks and roads and skateboard runs. In real life the streets weren't as simple as they were on the map. When I finally got to Kim's address, I saw it was an old red-brick block that had seven floors and went round in a square with the front doors facing a patch of grass in the middle. I looked around for their door. I couldn't quite remember the number, but I went up to one painted vivid green with wonky writing on it. When I got up close it said, *What's Behind the Green Door?* and I guessed it must be theirs.

I peered in through one of the windows and saw a bass and amp and a line of albums around the edge of the room. It could only be Vonnie's. Especially when I saw all her stiletto shoes hanging off the picture rail by their heels. No one else in the world would think of doing that. There was nobody home so I sat on the step with my bags around me and waited.

I heard her great guffaw echoing through the archway into the square before I saw her. I looked up and squinted into the evening sun, grinning and waiting for them to see me. Vonnie looked like the personification of summer. She had tiny Levi cut-offs on with a frayed fringe skimming the tops of her tanned thighs and a pale yellow shirt tied up at the front to bare her brown belly. Her feet were bare except for red nail polish and her hair framed her face in filmstar curls of golden sunshine blonde. Kim had on a top with jazzy instruments all over it and pedal pushers. Ruby and Fliss were with them too. They were all strolling in a lazy, sun-drenched way and they all had on shades so I couldn't tell when they would notice me. Kim screamed when she did and ran up.

'Lizzie! You came! Are you here to stay?' The rest of them gathered round as I told them I was and Vonnie strolled up behind, smiling.

'Looks like we're gonna get this band on the road,' she said. 'Cause for celebration!' And they all cheered.

Vonnie opened the door and Kim and I fell in after her with my bags, chattering and laughing. You could still smell the paint from when they'd decorated. The living room with the kitchenette was splattered with fluorescent colours, green, pink and yellow, that they'd just flicked everywhere, like modern art. Vonnie's room was red and black with lace and leopardskin everywhere, like a sex kitten's boudoir. Kim's was electric blue and the bathroom the same glossy Day-Glo green as the front door.

And mine, mine they'd left for me to do as I liked. I was glad. I'd been designing it in my head ever since I'd heard that there was a room for me here, a room that wasn't my mum's or Arry's, but totally mine. I was going to do it black and white with groovy op art patterns all over it. We plonked my bags down in the bare room and went through to where Vonnie was making up rum and coke in a plastic mixing bowl. There was a back door onto a balcony with the pub chairs and table on it, so we went out there for the evening breeze. Vonnie put a Nina Simone record on, which was just right — mellow and sweet to match the air. Everyone was asking about me doing a runner from Arry. Now that I'd left him, I was glad I'd had a boyfriend. It made me feel less of an innocent know-nothing up from the country to be able to talk about men and relationships with Vonnie. It sounded good, the way I'd just upped and left him like that. It made me sound better than I really was.

'Was it true love or just lust?' she asked.

I shrugged. 'Neither, really,' I replied and we laughed like we knew a thing or two, although I didn't really know what was funny or clever about it.

'Now you've got the first one out of your system you can move on,' she said sagely. 'It's never bad to add to your list of experiences. In fact, there's no such thing as a bad experience, only an old one.'

I don't know where she got the things she said from. It was like there was a book of cool things to say and do that only she knew about.

We talked about love while the sun went down. Kim had a crush on someone but wasn't in love. She'd lost her virginity by now, but not to the person she had the crush on. Ruby had had a few boyfriends but was trying to be celibate so that she felt like a virgin again next time. 'It takes six months, apparently, for your hymen to grow back,' she said. Vonnie roared with laughter, so I knew it wasn't true. Fliss was having an affair but not a relationship because he had a live-in girlfriend. She liked it that way. Vonnie denied she was in love with Billy, but everyone else decided she was. Looking at the way she lit up when she talked about him, I had to agree.

'Well, I might be *in love* with him for the moment, but I don't *love* him,' she retorted, flicking her hair. The blonde glowed against the darkening sky as though the sun's rays were trapped in it. 'When you *love* somebody they have a hold over you. I can't imagine ever letting anyone have a hold over me.'

I couldn't imagine it either, not even Billy Diamond.

'You're *infatuated* then,' said Fliss.

Vonnie cocked her head on one side and blinked while she considered it.

'Maybe,' she conceded. 'He certainly *satisfies* me.' She sat there like the cat who got the cream while we all whooped and raised our glasses to her and my tummy flipped over at the thought of being satisfied by Billy Diamond.

As it got chillier we went inside and Vonnie changed the record to LaVern Baker. She danced around singing along and I joined in. I could keep up with her now Julie had shown me some steps. We got ideas for moves you could do if you were playing an instrument in a band. Vonnie got her bass out. She'd obviously thought about it a lot. She plugged in to her amp in her bedroom next door and came in as far as her lead would let her to play along to the Stray Cats. She was actually pretty good. She'd learnt how to do a twelve-bar bass line really fast in several keys. Sometimes she stood still in a pose, sometimes she shook her leg like a rocker, sometimes she hung her bass way down low and held it to the side of her, swinging it as she played. She could even do a jump at the end of a song and still hit the right note. She looked so amazing, this tiny glamorous wild thing thumping out bass lines that shook the floor on this bass that was nearly as big as she was, her sexy bare legs kicking out from under it. I couldn't wait to get my guitar, or piano, or whatever it was I was going to play.

'We'll go to the Record and Tape Exchange

tomorrow and have a look,' she said. Kim had to get a saxophone somehow, too. For now she got out her kazoo to work out the brass parts, and she and Ruby put their shades on and did steps like the Blues Brothers. Ruby had played trumpet for the Girls Brigade band when she was at school, and her mum still had it somewhere. She'd get it next time she was home in Leeds. Kim said that Nick had already been collecting drums and bongos and anything else she could hit and get a sound out of. Fliss looked at us, shaking her head.

'What are you going to play, Fliss?' I shouted over the racket, doing a Chuck Berry skedaddle across the room.

'Nothing with you lot,' she said. 'Girl bands are always really crap.'

'Not any more,' said Vonnie. 'Not now there's us. We're gonna be the first girl band that's as good as any blokes' band. Lock up your sons! Here come . . . '

We all looked at each other. We needed a name. We started shouting out names and writing them on the wall so we wouldn't forget them. Everything seemed like a brilliant name at first, but when we looked at it again it seemed really stupid, like when Kim thought of the Spacehoppers. Vonnie wanted a name like Attack of the Fifty-Foot Women or the Faster Pussycats after some films she'd seen. We scoured Kim's and Vonnie's records for titles of songs that would make good names. We soon had a whole wall covered with words. Voodoo Voodoo, the Red Hot Mamas, the Thunder Birds. We nearly

243

went with that one. The Speed Queens, after the washing machines in the launderette. The Water Bunnies after the tampon machines in the toilets. The Vonnettes. That was one of Vonnie's.

We thought about what songs we would do too, and what our individual band names would be. I thought my brain would short circuit with all the energy crackling round the room. We finally went to bed — me on two foam cushions off the back of the chairs, Ruby on two off the bottom, while Fliss crashed in with Vonnie. The fireworks were still going off in my head. Ideas for names and songs and tunes and stagewear kept exploding and the sparks showering down into my veins. I couldn't wait to get up again. I thought briefly about Arry and what was happening back in the bedsit right now. I couldn't believe it had only been that morning that I'd seen him. Already he was a million miles away, a million years ago.

★　★　★

Before now, I'd just seen glimpses of how life could be. Snatched moments from other worlds that I had somehow gatecrashed to be a part of: a visit to Vonnie's room, a gig here and there, a weekend stolen from other people's lives. But I'd always had to go back to my own boring world afterwards. That night, that weekend, I arrived in Wonderland and finally got to stay.

On Saturday they took me to Portobello and we sifted through clothes and records and I found some cheap Sixties tops and a pair of ski pants and a paisley minidress that would suit the new me. I found some lacy tights too, just like the ones I'd seen in Julie's old pictures. Vonnie seemed to know loads of really cool people and whenever she got the chance she referred to us as 'my band'.

'Yeah, I'm just heading up the Record and Tape to check out guitars wiv my band.'

Or, 'Nah, sorry I can't — got a rehearsal wiv my band.'

I liked it when she introduced me as 'the new guitarist in my band'. I'd come a long way since I was just her annoying little sister's sniggering best friend.

I guessed it was guitar I was going to play then. It was fine with me.

We wandered up to Notting Hill and looked at the instruments. There was so much stuff I needed, none of which I could afford. I saw a couple of guitars I liked the look of, but I didn't know anything about guitars. Vonnie knew the bloke in the shop and he let me try them. The old me would have been too shy, but with Vonnie and the band there I didn't feel so silly. A lot of the blokes in the shop were looking at us as though we'd wandered in to the men's loos instead of the ladies'. But nobody could make you feel you were in the wrong place when you were with Vonnie. She bought some new bass strings and invited the bloke in the shop to our gig when we played.

I'd never felt so surreal, and so real. It was surreal how real I felt.

We had chips and tea in a caff and followed

Vonnie into Boots, where she used all the testers to redo her make-up before heading over to Billy's. She arranged to meet us at Gossips later and ran for a bus as best she could in her pencil skirt. It was so tight she had to hold onto the handrail and jump herself onto the bus platform with a little bunny hop. She turned and blew us a kiss like Marilyn Monroe in her shiny new red lipstick.

I went back home with Kim and Ruby and sorted out an outfit for later. I'd found a lamé top with a big bow at the front and cutaway shoulders, in a bargain box for fifty pence, which I washed quickly in the sink and dried with Ruby's hairdryer. All I had to do to the ski pants was take them in a bit round the hips, so I sat cross-legged on the floor and backstitched by hand. Ruby let me borrow some winklepickers to finish the outfit. I painted my eyes into points that almost reached my temples, puffed up my hair at the crown and curled my sideburns round my cheeks so my look was like Audrey Hepburn's in *How to Steal a Million*.

Gossips was this club in a basement where all these people that you'd want to know hung out. I just followed everyone and didn't say much and hoped I looked cool instead of shy. Vonnie had got some speed from somewhere and she cut it up expertly on the back of the toilet as the four of us huddled into one cubicle. I didn't stay shy for long. I don't know who I talked to or what I said, only that by the time we left it was getting light and I thought everyone in the whole world was my friend and my jaw ached like crazy from chewing and talking. I'd even been able to answer Billy when he spoke to me.

'Here for good this time, hey, Liza Doo?'

No one had ever called me Liza Doo before. He probably just didn't remember my name, but I didn't mind. It made me feel special that he'd called me anything at all. I loved being Liza Doo. It was a lot better than Lizzie.

'Yeah,' I replied, managing to make eye contact with him for half a second before I looked away to Kim and giggled.

'A mate of mine might have a guitar for sale,' he said. 'It's pretty nice — an Epiphone semi-acoustic, late Sixties I reckon — could be a Casino. I think one of the tuners might be broken but get Archie's to give it the once over anyway.' I nodded as though I knew what he was talking about. 'But you should get a good deal on it. I'll catch up with him and let him know you're interested, yeah?'

I nodded and smiled.

'Sweet,' he said and winked, and pulled Vonnie onto the dancefloor to fling her around to some wild old bop tune that had started up with manic bongos and screeching saxophones.

★ ★ ★

On Monday Kim took me to the DHSS on Shepherd's Bush Road to sign on. We had to sit there for hours waiting for the Turn-o-matic to flip round to my number, but at least we got the name the Turn-o-matics out of it. Kim filled out her forms for her furniture claim so she could get a saxophone. It looked like I wouldn't get any dole for ages, because I'd left the Golden Egg of my own accord, but Kim said we'd be OK. Even though I'd nearly used up all my money, I somehow knew we would be. I wasn't going to starve or run out of tampons. Mostly because they all knew how to nick stuff when they needed it. Or even when they didn't need it, but just because they could.

Vonnie took me round to Midge's to look at the guitar. It was a gorgeous turquoise blue and I knew it'd look fantastic against my black and white clothes. Vonnie lent me the cash to buy it there and then because she couldn't wait to start the band and become a big star. I found a dog-tooth-check women's suit in the Notting Hill Housing Trust shop to go with it. I took the skirt in and up.

I began to see myself as another character, as if I was in the audience and Liza Doo was up there on the stage. Liza Doo was everything I wanted to be. She looked like someone who should be a Sixties filmstar or singer but played guitar like she was in the Rolling Stones. I was a big Liza Doo fan. I knew every outfit she wore, every pose she struck. I sang along with every lyric she'd written. I got so I was desperate to meet her, the way you are with your idol when you go to see them play. Every moment was like a step nearer the stage, the way you tried to squeeze your way through the crowd into the front row, just in the hope that you could reach up and touch them when they strutted forward to the front of the stage. When she looked out into the crowd and met my eyes she made me feel special, like I was a somebody.

Nick brought round her weird collection of drums and set them up in the corner of the living room. Ruby got her trumpet from Leeds and we started to stick egg boxes up on the walls to soundproof our rehearsal room while she was practising and the neighbours banged on the wall. We put Vonnie's amp against the wall with nobody on the other side. She brought in her huge mirror so we could work out our poses. Kim bought a saxophone second-hand out of *Loot* and when my dole finally came through I bought a Fender amp from the Record and Tape and plugged in.

It was the biggest noise I'd ever made. I was glad I hadn't been able to plug in before, when I was learning how to play with a plectrum. I worked out the chords of 'Wild Thing' and it became the first song we played together. It was easy because we could all play the same thing over and over, and it didn't seem to matter if we weren't particularly in time with each other. We did it much faster than the Troggs, a kind of punky, garage version. Then, when I hit a bum chord by mistake, we discovered you could do the same thing but sing 'Louie Louie' over the top of it.

It felt really good to hear this glorious, awful racket and know we were the ones making it. We couldn't stop grinning at each other and ourselves in the mirror the whole time. We sounded pretty bad, but we looked great. Vonnie learnt the bass lines to all these cool tunes, like

'Big Noise from Winnetka' and 'Peter Gunn' and 'Green Onions' and 'Psycho Killer', and I worked out the guitar riffs to go with them. At first I just played rhythm, but after a while the fingers of my left hand got the hang of doing cool little licks in between the chords and my right hand could pick out the separate strings to do runs without hitting a duff note. Kim and Ruby eventually learnt how to stop splitting notes and laughing while they played, and built the songs with jabbing harmonies that led to high, loud blares of sound on the choruses. Nicki Stix drummed like a banshee. To her delight, she started getting biceps like a boy.

At first we all sang along, or shouted, unless Kim and Ruby were blowing or the rest of us were trying to do something a bit difficult on our instruments. Trying to sing at the same time was like patting your head and rubbing your tummy. Nick and Vonnie stopped trying, which just left me.

When we got a few songs together enough, Vonnie said, 'OK, we're ready to audition a singer. I know a couple of girls who'd be really good. I'll get them to come down.'

After a pause Kim said, 'I thought Liza was singing?'

I guess I'd thought so too, but I didn't want to look like I had.

'Only while we're practising,' I said quickly. 'Vonnie's right, we'd be better with a front person.'

Ruby and Nick agreed with Kim and tried to make me be the singer, but I could feel Vonnie

250

looking me over and I knew she didn't think I quite had it.

'I think Liza looks coolest just playing guitar,' she said, studying herself and me in the mirror. 'I think it'd look better if we either stood together to one side like this . . . or went either side with a front person in the middle like this . . . ' She posed us as she talked. 'I personally wouldn't want to sing and play bass. I mean, you can't do much, can you, if you're tied to a mic and an instrument? A front person should be free to go a little crazy, throw themselves around a bit. We don't want to be boring, do we?'

Nobody said anything.

'But hey,' she added. 'That's just me. If you all think different, fine.' She shrugged and leant across to pull a cigarette out of the packet on her amp, lighting it and taking a long drag before poking it between the strings on the bass head to get good rock and roll burn marks on the wood. She started up a riff.

I watched her playing her bass and sucking her cheeks in, the cigarette smoke curling around her like adulation. It was true. She did look much cooler pouting mysteriously than if she suddenly had to come forward to a mic and burst into song. And she was right. I did want to look like that, standing either next to her or the other side of the singer, pouting mysteriously myself.

'I agree with Vonnie,' I said. 'I'm not a front person.'

'I didn't say that.' Vonnie smiled, but I knew. She didn't have to.

24

Beth

Kim phones me with updates on Vonnie's progress. But since I have met Jesse the whole nightmare seems far away. I like it better that way. I am glad I haven't seen Vonnie in her sick bed, lying there like a fucked-up old junkie. It makes it easier to be removed, less *involved*. Well, that's what Toby wanted, wasn't it? This is how I justify myself to myself. Though even I know that, of course, it is not because of Toby that I have taken myself away.

Being with Jesse and making music has become like a drug for me, only better. He has made me feel good when I didn't think I could and numbed me to the pain, like all good drugs do. I can hold the phone and let Kim offload into my ear without it really going in. I can listen without hearing. It is such a relief. It doesn't affect me, whatever the news is.

I laugh along when Kim tells me Vonnie lifted her head and said, 'All right, little sis?' and asked her to sneak her a fag.

'That's great!' I enthuse, when she tells me Vonnie has agreed to go into rehab.

'It'll be a new beginning. She can start over,' I agree, when Kim makes plans to get Vonnie a transfer away from her old flat, and all the bad news types that hung around there.

'She'll be OK,' I soothe when she tells me Vonnie fell back into unconsciousness, when Kim was only gone for a minute to get her a cup of tea.

I listen and say what I hope are the right things, but my mind is elsewhere. All I can think about is when I'll be with Jesse again. I suppose I am heartless, but I can't help it. It's as though we've all fallen overboard and my survival instincts have taken over and found a way for me to stay afloat while the others cling to each other and drown. I want to live, I hear myself decide.

I want to live.

I have begun to not pick up when she rings. This pleases Toby.

'You can't be there for her twenty-four seven,' he says as I stand with my hand hovering by the receiver while Kim reports onto the answerphone near midnight. 'This is just too late to call someone. We have our own lives. Some of us have jobs to get up for. Phone her back in the morning. You've got to be less . . . *selfless*, Beth.'

I turn away guiltily to catch my reflection in the mirror, a wicked twitch playing at the corners of my mouth. *OK*, I think. *I will*. As if I needed any encouragement.

* * *

On Tuesday I close the door behind Toby and race upstairs to get ready for my day with Jesse. Getting the clothes right is hard. I don't know what to wear any more. Over the years I have settled for a style I imagine is suitable for a wife of a cool exec — fashionable but age-appropriate, designer, expensive. I have learned how to spot a good cut for my figure, a fine fabric that will hang and move well. But since my love affair with the retro clothing craze of my youth, nothing has excited me. Nothing I have put on has made me think, *Yes! this is so me!* I can look in a changing-room mirror and appreciate a bias cut that has narrowed my hips, or a neck line that has structured my breasts, but the woman facing me has rarely been someone I recognize.

I see that retro styles are around again. Fifties prints on bell skirts and handbags, Sixties suits with shiny patent belts. I am drawn to them on my anonymous drifts around Bond Street, pull out the fabrics and handle them, but never try them on. I know too well that rather than the punky rock chick of my youth, it is a faded photograph of my mother on her honeymoon in the Isle of Wight I will be most reminded of in the changing-room mirror.

Trying to find clothes in my wardrobe that best represent me, or the me I want to be, are what make me late on Tuesday morning. Not Wife of Cool Exec, for sure. Not Rock Chick, not somebody's mum. What am I to him? In the end I dig out some old biscuit cords with worn knees and a good cut around the bum and put them on with a faded flowery shirt. Laid back but a bit *muso chic*. Not exactly Seventies retro, but with a reference to it, a hint.

As I head down the street I turn back, and

rush upstairs to change. He'll know I've thought about it, tried. Something about the cords and shirt together is too matching and obvious, too *Woodstock*. In the end I keep the shirt but wear it with the same jeans I wore when he saw me last, still unwashed. You can't try less than that, surely?

'Sorry I'm late,' I grimace at his door, breathless from near-running and nerves.

'Rock 'n' roll!' he smiles. 'I wouldn't expect anything less.'

When I was away from Jesse I was sick to the stomach with nerves about seeing him again. How I'd look to him, what I'd say, how I'd keep this up, whatever this is. Bracing myself for the moment when the bubble bursts and he realizes what I am. The moment I see it in his eyes that the feeling we shared is over, or was just imagined, not really ever there. The moment he feels foolish, for me, and for himself for indulging me.

But as soon as we meet and he smiles, the fears vanish. He, our connection, seems more real than anything I can remember. Conversation is easy, like breathing. It just happens. Like meeting someone else who shares your language in a foreign country. The language of gigs and songs and music, the things we don't know the words for. It is so good to speak them again. He likes my ideas for his demo songs, and gets the tracks up to record them. He makes suggestions — cutting out sometimes, louder, more rocky here, higher up the keys, more chimey there.

'Chimey?' I tease.

'You know what I mean,' he answers. And I do. Somehow his being there makes it easier instead of seizing me up, and I soon find something chimey to put down. It's hard to believe he is as uplifted as I am, but he is, I can feel it.

When I check the time and it's six o'clock I force myself to separate out, prepare to go. We grin at each other, both alight.

'Music's like sex,' he says, his eyes keeping hold of mine. He has a way about him that is unsettlingly sexy in someone so young. 'So much better with two.'

I laugh and give him a goodbye hug.

'See you Thursday,' I shout, skipping down the stairs.

25

Liza Doo

It was Billy who gave us our name. He wasn't even trying. He just called round one time for Vonnie while we were practising. I looked up from my fingers trying to learn a Bo Diddley lick to see his shiny brogues loping into the room. I stopped playing, of course, and blushed. We all did, even Vonnie. I'd never seen her shy.

'Billy! Don't you ever knock?' She gave him a shove, but it didn't stop him crushing her little shoulders into his chest while he kissed her neck.

'I didn't wanna interrupt,' he replied. 'Don't stop on account of me.' He sat down on the sofa in front of us, hitching up his suit pants and spreading his knees wide. We all giggled and shuffled our feet.

'Hey, come on!' He clapped his hands and grinned. 'You're not gonna let me put you off, are you? You gotta get used to playing in front of people. That's the point, ain't it? It's only me.'

Only Billy Diamond. I looked to Vonnie to see what she would do. She put her hands on her hips.

'Are you on the guest list?' she asked.

'Well, I sure hope so,' he winked. 'The bass player sent for me to be her groupie tonight.'

Vonnie's face broke into a grin she couldn't help.

257

'Well, you better be worth a free performance,' she purred, bouncing on one hip like a Mae West kind of sex kitten. She mussed up her hair and put one leg forward with her bare foot on tiptoe to balance the bass on her thigh for her starting up pose. Her stretchy Spandex sheath dress rode up above her knee.

'OK, girls.' She turned the volume up on her amp and picked up a plectrum. 'Let's go for it. How about 'I'm a Woman'?'

I wished she hadn't said that one. We were doing a punky version, and had changed the words so that they were suitable for modern rock chicks like us. I was embarrassed to sing them in front of Billy. They were supposed to be feisty and feminist, but I didn't feel very feisty and feminist when he was around. I'd never be able to sing them right. It was hard enough to remember all the lyrics as it was. And I wanted to be cool and pouty like Vonnie when Billy was there, not screeching over the top of the racket and pulling ugly faces while I sang.

But before I could suggest something else, Nicki Stix was counting us in and all I could do was jump right in too. I couldn't look at Billy. But I knew I couldn't just look at the floor either. I hated anyone looking at me when I didn't want them to, but there was nowhere to hide when you were in a band. So my only choice was looking stupid when Billy looked at me, or looking cool. I decided I'd rather look cool. I closed my eyes and pictured Liza Doo, the way I'd been dreaming her up, my idol, and I imagined myself into that picture until she took over my body, pushing out the awkwardness, posing my limbs and letting my fingers fly.

I kept my eyes closed all the way through the first verse. When I braved opening them again to shout, *'I'm a WOMAN!'* I was staring into Billy's grinning face. He was nodding his head and tapping out the beat on his knees. Our eyes locked for a moment and I felt Liza Doo smiling back at him as she spelt out *'W.O.M.A.N.'*

Something about playing to an audience, even if it was just one person, lifted us up. We went into my favourite verse, when we took a turn dropping out of playing and sang a line each. Nick started with, *'I can beat out the beat till you're out of your seat and shaking through and through,'* and then Vonnie drawled her line, *'I can drive you wild with a wink and a smile and pump out a bass line too.'* Ruby and Kim leaned together to sing, *'I can play on your horn, keep you up until dawn, and still have plenty to give,'* and I screamed out the last line, *'I can do some mean licks and show you some tricks till you really know how to live.'*

Billy whooped and hollered, *'All right!'* as we went into the chorus. We played the best we'd played so far. It was like the whole thing suddenly made sense. You were there for a reason. It was as though that person watching and listening was the missing part that at last let the electricity flow round the room. We were all connected, without talking, without touching. The music made the leap between us and turned us into something bigger, something stronger, currents slipping into each other and creating a storm. The me that I thought was set in stone, forever trapped inside, struggling and small and alone, broke down and dissipated outwards, joining forces, no longer separate but a part of things, fluid and free. By the end of the song my parts all came back to me and I stood there tall and strong, rebuilt again as Liza Doo.

We grinned at each other as Billy whistled and clapped and we went straight into 'Wild Thing'. We played like we were Wild Things too, and I even began jumping about until I fucked up the chords, but it didn't matter. We all laughed and carried on. We played every song that we knew, all seven of them, because we didn't want to stop. Billy sang along, bouncing his legs up and down, his hands playing drums and pianos and double basses and guitars and whatever other instruments he could find in his head. At the end of our set he cheered and skidded forward off the couch, landing on his knees in front of Vonnie, his hands clasped up to her in worship.

'Amen!' he cried, in a mock American drawl. 'Or should I say, *Awomen?*'

Vonnie looked down at him with a sexy smirk on her face.

'No, you should say A Goddess,' she retorted, and we all collapsed laughing. We turned off amps and swung off our instruments and pushed our hands through our hair and lit cigarettes. Having an instrument made you feel powerful, like a cowboy with a gun. I leant my weapon against the side of Vonnie's Marshall Stack, while she leant hers on the other.

'Good job, Liza Doo,' said Billy over Vonnie's

shoulder as he scooped her up and swung her round before collapsing on the couch with her across his lap.

'We're auditioning singers next,' said Vonnie. 'Can you fink of anyone, Billy?'

'What's wrong with L'il Liza, here?' he answered. 'She's doing good, man.'

Vonnie watched him as he winked at me, and turned to look at me herself. She began to jig her foot up and down.

'Nah — we want a proper front person,' I said.

'Liza doesn't want to,' said Vonnie, turning her face back to Billy. 'She wants to be cool. Like me.'

Billy pulled a jokey shocked face at her, then me, then her again. He grabbed her round the waist and twisted her over to pin her down on the couch and tickle her while she squealed and kicked her bare legs.

'Well, just *everyone* wants to be cool like you,' he teased. 'Ain't that the truth, Liza?' I laughed as I trailed through to the kitchen with the others to cool off out the back. There always came a point where you had to leave Billy and Vonnie alone. We heard Billy carry on, 'We all just pray to the Lord Above every day that we could only be just the teensiest bit as cool as you.'

The teasing and screaming died down and turned into whispering and giggling, and pretty soon they went through to Vonnie's room. Kim put a record on so we wouldn't hear anything. We all tried to think of things to say and acted as though we weren't imagining what they were doing in the bedroom, pretending we weren't at all jealous of being swept off by this gorgeous guy and *satisfied*.

'I hope we get groupies,' said Ruby, and the prospect cheered us up again. We talked about the band, and what we were going to do next. We needed a singer and our own songs. I got out the lyrics of some I'd been writing, and we went back inside to start working them out. I based my songs on Sixties riffs and chords, but I wrote them about being a girl in the here and now, rebellious and free, doing our own thing — like the boys had written about back then, and have done ever since.

Billy came back through while Vonnie put herself together again for going out.

'So, Billy,' said Nick. 'What do you think, really?'

Billy nodded. 'You're getting there,' he said, 'for sure. You look great. Super cool. And the kind of music you play — you're well rockin'. You just need some of your own stuff, but I like the covers you do. It's good to have a few well-known tracks when you're starting out.' We listened to him like he was a guru. 'And your style — I like it. It's raw. A crazy mix of stuff.'

It hadn't occurred to us that we might have a style.

'What kind of stuff?' asked Nick.

'Well. Liza's guitar, that has a kinda Sixties garage psychedelic surf feel about it.' Sixties garage psychedelic surf. I didn't really know what it was, but I liked the sound of it.

'And Vonnie's driving bass, jazz and blues riffs played in a kinda punkabilly way. And those horns jabbing in with injections of soul. But the way you play is dirty, not smooth.' Ruby and Kim looked at each other proudly. They'd been practising loads to get the dirt out of the sound of their instruments, but something told me they might not any more.

'And Nick!' He put his hand out to her for a high five. 'Your beats, man. Wicked. You drum like you're the jungle telegraph.' Nick wasn't one for being girlie around men. But even she blushed with pleasure at Billy's admiration.

'And all of yous together — I guess it shouldn't work, but it does. You're kind of, I dunno. Loose. But. It doesn't seem to matter.'

As he said so Vonnie came into the room, catching the tail end of what he was saying.

'Loose?' she said. 'Are you calling us loose?'

'Only in a good way,' he laughed.

'Loose,' she repeated, and the word took on some kind of significance as it hung in the room between us. She took the lid off the red lipstick she had just applied and turned to the writing on the wall. 'How do you spell it?' she asked, and Kim and I spelt it out together as she wrote it big and bold in the middle of all the other band names. She stood back and we all looked at the word, full-bodied, glistening scarlet as though it was written in hot blood next to the spidery limbs of the other names, like insects swatted on the wall.

'It'd look good written on my kick drum,' said Nick, 'when I get one.'

We loved what the word meant: loose music played by loose women. After a while the word itself stopped making any sense, the way words do when you think about them too much. But even then, there was something about the way it looked, with the juicy, womanly double O in the middle, that made it somehow right. Something about the sound of the word, beginning with a la and ending in a hiss, that sounded like a description of sound itself. We were grinning.

Liza Doo suddenly reached out and grabbed her imaginary microphone and shouted, 'Hello, London! We're Loose!' and everyone clapped and cheered.

That was the moment I felt like a rock and roll star. I think we all did. It was the moment that we knew was the start of everything. We just knew.

★　★　★

We put the word out that we needed a singer, and they swarmed round like we were honey. We didn't need to advertise or anything. We were just somehow right at the centre of the universe, able to pull people in to orbit round us just by walking down the street or hanging out in a club. Instead of me wanting to be in with everyone else, they wanted to be in with me. It was weird at first, but I soon got used to it. It felt better that way round. I felt my limbs begin to move with ease and confidence with everything I did, like a butterfly finally breaking out of its cocoon and stretching out. I knew what it was like to feel good.

We shopped for a singer the way we shopped

for clothes and records and a good time, our eyes and ears always alert for a colour or a shimmer or a beat or the guy with the drugs. It was Vonnie who spotted Ava, standing on a stool behind her clothes stall on Portobello at the end of the market on a Friday, shouting out, 'Everything one pound, one pound only!' Vonnie came back to the flat with a leopardskin leotard and Ava's phone number.

'I found a great singer today,' she said. 'I swear she's the one. She can come round Sunday if we're all here.'

'Where did you hear her sing then?' asked Nick.

'I didn't.' Vonnie shrugged. 'But I know she'll be great.'

Nicki Stix rolled her eyes. We'd auditioned a few of Vonnie's discoveries already, only one of which she'd actually heard singing in a club. Mostly she went on how they looked. So far she'd brought round a rockabilly girl called Ginger, who worked on the door of the 100 Club and looked like Rita Hayworth but was tone deaf, a transsexual she'd picked up on Westbourne Grove who was beautiful but sang like Chas, or Dave, and a woman called Desiree in a long black wig and a rubber cat suit. She wasn't a bad singer, but when she found out she wouldn't be paid up front said she couldn't afford to waste her time and would rather stick to being a hooker. I don't know where Vonnie found her.

The rest of us had brought along a few people, too; someone we'd heard about, or seen busking or doing backing vocals for a band. We auditioned about nine before Ava. Nobody was right somehow. A couple of them had voices we liked, but one was a New Romantic and the other turned up in dungarees and admitted she was a student.

We knew what Vonnie meant though, the moment Ava burst into the room. We all chose her like Vonnie had, without her singing a note. I prayed she could sing. She was Puerto Rican with skin like toffee and had her long dark hair braided and stacked on top of her head, almost like a beehive but in a mess, as though it had psychotic bees whirling angrily round it. Even without the beehive she was tall and skinny as a scarecrow, wearing a corset and a pair of luminous stripy leggings with biker boots and a tutu. She reminded me of Jemima, the rag doll I had when I was a girl.

She screamed in delight like a big old queen when she came into the room and saw us standing around nonchalantly in our poses, and clasped her hands to her bony chest.

'Oh my God, dahlings! Look at you! You're all so bootifool!'

Her gap-toothed beam was as wide as her face. We asked her which of the songs we did she knew, but she hadn't heard of any of them.

'But don't matter, dahling. Jus' give the microphone to me and I sing for you, I show you.'

We were embarrassed that we didn't have a mic for her, and worried that it might make her leave, but she didn't.

'No problem, honey, no need. You can hear me, no problem.'

She struck a starting up pose in front of us, arms up like a flamenco dancer. She was the only singer we'd had who'd stayed facing us as we began the intro, as though we were the audience. It said it all. Some people were just born to be on stage. We played the chords of 'Wild Thing' and she improvised over the top. You couldn't call it singing exactly, but she had an amazing voice, husky and mellow, like spliff. We all just fell in love with her as she began to perform in a growl, fluttering her false eyelashes at us and throwing her limbs into over-dramatic poses. As we heated up she rolled her Latin American tongue and rapped in Spanish, starting to bounce, with her tutu flapping up and down in opposite momentum to her body, revealing flashes of her pink pants worn over the top of her tights.

'Arriba, Arriba!' she squealed as we headed for the middle eight, and grabbing some maracas she began skipping thunderously around us in her boots. Her beehive started to unwind and she jumped up on the sofa and flung her head around in circles so that the plaits cut through the air like helicopter blades. It wouldn't have surprised me if she had taken off and sliced her way up through the ceiling.

We went for a crashing extended rock and roll ending to the song; Ruby and Kim with their brass raised high, blaring like colliding car horns, Vonnie swinging her arm round and round as she thrummed, me sinking to the floor and pretending to play guitar with my teeth and Nicki Stix kicking over her bongos. Ava leaped up in an attempt at the splits and crashed through the sofa on her way down. We all rushed to her rescue as the sofa cushions immersed her, the drone of feedback from our dropped guitars merely a backing track to the peals of Ava's hysterical laughter.

'Now you know what I meant by a front person,' said Vonnie smugly after she'd gone.

★ ★ ★

We made Ava a tape of all the covers we did and wrote out the lyrics. Then we taped us playing the songs I'd written live into Vonnie's ghetto blaster, with me leaning into the inbuilt mic so she could hear how the tunes and lyrics fitted.

I had three that were totally finished. '*You can have your fun while I'm around, You can tie me up, but boy, don't tie me down,*' I yelled towards the matt black box.

'*Girls (Yeah!) We're taking over the world. (We're taking over!)*' It really felt like we were, too.

And then a manic rockabilly number, '*There's a lot of things I am, Yeah, I guess that may be true, But there's one thing that I'm not and that is answering to you, NO I DON'T ANSWER TO YOU-HOO!*' I shouted as loud as I could over the musical frenzy, loud enough for my mum and Mr Grundy and Arry to hear me back in their sad little worlds, wherever they were.

26

Beth

By the time of Jesse's next gig — an open mic at Cassady's the following Saturday — I have become a different person. Or maybe it's actually that I'm more me than I have ever been. I have been making music every day of the week, from the minute Toby leaves in the morning to the time he phones to say he's on his way home, when I have to summon up all my effort to switch off and think about dinner.

And sometimes in the night when I can't sleep for the veins of melody pulsating around my body, I creep downstairs to sit on the steps of the French doors, smoking and humming.

I have been to Jesse's all three days he was in and at the piano at mine the days when he wasn't. I have developed a piano style, a strange mix of cod grade four classical training and Ray Charles Made Simple. It is something utterly new to me, new and miraculous, like a baby, I imagine. Something like that. I'd abandoned piano when I got my guitar. Guitars were jagged and loud and thrilling. I liked being able to hit the strings. I liked the way with one delicate little tap of your girlie shoe or bare toe on the fuzzbox you could distort and explode the sound made by your little finger into some kind of raging monster. I liked the way you could pose with a guitar. The way you could become so *other*.

When we made a bit of cash playing, I did buy a keyboard, the old Farfisa in the attic. It was after I'd spent hours in Honest Jon's and Vinyl Solution searching out *Sixties garage psychedelic surf*. I discovered the Pebbles collections and Question Mark and the Mysterians and fell in love all over again. The three-note repetitions on the organ, big as symphonies. So when I saw a Farfisa I bought one, to play when we recorded our demo. I wasn't going to play a keyboard live and run the risk of looking like I should be in Yazoo. I learned how to play organ riffs like Booker T or the Doors, and I wrote a few songs on it when I got better at writing songs and my knowledge of the chords on guitar was too limited. But apart from that my relationship with the piano faltered and died. It's why I could never bring myself to play Toby's baby grand when he got it. It was like trying again with someone when you know you'll never get back what you've lost. Too late, is how it always felt. Over.

But now I see it could never be over. However little I've practised over the years, however limited my dexterity, however unable to stretch an octave. I will never be a concert pianist, that's for certain. But I can create the perfect piano for Jesse. It needs to be simple, scarce and elusive to allow space for Jesse's beautiful voice. Too much would be . . . too much. By the end of the week I can play the pieces perfectly. By Friday it flows. I don't have to put each hand down separately on two tracks. I'm embarrassed that I had to in the first place.

'Why be embarrassed about getting better?' Jesse asks me. 'Shouldn't you be proud of that?'

He has a way of saying things that stops my anxieties in their tracks. He makes me see things in another, better way. He turns them round and gives them their marching orders. Yes, I think. Now that you say it, I am proud.

Toby is so busy with Eye Candy's launch and promotion we hardly see each other. On Friday night I become braver. He has his back to me in the kitchen, getting a beer out of the fridge.

'Tobes, you know that boy that came round to see you when you were away? He's playing again tomorrow.' I see his shoulders stiffen and he chucks the bottle top into the sink and takes a deep slug before scraping a chair back and sitting down at the table.

'Look, I know you're stretched to the limit with Eye Candy. But it'll be nice for you, take your mind off it. It won't be work.'

'Beth, it's always work. Why else would I be going?'

'Because you might enjoy listening to someone great playing live for a change?'

He rocks back on the chair legs and looks at me.

'So he's *great*, is he?'

I feel myself get hot. Toby has no idea I've been working with him all week. He hasn't asked. My beating heart tells me now is the time to say.

'I think he might be,' I reply, getting ready to tell.

'What makes you think that?' he asks.

'I've heard him,' I say, and take a breath. 'And seen him.'

And I've been playing with him all week. I hear the sentence in my head, and try to force it out.

'Oh yeah,' Toby remembers. 'He came by in person with his demo, didn't he?'

'Yeah, that's the one. Jack told him to.'

At the mention of Jack, Toby finally looks like he's taking an interest.

'Come on then,' he sighs. 'Where's this demo? Put it on while I order the curry. It'll kill the time while I'm waiting. I'm fucking starving.'

I stand for a moment, waiting, but my words don't come. Toby is out of his seat and I move to let him past me to get the phone. I go through to the lounge to start the demo CD, still in the player. I am nervous as Toby comes through to listen.

'Where's the cover?' he asks, and I pass it to him. He flips it over and looks inside.

'No photos?' I shake my head.

'What does he look like?'

'Oh, you know. He looks the part. Dark, messy-ish hair. Scruffy. Not very posey. Not yet anyway.' I hear myself giggle. 'Good looking, I guess.'

'How old is he?'

'Nineteen. Well. Round about nineteen. I should imagine.'

Toby listens for a few seconds to the quiet picking and soft, near-spoken first verse, then skips the track to 'I Don't Believe'.

'Oh,' I jump in. 'It does get going in a minute. He builds it. He doesn't just do the usual acoustic stuff.'

'Well, he shouldn't start a demo with it. It's gotta grab you straight away.'

'Just give it a chance.' My hand reflexively touches his arm to stop him jumping forward again. The number redial to the curry house finally puts him through and he relents, flopping back in the sofa and placing our usual order. When he's done, track two has reached the middle eight, glorious as the elements them-selves. The guitar is so deep and dark it seems to slip under me as though I am on a river at night, his voice howling around like the wind. It affects me so much I have to look away, reaching for the demo cover and pretending to examine it. I steal a glance at Toby. He pulls his 'quite impressed' face — raised eyebrows and a down-turned pout — and nods. He lets this one play to the end and sits through 'Out There Somewhere', listening.

When I care too much about something I'll do anything to look unbothered. I've already left the room by the final fade, setting out plates on a tray and cracking the tops off two more beers. When I bring them through Toby has turned the TV on and is watching another repeat of *Friends*.

'Yeah, he's got talent,' he says as I set the tray down on the old wooden trunk we use as a coffee table.

'Well, Jack must've thought so,' I reply, offhand, and curl on the couch next to him. He puts his arm round me and pulls me in to kiss my head.

'OK, we'll go down tomorrow,' he concedes. 'What lousy dive is it this time?'

273

27

Liza Doo

I thought it was the beginning of everything, but it turns out it *was* the everything. It went by so fast. Not a lifetime but a moment, like a shooting star.

How we got to have our moment, our glorious blaze across the sky, I don't know, but it was all down to Vonnie, that's for sure. Vonnie was good tender in those days. When our rehearsals got too much for the neighbours and they complained to the housing association, Vonnie got us free rehearsal space at Westbourne Studios by flirting with the guy who managed the nighttime rehearsals. If all the rooms weren't booked up for the Red Eye session we could use the room for nothing but one of Vonnie's smiles. Vonnie's smiles were worth a lot back then. Slash, a guy in Ava's house, was a roadie for the Bad and The Ugly and, as he was between tours, ferried us and our stuff back and forth in his transit van. All it cost us was the petrol and the promise of a flash of Vonnie's thighs as she sat up next to him while we all squatted and hunched amongst the equipment in the back. People often stopped and stared at us as we hefted amps and instruments in and out of the van. I felt so invincible I could have picked up a Marshall speaker with my little finger.

In the rehearsal room we all turned up even more. Now Ava had a mic she no longer had to shout over us and we found out just how great a singer she was, her purrs and growls and squeals and whistles now audible over the din. Stix got to play on an actual drum kit. With a proper PA we actually sounded like a band. The whole opposite wall was mirrored and as I watched and listened to us I was blown away. It was just the band I would have wanted to be in if I wasn't. I would have ached with jealousy, if I wasn't right there, at Ava's right shoulder, one of a pair with Vonnie on her left, egging her on like angelic demons, or demonic angels. Or maybe we were one of each, Vonnie's golden halo of hair shining as though she was lit up by a ray from Heaven, mine blue black as raven's feathers casting my face in the shadows, while Ava tore between us like the possessed.

We soon had a set of songs that we could play through, one into the next, without fucking up too much. We knew we were ready to play when we sorted our coming on song. You had to have a good coming on song. I'd found an LP at the Chicken Shack that I'd bought to put the cover on my wall — the soundtrack to an old film, *Beat Girl*. We'd played it for a laugh. But the title track was amazing, a thrilling twangy riff on electric guitar and brilliant beatnik words. We worked out a way of joining in with the record one by one, so that by the time the track finished it was just us playing.

The DJ would play the record, then Stix would come on stage first, which would be great because everyone would assume she was a bloke. She'd start drumming along, while I took to the stage, flinging my strap around my shoulder and joining in with the riff — dang de la lang dang da da da dang da da dang dang — building up the tension until Vonnie made her entrance. That would make everybody sit up and take notice. Vonnie would slink on smoking and plug in her bass, tossing her gold hair and her cigarette and joining in on the riff way down low on the E string so the floor would vibrate. Kim and Ruby would come on together next, Ruby in a swishy dress and Kim with her quiff on end and a cool Fifties shirt. They would swing from side to side together and come in low and moody on their horns. There was an instrumental bit with Adam Faith talking about this beatnik chick, which we played along with.

And then we'd suddenly all blast the track away while Ava would leap on stage shrieking as we took over, a dozen bpms faster, a hundred kilowatts louder.

It took some rehearsing. But it was worth it.

By the time Vonnie got us our first gig we were still rough but ready. I was nervous, but hungry for it too. And the hunger outstripped the nerves. And anyway, it wasn't me. It was Liza Doo. And she could do anything.

Vonnie blagged us on to the gig, bottom of a bill of five on a Monday night at the Enterprise in Chalk Farm. Because it was the Enterprise we worked out the *Star Trek* theme tune for an encore especially. The only people who saw us were the members of the other bands and their

276

mates and ours. But it didn't matter. It was enough that they treated us as one of them.

Guys in bands treated you differently when you were in a band yourself. They couldn't just swagger about knowing you were impressed. They couldn't help but be impressed themselves. You were their equal but, because you were a girl, even more equal than them. Boys were expected to pose around with instruments showing off. When girls did it it was like being in a parallel universe where everything was the wrong way round.

When I dared to look out across the faces watching us as I played, that's how it felt. We only fucked up once or twice. Only once when we had to stop completely and start again. It didn't matter. We roared with laughter and went from the top. We got a bemused round of applause when we finished, but it wasn't enough for us to play *Star Trek*, so we leapt off the stage and stood at the front, cheering for ourselves, shouting, 'More! More!' Billy and Fliss and Stan and everyone joined in and wouldn't stop until we got back up on stage to do *Star Trek*. The guy running the night shooed us off after that, but while we were packing up he came and asked us to come back, higher up the bill and on a Friday.

Once we'd put our instruments in the backstage room we took speed and helped ourselves to the rider. We weren't paid but we got a crate of free beer. It was worth playing just to get a free night out. When we headed back out we all got chatted up, not just Vonnie. I got a pair of guys from Liverpool in black drainpipe jeans and Chelsea boots, eyeing me from beneath their heavy fringes and corduroy caps as they leaned on the bar. They dug my hair. By now I'd got the whole Supremes thing going, with the points down to the corners of my mouth and the back bouffed up high at the crown. I was wearing my dog-tooth-check suit with a pair of white plastic boots I'd nicked from Sweet Charity. One of them, Joey, asked me for my phone number, but when I said I didn't have one he said, 'It's cool. I'll see you on the scene,' and gave me a flyer for his gigs. I hadn't realized until I saw him setting up his Vox Continental that they were from the headlining band, the Happening.

In Slash's van on the way home we decided we had to have a phone. We didn't want to miss out on all the guys who wanted to call us to go out with them, or more importantly, to play sets at the nights they were running in underground clubs. We were on our way.

28

Beth

Part of me — most of me — wishes Toby hadn't agreed to come. I've got to tell him I've been working with Jesse, but I seem to have missed my chance, the right moment. What am I going to say now, when I introduce them and it all comes out? Jesse has no idea that Toby has no idea. He says he's not bothered about Toby coming to see him, but I am. He wouldn't have come into my life if he hadn't wanted Toby to see him play, to help him get somewhere. Some kind of skew-whiff moral code makes me determined that I do my best to get Toby there. Like it's my vocation or something.

'The thing that matters is that dropping my demo off brought me you,' says Jesse on the Friday. 'It can't get better than that.'

But I know it can. Toby transforms lives. His chosen few are rocketed into worlds they didn't know existed. He helps them adapt as they learn to move without gravity, breathe without air. He's kind of like God, or evolution or something, giving them wings and gills.

All I can do is twiddle around a few keys on a piano. I can't even play with Jesse live, although he asks me to.

I tut when he suggests it, of course, and give

him a *Don't take the piss* look.

'Why not?' he says.

'Don't look at me with that serious face,' I say. 'Don't feel you have to ask me, for Christ's sake! I'm not that sad. Of course I'm not going to play with you live!'

'Why not?' he asks again, either incredulous, or doing a good job of pretending to be.

'Fuck off, I'm not a charity case,' I say, suddenly heated. I don't know why am I so upset. I look away.

'I wouldn't ask you out of pity,' I hear him say. 'Or to make a fool out of you. Or whatever warped thing it is you think I'm doing with you here.'

When I say nothing he says, 'I wouldn't play with someone I don't rate. Ever.'

When I say nothing again he says, 'Is this another of your weird *I'm too old* things?'

'I am too old,' I finally turn and reply. He gives me a look and raises his eyes to the ceiling. 'You'll look like you're doing a concert with your mum.'

He throws his head back and guffaws then, a contagious belly laugh, and I can't help but catch it. I give him a shove. 'Fuck off, you know it's true.'

'Why?! What on earth were you thinking of wearing?' he manages to get out through the giggles. 'A hair net and support stockings rolled down to your knees?'

The image of the audience view of me sitting at the keyboard with my knees splayed beneath in a tweed skirt and slippers makes me roar. 'I said mum, not granny!' I gasp. 'How old do you think I am, exactly?!'

We're doubled up. It's not even that funny, but it's one of those times something really gets you in your ticklish spot, made worse — better — by it killing someone else too. We can't stop laughing.

'You could wear shorts and take your lyrics out of your satchel,' I snort. He rolls back in fits. I haven't hurt from laughing like this in an age. It feels great.

'Seriously,' I say when we eventually calm down. 'Yes, your songs are big enough to take arrangements and other instrumentation when they're recorded to make the best of them, and maybe you can sometimes do concerts with other musicians and even whole fuck-off orchestras when it suits, but. The thing you have when you play these little clubs live is . . . you. Your songs. Your guitar. Your voice. You're beautiful. You really are.'

I can't believe I've said it. For the first time it's me that's unsettled him and he blushes. He doesn't know where to put himself.

'Aw, shucks,' he finally jokes. We laugh again. 'I'm all embarrassed now.'

'About time,' I joke. 'You're far too self-assured for someone your age.'

'Telling me things like that's really gonna help,' he smiles.

'Unfortunately you have to know it. Life is too short. Don't miss your chances. Leap on them and live it. Don't let it all just slip away.'

The words *slip away* make me check my

watch. It's time for me to disappear.

'It's true what they say,' he says as I gather my stuff.

'What's that?' I ask.

'Old people are so wise.'

I cuff him round the head and say, 'Less of your cheek. If you've finished your homework go and brush your teeth. I'll know if you haven't.'

'How?' he asks, innocently. *When you kiss me*, I think, and wonder if that's what he's inferring.

'Mums just do,' I say, to cover up the thrill running through me.

I can't stop grinning like an idiot all the way home on the tube. We have a rapport, there's no denying it.

★　★　★

When it comes to it I am glad Toby makes us late for the gig. It's a bit of a washout, the only people there obviously the most loyal of friends. I can hear Toby's silent groan as we walk in the upstairs room of the pub. A dreadful Scandinavian girl is trying to imitate Marlene Dietrich, accompanying herself with a tinny accordion sound played on a Casio. Only her table of friends clap. We lean on the bar at the back with plastic glasses of lager. My eyes skim the room for Jesse and I am relieved not to spot him.

As she leaves I joke with Toby, 'You'll have to be quick if you want to sign her.' He is not particularly amused.

'Jesus wept,' he sighs as he shakes his head. 'What's wrong with these people? Why doesn't anybody tell her and put her out of her misery?'

This has been a mistake, I think. I shouldn't have dragged Toby here. I should have waited for a good gig, something with a vibe. Toby is never interested these days unless it's ready. He's not going to get a sense of Jesse's talent through the whiff of *amateur* in the room.

When Jesse comes up the stairs he is alone. His mates haven't even turned up, no Mickeys or Amies shuffle in behind him. He heads straight for the 'stage' set up in the corner and plugs in and tunes. Toby is yawning and rubbing his face, so I nudge him to say, 'That's him.'

I have to admit, Jesse doesn't look anything special. He chats with the sound guy huddled in his hoodie over a small desk in front of the 'stage'. Jesse drags a stray stool from the side of the room and perches in front of the mic stand. His entry into his set is too casual for Toby. It's hard to tell when he finishes tuning and when he starts playing. But suddenly he is halfway through a song. There aren't enough people for him to have to overcome chatter. It's more like having to bring corpses back from the dead. I'm embarrassed for him. I decide I'll wait through three songs and, then put Toby out of his own misery by gesturing that we should slip out without Jesse noticing.

But it is only me, losing my faith for a moment. As I check our escape route, noting who to creep behind to stay unseen, I see punters gradually drifting upstairs from the pub below to check Jesse out. They've heard him when the jukebox stopped playing. I close my eyes so I can stop trying to see through Toby's and listen. Without the sad surroundings he is as sublime as ever. There is applause when the song ends. He starts 'I Met Someone', and it's just me and him. I mouth the words and hum my own harmony, my fingers twitching with the piano line I've woven around his guitar.

When I open my eyes I find Toby looking at me, quizzical but smiling. It is the fond, amused smile of a dad taking his sixteen-year-old daughter to see her pop hero. He takes a lighter off the bar, flicks it alight and passes it to me to sway in the air. I slap his arm away. All the same, he claps at the end. The room is fuller now. Some girls have arrived that Jesse says hi to as they head straight for the front and sit cross-legged on the floor. Toby nudges me and jokes, 'Do you want to join your girlfriends?'

'Fuck off!' I laugh. There are too many heads in front of us now to be able to see and it is Toby who moves forward for a better view. When Toby watches a performer seriously he really does. He is, after all, an expert. His reputation isn't for nothing. It is built on a true ability to spot talent. He has broken so many artists and bands over the years that he had faith in — weird, indie bands to start with that no one else could see would be able to make it big. It came from a true passion for good music, in the beginning at least. It is one of the things that made me fall for him. I hope that seeing Jesse will ignite that passion again, after these last few years of sure-thing pop. It's made him enough money to be able to take a risk again.

At the end of Jesse's set he applauds. Not one to hang around, he walks up to where Jesse is winding up his lead at the side of the room. I follow nervously.

He puts his hand out to Jesse. 'All right? I'm Toby. You brought a demo round for me.' Jesse shakes his hand and glances at me just behind Toby's shoulder. 'This is my wife, Beth,' Toby adds.

'I know,' smiles Jesse, giving me a nod. 'Hi.'

I am frozen.

'Oh, yeah, of course. You met,' says Toby.

Jesse doesn't turn a hair. 'Thanks for coming down,' he says, looking from me to Toby. 'I appreciate it.'

'It was actually a pleasure,' says Toby. 'You managed to turn the place around. That's quite impressive. Do you gig a lot?'

'Yeah, I usually play somewhere once a week or so. More when I've got new songs to try out.'

'Good. Do you always play alone or with a band ever?'

My heart lurches into my mouth, but Jesse is cool.

'No, it's just me.'

'And have you had any interest yet from the industry?'

'Yes, but not a deal as yet.'

'What are you hoping for?'

'I don't know, really. I'll see what's offered, I suppose.'

Toby nods, sizing him up. I cringe behind him.

'So where do you want to be in a year's time?'

'In a year's time? I'm not sure. I haven't really thought about it.'

'Haven't you?'

Toby's aggressive line of questioning is beginning to make Jesse uncomfortable. He seems relieved to be interrupted by his friends coming over and hugging him hi.

'Hi, Chloe. Hi, Jaz.'

'Jesse! Hi! Sorry we were late. You were great! This is Pee Wee.'

'Hi, Pee Wee,' says Jesse. Pee Wee is a stunning Asian girl with huge eyes and long black hair swathing her tiny shoulders like a luxurious fur cape. She kisses Jesse hello on the cheek. I feel a stab of envy. I wish I could be more territorial over him, slip my arm into his or something, just to let the girls know I'm something special to him. But I can't. I stand behind Toby, like nobody.

'You were wonderful,' she breathes, flicking her hair and wrapping us in a waft of coconut oil. 'Thank you so much. Can I get you a drink?'

The girls head for the bar.

'Sorry about that,' says Jesse. 'Sorry, what did you ask?'

'It's OK,' says Tobes. 'The chicks love it, huh?'

Jesse is embarrassed. 'Well. I hope so.'

'Is that what you do it for?'

'I'm sorry?'

'You know. Chicks. Adulation . . . '

'Toby!' I scold, laughing uncomfortably. 'Take no notice,' I say jokily to Jesse.

'I'm only asking what drives him,' says Toby. 'It matters. The drive is the most important thing. More important than the talent. You have to want it more than anything.'

'It depends what you mean by 'it', I guess.'

'What does anyone mean by 'it'? If you don't know, you'll never get it.'

Jesse nods with a wry smile. 'I'm sure that's true.' This isn't going well. 'Excuse me a sec,' he says and grabs his guitar from the stand to make way for the next act. We shuffle off the edge of the performing area. I collect Jesse's pedals and tuner as he puts away his guitar and pass them to him.

'Thanks,' he smiles at me. I am relieved to see it is a nice smile. I hope my smile back conveys my apology.

'Anyway. We're going to make a move before we get trapped in here with this lot.' Toby nods his head towards the stage, where a fiddler and a penny whistle player in a jester's hat are getting ready to play.

'Right,' says Jesse. 'Thanks for coming down.' He and Toby shake hands.

'You're good,' says Toby. 'Keep at it. Have we got your number?'

Jesse looks at me.

'Yes, we have,' I say.

'Cool. I'll call you.' He puts his hand in his jacket pocket and hands over his business card. 'Call me if I haven't in a week or so. I'm just up to my eyeballs.'

'OK. Cheers.' Jesse turns to me, touching my hand as he kisses me on the cheek. 'Bye Lizzie,' I hear him whisper. 'Thanks for coming.' He squeezes my hand before he lets it go.

'I'll look forward to your call,' he says, to both of us as we leave.

But he's looking at me.

29

Liza Doo

I don't know if we were talented or not. We had something I guess, in that time, in that place. But Toby is right. It is the hunger that counts, and we were ravenous.

We played the Enterprise again, third on the bill on a Friday night. We had an audience that wasn't just the bands and their mates and ours. There were more bands' mates, our mates had brought mates, and there were even several paying punters, coming to see the Happening, who'd had a good write-up in *City Limits*.

This time I hung out with Joey Dietrich backstage, giggling against the wall as he leant in to me to give me a blow-back. He invited me back to his place, but I said I had to help unload the van the other end.

'See you around though,' was my parting gift, and I snogged him goodbye. I loved that I preferred going back with the band and lugging equipment to a guy. Boys were no longer the destination in themselves, just a stop on the way.

'Good girl. Keep 'im hanging,' said Vonnie, approvingly. 'He might be useful.'

Her boyfriend proved pretty useful too. Rebel Yell were big on the rockabilly circuit, and got paid good money for doing gigs on rocking nights. They'd even done a John Peel session. We couldn't support them when they played as we weren't strictly rocking, but he told everyone he knew about us. All he had to do was drape his arm around Vonnie in that way they had of seeming to wear each other.

'My girl's in a great band,' he'd say. 'You should book 'em.' And the club owner would take one look at Vonnie, gleaming out at him from Billy's shoulder like a rhinestone, and go, 'Are they all like you?' Billy would wink and reply, 'Almost.'

'Almost is good enough for me,' would come the reply. And the guys would laugh together in that *I'm a guy, you're a guy* way. But it was us that laughed last, and longest. I was happy to be Almost Vonnie.

'You only get gigs because you're girls,' scoffed Fliss, as though it devalued us somehow, and meant we didn't count as a proper band. But it didn't matter to us. Pretty faces weren't our weakness, they were men's. Pretty faces were our strength. They might not have been if we couldn't play. But we could, just well enough. Individually we might not have made the grade. But something about us added up. Together we were greater than the sum of our parts.

The band subsumed me like a fever. It took us all that way, raging through our bodies so that the rest of life became vague and unimportant, shut outside the door like background. Gigging became our life. We played every gig we were offered until within a year we were performing around London three or four nights a week.

Vonnie gave up her day job. She didn't need it any more. The band was what we did, what we were. We just wanted to carry on like that forever.

I don't remember what we did when we weren't playing, unless we were fuelling the fire by rehearsing or touting for gigs or buying stagewear.

I don't remember eating, but I do remember driving around at three in the morning, suddenly starving after playing, looking for kebabs.

I had only the vaguest idea of chart bands in plus-fours or ra-ra skirts on *Top of the Pops*, but knew every band we were on that London circuit with; blues, R 'n' B, soul and jazz bands, ska, psychedelic, psychobilly, rocking bands — sometimes bands that played a manic mixture of it all.

All I remember about signing on is the queue of sad, grey people that I didn't really belong to, and the lyrics I wrote as I waited amongst them in the dole office.

I don't know what was going on with my mum, only her silence at the other end of the phone line when I got round to calling her and filling the space with news about how well we were doing.

I can't recall all the boys I got off with, only the sense of them out there watching me and waiting while I came off the stage, and comparing notes with the other girls the days after when we got rid of them.

I don't remember sleeping, only crashing out when there was no more life to squeeze out of the day and waking up looking forward.

I don't remember crying.

All I felt about the past was glad it was over. I didn't worry about the future. I was living in the moment for the first time. Whooshed up into a Technicolor kingdom and never wanting to click my heels to go home.

30

Beth

On Monday night I try to wait until Toby mentions Jesse and what he's going to do with him, but he doesn't. All I've done is text Jesse to say he was great. I haven't wanted to speak to him until I've got some good news from Toby. After a couple of hours my patience gives out and I broach the subject.

'So have you called Jesse Porter yet?' I say after dinner, when I've run out of the usual questions about his day at work.

'Nope,' says Toby, with a decisiveness that bugs me.

After a pause I ask, 'Any particular reason?' I try to sound unconcerned.

'Yeah.' He spears some tempura and dips it in the sweet chilli sauce and I wait while he shovels it into his mouth and chews. I take a swig of Tiger beer to swallow down a sudden violent hatred that wants to spew all over Toby's cockiness. I hate that power thing that comes with big egos, that ease people get about keeping others hanging on their words, that smugness. *Fuck off*, I think, *you're not going to make me fucking well ask again.* But I do.

'So? What is it, then?'

'I'm waiting for him to ring me,' he replies.

'But you said you'd call him,' I say, trying to keep the indignation out of my voice. 'He'll be waiting for your call.'

'Well, he shouldn't,' says Toby. 'I told him to ring me if he hadn't heard. I want to see how long it takes him.'

'But you told him to give you at least a week,' I say. 'Of course he's not going to ring you yet.'

'If he's got any drive he will,' Toby replies. 'That's the thing I think he's missing. He's got talent for sure. But he doesn't want it badly enough.'

I pick up my beer for another swig. My hand is trembling. 'How do you know?' I keep it light, with a just-out-of-interest tone.

'I don't for sure. That's why I'm waiting for him to call me.' Smug bastard.

'I don't see how you're going to know from that. You said you'd call him or that if you didn't within a week for him to call you. It doesn't mean he hasn't got the drive to succeed, just because he does what you ask him to.'

'Well, we'll see.'

I stop eating and pick up my plate, scraping what's left noisily into the bin. My passive-aggressive stance makes me feel more furious than ever.

'What's eating you?' Toby asks.

'Nothing,' I reply, my automatic response. 'Whatever. I just don't think it's a fair way to play him, that's all. Anyway, I don't see why you're not rushing to nab him. You usually do when you see something that special. When was the last time you saw someone with that raw talent?'

Toby coolly cocks his head on one side and thinks about it. 'Yeah, I guess it's been a while. But maybe this is what I'm saying. Raw talent isn't enough. In a way it's kind of old-fashioned. It's about so much more these days. I'm not sure he'd sell. It's a difficult market. I don't know how I'd promote him.'

Sales and marketing! Does everything these days always have to come to this in the end, even in my own kitchen, in a row with my own bloody husband?

'I don't think talent ever goes out of fashion, does it? If so, maybe it's time for a bit of a revolution. Maybe there are a lot of people who don't buy records any more who might do if there was someone out there singing proper songs that mean something.' I sound like a child as my voice rises but it doesn't stop me. 'Maybe you could afford to take a bit of a risk and put it out there instead of playing so fucking safe for a change.'

'Christ, Beth, what's going on? What are you having a go at me for? Jesus!' He doesn't wait for a reply. 'This is all I need when I finally switch off work for once. Anyway, since when do you care about who I take on and who I don't? You're never usually that bothered about my job. You can't even keep an eye on what's going on in the studio lately. Ady says he can never get hold of you and he phones me direct now. That's another hassle I could do without. The Wires demo session was a total mess. Where the fuck were you?'

Toby is too good at arguments. He always

sticks to his winning strategy — the best form of defence is attack.

'If you want to be involved you can start there instead of getting on my back about how to go about signing new acts, which, incidentally, I've been doing pretty successfully for twenty fucking years.'

He storms out, leaving me to stare at the reflection of myself in the French window. *This is what has become of us*, I think, as the woman in the window turns and clears the table.

★ ★ ★

After a long soak in the bath I apologize for having a go and interfering. Toby apologizes for being tired and overworked. I apologize for neglecting the studio and promise to get a hold on it again. Toby accepts. We are on automatic. We are all right again. Not joyous and closer, the way you are when you make up when you're in love, but all right. It's been enough for a long time, but now, suddenly, it doesn't feel enough. Now that I have remembered what it is to feel, *really* feel. It almost feels worse than anything, feeling *all right* with somebody. Is this what it always comes to? How long have we picked our way along like this? Skirting around the hard parts until we find the channel that leaves us to carry on, mutually *all right*?

Toby goes to work out in the gym room to tire himself out so he can sleep and I have a crafty fag out the kitchen window, staring again at my woman-in-the-kitchen scene and trying to find feelings for Toby. What do I feel for this industry executive whose house I live in, who loves the sound of his own voice and pauses for dramatic effect to keep me hanging on his every word? Who talks about sales and marketing when this new music has come pouring into my heart, filling and breaking it at the same time? Who is now in the basement thrashing himself backwards and forwards on a rowing machine to unwind. All I can summon up is a feeling that he is a ridiculous stereotype that I'd laugh at if he was on the telly. Surely we both would?

He wasn't always like this. We had something once. I don't know if he was exactly my type, but then your *type* is not always the best thing for you, as I found. He was the safe one I clung to, after the dangerous one had swept me out of my depth, the one who pulled me back to the shallows.

31

Liza Doo

Vonnie was the only one who thought about the future. I guess that was what made her Vonnie, and us *Almost Vonnie*. She couldn't wait for the future. The rest of us were content in the place we'd got to; we thought we'd already arrived, but it was just a stage of the journey for Vonnie. She had somewhere in her sights the rest of us hadn't even imagined.

While the rest of us were more than happy with showing off and posing about and the extra cash in our pockets, Vonnie was taking care of stuff, sorting out photo sessions, having flyers photocopied and organizing us all into pairs to go bill posting in the middle of the night. She booked studios to record a demo, and sent gig tickets to friends for their friends of friends who knew someone who worked for a record company.

We recorded three songs for our demo, 'Beat Girl' and two of our own, and sat up all night cutting out covers for the cassettes. We'd used a picture from the cover of an old pulp-fiction paperback called *Loose Women*, cutting out photos of our own faces and sticking them on the bodies hanging out on a street corner in their tight trashy sweaters and slit skirts and stockings — apart from Nick, whose face we put on a bloke cruising past in his car. To be honest we didn't look much different from how we did in real life. But it was a cool picture.

Vonnie had a sharp eye for spotting which of us a guy liked best, and she'd assign whichever one of us it was to do the dealing with him. Usually it was her, as most guys fell in love with her on the spot, or Ava if the guy was brave or a bit crazy. Not all blokes had the confidence to deal with them. Guys who were more old-fashioned, liked big tits or were rocking were passed to Ruby; guys who were shy around girls were Kim's. Nick got the lesbians and women haters and any other blokes who couldn't be flirted with: she could talk to them man to man. And I got anyone who was into the Sixties revival. I guess that's how come I was allocated Toby. He was wearing a button-down shirt when he came to one of our gigs and we mistook him for a mod. But it turned out it was just that he had a job, at a record company, and had come straight from work.

He came up to us when we were packing our equipment away.

'Cheers for the ticket,' he said, and we all looked up at him to see who he was. None of us knew how he'd got the ticket, but we figured he must be someone if he'd got in for nothing.

'Hi,' we all smiled simultaneously.

'Thanks for coming down,' said Vonnie, checking out his clothes and glancing at me. I snapped shut my guitar case and straightened up, smoothing down my white Vandella dress and wiggling to the side of the stage to chat to him.

'I'm Toby. From Flipside Records.'

'Liza Doo.' I offered my hand for him to touch. He was quite good looking for a square, with his sharp blue eyes giving me an amused look as he pushed aside the fringe of his straight, dark hair and took my hand for a moment.

'Pleased to meet you, Liza Doo,' he grinned. I smiled. I'd heard of Flipside. I'd seen some of their singles in Rough Trade Records. They had a retro-looking label in baby pink with black writing made out of music notes and piano keys down one edge, which is how come I'd noticed their records and pulled them out to examine them. They had some really cool bands signed to them that we'd seen on the circuit, like the Stingrays and the Bold Three. These days they were only playing the really big venues, like the Astoria and Camden Palace.

I could really see the name Loose going round and round on that pink label on a turntable. It was why we'd sent them a demo.

'Thank you for coming down, Toby from Flipside Records,' I said. 'Got a smoke?'

Toby reached into his Harrington pocket and pulled out ten B&H, offering me one, which I waited for him to light.

'The pleasure was all mine,' he replied. 'I like your band.'

'Well, thank you,' I said, taking a drag and blowing a smoke ring. 'I like your label.'

Toby looked a bit chuffed, and hid it by lighting up himself. 'So how do you know about us?' he asked.

'We know our stuff,' I replied. 'And we played

with the Bolds a couple of times before you made them big and famous.'

He chuckled appreciatively. 'Well, I wish I'd been there,' he said. 'We could have met so much earlier.'

'Better late than never,' I replied.

'True,' he nodded. 'And anyway, could be the perfect timing. We're on the lookout for a new band right now. I like the demo you sent. It's kinda raw and exciting. I like the energy. I played it to the rest of the guys at Flipside. We think you've got promise.'

I raised my eyebrows and leant on the speaker to appear unimpressed. Even though I was totally impressed. 'So where are the rest of the guys at Flipside?' I asked.

Toby leant on the speaker too. He pushed his hand through his fringe again. 'To be honest, they didn't reckon a girl band could cut it live,' he said.

'So what are you going to tell them?' I asked.

'That they each owe me a tenner,' he replied. We smiled. 'When's your next gig? I'll be sure they come.'

I shrugged. 'Their loss if they don't.'

'True,' he said, laughing, and handed me a Flipside business card with his number on it. I took it and passed back a flyer with our gig dates on it from a stack on the speaker. Toby stood looking at it for a moment. 'OK. I'll call you to let you know which one they can make it to,' he said.

'Sure,' I said. 'I'll see if I can get them on the guest list if you're gonna make them skint.' I liked having the power to say such a thing. It made me feel master of my world and theirs and the whole damned universe. 'Although you could always shout everyone in with the proceeds of your big win.'

'You're gonna have to prove it to them before they part with their money,' he laughed.

'Then you'll be flush at the end of our set and you can buy us all a drink,' I replied. I was practically beside myself with how fucking cool I was.

'It's a deal,' he said. 'Good to meet you, Liza Doo.' We touched hands again and locked eyes for a long second. His were shining like mirrors and in that moment I could somehow see myself reflected in them in all my glory. I liked what I saw. I was like a screen siren, projected huge and flawless. I could only agree with him. It certainly was good to meet Liza Doo.

★ ★ ★

Being the contact for Toby gave me a power in the band, a power that was even bigger than Vonnie's. Toby was the first one who had proper pull, who made us all see that higher level that Vonnie had seen while the rest of us messed about. He asked for Liza Doo when he called and the others gathered round to hear me impart what he had to say. He told me which gig he was going to bring more people from Flipside to, and that he thought we were the best band around at the moment and was going to stick his neck out for ours to be the next record they released. Kim and Ruby and Ava and even Nick squealed and leapt around in excitement when I told them.

Vonnie was cool about it.

'Yeah, well, don't get carried away. We better get some more rehearsals in before they come down to see us. Not that it's EMI or anyfink but we don't wanna fuck it up. It's a start.'

She always had to say something like that, something to keep Toby and Flipside in their place and let us know she had bigger ideas. It didn't bother me, though. In fact it just made me stronger, especially when Ruby rolled her eyes when Vonnie came in to rehearsals one day saying, 'Just keep cool with Flipside. We might not have to do a little record first. We could go straight to getting a proper deal — I've got this girl coming down to the gig who's got a mate that works for Island Records.'

When I look back that tiny gesture was a huge, significant moment — the sign that the power balance had shifted between me and Vonnie. The roll of Ruby's eye where there should have been a *Wow*. A tiny thing, like I said, that nobody mentioned or even noticed particularly and I don't think I was even aware of what it meant at the time, but looking back, it showed everything. It didn't help Vonnie that she wasn't round our place much any more. She stayed at Billy's pretty much all the time. Who wouldn't? Nick shifted her stuff out of the lounge into Vonnie's room.

It meant that Vonnie wasn't the first to know any more, but the last. How could that ever be right? I should have seen that it couldn't, but my own glory began to shine so brightly it blinded me. When I was alight I didn't see anything else around me, and I wouldn't have wanted to, even if I could. I got confused, somehow believing in my crown of white gold, as though I was a worthy successor to the throne and not a pretender at all.

★   ★   ★

My hair had got so long it took a false hair doughnut and practically a whole can of hairspray to hold it up in a bouffant. It was starting to be more the size of Dusty Springfield's than the Motown girls, which was why I started thinking about peroxiding it white. Getting into that whole psychedelic scene played its role, too. I began to love how Rolling Stones chicks looked, Marianne Faithfull and Anita Pallenburg, cool enough to go out with two Rolling Stones at the same time. I liked how those painted Sixties eyes stared out knowingly under innocent bleached fringes. I wanted to look like that. After all, I was knowing too.

I spent a week between gigs indoors, turning the bathroom into a chemistry laboratory, bleaching and bleaching the darkness out of my hair. It turned it to straw, but I loved it. It was so easy to back-comb. I let the bits I used to comb into a side parting flop into my eyes and still bouffed the rest but left it a bit messy, as though I'd just tumbled out of bed with a Rolling Stone myself. Without pinning it into a beehive my hair fell around my face. I drew my eyes and eyebrows sharp black and bleached out the rest of my face with the palest foundation and skin-coloured lipstick. I looked like a photograph taken by David Bailey. I found a Mary Quant op art dress in Ken Market that I wore over lacy tights.

Everyone was, like, 'Wow!'

Everyone except Vonnie. She'd spent the week round at Billy's and hadn't witnessed the metamorphosis as my hair turned from purple to orange to yellow, like a rising sun. She didn't see me until the sound check of our next gig when it was all done, and it was a shock. She did a double take. In fact, we both did. Because she had bleached the honey out of her hair and gone peroxide blonde too. The chemicals had swiped the curl out of her style and for a split second it was like looking in a mirror for both of us. I guess it was a better experience for me than it was for her.

'Why have you gone and copied me?' she blurted out, wiping the excited grin off my face.

'What? I haven't,' I protested. 'I didn't know you were going to bleach yours too.'

'Well, I've been blonde for ages,' she frowned. 'It's my thing.'

I looked to Kim for support.

'You don't own the rights to having blonde hair, Vonnie,' she said, reasonably. 'Anyway, yours was a different blonde. Liza didn't know you were going white blonde. Besides, loads of your friends are blondes. What's the problem?'

'It's obvious what the problem is!' Vonnie retorted. 'The whole look of the band is out. I thought we were all happy with our roles. It looked right with her being dark and me being blonde.'

I looked to the others and they seemed as bemused as I was.

'But it's not like we planned it that we should have different colour hair or anything. We never said we always had to stay like that forever. What's the big deal?'

'Well you should have said you were going blonde. I would've done something different,' she snapped. 'I feel really stupid now, going on like we're a pair of fucking Barbie dolls.'

She stormed off in a huff. Ava went after her calling, 'Dahling! Dahling! You look fine you both, my bootifool, bootifool twin dollies.'

It probably didn't help Vonnie's mood much, Ava calling us twins, or dollies.

Kim pulled a face. 'Ignore her,' she said. 'She's just jealous.'

I tried to forget about it and believe she was jealous, but I couldn't. At least, not until later on. I discovered it was true, the thing about being a blonde. Blokes just went all gooey over you. It was like you rendered them helpless, like your hair was made of kryptonite, drawing their strength away through their eyes as they stared. As we played and I walked forwards, leaning my guitar on my thigh and placing my foot on the monitor for my solo, I felt myself fill with the power from their eyes upon me. When I clanged the last jibing discord of my solo I looked up through their cheering and my new long fringe, straight into Billy's eyes, burning back at me like smouldering coals from the side of the stage.

It was a reversal of the first time I saw him, when I was just me watching from the audience and he was on stage, only then I thought he was looking at me, but he wasn't, he was looking at Vonnie and couldn't see me at all. This time it was me on the stage and he was watching, and this time there was no doubt. It was me he was seeing. I got so locked into his eyes I missed coming in with my backing vocal. It was Ava wildly leaping into my peripheral vision that reminded me, and I moved up to the mic and joined in. I shook my fringe to the side and glanced back at Billy and he smiled at me and I smiled back.

That was the time. The time I came off stage after our last encore — our third — and people were slapping me on the back and staring at me in my halo like I was some kind of vision. And I saw Billy in the corridor and knew I'd have to squeeze past him. And I could just tell that he knew I was coming and he didn't move or look away. And as I got close I dared to look straight into his eyes again as my body brushed against his.

And that's when he winked and said, 'Ullo, Little Miss Sixties,' and I knew I could have him if I wanted.

That was the time.

★   ★   ★

For a moment there I was as good as Vonnie. Ever since I'd first met her, being Vonnie had always been the thing I wanted most, my highest aspiration. I couldn't ever have imagined wanting to turn out any other way. For a moment there I forgot who I really was. It all went to my head like a snort of amyl nitrate. A big explosion in my brain that blew to smithereens any idea I might have had of who I really was. I had already been feeling as good as I thought I ever could, but having Billy's eyes on me, knowing he wanted me even though he already had Vonnie, I actually got a glimmer of what it was like to love yourself. Looking through Billy's eyes I couldn't help but love what I saw. It was amazing. It wasn't just me; it was everything. The world was a different place — life was a different experience. Imagine if you felt like this all the time. You could do anything at all. At least, you felt you could. And that was the vital thing in life, wasn't it? Feeling that you could do anything made you able to. It was all about confidence. Confidence and the desire to do it.

Desire was the other thing I learned from Billy Diamond. Desire made me feel as though any love I'd thought I'd felt before had been me watching it in a movie and not experiencing it myself. My body hummed with excruciating joy, or blissful pain, depending. When I watched him take Vonnie home it was agony; when I saw him glance at me over the top of her hair it was ecstasy. When he was around I could feel my whole being kind of opening up and yielding to him, my pupils widening, my lips parting, my skin softening so much it felt as though it was melting right away.

I felt oozy like butter in a hot pan, ready to fry. Whenever he touched me I could feel the scorch on my skin for hours afterwards. I don't know if he touched me a lot, or if I just noticed it every little time he did because it made me sizzle. But it seemed to me that he was touching me a lot more than he did before. There were always lots of little reasons to, like lighting my cigarette or handing me my guitar case. Sitting next to me if he was ever in the van or on the tube or on our sofa, he would splay his knees wide so I could feel the heat and tautness of his thighs alongside mine. Looking down at my lap, narrow and smooth in its pencil skirt next to his rocky slabs of muscle, made me feel dainty and petite, fragile, but not in the way I was fragile before, cheap and easily broken. I felt fragile in a precious way, something to be treated right and handled with care. I finally felt I knew what it meant to be feminine. I was dripping with it. Next to a man like Billy you couldn't help but be all woman.

I don't know why, but somehow the bleach-white hair lost Vonnie her shine. Maybe it was because she'd bleached and coloured it so much over the years, or maybe it didn't suit the gypsy tone of her skin, but whatever it was it didn't quite work. Whereas mine rang like platinum, Vonnie's held the soggy non-colour of a dishcloth or a mop. A load of it fell out and broke off too, which is why she didn't dare put more dye on it. She tried a few less harsh temporary colours, strawberry blonde or light auburn, but whatever shade it was it couldn't cover up the dullness underneath. I knew it must be awful, but I couldn't actually feel for her. I didn't have any feelings left over for anyone after Billy and myself. Over the next few weeks Vonnie wore her petulant frown more and more, until it became boringly normal, instead of a glorious, impressive moment. She was snappy and ready to argue with everyone at rehearsals. She would often turn up from Billy's late, looking tired. The excitement over the interest from Flipside only made her sulk more.

'What's your problem?' Kim asked. As her sister she was the only one brave enough to challenge her.

'It's you lot that's got the problem,' Vonnie scoffed at us. 'You're all just losing your heads over stupid little things. We need to keep it togevver and hold out for the best deal.'

'We're not losing our heads,' Kim retorted. 'It's not as if getting a record out on Flipside's going to ruin our chances for anything else. I mean, look at the Stingrays.'

The Stingrays single was being played on the radio and rumour had it they might get to be on *The Tube*. But somehow having this pointed out only made Vonnie more bad-tempered.

'Well, if that's all you want out of life, suit yourself,' she said. 'I think we can do better than that, but if you don't want to listen to me, fine. Fucking fine.' She wrenched her bass strap over her head and flung the guitar onto the sofa as she flounced out. Ava was the one who always went after her, but she never managed to help. In fact, she usually made things a lot worse.

'Vonnie dahling!' she shouted. 'Is it you time of month? Is all is, yes? No? Is because you hair so bad disahster? No worry, dahling, what you need is a wig, I got some you can try.'

The rest of us looked at each other. We couldn't help it; we got the giggles really badly. Vonnie was only outside the door, swearing at Ava as she pulled strands of her hair about, but we couldn't stop. We tried to play another song, but Kim and Ruby couldn't blow a note. Nick and I played as best we could bent over with laughter. Our bum notes only added to the comic effect. I was crying deliriously. My euphoria far outstripped the funniness of Ava suggesting Vonnie should wear a wig. It was something about the joke being at Vonnie's expense, us all ganging up together conspiratorially to laugh at her. It just wasn't allowed to laugh at Vonnie; the social order of things made it taboo. She was above the law, which made us real renegades to dare. It was mutiny. And that made us feel so good. Girls are cruel. I felt I was getting my own back on every popular girl who had ever sneered at geeky me. It was a sweet revenge, a fingers up.

Unfortunately, I was so creased up I didn't notice her come back into the room. I unscrewed my teary eyes to see a blur of her coming at me.

'And I'm fucking well sick of this bitch nicking all my ideas all the time.'

'What?' I said, the laughter stunned out of me. 'What the fuck are you talking about?'

'You know what I'm talking about and don't act like you don't,' she screamed into my face.

'The way you hold your guitar on your thigh. The way you smoke and stub your cigarettes out. The way you swing your handbag when you walk. And now this blonde thing's the last straw. Don't deny it, you know full well you've got your whole persona off of me. That's my identity you're stealing and it's fucking creeping me out. Fucking well lay off.'

She shoved me in the shoulder and kicked over my amp as she stormed out. I tried to laugh it off but I was shaken. I stood with my palms out helplessly and said, 'What's she on about?' My hands were trembling.

'It's her blonde that's the last straw,' Nick tried to quip, but the urge to laugh had gone. I looked at Kim, I guess for some kind of support or comfort. But she couldn't give it. She looked uncomfortable.

'I think p'raps I'd better go after her,' she said, unclipping her saxophone and laying it down. 'I don't know what's up with her.'

I felt foolish. I wished I'd stuck up for myself, or at least that now somebody else would stick up for me — say Vonnie was mad or out of order or all wrong. But nobody did. I took off my guitar, picked up my buzzing amp, switched it off and lit a cigarette. I couldn't hide my embarrassment. Ruby put the kettle on and Ava gave me a bone-crushing hug, which only made me feel worse and that I was about to cry.

'Don upset you my dahling,' she said, 'no matter.' We knocked the rehearsal on the head. I could feel everyone in the room was sympathetic to me but it didn't help. The one thing nobody said was that I wasn't copying her. I started to protest too much. I couldn't forget it, even when Nick told me to. *How dare she? . . . She's never been into the Sixties, that's my thing . . . I didn't know she was bleaching her hair again . . . I've always smoked like this . . . I don't even know how I hold my fucking handbag! . . . I can't believe she's so petty! . . . Don't you think that's petty?*

I went on and on. I was pumped up with the righteous indignation of someone who deep down can't deny the grain of truth in the allegation against them. It was as though the grain of truth niggled inside like an infection I couldn't stop prodding, causing a big swelling abscess of complaint. The grain of truth hurt. Putting the bleach and the cigarettes and the swinging handbags aside, I knew that I had no idea what kind of woman I would have become if I had never met Vonnie. But it wouldn't have been the one I was now. The one that I loved.

Somehow that didn't make me want to admit it, or apologize. It made me mad. It made me want to assert myself even more. It made me want to obliterate the grain of truth, and the person who had spotted it there and revealed it for all to see.

32

Beth

Next day I call Jesse and apologize on Toby's behalf.

'Toby's really sorry — he wanted to call you yesterday but he's just so snowed under with work. He thinks you're great. He says it's fine for you to call him.'

'When can you come over?' is Jesse's reply. 'I've got this new song and I need help with a break or something. Listen.'

He plays it to me over the phone. It's far darker than anything I've heard from him before. Instead of his usual delicately rambling melodies he is jamming hard on a taut funk riff, at first rant-singing low and nasty, his voice bubbling into a bitter melody and then simmering down again. It works. His musicality makes him rhythm personified and I can feel myself immediately moving to his beat. Jesse scrabbles to pick the phone up again.

'I don't know how to get out of this — I'm caught in a cycle. It needs to go somewhere.'

'Yeah — you need something to lift you out, suspend you for a bit before you drop into it again. It's fucking great. What are the chords?'

I scribble them down, and the main thrust of the lyrics he's got so far. 'Drive', it's called. *I got the drive, you got the wheels, let's put this monster in motion . . .*

From what I can make out, it's an anti-corporate protest song. It thrills me.

But is it marketable? a voice gatecrashes into my head. Fucking Toby.

'Look, I've really got to go to the studio today,' I say. 'But I'll have a go with it. How's tomorrow?'

'Tomorrow's great. Actually no, bollocks, it isn't — I've got college stuff to do to hand in on Thursday. How's Friday? Please say you'll come and save me from this black hole.' *It'll be you saving me,* I think. And then I say it.

'It'll be you saving me.'

I take a breath and shut my eyes. There's a silence.

'In that case,' he finally replies, softly, 'I could toss everything else off and you could come tomorrow.'

It throws me. My fear was that it would make him back off me, not come towards me, arms open. I can't remember the last time someone dropped everything for me. Did anyone, ever?

'Or today?' he offers at my silence. 'I could come to you. Where's your studio?'

'No, it's OK. I'm fine, really.' I can't handle it. I make it a joke. 'I can survive till Friday.'

'Are you sure you're all right?'

The words *all right* make me want to cry. I suddenly feel close to him, the kind of closeness that makes me believe he knows me without my having to explain, that makes me want to tell him everything anyway, even though he just knows it. And for him to tell me every little thing

314

about him. Although I feel I know him inside out, too.

'Really. I'm fine. I'll be fine.' I say instead. It's not enough. 'At least, I will be now I know I've got Friday. With you.'

'Fuck it — at least come on Thursday. I can get to college first thing and be back.'

'No, really — Friday's good.'

'Yeah, but.' He sighs a low sigh. 'I can't wait till then. To be with you.'

I can't believe what I'm hearing, but I can too. It makes no sense, this boy, me. But it is, at the same time, the only thing that makes sense to me right now.

'OK, Thursday. I'll see you Thursday.'

'Brilliant,' he says. We both laugh.

'Yeah. Brilliant,' I say.

The conversation is over, but I want to keep him on the phone, to say more to him and for him to say more to me.

'Jesse?'

'Lizzie?' I love him calling me Lizzie. I feel sixteen. Especially when I can't think what to say. I laugh again.

'Nothing. Just . . . nothing.'

He laughs. 'OK.'

'Have you still got Toby's number?' I suddenly add, and then wish I hadn't mentioned Toby.

'Yeah, I do,' Jesse replies, and it doesn't matter that I've mentioned him. After all, he knows about Toby. Something about the way we mention him, lightly, like he's just some industry guy he met through me that he should call, makes him not matter. Toby can't spoil things.

315

'So you'll call him then?'
'Yeah, I will.'

★ ★ ★

He doesn't phone Toby. At least, I assume not.
Toby doesn't mention it. Whether that means he
hasn't phoned, or Toby's forgotten to mention it,
or chooses not to mention it as some way of
holding power over me I don't know. Fuck it. I
hold on to what power I have by not asking.
Pathetic. Childish. I don't care.

I push it to the back of my mind, filling my
head with Jesse's song and my work at the studio
instead. I realize I enjoy going there. Ady's a
laugh, just your regular south London guy,
working as a studio manager since he stopped
being a drum roadie for the Death Rattle
Junkies. Still wears black jeans and his thinning
hair in a ponytail. He flirts in a harmless way,
just because he doesn't know how else to relate
to a bird. He is relieved to be able to stop
bothering Toby with the things that go wrong.

Although technically his boss, I discover my
innate female ability to organize and adminis-
trate, and begin to take over all the jobs that
make us end up as secretaries, PAs and coordina-
tors. I tidy the place up a bit, and clean. Ady is
relieved about that too. He's the sort of guy who
says, 'Where've you been all my life?' In fact, he
does say it.

'I don't know, Ady,' I reply. 'I don't know
where the fuck I've been. Let's just call them the
missing years.'

We have a laugh. In quiet moments I tiddle around working out possible middle-eight breaks for 'Drive' on the state-of-the-art keyboards, the world's samples at my finger-tips. I sit in on a couple of recording sessions and watch and learn. It's great to be out of the house. I don't know why I haven't been coming here every day for years. What have I been doing with my time? What have I been wasting my life on? Life suddenly seems precious and urgent and vivid. Every moment counts. I can't wait to get up in the morning and start my day.

'You're looking great,' Ady compliments me on Wednesday. 'What are you on?'

It's ironic, really. Recently I've just been throwing on my scruffiest, most comfortable old jeans and a crumpled shirt and letting my hair either hang without styling it or scraping it back into silly titchy bunches that Ady pulls as though we're still at school. I often even forget to put my eyes on. I don't bother with the frequent anxious checks at my reflection, until Ady mentions I'm looking good.

I peer unflinchingly at my face in the mirror in the loos. I see what he means. There is a vibrancy showing, like something, a shell or a petal, has opened to reveal its inner self, the thing it's been protecting. Even without kohl my eyes seem bigger and brighter, as though they are letting out warmth and light like candles in windows.

My body is somehow less composed — relaxed and loose like improvisation, and, depending on my mood, dancing when it feels like it, or slumping when it's tired, like a bloke. My clothes don't

317

look so embarrassed. They sort of hang around like I'm cool to be seen with, not worried if my body wants to peep out for a while. The fact that I've hardly eaten helps. My flesh lies more comfortably across my bones. I don't look younger really, just more alive. Something about me, everything about me, is different.

I think it's love that I'm on.

What else can it be but love?

'Whatever it is, can I have some?' asks Ady.

I smile the slow smile of someone with a sweet secret.

'If you're very lucky,' I reply.

★   ★   ★

On Thursday my morning routine with Toby goes by in slow motion. Each moment seems weighed down with heavy significance. I savour the sweet familiarity of it with a sadness I don't expect casting shadows over my thrills of anticipation. I brew coffee and slice up fruit and make toast and find Toby's keys and wallet. Why can men never find anything at home? Is it because they never look? Do they just shout *I can't find my keys, I can't find my wallet* before they've even tried? Our routine is so embedded that I can't remember the last time Toby had to shout these things. For I have found them and placed them in his hands before he's even got round to thinking of them, every day for years.

We reach for each other for a peck on the mouth as he picks up his bag to leave, knowing the other will be there, right where we expect them. As I hold the front door to close it behind him he surprises me by turning back round to ask, 'What are you doing today?' *He knows*, I think, and we look at each other for a split second that feels too long.

'Making music,' I answer. He raises his eyebrows in a bright smile.

'Good,' he says, and I realize he knows nothing. 'You know,' he adds, 'Ady's really happy with your input at the studio.'

'Good,' I say too, and smile back.

'Thanks, Beth. I appreciate it. It really helps me, to have that off my plate.'

I lower my eyes, heavy with guilt. It is a shy and awkward too-intimate moment, the type you have with strangers. 'What time are you home?' I ask.

'Late, I expect. We've had a hitch getting Eye Candy on the Radio One playlist. I've got to sort it today or we're fucked. I'll call, OK?'

'OK. I'll get something for dins we can do quickly. Take care.'

'Bye, hon.'

'Hope you get it sorted.'

As I close the door behind him, I realize the time he came home after Japan is the only time I can recall him having to come home to an empty house. I am always here to come home to. In fact, it is something he often mentions.

'You're so nice to come home to,' is his most used compliment, as he flings himself in front of a TV dinner after a bad day at work. I have always found it sweet, but as I head upstairs to get ready for Jesse I hear a voice inside, and it's my voice, say, *It's not enough.*

I think I always wanted to be more than something nice to come home to. Didn't I?

33

Liza Doo

The night Flipside came to see us at Dingwalls was the night I burned my brightest. I was all lit up, like a neon star, glittering darts of silver shooting out into the dark of the audience from my tinsel hair. Toby brought another couple of guys down with him. It was me he introduced them to as I squeezed past them at the bar. The place was packed because we were supporting Screaming Blue Murder, which meant there would be press down, too.

I stopped and said, 'Hi,' and smiled graciously all round, accepting a drink from Toby. I could feel their eyes on me still as I left them to head backstage, so I made sure I swung my hips with just the right amount of rock and roll insouciance for their benefit.

The atmosphere was good enough to cover the fact that me and Vonnie had ignored each other since she'd had her go at me. Even Vonnie forgot herself for a minute and got excited with the rest of us. Screaming Blue Murder's following were a good, up-for-it crowd, not the sort to stand as far back as they could with their arms folded, challenging you to impress them. They were already jostling at the front to the DJ's records, so we didn't have so much work to do when he put 'Beat Girl' on the turntable. They were the kind of crowd to appreciate a song like 'Beat Girl', too. They were already dancing as I came on stage and I met their wondrous gaze as I plugged in and riffed along with the record and Nicki Stix.

Locking eyes with the audience as you were performing created all the more potent a brew, like — I imagine — looking when you're having sex, or stripping. I felt Vonnie's presence as she took up her place to my left, but I carried on staring out from where I was at the front of the stage. As the glorious bass joined in with the riff and shook the stage, I watched several pairs of eyes swing to take in Vonnie. But I didn't see her come forward, and she didn't hold their gaze. The eyes returned to me. The crowd was mine. When Ava came bounding on I stepped back and let her have them.

I played like I'd sold my soul to the devil. We all did. We were amazing. We were a tough act for Screaming Blue Murder to follow. We could tell by the way we drew them out from backstage to check us out from the side, and the way they were trying to hype themselves up before they went on after us. Not many bands were upstaged by a bunch of girls back then. It wasn't a threat they'd ever considered.

When we came back out into the crowd after our set it was as though we were already famous. People just wanted to know us. A couple of guys even wanted our autographs, but they weren't from London. Some Japanese girls wanted their photos taken with us. Whenever we caught each other's eyes we grinned. Some guy gave up his stool for me at the end of the bar and I let everyone come up and buy me drinks.

Toby brought his mates from Flipside over to say we were great, and we shared a triumphant look. I think I may even have winked at him. His mates were a bit shy in my presence. They were organizing a showcase gig for the best bands around and he said we were on the line-up for sure. Flipside was going to pick their next act from it. He said we had a great chance. In fact, 'all sewn up' was the phrase he used. As I smiled I glanced up at the mirror behind the bar and met Billy's eyes in the crowd.

It happened several more times. Wherever I was, coming out of the loo, chatting to a group of friends at a table, or dancing with a bunch of guys who couldn't believe their luck, I would look up into a heaving sea of people and find Billy's eyes, always Billy's, waiting to meet mine. No matter who else was around, who else was looking, it was always Billy's that tracked me down and shone on me, like spot-lights. The more the place filled up with people, the more it was only me and Billy there.

And then it happened, the moment I had been dreaming about since I first saw him. I thought I was dreaming still at first, as I stood at the bar with my back to the stream of bodies surging through. I heard his voice, low and urgent, speaking into the back of my neck and making the hairs there stand up on end. 'I want you,' he breathed, and I looked round to catch him but he was already gone. And then later, as I moved through the bodies, a hand smoothing my bum, tightly packed in a figure-hugging Chinese silk minidress. I looked down and the hand was gone, but the voice was there in my ear, 'I gotta have you, Liza Doo. You're driving me crazy.' I glanced around but he had slipped away again as I was propelled through the crowd.

I tried to keep my head. Somewhere in the back of it a voice was telling me it was wrong and I tried to listen, but it kept getting drowned out by the roar of desire surging around my veins.

When Screaming Blue Murder came on I pushed through to the front with Kim and Nick and let my body be taken over by the music and the crowd for a while. But I could feel the pull of Billy behind me. I knew exactly where he would be if I went to find him. He was leaning on the corner of the bar, hanging back in the shadows, waiting. I just knew it. It began to feel like a struggle, just staying where I was, as though I was fighting against a strong, strong current.

'Where's Vonnie?' I shouted into Kim's eardrum.

Kim gestured to the room backstage and held a finger over one nostril and snorted.

'She's really gone,' she shouted back, between songs.

I made a going-for-a-smoke sign and she nodded, and I gave up resisting, allowing the drift to carry me backwards. I watched the crowd spill into the gaps that formed in front of me as the band powered away into the distance ahead, until I found myself caught in the slipstream where the room narrowed at the bar. I didn't look but I knew Billy was there just behind me. I was shaking like a water diviner at the source. I felt him move away from me, squeezing through the bodies towards the rear exit. I tried to stop where I was, clinging on to the corner of the bar but I suddenly felt faint, that I was struggling for air. I turned and felt my way through to the back door leading onto the lock.

The coolness of the night air thrilled my skin, like soft, fresh sheets. I gulped it in as I moved down to the canal and strolled along the towpath towards the dark bridge. As my sweat dried cold I shivered and rubbed my naked arms. That's when I felt his warmth radiating next to me. I turned my face towards him and his mouth was on mine, his stubble rough against my cheek. I dissolved into him, into the moment I had been moving towards, as though it was beyond my control. Nothing mattered, only this kiss. Every other moment would have its fleeting spark of life and perish, but the time I was kissing Billy was eternal.

I was shocked out of my bliss by his body suddenly slamming the breath out of me against the dank stone wall of the bridge. I remember hearing the silk of my minidress ripping as he yanked it up and then the good hurt of him shoving into me. It was urgent, violent, and made me scream with pain and ecstasy, too loud, so that he had to cover my mouth with his hand. I couldn't breathe and as he kept pushing into my body I felt myself falling away. I tried hitting his shoulder to let him know I was suffocating, but my fists made no impact. Part of me didn't care. My orgasm kept washing back over me and I thought, *This is how I will die, drowning in love.*

When he let me go I collapsed. My legs just weren't there. I came back to earth as he helped me to my feet and I heard myself giggling about it.

'Look what you've done to me,' I breathed, as sexily as I could, readjusting my clothes and checking for damage. My skirt was split to my knickers, but it didn't matter because my knickers were split too. I removed what was left of them and threw them in the canal. I was still breathless and all over the place. Billy shushed me suddenly and peered out from under the bridge.

'Fuck. Someone's coming,' he whispered, and we slunk back into the shadows. I held onto him to try and get my strength back. A group of people came down to the canal, but stopped where they were to light a spliff.

'No one we know, I don't fink,' said Billy. 'But we better go back in separate.' He pulled away from me. 'You all right?' he asked.

'Getting there,' I smiled as best I could.

'OK. Well you better hang back for a bit and sort yourself out. Anyone asks I'll say I haven't seen you.'

He tucked his shirt back in and checked the front of his trousers as he stepped out of the shadow of the bridge, lighting up as he loped along the towpath.

'Billy,' I whispered, but too late. Even if he had

326

heard me he couldn't have turned back by then in case anyone was watching.

I took some deep breaths and began to feel my body coming back to me, the imprints of Billy's body stinging on mine. I slunk back to the other side of the bridge to catch some light from the street above and checked the backs of my arms and legs. They were raw and bleeding in several places where I had been scraped on the wall. I wiped off the dirt and green slime, and the blood that was trickling down my leg. I waited until the spliffheads had gone and then tried to walk without staggering back to the club. I went around to the front entrance to buy myself some more time, and also because it was nearer the ladies.

Ruby was in there, hanging over the sink waiting to chuck.

'State on you!' she slurred as she looked up at me through bleary eyes. 'You look like I feel, mate.'

We looked in the mirror at ourselves. I was glad Ruby was so out of it. It was obvious what I'd been doing. My lips were overblown from snogging, chafed raw around the edges and on my chin by Billy's rough face. My make-up and hair were all over the place, the dress fastenings open, a breast halfway out of my bra, cuts and red marks all over me. I splashed cold water over my face and borrowed Ruby's foundation from her handbag, covering up as much as I could.

Kim burst in.

'Where've you been?' she said. 'You've been gone ages.'

I staggered a bit and leant over the sink.

'I'm off my face,' I said. 'I went out to throw up and fell over. Look at my skirt!'

I showed her where my skirt had split and she laughed at me.

'Classy bird,' she said, going into a stall for a wee.

Pretending to be drunk was the best way to deal with it. I headed back out into the gig and the middle of the crowd, scouring it sneakily for Billy. But I couldn't see him. I couldn't feel where he was any more, either. But something about the way I was, weak, torn and battered, made me just want to be flung around for a while by the surges of the crowd, like so much ravaged detritus.

*   *   *

The next day I tried to get out of bed and fell. I could hardly walk. I hurt all over.

'You had a good night then,' Kim said when she got up and saw me nursing my split lip in the bathroom. I blamed my marks on the crowd surfing I'd done.

'Fuck, I wonder what happened with Billy and Vonnie,' she said, and my blood ran cold.

'Why? What went on?' I asked.

'Fuck! How did you manage to miss it? Didn't you see them? As we were leaving in the van they were having a fight in the street. He was trying to get her to come home with him, and she was screaming at him that she could smell another woman on him. He was dragging her along by her hair in the end. It was mad. Christ, you must've been well gone.'

I realized I hadn't missed it. I suddenly remembered the whole scene. How I'd tried to catch his eye again after the gig finished and never managed to, as though someone had pulled the plug on my electric glow. How I'd tried to pass him whenever I'd got the chance and touch him casually, secretly. How I'd tried to say something to him, anything, just be with him somehow, how there never seemed to be the chance. How he was suddenly always with Vonnie, who was glassy-eyed with God knows what drugs. How he hadn't seemed to notice me at all. How I'd heard her accusing him, saying she knew he'd been with someone and how he had denied me, over and over again. How he'd taken her home with him to sleep with.

How in spite of all this, I still felt he was mine.

★   ★   ★

That night, everything turned. It was as though that one stupid act had nudged the planets out of kilter, just when they were about to line up in perfect synch for us. I reached out to chip off one piece of moon too many, and the whole rock toppled around us like rubble. Whatever made me think someone like me could ever step over someone like Vonnie to get someone like Billy?

Turns out Vonnie had to have her stomach pumped that night. Billy took her to A&E when she tried to jump out of his third-floor window and he realized she'd done some bad acid on top

329

of whatever else she'd taken. He was still at her side when Kim went to see her the next day. I said I was too hungover to go.

'Vonnie's flipped out,' said Kim when she came back. 'They think she's just had a bad trip, but they're not sure. They're keeping her in for a bit. Billy's beside himself. She keeps raving on about him screwing somebody else.'

I became aware of my heart beating then, and it seemed to beat louder and louder as the days went by, until it was all over. It was like the drum of a bloodthirsty tribe coming ever closer, pounding in an angry procession towards me. I couldn't stop hearing it, especially at night when I lay on my pillow and listened to them advancing towards me. 'You! You! You!' it seemed to accuse, as though that was the worst thing I could ever be charged with.

Everyone was spooked about Vonnie, so nobody noticed my constant state of fear. How I would tremble at the mention of Billy's name, or look away at the mention of Vonnie's. I tried not to give myself away, joining in as much and as little as possible with the debate about whether Vonnie was mad or whether Billy really had done something.

'Did you see him with any other girls, Lize?'

'Me? No. No, I didn't see him with any other girls. But I was fucked, man.' I blushed as I realized the raw truth of what I'd said, but nobody seemed to see.

★   ★   ★

330

Billy smuggled Vonnie out of hospital when he overheard a doctor say something about a psychotic episode and that he was referring Vonnie to a psychiatrist.

'Christ, Billy! What the fuck are you doing?!' Kim said when he turned up on our doorstep with Vonnie hanging off him like a scarf, wrapped up in a mac over not much else. I skulked about shiftily in the background while Kim and Ava fussed around her, making sweet tea and swaddling her in cushions and blankets on the couch. She was a bloodless pale, her skin and hair and lips colourless, almost transparent. She seemed sort of hollowed out, as though something had taken scoops of her from the inside. Her hair was clumpy and sticking to her head where she'd been sweating and writhing in bed. Only her eyes were dark, not their usual radiant green but an anxious, metallic grey. She collapsed into the cushions, limp and bedraggled and quiet.

'Are you sure she's well enough to come back?' Kim whispered dubiously to Billy when she drifted off into her own mind again.

'She's just had a bad trip, that's all,' he said. 'Last fing she needs is shrinks fucking wiv her head. She'll be right as rain now she's outta that place.'

When it looked as though Vonnie was sleeping soundly he said he'd better be going, but as soon as he said the words Vonnie snapped awake and struggled to get up to go with him.

'Aw, c'mon Von,' he said. 'Lie down. You need to rest.'

331

But she wouldn't have it. 'Why are you going? Why don't you want me with you?' she flashed at him, her paranoia buzzing again like an electric fault.

'It's not that, Von. You're not well enough. I've just got stuff to do. Be reasonable. I don't know nuffing about looking after people. You should be wiv your sister and women and that.'

'What have you got to do? What's more important than me?' She grabbed his lapels with her feeble fists.

'Kim, help me out here,' he pleaded. 'Talk some sense into her.' Kim and Ava tried to reason with her and settle her down again. She began to recover her strength and wrestle against them as they gently pushed her back onto the couch.

'You're not going anywhere like this, Vonnie,' said Kim firmly.

'Well, if he loved me he'd stay with me,' said Vonnie, her voice rising, still fighting to get up and at Billy. 'Why won't you stay with me? Why do you want to go? What have you got to do? Who are you going to see?'

Billy tried to shush her as patiently as his hot-headed temperament would let him. 'I'm not going anywhere, I'm not seeing anyone,' but she kept on. In the end his nerves frazzled and snapped.

'Fuck's sake, woman,' he yelled, shoving her suddenly with a violence that shocked Kim and Ava. But not me. 'Stop being such a fucking paranoid bitch.' Kim stepped in and put a hand on his arm to remind him that that was exactly the problem.

'Billy,' she pleaded. 'Couldn't you at least stay the night?'

I could see him trying, but in the end he couldn't think of a good enough reason not to stay. Only he and I knew that I was more than a good enough reason. Discomfort was crawling up my spine and around my neck like shingles. Vonnie was trying to keep Billy away from trouble, and there it was under the very same roof. Not that I felt much like trouble, the way Billy was treating me. He wasn't treating me like anything at all. It was as though I wasn't there. I was invisible to him. I hung like a shadow, following what Kim and Ava did. I helped to clear Nick's stuff off Vonnie's bed to give them some privacy. Billy carried her into her room. She looked tiny in his arms, like Fay Wray. As Ava closed the door I glanced in and saw Billy lie down with Vonnie, enveloping her in the nook of his big arm as he kicked off his brogues.

We sat in the next room in reverent quiet as dusk fell, only moving to rush to the door and hush Ruby and Nick as they burst loudly in. Kim shepherded them into the lounge and we huddled together and told them in whispers what had gone on.

'What do you reckon, though?' asked Nick. 'There has to be a reason she suddenly flipped out like that. Most blokes are bastards. I bet he did fuck someone else.'

As she spoke, Billy silently rounded the corner in his socks and entered the room behind her, where she sat cross-legged on the floor.

I'd been trying to join in, so I didn't look

guilty to the others. But as I looked up at Billy I felt as burnt up with guilt as a witch. His eyes looked through me as he took us in, sitting around in our coven.

'You're right,' he said, as calm and steady as truth itself. My heart was about to explode, as though he'd just thrown petrol over me and was reaching for a match.

'Billy,' I gasped. 'No!'

Nick swung her head round in horror and instinctively held her arm up in front of her face. She assumed from my reaction that he was about to hit her, but he stayed back with his palms spread.

'Fuck's sake, what d'you fink I'm gonna do?' he said, with a convincing mix of little-boy hurt and a man's anger, the sort that makes women helpless over guys like Billy.

'You're right that most men are bastards. You coulda accused me of that in the past and I ain't always been a saint, but Vonnie's the only girl I ever loved. I'm madly in love; surely you can see that? I'm outta my mind wiv worry here.' He wiped at his eye and pushed his hand through his hair, turning away slightly as though he had to collect himself. We all lowered our eyes, ashamed.

'Look, fink what you like about me. But I didn't do that to Vonnie. You might not trust men and you might have good reason not to, but fink about it. When the fuck do you fink I had the chance to fuck some girl that night? I was around all night. You all saw me. Kim? Ava? Liza?'

He looked right at me, as though he was an innocent man appealing to the better nature of a random member of a jury. 'And even if you fink I had the chance to chat up some bird in two minutes and convince her to fuck me right there and then in a toilet or down some alleyway, what sort of girl do you fink would do somefing like that? And all right, there might be such slags, but d'you really fink I'd be interested when I've got a girl like Vonnie?'

He was looking at me as though I should answer him. I stared at him, unable to believe what he was doing.

'Well, do you?' he asked again as I stared at him in horror. With the girls' eyes on me too, all I could do was shake my head no. He looked to the others and one by one they shook their heads or said, 'No, Billy.'

He dropped his beseeching shoulders then, and let out a vindicated sigh, blowing the strands of his collapsing quiff out of his face. He sat down on the amp with his elbows on his knees and his head in his hands. We didn't know if he was crying. In the awkwardness, Ava went over to him and put her arm around his bent frame.

'We so sorry, Billy,' she said. 'We were just being stupid girls, you know?'

'Yeah, sorry, mate,' said Nick, leaning over and patting his knee. 'I didn't mean it.'

'It's all right,' said Billy, looking at her with intense liquid eyes. 'I'm just . . . overwrought, you know?'

They all made comforting noises and Kim started looking in the kitchen for something to make for tea. Ruby put a record on. I stayed where I was on the floor, like a piece of dirt that someone had brought in on the bottom of their shoe. Not only had Billy denied me, he'd managed to make me deny myself. The graven image I had so carefully created and perfected and worshipped was toppled and I felt myself returned again, insignificant as ash, dry as dust.

34

Beth

I climb the stairs to Jesse's room. When I enter he is not hunched over his recording equipment or putting the kettle on as usual, but standing in the middle of the room waiting for me, his arms hanging at his side, not knowing what to do. He steps forward as I come through the door, and then stops, thrusting his hands in his jeans pocket.

'Hi,' I smile, closing the door behind me.

'Hi,' he replies, scratching his head before replacing his hand in his pocket. I put my bag down on the floor and stand three paces from him. He rocks out onto the edges of his bare feet and looks up at me shyly through his hair and we laugh with embarrassment. Then we both take an awkward step forward to kiss each other hello on the cheek. We both go to the same side of each other's face, laugh again, then both go to the other side. Our eyes meet properly for the first time. I become wrapped in their deep, luxurious, velvet brown. I watch his pupils dilate as he looks at me and see myself slipping into them as his face comes near and his soft warm lips meet mine. Our eyes stay open to each other, our noses touch. He rubs mine with the end of his and we smile again. He puts his arms around my shoulders and pulls me close to him, placing his face in my hair. I put my arms around his waist and lay my head in the crook of his neck. We begin to sway slightly from side to side, dancing to a silent music. I slip my feet out of my sandals and creep my toes forward until they are over his. I feel him sigh, his breath a tender stroke on the back of my neck, and he lifts me slightly to place my feet over his.

Jesse begins to waltz me, jeans to jeans, breast to breast. The feel of his hands on my back warms me like the rays of a summer sun. I hold him tighter and place my lips against the soft skin of his neck as he rocks me. We feel a perfect fit. I feel the right size, big and small both. I am everything in his arms, strong as a mother, fragile as a baby, protector and protected. He is no longer just a skinny boy. Close like this he is a man. We are both old enough, and young enough.

I slide my hands into his back pockets and pull him into me, aware of the bliss beginning in my jeans as they press against his. His hands move up to my head, smoothing my hair away from my face and holding it so he can look into my eyes again. He pulls me in and kisses me deeply. We both keep looking. I have never looked into eyes before as the passion takes over. I have always been too afraid. The intimacy is almost unbearable. I discover it is the most erotic thing.

When we can no longer stand he walks me to the bed and lowers me onto it. Lying next to me he unbuttons my shirt. He slides the straps from my shoulders and kisses my breasts. I take off his

T-shirt and we kiss some more, stroking each other's skin.

'You are beautiful,' he says.

'So are you,' I say.

He unbuttons my jeans and I unbutton his and we tug them off each other. Our hands explore each other, gently and slowly, and he pulls me on top of him and we move together as though we are already making love. When I can't take any more and have to close my eyes, he stops and waits for me until I open them again. We laugh. When it happens to him I do the same. He finally rolls me onto my side and moves down, pulling off what is left of my clothing. I run my fingers through his hair and watch him kiss my body, for the first time unashamed, until my need of him becomes too great and I pull him up. He kneels above me and I slip down to kiss him, always still looking into his eyes. I am a virgin in this, this soul-window sex. I feel a heady mixture of innocence and knowledge as I look at him. He soon has to stop me, and he moves me up the bed again, taking my face in his hands and kissing me as he pushes into me.

'I love you, Lizzie,' he says, his eyes shining deep into mine.

'I love you too,' I reply. And this is how we make love, his hands around my face, mine around his back, mouth to mouth, eye to eye. We come together still kissing, still looking, and fall asleep that way, like a key in a lock.

35

Liza Doo

We cancelled a couple of gigs while we waited for Vonnie to get back to normal. It was hard to tell when that was, as she hadn't ever really been very normal in the first place. Billy came and went and I got used to it. Used to the nod of vague acknowledgement in front of the others that sealed another layer over what had happened between us, as though it was an ugly crack, until even I couldn't tell it had ever been there. I got used to the heavy weight inside, the sickening tangle of anxiety, guilt and heartache. I got used to the old me returning and the feel of it spreading through me like a degenerative disease that began to take control of my actions again: the awkward, unsure steps, the clumsy handling of a guitar that felt strange in my arms, the burn of self-consciousness crawling over my skin like an inflamed rash.

I tried to block out the sounds from Vonnie's room as she and Billy fought and, more still, as they made up. But I could feel them filtering into me like smoke.

I tried to concentrate on the gig we had coming up, the Battle of the Bands Showcase at Bay 63 that Flipside had booked us into. I tried to focus on the fact that it was our Big Chance, that if we could just make it through to that moment maybe all this wouldn't matter. Maybe it would move us forward and we could forget about it, put it down to being just one of those rock and roll things that happen. Maybe it would take us to that other place that Vonnie had envisaged, where she would meet a famous rock star and forget all about Billy.

Maybe I'd have felt a whole lot less worried about it if Rebel Yell weren't playing at the showcase too.

The whole thing didn't seem to rock Billy the way it did me. I kept trying to hang on to myself and get over it, but with him it was as though he didn't even have anything to get over. Even his concern for Vonnie waned, once he could see she would survive. His time away from ours became longer as every day he went off to rehearsals, and most nights he set off for gigs. It soon made Vonnie recover enough to get herself to his gigs. We tried to stop her and make her concentrate on getting our own band together for the showcase, but even though she was desperate for us to beat Rebel Yell she couldn't stop her obsession with Billy. The two things pulled her in opposite directions at the same time, so her nerves were as strung out as over-used elastic. We tried to get rehearsals going, but Vonnie arrived late and left early, and when she was there, she wasn't really. She'd end up running off to catch the end of Billy's set so he couldn't take home any other girls.

Billy began to get annoyed.

'Don chase 'im, dahlin,' Ava advised. 'Guys

don like. You lose you power over 'im. Stay cool like you don care.'

Vonnie tried to stay cool like she didn't care, but it didn't work. Billy stopped coming round to ours at all and Vonnie finally cracked at eight one morning, when she was still awake, and went round to his place.

It was the week of the showcase and we were all getting edgy. We'd booked a four-day block of rehearsal space leading up to the gig, just to be on the safe side. We hadn't needed to rehearse so solidly since the early days, when playing a bar chord all the way through a song was an achievement. But with the state of Vonnie and the two missed gigs — like I said, we were getting edgy.

It was Ava who got most impatient that Vonnie was still late, even when we were in a studio now, paying by the hour.

'Ah, forget it. This is crazy,' she huffed, giving up on trying to rehearse a bass-heavy number without the bass. She whacked her mic down on its stand and paced about as though she was in a cage with us. 'How am I supposed to get into it when it's like this shit? I have to perform, you know? I have to have something to help me, how you say? You know, give it some, make it happen, you know? I can't do like this, with nothing to support me. It's me at the front here, trying to get this across. When it's shit like this behind me I jus' make a fool a myself.'

She eventually stopped stalking about and sat on the drum rise and sulked. We stood about awkwardly, caught between our own frustration and trying to calm Ava's. Ruby sat on the floor next to Ava to soothe her while Kim and I went out to get coffees and cakes from the Lisboa for breakfast.

It was the first time I'd been alone with Kim for more than a few seconds since the whole thing happened with Billy. As we walked along together in silence I remembered why I'd been avoiding her. The worry over Vonnie had trampled over her features as though they'd broken in, new shadows residing under her eyes like squatters. Being her best friend I knew I should be the one she could talk to about her sister, and how she herself was coping. But being the cause of it all I couldn't bear to. And Kim being my best friend, I felt as though she would just be able to tell what I'd done if we were alone talking about it, just by looking into my eyes for a second. The shame in them would give me away, like the silver of minnows hiding under rocks.

Running this errand our eyes didn't have to meet, as we walked along, queued and made our purchases. On the way back I asked her if she was all right and she said yes.

When we got back, Vonnie had arrived.

Billy hadn't had another girl at his place, which is probably why he'd got as angry as he did with Vonnie. She'd tried to cover up her black eye with spot concealer and purple eyeshadow, but we could tell when, by the end of the rehearsal, the swelling was up and the eyeshadow had sweated off one eye but not the other. Nobody mentioned it.

343

Ava carried us through those rehearsals. It was a relief to have her in front of us, taking control of the set list and songs, allowing us to work the mechanics behind her and look down in concentration at our instruments. As long as our fingers welded the notes and chords together we created a strong enough chassis for her to steer.

Without us really noticing Ava had become slick and professional. She had tamed her wild vocal cords so that they behaved as she bid them, only letting their whoops and squeals fly when intended, rising from their husky, earthy tones like horses over fences. Her voice had become quite beautiful, and when I relaxed enough to look at her in the mirrored wall opposite I saw that so had she. She always had been in her mad way, but now she had become sophisticated, sort of like jazz.

She had set her frenetic, tight-wound plaits free into a soft, relaxed tumble of curls that she sometimes let cascade around her shoulders and sometimes smoothed back into a chignon. The fluorescent frills and raggy tutus and enormous boots were gone, replaced by streamlined black dresses or ski pants. When she moved, it was dancing, not just leaping around like an over-excited kid.

Towards the end of the second day's rehearsal I felt a glimmer of hope return that it was all going to be OK. We were going to pull it off. Kim locked the front door at night and hid the key so that Vonnie couldn't go to Billy's in the early hours, and with us all practising together all day we felt our band spirit returning.

'We're gonna be great,' Nick grinned at everyone when we pumped through a perfect set to finish up the session. 'Let's go for a drink.'

We started packing up, but Ava seemed dissatisfied. 'Don you go celebrate yet. We still got lots a work to do.'

She'd been picking at Nick's drumming all day, telling her to tone down because she couldn't hear herself sing. You could tell it had been getting on Nick's nerves by the twitching of her jawbone she'd copied off men in the movies, as she silently followed Ava's orders.

'Oh, come on, Ava, lighten up. There was nothing wrong with that last set.'

'Mmnn,' Ava replied with a downturned mouth and an unimpressed shrug. 'We could be better.'

Nicki Stix's patience ran out. She let out an exaggerated sigh and flung her sticks down. 'Fucking how?'

'I just think we could be a little smoother, you know? Not so rough, not so kind of punk. Is a bit outdated now, don you think so?'

'*What?*' said Nick, incredulous. 'Fuck's sake Ava. Now's a fine time to be saying we should change the whole sound of the band. We've only got two days to the gig, you know.'

'Yes I know, but we could at least drop a couple of the more stupid songs, you know. Like 'Don't Answer to You' maybe, and 'Girls Are Taking Over'. They're jus' a little bit, I don know. Like, old-fashioned or something.'

The rest of us glanced at each other. This was about more than Nick's drumming.

'What are you trying to say, Ava?' said Vonnie, putting her hands on her hips menacingly.

Ava shrugged casually. 'What about doing some more soul sort of thing?' she suggested.

'Soul?' Nick said, like she was spitting out a bad mouthful. 'Like what? Paul Fucking Young? We haven't got any soul songs.'

'Actually, I have,' Ava replied, coolly. She met our stunned stares with a big smile. 'I've written a couple of soul ballads.' Only she pronounced it *ballaads*. 'If you want I can sing them for you.'

She rummaged around in her shoulder bag for her lyrics before anyone said anything.

'I wrote down the chords for you,' she said to me, handing me a torn-off scrap of lined paper. I took it and looked at it blindly, not knowing what else to do.

'But — Ava, that's great and everything, but don't you think it's a bit late to learn new songs right now?' Ruby attempted. 'For this gig at least?'

'Yeah, it's a bit sudden,' Kim agreed. 'We've only just got back on track. Can't we just keep the set as it is for Friday?'

'So you don even wanna hear them?' Ava said, a flash of her hot temper bolting through her eyes. 'Is OK for you; you don have to stand at the front and sing your stupid words like you mean them and have all the men think you're lesbienne. How we gonna get on in this business if they all think we're some bunch of man haters?'

'Ava!' Ruby exclaimed. 'Don't be ridiculous! No one thinks we're man-hating lesbians!'

We all laughed at that, except for Vonnie, whose mood was building like a darkening sky.

'Yes they do,' said Ava, and we stopped laughing.

'Like who?' said Kim.

Ava shrugged and twirled a tendril of hair around her finger. 'Jus' some people.'

'Yeah, right,' said Nick. 'Sure they do. And anyway, even if they did, what do we care what anyone thinks?'

'It wasn't jus' anyone,' Ava retorted. 'It happened to be some important guys from the industry. One of them was Screaming Blue Murder's manager, actually. He gave me some really good advice after the last gig, but if you're too stupid to hear it, fine.'

Vonnie's voice was low with rage. 'What did he say?'

'I don know if you really wanna hear it,' said Ava petulantly.

'Yeah, maybe we don't,' Nick said in a huff. But the rest of us did.

'Just tell us, Ava,' said Vonnie, with enough insanity threatening in her eyes to make her.

'Well. Don get me wrong. He thought we had promise, for sure. That we were good as far as that kind of gig goes. But that to take it to the next level, we have to make some changes. Like, it's a real good gimmick for us to be all-girl band, but we're not using it right. We look OK, all pretty and thing, but it's better if we wore more up-to-date clothes, like the ra-ra skirts and stuff like that. And all-girl band should appeal to men, you know? Not make out they don need

347

them by singing this kind of song.'

There was a very long silence while we digested this information. Even Vonnie's confidence in how we were, how we looked, the music we played, seemed rocked. Finally Nick said, 'Ra-ra skirts?'

And then louder, 'Fucking ra-ra skirts?'

That did it. We all fell about, even Vonnie. The thought of Nicki Stix sitting there drumming in a ra-ra skirt was the funniest sight I could imagine. Ruby hitched her dress up round her chunky thighs and started dancing like a student. Nick joined in, pulling down Ruby's frilly net petticoat and putting it on, winding it round and round the waist and dropping her jeans. She jumped around with her trousers round her ankles, showing her holey grey pants and the skinniest, whitest, hairiest legs you've ever seen on a girl. It was hysterical. Vonnie, Kim and me were rolling around on the floor with laughter, just like we had done way back when we were teenagers.

Ava's authority in the room had evaporated, so that we hardly noticed as she picked up the pieces of her songs and muttered something about us proving him right as she stormed out, trying ineffectually to slam the heavy soundproof door, which slowly shunted shut behind her in its own time.

★   ★   ★

Ava didn't show the morning of the next rehearsal. We were kind of glad at first, as we nursed our hangovers from the night before and set up and attempted to play. But as the hours slipped away we became more and more nervous. Never having been someone who had to wait for others to turn up late, Vonnie was furious.

'Who the fuck does she think she is?' she snapped, strutting out to call her on the payphone, to no avail.

It was mid-afternoon when she finally arrived, keeping her coat on as she stood and faced us in the middle of the room.

'Where the fuck were you?' yelled Vonnie. 'That's five hours you've wasted. There's no way we can work out your new fucking songs now.'

'I got the impression you weren't gonna work on my *new fucking songs* whatever,' Ava replied calmly, staying where she was without taking her coat off. Despite the fact that she was standing her ground there was something nervous about her.

'Well, you didn't exactly give us a chance to talk it through, did you?' Vonnie replied, turning her back to her to retune the bass. When she sensed Ava still hadn't moved she looked over her shoulder at her. 'Well, don't waste any more fucking time,' she said disdainfully.

'I don intend to,' said Ava quietly and, clasping her hands together, she seemed to take a breath before she said, 'That's why I'm leaving your band.'

We all stopped what we were doing and stared. Only Vonnie could find a voice. 'Leaving? *Our* band? But it's your band, too . . . What the fuck are you talking about?'

'I'm sorry to let you down. But I think very deeply about this last night and is no thing against you guys you selves, is jus' — is not right for me.'

We all leapt into action then, the way you would at the scene of an accident, or hope you would. We gathered round her, pleading with her to stay, promising to work on her songs, apologizing for laughing at ra-ra skirts. We thought she just needed to be fussed over and given some attention. But no matter what we said nothing would sway her until Ruby burst into tears. Ava softened to us then, suddenly the old emotional Ava, crying herself. They hugged each other and laughed, and I thought everything was going to be all right.

'Let's just all pull together and get through this gig,' I said, watery-eyed myself. 'We'll play the best ever and we'll win, and then we can really sort out the direction we want to go in. We'll do whatever song you want for the single, Ava, and we'll have a brand-new start.'

Ava took some tissues out of her bag and wiped her eyes. She blew her nose and shook her head. 'You don understan'. I can't play the gig if I wanted to.'

We chorused together:

'Of course you can!'

'Why not?'

'You'll be fine! We'll cut out those songs and just do a shorter set.'

'No.' Ava pulled away from us. 'I have to tell you somethings. That manager guy I tell you about? I meet him last night. I'm *sorry,* but I didn't think you were gonna come with me on this. He offered me to be my manager if I go solo. He thinks is right market for solo female singers. He wants to make the big time with solo jazz funk pop fusion kind of singer, you know? A bit sophisticated. Will be jus' my first name, Ava, like that. And he has this producer he can put me with to make songs together. I tell him I think about it, but I have this gig, and he say I can't do. Not if is for band to get record contract. I have to sign, what you call it? Like exclusive contract with him. He say is no good me singing with you if you get contract with Flipside.'

She stopped to take a breath.

'Ava — don't sign it,' I jumped in quickly, grabbing her arm. 'Please. At least leave yourself the option of both chances. If you still don't like what they offer at Flipside, you can go for this other guy then, whatever he's offering. Ava, he can't make you do this. He's just a manager — it's not a deal or anything.'

Ava looked at me sadly. 'I'm sorry, Liza. I don want to mess it up for you, but this band is your dream, not mine. Yes, I've had lot of fun and I'm grateful to you guys for having me the singer, but. My dream is always to be a singer. A popular singer, you know. Well, I go home las' night and I think about it and today I go to sign the contract.'

'No, Ava — don't sign it yet. What's the rush? Think about it.'

But we'd misunderstood her foreign muddle

over tenses. She had already been to sign the contract. I tried to persuade her even then, saying a quickly drawn-up contract couldn't stop her. I begged her to sing with us just one last time. Just to give us a chance with Flipside. But she wouldn't.

'What's the point?' she asked, and I could see that, for her, there was no point.

She had a meeting to hook up with the producer the day of the gig anyway, and the weaselly manager had booked her in to a swanky studio the following week to get working on her demo. It was all suddenly happening for Ava.

When she'd told us all there was to tell, and we were all argued out, she kissed us all as we stood about helplessly and told us she loved us.

As she left she said, 'Anyway, what's the problem? Liza can sing, like before, no?'

★   ★   ★

Up until then I had just assumed we would be calling Toby and pulling out of the gig. As Ava swept out of the room and out of our dream, looking every bit the star, we were left with her parting words hanging in the air. I felt sick, as though they were toxic. I glanced up into expectant faces.

'Don't look at me,' I said, 'I can't.' I wished she hadn't planted the thought in their minds. 'Really, I can't,' I said again for emphasis, but nobody let me off.

'Why not?' said Kim. 'You've done it before.'

'I haven't. Not at a gig. Not in front of anyone.'

'So? You can do it.'

'Yes. Go on, Lize. You'll be fine.'

'You'll be brilliant.'

Their hopes were rising again, as mine were sinking.

'No way,' I was shaking my head. 'I'll die.'

'Oh, c'mon Liza. What else can we do? We can't let a chance like this just blow right on past us.'

'Yes — you can sing, you know you can. And you know all the words. Look — we've got a couple of hours left today, and we've got tomorrow. At least give it a go.'

'Go on, Liza!'

When Vonnie started chanting, 'Liza! Liza!' and they all joined in, I relented.

'I'm only doing this today, though,' I said, my hands trembling as I picked up my guitar. They all cheered as I lowered the mic stand to my level, and rushed to take their places around me. 'I won't be good enough and you'll see it and I'll be phoning Toby tomorrow and we'll be pulling out. OK? There'll be other chances along the line. We'll get another singer and try again — '
But I was drowned out by Nick's drums thundering out the beginning of 'Beat Girl'.

By the end of the session I thought they would realize that it was no good. But instead they were charged up, ready to go. They hadn't seemed to notice how bad I was. I kept protesting that I couldn't handle playing guitar and fronting the band at the same time, that I had to cut out some of my lead and just play rhythm, that my voice was weak and I couldn't remember all the words. But they just kept encouraging me, saying I was fine.

'LISTEN TO ME!' My voice rose with panic and the need to be heard. 'It's not good enough. *I'm* not good enough.'

I began to cry distraught, terrified tears. It was Vonnie who came and put her arm around me. Kim came the other side of me and did the same.

'You're really good, Liza,' I heard Vonnie's gruff voice in my right ear. 'We wouldn't let you do it if you weren't, I promise. We wouldn't wanna stand there with you anyway, would we, if you were shit?'

'Please do it, Liza,' said Kim's in my left. 'For us.'

I remembered the thought I'd had, that if only we could get through this gig and get a record out with Flipside, maybe the whole mess I'd made with Billy would slip away into the past, the way you forget how sickness feels when you're better, or being cold to the bone when you're warm. Maybe if I could do this I could redeem myself and make everything all right again. Maybe they were right and I was wrong, and I could do this.

'Let's see how we sound tomorrow,' I answered through my sobs. 'We'll give it till lunchtime before I call Toby.'

36

Beth

I kneel in the attic sorting through all my relics; photographs of myself and my friends forever fixed in our prime, gig posters and flyers, magazine reviews. I am supposed to be carrying on with my spring cleaning. But I am not sorting out and throwing away. I am reliving the past. I coo and examine and laugh and exclaim out loud, 'Oh! This was the time . . . ' I handle the items carefully, as though they are valuable treasure to be cherished, not dumped and left like so much dusty junk. I can feel the late afternoon sun on my face, airbrushing my nostalgic smile with a rosy tint, as it slips imperceptibly away, like youth.

★ ★ ★

'I love everything about you,' Jesse says, as he pores over the old scrapbooks of my life he has insisted I show him. 'Tell me all there is to know.'

I don't know why he is so interested in me, but he is. He makes me feel that my past is not an embarrassing secret to be hidden away, but something to be proud of. He is impressed with the write-ups in the gig pages, the way we looked, my rock and roll stories. I'm surprised how many there are. They add up to a body of evidence, the sheer volume of them proof that we really happened. Seen through his eyes, they remove any trace of doubt that we were ever really there. He looks at me as though I was somebody.

When I joke about this he doesn't laugh.

'Of course you were somebody,' he answers, refusing to make light of me. 'You still are somebody. You always will be.'

'I was only joking,' I say quickly. Jesse often doesn't get my jokes.

'Well, don't,' he replies. 'Your jokes aren't funny.'

'Thanks,' I retort.

'They're always at your expense. And I'm not going to laugh at you. You're always putting yourself down. I won't have it. Stop taking the piss out of my girl.'

I love it when he calls me that.

'Sorry,' I say automatically.

'And don't bloody apologize for her either,' he tells me off. 'Do you wanna start something, mate?' He playfully shoves me, defending me against my own verbal abuse.

After a teenage tussle we collapse on his bed again and I let him win.

'You're my hero,' I tell him as he pins me in a tender and delicious way to the bed and kisses me.

'It's a dirty job but someone's got to do it,' he replies, lifting my shirt. 'Stand back — I'm going in.'

★　★　★

I see Jesse every possible moment. When we're not making love we're making music as though it's going out of fashion. Well, it seems as though it is, to me anyway, to us. I am in a strange and beautiful elevated place, where songs and melodies come to me like spirits to a shaman. I even play guitar again, and sing songs I have written for Jesse, eyes open and staring into his. He cries.

'No one has ever written a song for me before,' he says.

'I bet they have,' I reply. 'You just don't know about it.'

'Why would anyone but you?' he says. 'No one else knows me. Only you.'

'I'm not the only one who loves you,' I say. 'I can feel it when you sing. Can't you? Something you have, something you are, makes us all fall in love. You make us all feel . . . special.'

'I don't know about anyone else,' he replies. 'All I care about is you. And you should feel special. You are special. It's nothing to do with me.'

But it is something to do with Jesse. It is everything to do with him. He makes me believe in myself again, looking at myself through his adoring eyes. When I am with him I leave all my weakness and failing behind. I reinvent myself as a strong, brave, wise, beautiful person, the woman I always hoped I would be. I can be that, with Jesse. I start to believe maybe it's not too late. I start to see glimmers of hope for the future. I start to imagine grasping for them.

It's true what they say about love.

357

It makes you feel as though anything is possible.

I can't even feel guilty about loving him when I'm supposed to love only Toby. I discover the answer to the age-old question. You can love two people at once. My heart has swelled enough to love a million people, let alone two. I don't stop loving Toby. In some ways, it makes me love him more. It makes me remember that he made me feel good too, once. Being with Jesse has made me separate out from Toby, become my own person again, so he is no longer responsible for my happiness. It makes me able to be friends with him, now that I am being fulfilled elsewhere.

The trouble is, of course, that *elsewhere* begins to feel like home. It feels wrong, leaving Jesse to come back to my reality, as though everything is back to front. When I am away from him, alone, things are so confusing and I ache over our age difference and the fact that I am married to someone else. When we are together, the worries disappear and everything is simple. He makes me happy.

I start to believe the solution is obvious.

Jesse and I are in such perfect time with each other that he voices it, just when I have begun to dare think it. 'Be with me, Lizzie,' he says. 'I can't bear being without you. I want you to always be with me.'

'You know I am,' I say. 'Even when I'm not actually here, I'm always with you.'

'Which is why you shouldn't ever not be here,' he says. 'Come to me, Lizzie. You can't let love like ours pass you by. What else matters, really? I will wait for you. This is a once in a lifetime love.'

★   ★   ★

Being someone else as well as his wife allows me to feel for Toby in a way I couldn't before. I can engage in his life and sympathize with his latest worries over work. Somehow the fuck-up over Eye Candy's single not making the daytime playlist has not been rectified. I'm not sure if Toby has ever been unable to make something all right at work. My newfound heart goes out to him when he comes home at midnight, the tension pulling together his brows and tightening his mouth like stitches. He talks me through the ins and outs of the mess while he smokes blow in an effort to wind down enough to sleep.

'Christ, we've paid the pluggers enough . . . without it we're fucked.'

'But all the other promotional stuff's going OK? They're doing the chart shows and kids' TV, aren't they? And that support slot with the Superstar winner — what's his name?'

'Yeah, all that's sorted. But it ain't worth shit without the radio play.'

'Well, maybe it will be,' I try to console. 'Maybe some other stations'll play it. Maybe the track'll catch on anyway.'

Toby gives me a don't-be-silly look.

'Why not? If it's a good track.' After a silence I say, 'Is it?'

'What?'

'A good track?'

It seems ridiculous suddenly, that I haven't even heard this band that has been Toby's world for however many months. I've seen the photos (gorgeously cute Japanese chicks in bright bunches with long socks and miniskirts) and the artwork (cartoon versions of gorgeously cute Japanese chicks in bright bunches with long socks and miniskirts). I've heard the songs in their demo form before the band was put together.

Toby is looking at me like I've gone mad.

'Well?!' I ask again, laughing. 'Do you even know if it's a good track or not?'

He cracks a smile then. 'Um . . . ?' is all he can say as he tries to decide.

'Play it!' I say. He groans.

'Go on!' I urge him. 'Let's hear the fucking thing!'

I raid his bag for a copy and put it in the CD player, turning up the volume and doing what I imagine is clubby dancing when the inevitable sample starts up. Toby laughs at me. It feels good to have the power to cheer him up. The track has all the right ingredients. The beat is infectious, perfect to dance to. An oriental-sounding instrument plinks an oriental-sounding intro. Then a gong heralds a repetitive catchy rock guitar riff coming in, giving it the right amount of raunch, followed by girlie processed voices ooh oohing together and then taking a line each as the verse begins. A cute Japanese lisp to the singing gives it its one element of identity, the one clue that it's this band and not Girls Aloud, or Britney, or Kylie, or Rachel Stevens, or

J Lo, or, or, or. After the chorus there is a break while the girls chant a version of the play-ground lines, *We are Japanee-eze, if you ple-ease.*

I stop mid-hop and look at Toby. 'Did I just hear that right?' I ask in wonder.

Toby twitches his bottom lip to show shame. 'I'm afraid so,' he admits.

I shake my head in mock horror. 'You can't do that!' I exclaim.

'I know,' he agrees, and we throw our heads back and guffaw like it's the old days.

When the track's over I flop back onto the couch.

'It's fun to dance to,' I say, 'Well-produced, catchy . . . ' I run out of things to say.

Toby looks serious again. 'Does that make it good, though?' he asks. It throws me. He never asks me anything. He never needs to. I can hear an inconceivable note of self-doubt in his voice, a plea for reassurance.

'Well — yeah,' I say. 'Of course it's good. For what it is. I mean, you know it's not my kind of music, but it's the perfect formula. C'mon, Tobes. Stop worrying. It's a sure-fire hit; you know that.'

'It better be. It'll lose us a shedload of money if it isn't and my neck'll be on the block,' he says grimly, and rolls another joint.

We lounge on the couch together getting amicably stoned. The only thing that sticks with me from Eye Candy's track is the twangy guitar sample, repeating on me like barbecue sauce after a fast-food takeaway. Somewhere in my warping head I lose the actual notes of it and they re-form as the 'Beat Girl' riff I used to play on guitar.

'Hey — that's the track you should get Eye Candy to do,' I murmur to Toby's feet, as we lie head to toe on the sofa.

'Whassat?' he replies from the other end.

'That song my band used to do. Remember it? 'Beat Girl', from that Adam Faith movie.' I start to dang-de-lang dang the refrain, but he butts in.

'Course I remember it. It was great,' says Toby affectionately. It feels like the first time we've talked about me being in a band since I was. I'm surprised he isn't surprised, just takes it in his stride as though it was yesterday. I don't know what I expected — that he would give me his don't-be-silly look again and say, *What band? You were never in a band.* I would have believed him too, if he'd reacted that way. Instead I am spurred on. I struggle up onto my elbows with sudden enthusiasm.

'It'd be fucking brilliant. You could sample the riff and put it over beats, like they did with those Elvis songs.'

Toby struggles up too and we grin at each other crookedly, sharing the memory of the excitement of the track as it was, and how Loose played it, and the vision of how it could be redone now.

'That'd be fucking fantastic,' he agrees.

'I wanna hear it but my records are up in the attic and I can't move,' I say.

'Doesn't matter,' he says. 'I can hear it anyway. Can't you?' He nods his head to a beat and attempts to strum an air guitar. He makes me laugh. He has no idea how to play guitar.

'No, it's like this,' I go, sliding to the edge of the seat, legs splayed, playing guitar on my hip, picking out the exact notes with my imaginary plectrum as Toby cheers me on, almost back the way it was in the beginning.

37

Liza Doo

I didn't sleep a wink. I stayed up all night in my room going over and over the songs, reworking my guitar parts so they were easier to play while singing at the same time, smoking and freaking out. I tried to lie down and get some sleep but my thoughts were filled with horrible images of me fucking up on stage and Ava on *Top of the Pops*. I'd bring myself to with a jolt, and the sudden lurch of horror as my consciousness crashed in with the reality of what I had to do was worse than the constant sickening awareness of it while I stayed awake.

We could still pull out, I kept thinking to calm myself down, but remembering that Kim, Ruby, Nick and Vonnie — especially Vonnie — were depending on me made me know I couldn't. How would we carry on afterwards? How could I face them again? I couldn't imagine how the following evening would ever pass, when we were meant to be taking up our Big Chance, and weren't. What would we do instead — watch some other band up there doing what we were meant to be doing, taking our place? Or stay home drinking tea and watching telly? How would we pick ourselves up the day after and carry on? I was cornered and there was no way out.

I got through rehearsals on coffee and nerves. Maybe the adrenaline was a good thing after all, as, nervous as I was, somehow by lunchtime I'd clicked into my new slot. The band was thrilled with me.

'Liza, you're doing great. You're gonna be fine,' Kim beamed as we took a breather. By the time Slash turned up in the afternoon with his van to take us to the venue for the sound check I felt OK. *I can do this*, a voice said in my head, but it didn't sound quite like mine. I treated the sound check as my one dress rehearsal and really went for it. I blinkered out the other bands and Billy as well as I could, but not so much that I didn't notice we had the edge. The relief left me exhausted. As we all got ready in the girls' loos all I wanted to do was lie down and sleep. I splashed my face with cold water and jumped around a bit, but there were still hours before we were on.

I threw up in the sink and said, 'I can't last.'

While Kim looked after me as I sat shaking on the floor, Ruby and Vonnie went off to find me something to keep me going. Ruby came back with a bag of chips and Vonnie brought me a couple of lines of speed, which she skilfully chopped and lined up for me on the back of the toilet.

The speed kicked in and began careering through my veins as the first punters started arriving. I wished we were on first instead of last, so I could get it over with now. I tried to hold on but as the night progressed and the speed took over I felt my concentration slip. My energy drained away as the speed forced my mouth to gabble an incessant stream to whoever was there, mostly Kim. While Rebel Yell were on Vonnie gave me another line of speed. As I was taking it I heard Kim outside the cubicle rowing with Vonnie about how much she'd had to drink, and Vonnie swearing at her as they grappled while Kim poured the rest of her bottle down the sink. Vonnie slurred something and staggered out, and we followed.

'She's fucking rat-arsed,' Kim shouted in my ear. 'I hope she's gonna hold it together.'

I was aware of Billy's band up there and the crowd going mad, and then everything went out of focus as I watched my blurry hands tuning my guitar backstage and listened to voices echoing *good luck* around me. I don't know what carried me as we lined up by the stage ready to go on, but it wasn't my legs. Toby's mate was the MC, and I heard him say the word 'Loose' and then the 'Beat Girl' record kicked in and Nick's drums bashed along. I felt Kim's hand on my back propelling me forward and I was out there in the spotlight. I took up my former position, stage left, and fixed my eyes on a point in the middle distance as I plugged in and took up the riff. Being in my usual place calmed me and I tried to let the music take me the way it always did. Then I heard Vonnie's bass, or rather, I felt it, making the stage bounce beneath me like a safety net. When I felt Kim and Ruby taking their positions slightly behind me and further left and then their horns striking up good and loud like a shield of sound around me I remembered to breathe. It was going to be all right.

The distance from my side of the stage to where the mic stood in middle front looked like a thousand miles. I thought I'd never make it, but as the Adam Faith talking bit came in I knew I had to get there soon. As I made my legs move forward, the front of the stage looked like the edge of a cliff and my head spun as though I had vertigo. But somehow, somehow, I reached the mic and opened my mouth and at the same moment a big dismembered 'Yeah!' came shrieking back at me from my monitor. The voice didn't sound like it was coming from me, but it was saying all the things I felt I was mouthing into the mic, so I tried to trust that it was my voice I could hear and that it was in tune. Singing was like a nightmare where you're screaming and screaming and no sound is coming out. I felt as though I had been hacked up and my parts scattered around the room. My fingers playing the guitar were flung to the back of the stage to my amp, my voice in my severed head was screaming from the black box in front of me, my heart was on the roof. I didn't know where the rest of me was.

Next thing I knew the song had finished and the crowd was cheering and Nick was thumping out the beginning to 'Boy Don't Tie Me Down'. It was happening. I could do it. I just had to let time and music take me through it. I just had to ride it out. It felt like steering a raft over rapids. The momentum took you so quickly, the roaring sound blasted you away. There was only so much you could do. *Just hang on, Lizzie*, I thought. *Hang on.*

About four or five songs in, halfway through our set, I'd got more used to the assault on my senses, the confusion of light and noise and fear. There'd only been a few fluffed notes, no major fuck-ups, and I tried to be a bit braver, take control, do more than just hang on. I tried to steer. I looked into some eyes in the audience, I moved a bit, stepping up to put my foot on the monitor to take a solo when I could get away from the mic. I got a cheer. I looked around at Loose, to make eye contact with everyone. Kim and Ruby Red grinned and Stix winked at me. Only Vonnie didn't catch me. She had her head down and was swaying even though we'd finished playing the song. She looked pretty cool though, ready for action, so I signalled Nick to head on into our latest song, 'Happy Ever After'.

I knew all the words but it was a tongue twister, a quickfire list of things that made a girl these days happy ever after, none of which included meeting Mr Right or getting married or having babies. It was no doubt one of the ones Ava thought was too man-hating *lesbienne*. I didn't care, though. I'd written it after all, and I even had a split second's thought when the drums were beating in the intro, that maybe I could do it more justice than Ava could have anyway. I certainly meant every word.

The first verse blazed in, but as I went into the second something sounded wrong. I couldn't tell what it was at first as our sound in the monitors was so muddy, so I just carried on as best I could. I realized Vonnie had gone into the chorus early, so our bass notes, the roots of us, were loose and ungrounded. I tried to catch her attention but I couldn't step away from the mic as there were no gaps between the words and she wasn't looking up. She was swinging her hair from side to side across her face and hanging her bass so low it looked as though she was going to drop it. I realized the drink and whatever drugs she'd taken had got the better of her. She was in her own world, in her own key, totally oblivious to what the rest of us were doing in the song.

I didn't know whether to go into the chorus as I was meant to, or try to catch up with Vonnie at the middle eight. I started to stumble over my words as my mind tried to pre-empt where Vonnie's would go next. Without a solid bass it was as though my raft had broken in two, and I was trying to ride with one foot on one plank of wood and one on another as they hurtled over the undulating river, separating and widening beneath me. None of us were able to get Vonnie's attention, so we all just plunged ahead into the chorus. I suddenly felt the bass give way altogether as Vonnie realized she was lost. The rest of us swerved into the middle eight and I thankfully shrank back from the mic and stepped over to Vonnie to yell 'middle eight' into her ear. She grinned at me with glazed eyes and joined back in.

When we got to the next verse I'd totally blanked out the lyrics, so I had to sing the first verse again. We got to the last double chorus but Vonnie was all over the place. I just hoped we were drowning out her bum notes. We made it through but we were shaken. I couldn't believe it wasn't over yet. All I wanted to do was get off stage but we had to keep going. I glanced over to the sound desk and saw Toby talking animatedly into the ear of a boss-looking guy, who was shrugging and shaking his head. I felt my heart come back into my body, where it sank like a stone.

I had no idea what song was next on the set list. I turned my back on the crowd and asked Nick. When she mouthed 'Don't Answer to You' I felt my legs buckle and my balance go. I was toppling. I couldn't think how the song started, what the chords were, the first line. I shook my head. 'Let's drop it,' I shouted at her. 'What's next?'

She checked the list taped onto the bass drum. 'Taking Over,' she yelled back. 'Taking Over.' I fumbled my fingers around the chords. It was an easy basic rock riff over three chords that only modulated up once, the first song we worked out after 'Louie Louie'. Nick signalled it to Ruby and Kim while I told Vonnie. Nick counted us in on her sticks and I whacked out the chords and forced myself back to the front of the stage to sing. I couldn't look up from my fingers clutching my guitar neck for dear life, even though I knew it was the worst thing you could do at the front of the stage. The spotlight felt as though it was burning me alive. I wished it would. I felt really stupid. It was painful, having to go on when I didn't want to, singing, 'Girls are Taking Over the World', when I knew that we weren't.

★　★　★

We somehow got through to the end of the set. I don't know how. I became aware of the noise of the audience, shouting drunkenly over us, and I knew we'd lost them. I did my best to get them back, but the trying-too-hard made my voice shrill and shouty, and without Vonnie and her bass really there — the heart and soul of our band — I don't know. I just couldn't do it without her.

We finished with a not-bad rendition of 'I'm a Woman'. The relief of it being the last song made me raise my performance again, but as Vonnie tried to sing her lines she got her lips in a numb tangle and started sniggering. It was quite funny and she got some laughs and cheers, which she bowed to and hiccuped. I felt a big plastic smile stretch across my face like a dressing over a wound. Maybe if it looked like it didn't matter, it wouldn't matter. That's all I could hope for.

We went backstage and Billy came over, straight to me, gave me a squeeze and said, 'Well done L'il Liza. You did pretty good, consid'rin'.'

He had the smile of someone who could afford to be generous. Vonnie came crashing in behind me and fell over, landing in a heap and taking Billy down with her. He was in high spirits enough to find it cute and funny.

'As for you, Missus,' he said affectionately, 'what are you like?! Nuffin' but trouble.'

I just wanted to be alone and cry. Kim and Nick and Ruby gathered round me and said 'Well done, Liza,' and 'You did it!' but it only

371

made me feel worse.

'Come on, let's go out there and get really drunk,' Kim urged me, but I couldn't face going out there, or getting really drunk. I couldn't think of anything worse than unravelling even more than I had already. I was undone and all over the place as it was. Rebel Yell left the dressing room to go and party with their fans and the other bands, but I refused to go anywhere.

'Did we win?' Vonnie slurred from under the coat she'd pulled over herself as she lay crashed out on the floor. A flicker of hope sparked up in me that the speed and my shattered nerves made me think it was worse than it really was. Maybe it wasn't so bad, if you weren't in my head while we were playing. Maybe we had pulled it off, just.

We finally heard the MC take to the mic and the DJ, Si Kadelic, faded out the track he was playing, 'Girl, You Captivate Me'. Kim and Nick peeked around the door to hear the announcement of who'd won the record deal. A great roar went up when he said the name Rebel Yell and invited Billy's band back onto the stage to do another number. I felt my heart break at the bottom of its murky depths, sending ripples that I knew would reverberate back and forth between my shores forever.

'Never mind, chicks,' said Nick. 'We'll get another chance, ay?'

'Yeah, at least we gave it a go,' said Kim. 'We did well to get up there and play at all.'

'Yeah, it's not gonna stop us,' said Ruby.

'Come on, let's go and have a laugh.'

But I wouldn't and Vonnie couldn't. As Kim was putting Vonnie in the recovery position, she tried to get me to come out and have some fun.

'It wasn't that bad, Liza, really. You did really well.'

There was a knock on the dressing room door, and Toby was standing there. He was the last person I wanted to see, but I lit a cigarette for something to do and put on a bright smile and said, 'All right?'

'I just wanted to say sorry you didn't win,' he said, looking serious and a bit scared. 'I fought for you, but Joe was just into Rebel Yell and wouldn't be swayed, and . . . he's the bossman.' We nodded.

'S'OK, Toby,' I said. 'You don't have to be kind. I know we were shit.'

'You weren't. You weren't at all,' said Toby, coming to sit by me. 'What the hell happened to Ava, though?'

It made me feel better, telling the whole story to Toby. He made me feel like a bit of a hero, stepping in at the last minute, and he made me feel I didn't make a fool out of myself.

'Really, you were great, Liza,' he kept reassuring me. 'Joe didn't notice you weren't the real singer, I swear. He was pretty impressed when I told him. Maybe I shouldn't've said anything, but I just thought he should know what you were pulling off.'

'Thanks, Toby. Don't worry about it. You couldn't've done anything. I know we just didn't have it. *I* didn't have it.'

'That's not true,' he said, looking shyly into my eyes.

Trashed as I was, I could see that he really liked me, the way a boy likes a girl, not just because I was in a band. I didn't know why. Without Liza Doo I was nothing. But for a blissful fleeting moment the pain went away. I glanced up to see that we were alone, apart from Vonnie, still crashed out on the floor.

'You have it in a big way, Liza. You always will to me.' He moved forward and I let him kiss me sweetly on the side of my mouth, just as Vonnie was coming to.

'Where the fuck's Billy?' she demanded, fighting her way out from under the big overcoat. It made us both giggle.

'I'll give you a call,' said Toby to me, getting up to go. 'Don't be blue. You'll get your chance yet.'

I smiled goodnight and helped Vonnie to her feet.

'Billy's band's just finished playing again,' I told her. 'They won.'

'Fucking cunting BASTARDS,' Vonnie yelled, lurching out the door and pushing past Toby. 'I'll bloody fucking KILL'IM!'

Toby looked back at me to share another smile. He really did like me.

38

Beth

I flick through my collection of albums, brought down from the attic along with my old case of Loose performances and demos on cassette. I ended up with hundreds of records by the time CDs came along, and I had to start all over again. I come across some rare soul originals that I've never seen reissued — they'd be worth something now if I hadn't played them to death.

I find 'Beat Girl' and play it on my old Dansette. It amazes me that the tinny little Dansette speaker had enough power to shoot thrills that pierced me to the core as the old needle scraped its way around the scratchy vinyl in my room. But it did. It does still, the charge of the 'Beat Girl' riff making me leap around the lounge by myself, grinning with my air guitar. I only stop when I imagine how sad I would seem if someone suddenly looked through the window at this ageing glorified housewife behaving like a teenage boy.

It is a day I won't be seeing Jesse, so I head over to the studio with the album to sample it. Ady really gets it.

'Cor, this'll making a fucking great dance track,' he enthuses, immediately starting to scroll through his drum loops. We work well together, me and Ady, as he puts the beats together and I add extra riffs and hooks on various keyboard sounds. We get totally lost in it, and by the time we notice it's dark outside, we've nearly finished it.

'It could do with some live instruments over it, just to give it a bit of welly, you know?' says Ady, but we finish off for the day, burning a copy to play to Toby, and I head home.

Toby is back already. I burst through the door, yelling, 'Tobes, listen to this, you'll love it . . .' but stop when I hear him. He is in the kitchen, crossly banging about through the cupboards and fridge for something to eat.

'What's going on?' he says tersely.

I say, 'Sorry?' to buy myself some time. He's more angry than he usually is over regular domestic grievances, and I think he must have found out about me and Jesse.

'Where've you been?' he tries again, an easier one to answer.

'At the studio,' I reply, grateful that I have been. 'Me and Ady have been sampling 'Beat Girl'. It'll be great for Eye Candy, Tobes. Come and have a listen.'

I grab him by the hand to pull him into the lounge, diverting him from his awkward line of questioning.

'Beth, I'm tired,' he stresses, resisting my tug. 'And I'm starving. How many times do I have to tell you, when I come home I want to forget about the fucking music business?'

I let go of his hand.

'I'm sorry, Toby,' I quickly apologize. 'I'm just

excited about the track. I thought you were into the idea of Eye Candy doing 'Beat Girl' so I dug it out of the attic and took it to the studio and Ady sampled it. We've worked really hard on it. It's practically ready to go. Just bung their voices on and voilà. Number one hit, guaranteed.' My wall of exuberance is a good defence. He sighs to release his tension and rubs his forehead.

'OK. I'm sorry I snapped. I just wanna eat. Is it too much to ask that you make sure there's some food in the house sometimes?'

'I know. I should've gone shopping,' I placate automatically. Then, annoyed with myself, I add, 'It's just that the time ran away with us. You know how it is.' This I say pointedly. It's his usual line for staying at work beyond the call of duty. My irritation rises as it transpires that he hasn't found out about Jesse after all. It means his level of anger is completely about me not being home when he got in and, worse than that, not having stocked the kitchen.

I get a pizza and garlic bread out of the freezer and shoo Toby into the lounge to get over it. I am outwardly calm but inside angry thoughts are brewing to boiling point in my mind.

Somewhere along the line our marriage has slipped into this. A silent deal. It all comes down to money. Because Toby is the one who makes the money he is the one with the power. Everything he does is Important. Because I make no money everything I do is meaningless. I have no power, no value. I have to justify my existence by catering to his wants and needs. I don't know how or when this situation settled, but it did. I have been automatically following this rule as though it is an instinct. It is, after all, a fair deal. Who could argue with it, reasonably? That's the awful thing. Lately I have not been proving my worth and it has disrupted the unspoken agreement, causing it to bubble up to both our surfaces in indignant, tetchy splatters. His are justified. I am not pulling my weight. Mine aren't, which makes me all the more indignant and tetchy.

Until today, that is. What I have done in the studio with Ady might make me a breadwinner for once. As far as I'm concerned, that puts me on an even playing field and I stand my ground. Internally, at least. Externally I am sticking to the rules and making Toby his dinner, but inside I am not backing down. This might be the arrangement we've come to, but I swear I never signed a deal like this in the first place. I just got married. I am seething with fury at myself. How did I ever let this happen to me? How did I not know that getting married would turn me into somebody's wife?

I feel such a fool I could cry. But the thought of my affair with Jesse somehow soothes and strengthens me. It is the one act that blows all the rules to smithereens. Sharing myself with someone else is not my part of the bargain and I have had no right to do it. Not when my existence is being paid for by Toby. But I did it anyway.

'Rock and roll!' I say to myself.

Actually, I say it out loud by mistake as I take the pizza in to the lounge to have in front of the TV.

'OK, put your little track on. Let's hear it,' Toby says, misinterpreting my remark as a hint that I want him to hear the track. I laugh to myself. *Patronizing idiot*, I think, taking care not to say it aloud.

I put the CD on, though. *I'll fucking show you. You think it's just a silly little amateur project that you can pat me on the head about and dismiss, but it isn't. It's going to save your skin and maybe then you'll get some respect back for me, you shit.*

The violence of my thoughts shocks me at the same time as making me so high I'm giddy. I am right, though. Toby stops tearing off pieces of pizza and sits up with his mouth hanging open and a piece of melted mozzarella descending to his T-shirt. I am cool about it.

'Beth, that's fucking great,' he says, genuinely impressed. I can see his mind racing behind his wide eyes with music biz calculations for getting it out as quickly as possible as Eye Candy's follow-up single.

'Yeah, I know,' I shrug in a *What's the big deal? Didn't you know I was good at this?* tone and carry on eating.

When it's finished he presses play again and, stuffing in a huge mouthful of pizza, wipes his hands on his jeans and opens his laptop.

'OK, who owns the publishing?' he barks at me as he starts tapping away.

'I don't know,' I say. 'But whoever it is is owed a few royalties off it already.'

'When was it written, though? With any luck it could be out of copyright by now.'

Typical Toby. He sorts out the dull stuff of timescales and budgets, and books the girls into the studio to do the vocals at their earliest free slot between promotions. First thing in the morning I have to shift the studio bookings around them, and bring in some proper singers for the overlay. Toby sorts out all the preparations and finally, exultantly, snaps his laptop shut for the night. Apart from one thing, that is. My role. Still buzzing from my rebellious, rule-breaking new self, I say, 'So, Tobes. What's my fee?'

'Hmn?' he says, grabbing a last piece of garlic bread and throwing himself back on the sofa.

'What do I get for my part in it? The idea, the arrangement, the production and engineering with Ady . . . my time. You know. What'll I be paid?'

Toby is stunned, but tries not to show it. I am smirking and trying not to show that.

'I mean, you're the expert, but wouldn't I be entitled to a fee? Or some points on the record for my role?'

'You want *points*?!'

'I don't know — wouldn't that be the usual thing?' I sound so innocent but I am not. I know damn well what the usual thing is. I don't know why my relationship with Toby is suddenly such a battleground, but I do know that victory is sweet. My moment of clarity in the kitchen about our relationship has been proved to be the truth. Toby is so used to me having no monetary value that in all his calculations — something he is vastly experienced in and has done every other day for over a decade — he has completely missed me out of the costs and the payroll. Even now he can't quite see why I would want money for doing this.

'Well, yes, but . . . I thought you just wanted to do it.'

I laugh reasonably. 'Well, yes, I did. But surely that doesn't stop me getting paid for it?'

'Yes, but, Beth! You're my wife! I thought you were doing it to help me out!'

'Well I was. I am. But why shouldn't I be paid as well? Everyone else is, aren't they? Anyway, what's it to you? Don't you want me to earn my own money?'

'Don't be ridiculous, it's not that. It's just — well, I'll have to look into it legally. Because you're my wife it might look suspicious if you're earning from it.'

'But, Toby!' I stand up. 'I've done the work! There's nothing suspicious about it! Ady's going to get his cut, isn't he? Everyone who works on it is going to get their cut, aren't they? You're going to get yours, aren't you? Fucking hell! Because I'm your wife I don't have the right to be paid for my work?!' I'm striding around the room, throwing my arms about and shouting.

'Beth, just calm down.' Toby stands up and puts his hands on my shoulders to get the equilibrium back. 'I didn't mean that. You've misunderstood. You're overreacting. Shush.'

'DON'T SHUSH ME!' I yell and fling his hands off me. 'Who the FUCK do you think you ARE?!'

We stare at each other in amazement.

'Beth, what is going on with you?' Toby almost looks scared, if he ever could. 'Where's all this coming from? I'm sorry, it was an oversight. I just assume we're in it together. We are, aren't we? The money I earn is for both of us. That's never been an issue. We have enough, don't we?'

'That's not the point,' I say, and turn and walk out. But I feel bad. It's true, Toby has never called his salary *his* money. He's never had a problem with the discrepancy between the wages we've brought in individually over the years, but then, why would he have? When his buys him the power. What he earns makes my contribution look like pocket money. He's even called it that at times.

'It's good that you've got a bit of your own pocket money,' he has said encouragingly in the past, when I've been apologetic about earning jack shit. I never said anything. Maybe that's the problem. It's certainly me that's got the problem with it, not him.

I get my cigarettes out of the cupboard and stand at the kitchen door smoking defiantly, out in the open.

Or maybe I'm looking for problems, to justify my affair with Jesse. It's easy to find a whole host of faults in an old relationship when you find a newer, perfect one. There's none of this build-up of crap in the foundations, piling in like so much junk in the basement, too much hassle to sort through so instead you just shut the door on it. There are no foundations. No relationship, really, not yet. It's just the moments when he and I are together, a connection of souls. It could never turn into something as soul-destroyingly practical as this. Not with the love, not with the music we make together.

I remember now. That's what I started out wanting. Not this.

I decide it is time to tell Toby about my affair. I don't want to stick to my side of the bargain any more.

39

Liza Doo

The comedown from the speed was awful. Disappointment rained down on us in sheets, until we were soaked to the bone. We got asked back to the usual venues we played, but we said we were taking a break while we got a singer sorted out.

Somehow, we never got one sorted out. We talked about how we would carry on, the rest of the group trying to encourage me to sing and me trying to encourage them to get another singer. We tried a couple of people, but there was nobody like Ava.

Despite the hopeful aspersions we cast to comfort each other — that her manager was just a sleazeball who wanted to get into her knickers — he actually got it together for her. Looking back it was in a very minor way, but at the time we thought she was going to make the big time. We'd bump into her sometimes posing around Portobello Road in shades and a fake fur.

They marketed her as a kind of mix between Yaz and Sade and her music was somewhere between the two as well. Slick, with lots of smarmy midi sax solos and Latin-jazz percussion. Her video was on TV once or twice, and she did a small European tour supporting

Animal Nightlife. She put us on the guest list at a couple of her gigs. We slagged her off to each other, but we were jealous really. You had to hand it to her. She was out there doing it and we weren't.

It wasn't that we didn't want to. But however much we wanted it we just couldn't seem to make it happen. We thought we could — we'd done it before, hadn't we? We'd created this incredible musical genie out of nothing but our own spirits rubbing together. But now, however much we tried to lift ourselves and each other up, something wasn't right. The magic had gone.

I guess it was a few things happening, or not happening, at the same time that held us down. Perhaps if the right singer had come along it would have panned out. Or if I'd felt I could be the singer. But I just couldn't. Whenever I thought about being on stage at a microphone I got palpitations that threw my heart out of its regular four-four timing into frenzied freeform jazz beats that were so wild I couldn't follow them. They made me break out into a nervous sweat that drenched my clothes and I was sometimes even sick or fainted.

I knew I'd be all right on stage if I was just playing guitar, behind someone else singing. It was the thought of being out there at the front I couldn't handle. I hardly slept, because when I did I had nightmares where the edge of the stage turned into a precipice and I took one step too far and toppled over it. I'd wake up with a huge lurching feeling in my stomach as I fell, knowing I was about to be eaten alive by whatever monsters were waiting hungrily at the bottom. It was the start of my affliction, my years of panic. At first it was just fronting a band with a big crowd watching me, perhaps not such an irrational fear. But then it became playing guitar in front of anyone, which affected the only life I'd known or wanted. Then it was doing anything with anyone watching me. Eyes upon me felt like darts.

Then it was playing at all, whether I was being watched or not.

Then it was anything unknown, until I submerged myself in Toby's life, for safety's sake.

★ ★ ★

The rest of the band's belief in me made my panic worse, though they didn't mean it to. My body reacted as violently against their sweet encouragement as if it were allergic to it.

Only Toby made me feel all right.

He had called me, as he'd said he would, and we arranged to meet in Holland Park. I was glad to get away for an afternoon from the flat and the others. Toby was waiting for me on the corner of Campden Hill in dog-tooth-check Sta-presseds and a turtleneck. I blushed as I approached, at the knowledge that he'd tried to impress me, making himself more Sixties-looking than usual. I felt shy, like it was a first date, although I wasn't sure if it was one or not.

We began to stroll into the park. Something about the atmosphere was different from the times we'd met before. Maybe it was just that it was daytime. There was a sad reality to the turning autumn leaves and the mist of rain, too fine for umbrellas. I had my corduroy cap on so I didn't have to worry about it ruining my hair. As we walked through the gardens I felt as though I'd come back down to earth from some other place entirely and was experiencing it for the first time.

We wound up at the cafe, where he bought cappuccinos. He had talked the whole way, apologizing for the fact we'd missed out on our record, as though it was his fault. He tried to make it up to me by saying he'd get us free recording time so that we were ready for Flipside's next new band release. Someone else taking the blame lifted the pain off me for a time, like medicine.

'It's OK, Toby,' I said, still trying to be a bit cool. 'We're taking a break anyway, until we find the right singer.'

He tried to encourage me to sing too, until he noticed me trembling and wiping away the perspiration on my lip.

'The DTs,' I said for a joke when I saw that he'd noticed. 'No, seriously. I'm just a bit hungover.' He smiled but his eyes kept piercing into me until I said, 'Toby, I really don't want to sing.'

All he said was, 'Cool.'

'I know I should,' I said, pre-empting the usual arguments I came up against — *go on, Liza, you can do it, you'll be great, please* . . . But they didn't come from Toby.

He just shrugged and said, 'Why should you if

you don't want to? If being a guitar hero's more your thing, then that's what you should be. You make a damn fine one. You're doing this because it's what you wanna do, right? That's the beauty of your band, what's special about it. I've never seen a band show so much passion for the music they're playing. The way you dress in the style too, and really know the right riffs and licks. It's fucking exciting. I didn't know girls ever felt like that about music, unless they've got a crush on one of the band or something. That's why I'm your number one fan. So what's the point of forcing yourself to play a part you don't want to?'

Toby let me off the hook. I was surprised, but the relief was enormous. I laughed.

'You just think I'm a crap singer,' I said.

'What are you *like*?!' he replied, rolling his eyes in mock exasperation. 'I don't actually,' he went on, seriously. 'Your voice is fine. And you look amazing. But that's not the important thing, is it? To be a front person, you've really got to want to be a front person.'

The way Toby says things has always made him sound like the voice of reason. He has a confidence in his opinion that makes it seem as though it is the absolute truth. What he said was what I wanted to hear at the time. He made it all right for me to be who I was, even if that wasn't the singer. And he still liked me that way. Toby liking me was the only thing that made me feel I hadn't fucked everything up.

When he asked me out again I said yes.

Being with him was like a holiday away from

myself. He took me to his flat, a studio in the basement of his parents' house on Holland Park Road. I realized he was a rich kid. He wasn't the sort of bloke I usually went for, posh, with a job. He'd even done his A-levels and some kind of course in business. It was all the stuff I usually found unforgivable.

But somehow I forgave Toby. He was sweet to me. He couldn't help his background. And his family were lovely, even if they were rich. They weren't bourgeois rich, anyway. None of his brothers and sisters had moved out of home, either. Why would you? When nothing you could find out there was better than what you already had. They came from old money. I don't really know what his mother and father did exactly. Whatever they wanted, I guess. They seemed to have been society bohemians, surfing the eras. In the Sixties they had expanded their minds and hung out with the London *set*. In the Seventies they'd gone 'self-sufficient' in a crumbling farmhouse in Cornwall, using the Holland Park place as a pied-à-terre when they needed to come up to town to buy rustic furnishings from Liberty. In the Eighties they went into property, their investments doubling and multiplying like bacteria. They made money look so easy to get. You just needed to have it in the first place.

His brothers and sisters thought I was the coolest thing they'd ever seen, and his mum said I reminded her of her youth and that I'd got the look exactly right. She loved telling me all her glamorous stories from the time. I loved hearing them too. Toby was proud of me, and somehow looking like a rock and roll chick and saying I played guitar in a rock and roll band was as good as actually playing. Better than playing, just then, the way I was feeling. His family were forever showing me off to the other people around their huge dining table. *Do you know Toby's girlfriend plays GUITAR in a BAND?! Isn't it MARVELLOUS?! We'd LOVE to come to one of your gigs, darling!* But they didn't really mind that there weren't any. They just seemed to take me as I was. They made me feel at home.

Toby and I became an item.

It was round about the same time that Billy dumped Vonnie. Flipside recorded and released 'Red Hot' and they got single of the week in *Melody Maker* and a half-page feature with an interview and a list of their tour dates. They went on the road as the headliners and got themselves a following for a while. Billy was the pin-up in the band, and Vonnie suffered at the news that he was going out with some up-and-coming actress he'd met when he'd been asked to model for a Vivienne Westwood show. Ruby heard rumours through her rockabilly grapevine of some rocking bird claiming Billy had got her up the duff. I was glad I wasn't the only one to blame any more for breaking Vonnie's heart.

She and Billy had some ugly scenes before it was finally over. Vonnie's finale was to turn up at one of his gigs, get backstage and stamp on his double bass with a stiletto, making a great cracking hole. He retaliated by bringing round a case with the last of her stuff from his flat and chucking it through her window. It was on fire at the time. Luckily we got in and smothered out the flames with the heaps of clothes all over the floor. They yelled a few choice names at each other before Billy screeched away in his new '65 Mustang convertible.

I didn't think a man would ever get to Vonnie, but then I didn't know there were men like Billy. There were a thousand guys who would've killed to go out with her, but she wasn't interested. No one was right after Billy and she never really got over him.

She changed.

She drank a lot in her room and when she went out it was mostly with Weasel, a dealer, who gave her an endless supply of free drugs. I don't know if she was sleeping with him, or if just having her around was payment enough. He would tell her stupid things that she would believe, like he was a psychic traveller and spiritual guru and had been her master in a former life. Weasel gave me the creeps. When he was in the house I felt uneasy, the way you do when you see rat droppings in a drawer or a cockroach scuttling under the skirting board.

Sometimes we got her to stay away from him and have a jam with us, and we had a real laugh again, and sometimes she got really hyper and over-excited about how it hadn't happened for us yet, but our turn was still out there.

And other times she would shout at us that we had ruined her chances and that she was too old now she was twenty-four. Sometimes she would get paranoid and keep asking everyone, 'Am I getting uglier?' or, 'Is my bum drooping?' Which on Vonnie was just a joke. She scoured magazines about how to keep looking young, and would lie around the flat with weird things like fish paste on the non-existent lines around her eyes. She would suddenly decide she had to have a baby, as someone had told her it would make her more beautiful. And then she would disappear round to Weasel's again, and we'd pray she wasn't doing something stupid like getting herself pregnant.

Vonnie began to let herself go. She started wearing the same saggy leggings all the time with a pale-pink top, which started looking grubby and collecting stains down the front that were still there when she next put it on. Her clothes had always been raggedy, but never dirty like this, and she had millions of clothes so she could have had something different to wear every day for six months before she had to wash anything. Her hair always looked greasy and the roots were nearly grown out so that her hair was practically brown, of all things. She even had bad breath, and her teeth looked like they had a kind of nasty grey film over them. When I first noticed a sweaty, charity-shop smell around her I thought I was imagining things, until Kim mentioned it. It was frightening, somehow, on someone who usually drove us mad spending about two hours in the bathroom every day.

'Maybe she really is going crazy,' Kim said when we talked about her sometimes. 'Maybe a shrink should have seen her after all.'

But I don't remember us taking it seriously. How would you know whether she was going crazy or not? She was just Vonnie. She'd always been crazy. And we couldn't seem to adjust to crazy being a bad thing. All the cool people went crazy, like Jim Morrison and Marilyn Monroe. It was a comforting thought. In a way it just made her more of a star.

We probably should have done more to help her. But somebody actually losing it was too real for us, more than we could handle. None of us was strong enough. I didn't want to be around it in case it took me down too, like a contagious virus. She became another tripwire for my panic attacks. So did my guitar leaning on its amp in my room. And my lyric book. And then the letters from the DHSS that started arriving saying I had to attend the Job Club.

Eventually the whole flat was a minefield, set up to get me.

I saw more and more of Toby, until I was staying round at his more nights than I stayed at home.

40

Beth

I leave the scribbled pages of my new lyrics out around the house for Toby to find. I can't bring myself to tell him about Jesse. There is never a right time. I hope he discovers the songs I've been writing about an older married woman falling in love with a younger man and puts two and two together himself. It is cowardly, but although I say the words over and over in my head — *Toby, I've got to tell you something. I'm having an affair* — it never comes out.

It is days before he actually picks up the lyrics and reads them. I have hung back at the studio deliberately although there's nothing left to do there, so that I am back later than him and he is kicking around the house on his own for a while. It is something he's not very good at, as though he is staying at someone else's house and doesn't know where everything is.

He is sitting on the piano stool, somewhere he never sits, with the lyrics in his hands. And although he is doing what I hoped he would, my heart lurches as I come through the door with the horror of being found out, as though I'd accidentally forgotten to hide them away.

'Who's this about?' he asks, simply, looking up. His face is scratched with pain. I begin to tremble. It has begun. I wish it hadn't. What was I thinking? Even now, unable to answer, I move over to look at the sheet Toby has in his hands. It is 'Bittersweet', my perfect song. It couldn't be more of a confession if it was one. It tells everything like it is, pure and simple. I was proud of it for that, getting the whole story into two verses and a chorus. I felt I'd finally achieved something in the way of the art of songwriting, without being too wordy or clichéd or trite.

'Is it Ady?' Toby asks, sparing me for a few more moments.

'Ady?!' I exclaim in relief. 'What?! No! Of course it's not Ady! I'm not having an affair with Ady!' I'm gabbling in an almost giggly, over-excited way.

'Who then?' asks Toby. His questions are unbearably to the point.

'It's just a song,' I say feebly.

'Then what made you write it?' he says. I fall silent and turn away.

'Come on, Beth,' he says. 'Songs like this don't come out of thin air. I know something's happened. Now it's been pointed out to me, it's obvious. I can see there's a change in you.'

'In what way?' I ask, still unable to say the words that I've written down.

'You just . . . ' Toby sighs and I hear him get up and move about. 'I don't know. You're full of life again. You look great. You're not fretting about silly things or . . . I should have noticed before how quiet and lifeless you'd got.'

I let the silence admit my guilt.

'Who is it, Beth? Who've you fallen in love with?'

I sit on the edge of the couch and look down at my hands, gripping each other for moral support.

'It's Jesse,' I finally say, in not much more than a whisper.

'Who?' I can feel Toby turn and look at me, suddenly incredulous, as though he hadn't been expecting me to admit an affair after all.

'Jesse,' I say again. 'The singer-songwriter we went to see.'

It dawns on Toby who I mean.

'That *kid*?!' he exclaims. Then he laughs. 'You're joking me!' he exclaims again, as though he's delighted. I'm confused by his response.

'No, I'm not,' I answer, indignant. I was prepared for a lot but not being laughed at.

'Ohh, I see!' he says, and sits down at the piano again, picking up my lyrics. He chuckles and shakes his head. 'I thought you were actually having a serious affair. I didn't realize you just had a big crush on a wannabe popstar! Oh, Beth!' he laughs. He starts to come over and teasingly make up with me, maturely accepting of the odd crush or two of his foolish wife on a young boy here and there as her youth passes and beauty fades. I see red.

'It *is* serious!' I shout, standing up before he can get to me. 'It's not just a crush. Don't patronize me!'

'OK,' Toby soothes me. He is getting used to my neurotic outbursts. I sit down again. Toby's reaction is fair enough. *I'd* want to believe it was just a crush, if it was the other way round.

'I'm sorry, Toby. And I know it seems

ridiculous, but it's true. I am having an affair with Jesse.'

My voice sounds strange. I feel like a bad actress delivering poorly written lines in a play. Our lounge is suddenly like one of the little fringe theatres I've been to see friends perform in, with its over-the-top chandelier and the long, faded red velvet drapes, and my co-star walking across the stage and sitting back down at the piano as though he'll break into a musical number.

'What do you mean by an affair?' he asks instead.

'What do you think I mean?' I reply. 'An affair. We've been seeing each other. I'm in love with him.'

'Seeing each other? What do you mean by that? Sleeping together?' Toby's voice is emotionless. I nod.

'And is he in love with you?' Toby asks.

'Yes,' I say. 'He is.' I can't believe my own confidence in this. But there is no doubt in my mind that he loves me.

'That kid we saw at Cassady's?'

'He's not a kid.'

'Well, OK, that young man who isn't a kid but is still probably young enough to be your son. Him?'

'Yes. Him.'

Toby blows out loudly as he tries to digest what I'm saying. 'Fuck,' he says in disbelief. Then, 'How long has it been going on?'

I find it hard to work out. I feel I have known him forever, but it can only be, what? A few months? Weeks, even.

'It's not been long, Toby. It's really recent.'

He takes it in, thinking back over the time to spot the clues. 'That night we went to see him? Were you seeing him then?'

'No! Christ, no,' I say. 'It was after then. Well, he'd invited me to do some music with him. That was before then. But we . . . fell in love after that. When we'd been working together. It just . . . happened.' I dare to look up at Toby. He looks completely baffled and rubs his face as if it will help it to sink in.

'I can't believe it,' he says shaking his head. 'Why are you telling me now?'

'What do you mean? Why does anyone tell their partner something like this? I have to. You're my husband and I've been unfaithful.' I find it is a strange thing for him to have asked.

'But are you telling me because you're leaving me for him? Is that what you're saying?' Toby's voice is rising. 'You're going to run off and shack up with this boy half your age that you've only just met? Do you realize how fucking stupid that sounds? Christ, Beth, this is real life! What are you doing — living out the lyrics of Killing Me Fucking Softly?'

'No, I'm not. And what's so stupid about it?' I snap back. 'That's so typical of you! You can't discuss anything with me as your equal. You have to put me down and call me stupid when I tell you something as serious as this! Our marriage is in trouble and I've fallen in love with someone else and all you can do is make sarcastic remarks.' I promptly burst into tears. It feels odd to be the one crying. I had expected it to be the other way round. Toby sits in silence until my tears subside. I go to get a tissue to blow my nose and when I come back he appears deep in thought. He looks heart-breakingly sad.

'Why, Beth?' he asks.

'What do you mean, why?'

'What made you need an affair? Haven't you been happy?'

I think about it and shake my head. 'No,' I reply, and break down in tears again. 'It's not you. It's me,' I add through the sniffs and winded breaths. I can't believe I've actually said it. *It just happened. It's not you, it's me.* I can only think in clichés. But sometimes clichés are clichés because they're true. In this case I know it's the absolute truth. 'I've not been able to hang on to myself somehow. Somewhere over the years I got lost and — '

'And this Jesse has helped to 'find' you?' Toby suggests.

'You can sneer as much as you like,' I flare. Hysteria is rising like a storm brewing, I can feel it. 'But yes, Jesse has helped me find myself again. Is that so laughable? That he makes me feel worth something? That he thinks I'm talented and beautiful and, and . . . lovable? Is that something to scoff at? Then go ahead. Have a good old laugh at your pathetic wife.'

This wasn't the way the scene had played in my head — Toby, collapsed in distraught tears, me sad and wise and kind, comforting him. Not shrieking like a harpy with snot all over my face.

'I'm not laughing,' says Toby. 'I'm just finding

399

it hard to take in, that's all.'

'Well, you seem to be coping pretty fucking well with it,' I scream, and suddenly chuck a heavy glass ashtray at his head. 'Maybe this'll help you react.'

Toby ducks and it crashes into the bookshelf behind him. I watch my body's actions from somewhere inside, as though I'm a pilot finally giving up trying to steer a rocket that is burning up, shooting off into the stratosphere. There's nothing I can do to regain control. I am aware of turning the coffee table over and sending a few more things through the air in the general direction of Toby, then grappling with him as he lurches towards me and wrestles my flailing limbs to the couch. I am hurling abuse at him but I don't know what I'm saying. I am eventually still and he trusts me enough to let go.

I struggle up and reach for the strewn contents of the weed box.

'I don't know if that's a good idea,' he offers cautiously, as I attempt to control my shaking hands enough to skin up. I fling the Rizlas down again and cry.

'I can't do *anything* round here,' I blurt, amidst the gulping sobs.

'It's OK, it's OK,' Toby says, rubbing my hunched back. 'I'll get you something.'

He comes back with some of the sleeping pills he sometimes resorts to and a glass of water, and although I hear myself shout at him, 'What are you, my fucking head doctor?' I gratefully put out my hand and throw two pills down my swollen throat.

We are both shaken. I sob some more. We don't speak. Toby keeps stroking my spine though, until I lean back, exhausted, on the couch. When the sedatives have taken over and put me on autopilot, Toby helps me to my feet and leads me upstairs to put me in bed.

'Toby, I'm really sorry,' I say, tears, fat with remorse, spilling down my cheeks.

'Don't,' he says, pulling the duvet around me. 'Get some sleep. We'll talk in the morning.'

★   ★   ★

I've no idea what time it is when I come to. Daylight is streaming through the gap in the curtains and Toby isn't there. Panic rises as I groggily struggle up, remembering what happened the night before. It is two in the afternoon. I swathe myself in my big bathrobe and head downstairs. I have a raging thirst. I am startled to see Toby sitting at the kitchen table. He smiles at me in a concerned way. My eyes prick with hot tears.

'Hey, come here,' he says kindly, pulling out a chair. 'I'll make some tea.'

I reach for the kitchen roll and hold a piece to my eyes.

'Why aren't you at work?' I ask as I sit down. I feel terrible. Making Toby take time off work seems like the worst thing imaginable.

'I wasn't going to leave you like this,' he says. 'It's OK. It's only a day off work. No big deal. I'm probably owed a few.'

'This is awful,' I say, while he boils the kettle

401

and puts teabags in mugs. Toby agrees. When he sits back down with the tea he takes my hands in his and prepares to say something. Oh God, no, I think. I don't know what about.

'Beth,' he starts. 'I'm worried about you.' I feel guiltier still.

'You don't have to worry about me,' I say. 'I'm fine. Well. As fine as I can be.'

'Well . . . I don't know if you are.'

'OK, so maybe I'm not at my best right now,' I try to joke. 'But it's not the happiest of circumstances. Having to tell your husband you're having an affair.'

Toby presses his lips together, looking at me.

'That's just it, Beth.' He wants to say something else, so I wait.

'You're not.'

'Not what?' I reply, confused.

'You're not having an affair.'

Toby is in denial. Or maybe I didn't explain properly.

'What are you on about?' I say. 'Haven't you listened to a word I've said?'

'Yes, I have. Now listen to me, Beth, please. Don't start again.'

I'm too fazed to start again anyway, so I let him go on.

'I . . . you . . . ' He takes a breath and tries again. 'I was up all night thinking about everything you told me. I just couldn't believe it.'

'I can't believe it myself right now,' I join in. 'It all seems so surreal.'

'It *is* surreal,' Toby nods. 'It just didn't seem to make sense. It's all happened so fast. I mean, we only saw him play last week. And you said it was after then. But you were talking as though you've been . . . with him . . . for way longer than that. I mean, even if you'd seen him every day since then, which I know you haven't — how could you have fallen so seriously in love?'

It is my turn to be incredulous. Only last week? It can't have been! I open my mouth to answer and he holds up his hand to stop me.

'Beth, I called Jesse,' he says quickly.

'You what?' I reply, horrified.

'I called Jesse. He doesn't know you.'

I flush through with heat, though I'm too synthetically calm for anger to erupt. 'You did what?! How dare you humiliate me like that? That's so typical of you. Thinking you have the right to take control of everything. And what do you mean, he doesn't know me? Of course he knows me! He gave me the demo, I saw him play — *we* saw him play together, for God's sake — you've *seen* that he knows me!'

'Just let me finish, Beth,' he says. 'I mean beyond that. Jesse doesn't know you beyond that.' He emphasizes his words with a squeeze of my hands. I pull mine away and sit back.

'Well, of course he'd say that,' I retort. 'He's bound to deny it. For my sake.'

'He didn't deny anything.' Toby is exasperated with trying to get through to me. 'There's nothing for him to deny.'

'Toby, will you listen to me — ?'

'No,' Toby interrupts urgently. 'You listen to me. I called Jesse. I didn't accuse him of anything, I didn't humiliate you . . . I called him with the number off his demo and told him who I was, that I'd come to see him play, and that I'd said I'd call him. He remembered who I was, and was really chuffed I'd phoned, and . . . ' Toby pauses. 'He didn't react like someone who was screwing my wife, Beth.' He says it quietly, almost as though he doesn't want to say it.

I sit, frozen. I can't comprehend what I'm hearing. Toby goes on.

'We chatted for a bit about what he's doing, what his plans are. I asked if he was working with any other musicians, thinking about getting a band together . . . he said no, he's only ever been solo. Does he write with anyone else? No. Would he like to? No. He didn't sound in the least bit guilty, or . . . ' He stops for a while, waiting for me to say something.

'I can't believe this,' I say.

'Which bit?' he asks.

'That you can't believe anyone would have an affair with me, that you have the *nerve* to check up on me as though I'm some compulsive liar. Why would I make this up, for Christ's sake? And anyway, nothing you've said proves anything. I mean, what did you expect him to say? *Oh, hi — love fucking your wife, by the way?*'

Toby keeps calm. 'Look, I don't know what's going on here,' he replies. 'But I don't believe that boy would be so at ease with me if he was having a thing with you. He just doesn't have the guile. Even when I mentioned you — '

'You mentioned me? What the fuck did you say about me?'

'I just said my wife thinks you're great and that I should sign you up immediately.'

My heart is in my mouth. 'What did he say?' I ask.

'He said thanks. That's nice.'

'That's nice?!' I reply. I push my hands through my hair. A laugh escapes me like a bark. 'This is ridiculous. Absolutely fucking ridiculous.'

'You don't have to tell me that,' Toby responds. 'What is going on with you?'

'I *told* you,' I finally snap. 'I don't know what you're trying to do to me here, but look. Crazy as this is, I'm obviously going to have to *prove* to you that I'm having an affair. If you'd rather fool yourself by reading what you want into what Jesse said, when he was only trying to protect me, than believe your own wife, here . . . ' I reach for my mobile phone and turn it on. 'You want to see evidence? I'll show you some of his texts. Most husbands would want to be spared the details, but hey.' I impatiently tap through until I get to my inbox.

'Beth, don't do this,' Toby says quietly. I scroll through a couple of old ones from Ady and Kim. One from Toby a few days ago saying he was working late. There are no more.

'Bollocks,' I snap in annoyance. 'I've deleted them. Or maybe you did,' I add. I try and find Jesse's number in my addresses, but that's gone too.

'Just stop it,' Toby tries again.

'No, no, no. You obviously don't believe a word I say, so I'll just have to show you.' I scrape my chair back and march through to the sitting room for copies of Jesse's recent tracks and the stuff we've done together. I can only find the original demo he brought round to the house in the first place, out by the phone from when Toby got his number and called him. I rifle through my sheets of new songs, but none of them are in Jesse's writing, only mine.

'I was sure I brought some of his back with me,' I say crossly as I check through piles of CDs and drawers while Toby stands back in the door frame.

'Beth, stop,' he tries again. 'You don't need to prove it. *Just* talk to me, please.'

'OK, well, they're not here,' I go on. 'They must all be at *Jesse's*. But look, I'll play you some of his stuff on the piano.'

I sit and open the lid of the baby grand and begin to play our new music, anxiety at first driving my fingers to run a little too fast and land a little too loudly. Toby moves as if to come and stop me, but then hangs back listening. I have played so much recently that my hands soon find their rhythm and flow easily over the keys. I give a running commentary over the top, to show what Jesse's guitar parts do and what lines he is singing while I'm doing the harmony. When I've skipped through a kind of medley of Jesse's songs I suddenly stop and sigh.

'I didn't know you could play like that,' says Toby, sounding genuinely amazed.

'There's a lot you don't know about me,' I say back. I feel my shoulders collapse down despondently. 'All right,' I go on. 'I know it

406

doesn't prove anything, but why can't you just believe me?' I feel like a little girl as I look up at Toby's frame approaching and looming over me.

'Let's just talk about it,' he says, putting a hand on my shoulder. 'We can work through it. It doesn't matter. One way or the other. That's what I've been trying to say.'

'But it *does* matter. It matters to me. I matter. That's what *I'm* trying to say.'

I slam the piano lid down and go to the window.

'*I know!*' I swing round excitedly. 'I'd been with him when you got back from Japan! Remember? I got in late. I'd been to see him play by myself, as you weren't here. It was when I first got to know him. We didn't do anything, but I stayed the night at his place after the gig. Wait right there!'

I run upstairs and rummage through my jumper drawer for the pullover he lent me. I keep it at the back of the drawer, unwashed, so that I can smell it sometimes. I dash back downstairs with it.

'This is his jumper!' I hold it out triumphantly. 'He let me wear it home because it was cold that day. See?'

Toby comes nearer to inspect it, touches it around the V neck briefly and turns away painfully. 'If that's got a spliff burn in the cuff of the left sleeve . . . ' he says, 'it's mine.'

I don't want to look for it, but I do.

It's there.

41

Liza Doo

I guess the thing that finally broke us up — physically separating us and forcing us to live our own lives as though we weren't the limbs of a shared being after all — was getting notice from the housing association. We had a month left of our tenancy. It was only a short-life flat, which was why it was cheap. They put tenants like us in empty dilapidated flats to stop squatters getting in, until the proper housing associations or the council got round to doing them up.

They were finally doing up the block and selling the flats on the private market to get some money in. They couldn't guarantee we could be rehoused in Notting Hill, but they still had lots of flats further out, in Shepherd's Bush and Acton. They said they'd try and rehouse us together.

'It's fucking miles out,' moaned Vonnie in disgust. 'I'm not fucking living out there again.'

She started hassling the housing association she'd had her name down on since she was first living in London, and after turning up at their offices day in, day out, they finally offered her the attic studio on Lancaster Road. She was thrilled with it, and we saw something of the old

Vonnie return. She could have it forever if she wanted, and although we were all jealous we were glad for her too. Secretly we were all relieved that she had her own place and we no longer had the responsibility for the way she was. She would be all right, in a fantastic flat like that. We helped her decorate and move in.

Out of the rest of us, only Kim and I were officially down on the short-life and they offered us a two-bedroom flat with a three-month lease on an estate near North Acton tube. Ruby and Nick came with us when we went to see it, hoping there would be room for them too. There wasn't, really. The sitting room and kitchen were all in one and the bedrooms were too small to share. North Acton was a dump. It wasn't a place really, just somewhere a triple carriageway sliced through to carry traffic in and out of somewhere better.

We tried not to get depressed, and went to see Uncle Jim at the short-life to get him to show us something else. It was great when you got Uncle Jim. He was a soft old lefty who still wore long hair and sandals, and could never resist a crying girl with a sob story. He'd been paying for our rehearsals for years after Vonnie told him we couldn't afford the electricity bills. He let us see whatever other places he had on the books, sneaking Ruby's and Nick's names into our manila file.

We finally accepted a second-floor flat in a converted terrace on Hammersmith Grove. It was still a two-bedroom, but it had plenty of space, with high ceilings and big windows and a

409

vast sitting room. The kitchen was off the sitting room, but you could shut the door on it and Ruby and Nick said they didn't mind the fact that people had to walk through their room. A pair of suede-headed dykes from the flat downstairs — one dark, one bleached, in ripped jeans and T-shirts — banged on the door to say hello. We liked the look of each other. When we told them all four of us were hoping to live there, they invited us into theirs to see the boxroom they had going spare.

'I'll take it,' said Nick, and hung back with them while we went back upstairs to sort out rooms. I made Kim take the best bedroom that had a window you could climb out of onto a titchy balcony. Kim loved that sort of thing. I stood in the other room for a while and tried to picture my stuff there. It was a nice room too, with a happy feeling, but I just couldn't imagine myself into it. In the end I went through to the sitting room, where Ruby and Kim were planning how to lay it out and separate off a kind of corridor to the kitchen with curtains strung up so Ruby had more privacy. They both seemed pleased, excited even.

'Why don't you have the other bedroom, Ruby?' I said.

She said she would be fine in the sitting room and tried to refuse, until I said, 'It makes sense. I mean, I'm the one who won't be here much now I stay at Toby's. It means you can use this as a sitting room as well when I'm not here, if I keep my stuff down that end. If I put my bed here against the wall you can use it like a couch.'

410

Although she tried to argue for a bit, I knew they could see it was a good idea. There was a floor-to-ceiling inbuilt cupboard in the alcove that would fit most of my stuff, and I'd got a screen at the market I could put my clothes rail behind. I could see myself better in this room, with my things packed away and me here only some of the time. All the little bits and pieces of Fifties furniture I'd picked up from the market — a pair of bucket chairs, a kidney-shaped table with black metal legs and coloured blobs on the ends, a treble clef magazine rack — would be great in a sitting room.

'It would be better for rehearsing, if it's not someone's bedroom all the time,' said Kim, and we agreed and that sealed it. I remember thinking that my guitar leaning against my amp would look great just as an ornament in the room, even if it was never used.

We were all happy when we headed home.

42

Beth

'This is too weird,' I cry as Toby tries to comfort me. 'I'm not going mad, I swear. I don't understand this.'

I hate myself for falling into our usual ways of dealing with things — me behaving like an adolescent and Toby like a dad. At the same time I want Toby to be my dad. It does comfort me. I hate myself more.

'You're just not very well, Beth. You're totally strung out. Stop upsetting yourself and try and accept that you need to rest and get better. Then we can talk it all through.'

'You're treating me like a mental patient,' I wail. 'What are you going to do, get the men in white coats round and put me in a straitjacket and cart me off to some loony bin?'

I feel smothered by Toby's hug and break free from it. I can't stand this. I run upstairs and throw some clothes on, and run back down again.

'Where are you going?' Toby tries to stop me, but I am too quick, too desperate.

'I've got to see Jesse,' I shout, hurtling out the front door. I hear Toby shout after me as I run up the street but I have to get away. I head towards the tube station, half aware of passers-by worriedly moving out of my way.

'It's all right, I'm not a mugger — that's my wife,' I hear Toby cry when somebody challenges him.

At the tube I am stopped by the turnstiles. I don't have my card on me. I try to open the gate at the side for people with luggage and pushchairs but a large official stops me. I pretend to look for my ticket.

'It's on me somewhere,' I gasp, breathless, but he isn't having any of it. I have to go back to the ticket office and the ticket man asks where I want to go.

I stare at him. My mind is blank. I don't know.

Toby catches me up as I'm frantically searching the tube map for inspiration.

'I've forgotten which tube stop he is, that's all,' I say as Toby approaches, before he can say anything.

'Please come home, Beth. You're going to get me arrested in a minute.'

But I am too overwrought to listen to sense. 'It's Kentish Town. Or is it Tufnell Park?' I turn on Toby. 'This is all your fault. You're doing it deliberately. You've got me in such a state I can't think straight. I've been going there practically every day — '

'Come on, why don't you calm down, come back home, check out the address on his demo — '

'You just don't want me to see him. You want to lock me away. If I go home you'll never let me out.'

We've never been ones for scenes, let alone in

public, and Toby is embarrassed as people hover around to watch.

'I promise I won't. If you need to see him then you must. Come home, get the address, and then call a cab or something to get over there. Just please don't go running around on the underground in this state when you don't know where you're going.'

I feel myself prickling with the stares on me, and let Toby gently take me by the elbow and steer me home.

There is no address on his demo. Only his phone number.

'Why don't you call him?' Toby suggests quietly, in a helpful rather than confrontational way. It is strange that I haven't thought to do so. But I shake my head. I don't want his voice in my ear, sounding like a voice in my head. I want to be able to see him, touch him, hold him. I want the real thing.

'I can't,' I reply. 'I'm in too much of a mess. Just let me get myself together.'

Toby makes toast and forces me to eat it.

'I know where he lives,' I insist. 'I can picture the street so perfectly, but I just can't get the name of it. Something's happened to my head. What were those pills you gave me last night anyway?'

'Beth — ' Toby tries to interrupt, but I don't let him.

'I can't remember the number but it's a red door. I'm sure it's a red door. He lives in an attic room in a terrace. It's a quiet little street off that really busy road — oh, what's it called? Is it

414

Camden Road? Or Holloway Road? One of those. If I could just get to a bit I recognize I could find my way from there.'

'OK then.' Toby seems to decide something. 'Let me give you a lift. We'll go there and drive around until we find it.'

'We? Why would you want to do that?' I ask warily.

'It's all right, Beth. When we find his house you can go and see him and I'll come home. I can see it's something you have to do.'

Even through my suspicion, I can see that he is being genuinely kind. Taking charge of everything as usual, yes, but that's Toby. I can't blame him for being himself. Not when it's always been something I've accepted, and wanted from him.

He ushers me into the car and slides into the driving seat, glancing at me with a watchful eye, like a smart, friendly detective trying to get to the bottom of a mystery with the help of an insane witness.

He chats normally as he drives, as if this is a perfectly reasonable search for someone whose address we've lost that we really need to speak to. It is soothing, but it's creeping me out too. Is he nice, or sinister? I can't tell. Maybe he really is going to get me sectioned.

We come into Kentish Town past the old Town and Country Club, where we played once in our heyday and I got off with a guy in a Brian Jones mop top and purple velvet jacket. He wouldn't take off his shades until we were back at his pad in the soft glow of his orange lava lamp. Things

415

begin to look familiar.

'It's that way!' I lean forward excitedly. 'Take the next left.'

Toby drives us through the residential streets behind the main drag as I direct him left or right. We finally crawl down a street that looks right, and we watch out either side for a red door. I see it. I peer up to the roof but can't see Jesse's window from here. I am nervous.

'Do you want me to wait just until you know he's in?' Toby asks. He seems nervous too.

'No, you go. I can get home from here. I know where I am.' We look at each other sadly.

'We'll have a proper talk when you get in,' Toby says, adding, 'Beth? Just don't do anything . . . rash. All right?'

I don't know what he means, but I nod. I get out of the car. He drives on as I reach the door. There are no separate bells for flats, only a knocker. I knock.

I hear someone coming to the front door and smooth my hair expectantly. A young studenty-looking guy opens it.

'Yeah?' he asks.

'I'm looking for Jesse,' I say.

'Jesse?' he asks, quizzically.

'Top-floor flat?' I say.

'Oh, right.' He holds the door open for me and shuffles back to his room. I start up the stairs nervously, but as I climb the hope of reaching Jesse makes me begin to race, stumbling blindly. I just need to get to him, have his arms around me, and everything will be all right. I bash on the top flat door. There is no reply. I keep bashing.

Eventually, somebody opens the door of the flat below and peers up.

'I don't think there's anyone there, love,' he says.

I ignore the sarcasm and lean over the banister, grateful for any response. 'D'you know where he's gone? When he'll be back?' I ask desperately.

'Who?' he asks.

'Jesse.'

'Jesse? I don't know any Jesse. I think the last guy moved out. I haven't seen him for a while.'

'But he can't have!' I insist. 'I was here just the other day. With Jesse. Don't you know Jesse? Short, dark hair? A musician?'

The guy looks at me, shaking his head. 'I think I would have heard a bloody musician up there.'

I stare at him. He shrugs. 'Have you got the right house? There's a few student lets along this road. Why don't you try them?'

He goes back into his flat and I hear him laugh with someone. I stand looking round, trying to recall definite things but I can't. Wasn't this where the bathroom was? Maybe the guy's right. Maybe I've got the wrong flat. I descend the stairs and leave the house. I walk along the road checking for another red door, and then try a few of the other streets. There are a couple of red doors, but I have begun to doubt my memory. Maybe it was a brown door. Or this black one. I can't face knocking on any of them, in case I'm wrong again.

I stop being able to see the houses when the tears blur my vision, and I stop bothering to look. A car slows down beside me and its door opens. Toby leans across.

'Come home,' he says. I crumple into the car and Toby drives. I am beyond humiliation, sobbing freely all the way.

★ ★ ★

Toby runs me a hot bath and makes me go to bed for a sleep. He makes a surprisingly good nurse, bringing me fresh towels and drinks and tablets.

'This is mad. I don't understand where he's gone,' I keep saying between sobs, or variations of it, over and over.

'I know. Don't try to. Just get some rest now. We'll work it all out,' he replies, in his newfound therapist voice.

Somehow I do sleep. I am roused by Toby turning on the bedside light. He is holding the phone. For a wild moment I think it must be Jesse, but then Toby says, 'It's Kim for you. I said you were sleeping but she said she really had to talk to you.'

He hands me the phone and I say, as brightly as I can, 'Hi, Kim. How are you?'

'Um . . . ' she says, in a bunged-up, cracking voice. 'I'm afraid I've got some bad news.'

43

Liza Doo

Our change of address gave us a reprieve from the DHSS. We had a few months before they started to hassle us again about jobs, or rather our lack of them. They started calling us Job Seekers instead of the Unemployed and made us take proof of what jobs we'd applied for every time we signed on. At first they tolerated you saying you were an out-of-work musician, but they soon tired of it and said you had to apply for any old job. You could make it up to an extent, but it became almost as bad as a job itself, having to write a new load of fake letters and responses each fortnight. They had to get their unemployment figures down. The golden age was over.

Ruby and Kim found a smart way round it and went on the Enterprise Allowance, a scheme the Government introduced so they could call you Self-employed instead of a Job Seeker. They started their own 'business' as a freelance brass section, hiring themselves out for gigs and recording sessions. They had a card made up calling themselves the Bra Section and pinned it to lots of studio noticeboards. They did get a bit of work through it, but the main thing was the dole office left them alone for a whole year.

Kim got friendly with three skinny Mancunian lads she met at a studio, who weren't in a band as I knew it, but all stood around playing keyboards linked to computers and decks. They sampled some of her saxophone riffs and repeated them over their trippy, hypnotic dance music. There was a new club scene sparking up in Manchester and Kim started going up there at weekends to all-night raves in clubs and fields and old warehouses. She tried to get us into it, saying it was like discovering a whole new world where everything was fantastic. All you wanted to do was dance and love each other. There was a new drug too, that kept you going all night. I never went. I'd got to the stage with my new boyfriend where I'd slotted into his life, and didn't really think about doing separate things with my own friends any more.

After a while Kim started going out with a bloke called Boz, a DJ on the scene. I don't know what she saw in him, but she wasted a good part of her youth on him until he accidentally became the father of her child — a lot more than he ever should have been.

Ruby's life carried on as it always had. She kept on rocking, jiving at rockabilly clubs at the weekends with her rockabilly friends and dating rockabilly guys.

Nick seemed happy with the new gang of friends she met through living with the dykes downstairs. She finally tired of waiting for Loose to get it together and started drumming for a female heavy rock band from Birmingham that one of the dykes knew, called Ace of Spades. She learnt to drive and got a van, so she could rattle her way up the M1 for gigs, like the real thing instead of just a girl who played drums a bit.

I stayed at the flat in Hammersmith even less than I imagined I would. Mostly I went round to pick up more clothes, or make it feel as though I had something to do when Toby was busy. We jammed when I was round and sometimes talked about playing a gig, but it never went further than the talking about it. I had trouble controlling my panic whenever I wasn't at Toby's. Sitting on the bus or the tube as I headed over to the flat or to sign on I learnt how to live with my fears. I hid them well behind eyeliner and under hairdos and sharp clothes.

Toby's mum rescued me just in the nick of time, before I was due to begin my sentence at the Job Club. One of her friends had started her own fashion design company, Subculture, and she'd opened a stall in Hyper Hyper. She needed someone to work on the stall and Toby's mum thought I'd be *perfect, darling*. I signed off. It was just a walk through the park to get to Kensington from Toby's place, and it helped to calm my nerves every morning. It made sense to stay at his every night instead of Hammersmith. Toby got an A&R job at Virgin Records. We could set off for work at the same time, in the same direction. Getting up with him and leaving the flat together helped to ease me into normal life.

I saw Vonnie less and less. We visited her a lot to start with, she being the only one left who had a place you could drop in on when you went round the market. But then, going round the market somehow stopped being something you had to do every week, or every fortnight, or even every month.

The last time I remember talking to her I was embarrassed instead of proud to know her. I spotted her from a distance prancing along Golborne Road in falling-apart plimsolls, swamped in a luxurious fur coat so that she looked like a little girl dressed up in her mum's clothes. From that distance her face was a pure white heart with jet black slashes for eyes and a red rose for a mouth. She looked incredible.

But as she got close I could see her large sensual mouth was actually lipstick painted so it overlapped her lips onto her face, and her eyeliner was drawn too thick and wobbled and bled as it travelled over her lines. You could see the broken blood vessels around her nose that she had tried to cover up with powder, probably in the false, dusky light of her un-drawn curtains, which were just a bit of material pinned on the window frame that you couldn't draw anyway. She looked older than she really was. For a split second it crossed my mind to pretend I hadn't seen her. But I didn't want Toby to know that was something I could do.

When I asked, 'How are you?' she said, 'Suicidal.' Even when she looked the way she did Vonnie still managed to make *suicidal* sound like a cool thing to be. She said it lightly, with a shrug and a smile, but when I looked into her eyes she seemed two thousand light years away.

'There's no answer to that,' Toby joked out of awkwardness once she had passed, and we tried to laugh it off, but it wasn't funny really. Not when I think of it now. I told Kim and we wondered what we should do about it, but that was as far as any help I offered went. Kim did more, going round to help tidy up the mess in her flat and cooking her meals, but she usually got them thrown back at her with a curse or two.

It went back to the way it was to begin with, me hearing all about her when I met up with Kim. Only it wasn't so great any more, hearing about all the crazy things Vonnie said and did. Instead of hanging on her every word in wonder I had to steel myself to listen. I thought of it as my punishment, having to know and feel the horror that Being Vonnie had become. I deserved to lie awake at nights sweating as I replayed the increasingly nightmarish images Kim's tales had projected into my mind: the squalor she lived in that she wouldn't let Kim touch, the druggies and weirdos that were always around whose freakish beliefs and influence she valued far more than her own sister's attempts to help. The shrine of peculiar artefacts she began to obsessively mumble at, the occult voices she didn't understand why Kim couldn't hear. The superstitious rituals she had to go through or something terrible would happen: backwards down the staircase, three times round the lamp post, every step retraced exactly, over and over, so it sometimes took all day just to get home again from the shops.

The voodoo dolls were the worst thing, for Kim. They gave her such a fright when she opened the cupboard under the sink that she couldn't go back to Vonnie's for a long, long time. She thought one doll was Billy for sure. She thought one might have been Ava. She wouldn't tell me about the other one.

Patti and Jeff had to take over and they somehow managed to get Vonnie into hospital. When she came out they tried to keep her home with them, but she wouldn't stay. She was given tablets to help her and they did for a while, and there were a few more times along the way when the old Vonnie returned, triumphant.

As the area became more and more gentrified it seemed to sometimes take Vonnie up with it. She went out with some aristo's son for a while, who'd bought up the whole house opposite and converted it back from flats, and who thought he was oh-so-bohemian to go out with such a bass-wielding, stiletto-wearing, Grove-wise chick who knew all the dealers. He got her into modelling for a fetish-wear company and she was in a spread in a magazine published by one of his toff mates.

A wannabe filmmaker saw it and cast her in his short film as a hooker. There was a screening at the Electric and we thought she was going to make it after all.

But somehow she never did. She survived the ongoing years as best she could with her personality splitting into two halves and battling with each other — sometimes glamorous and starry, sometimes seedy and falling apart, a bit like Ladbroke Grove itself.

★ ★ ★

As for Ava, we stopped seeing her around. I guess she moved on. She had a couple of singles out. They didn't get in the top forty, but I've seen them from time to time in the boxes of records in charity shops. Her first single has a picture cover to launch her career — a photo of her posed on a lurid Eighties-bright background, her permed hair with Whitney Houston blonde highlights up in a pink bow, big hoop earrings, long white gloves and high heels, a black 'body' and, what do you know? A polka-dot ra-ra skirt.

It didn't get her as far as she'd have liked, but at least it got her further than us.

44

Beth

Jesse never comes to me again. I hope he'll suddenly appear when I am at my mum's house, that he'll somehow track me down and prove himself true, like heroes and knights and princes are meant to do, but he doesn't.

I still can't figure it out. I have come here to convalesce after my whatever-you-call-it. Nervous breakdown, I suppose. In other times I may have been thought to be possessed by demons and burnt at the stake, or hysterical and given a lobotomy or had my clitoris cut out. I should be thankful for that, at least.

I am in my old single bed in a tiny room up the few stairs above the kitchen to the eaves of the bungalow. Even though I have never lived here Mum calls it my room, and has decorated it with the things I had as a little girl. My old dolls are arranged in my kiddie chair in the corner, and my old drawings, poems, piano certificates and photographs of me in pigtails are hanging in frames on the walls. I have always thought her silly for keeping my childhood things, but now I am comforted by them around me, however sentimental that is.

Each morning I am woken by a shadow stealing into the room and my first thought is always that it is Jesse. But it never is. It is Mum, bringing me a cup of tea and moving to the window to draw my curtains and give me her daily brisk, cheery weather report.

Then she leaves and I sit up in bed with my knees drawn up and my hands around my mug of tea and weep, for the goodbyes I have to say. The images of everything that's happened replay in my mind like old cine film. The pictures of the awful things are sad enough, but it's the happy faces that are the most painful to watch. I just can't stop them floating into my vision, in agonizing slow motion. Vonnie, no more than a precocious fresh-faced kid, winks and smiles at me as she dances and strips. Just a teenager, with it all still ahead of her, she stalks down the Portobello Road like its queen, only stopping to throw back her golden head and guffaw like a drain. As a full-blown woman, posing with her bass, she soaks up her applause, turning to grin at me across the stage, the world at our feet.

And Jesse. Jesse waiting with a shy smile as I open my front door. His eyes finding mine as he leans into the mic and sings the words 'I Met Someone' to me, across the crowd. Turning around, just as I am about to pass him by after he's played, with the smile that let me in, the moment I thought was the beginning of us. The moment that I don't even know actually happened, even though it is so vivid and real I feel I could reach out and touch him even now.

And then Toby, with his anxious please-be-all-right grin waving to me from the platform, the moment that definitely did happen.

Toby has been sweet. As he put me on the train at Paddington he held me tightly on the platform for a long time and said, 'I'm so sorry I didn't see what you were going through. That I wasn't there for you. But it'll be all right now, I promise. I understand why you . . . needed Jesse. I love you. I always will.'

'I feel such a fool,' I say in a small voice, to the platform.

'Well, don't,' Toby says, squeezing my arm and lifting my trembling chin. 'There's nothing foolish about needing someone. I wasn't there. I'm the fool for letting you nearly slip away.'

As the whistle blew he lifted me into the train and shut the door.

'I'll miss you,' he said as I pushed down the window to kiss him goodbye. 'Get better. Don't worry about anything. And come home soon.'

He walked along the platform as the train pulled out of the station, and even broke into a run as the train gathered speed, until the platform ended. It was romantic, for him. He wasn't usually given to such displays of emotion. We watched each other until we disappeared out of each other's view.

I sat on the train, numb and dark and hollow, the way I had been ever since I got the news about Vonnie. It was as though a part of me died as well. Toby said I didn't speak that whole night, or the following day, or the night after that, whatever he said to me, even when he shook me. I didn't sleep or cry or eat or do anything apart from get up automatically to pee. I was glazed over, he said, like a cast of myself.

He was frightened and called the doctor, who gave me an examination and an injection of something, which made tears push out through my eyes. I slept for the morning then, and when I woke up I was back to my old self, or one of them. Not the hysterical shrieking one, or the silent, far-away one, but someone somewhere in between that he recognized as me.

Toby had had to go back to work after a while to try and sort out the Eye Candy disaster. He tried to make me go and stay with his mum. But I surprised myself, suddenly knowing the only place I felt I could be. It was my mum I wanted.

Maybe she could tell me how you were supposed to carry on with real life when it didn't turn out the way you dreamed it would.

* * *

Mum doesn't mention my red-rimmed eyes when I shuffle down in my old flowery-print dressing gown. It's funny, I quite like it now, although of course I refused to wear it when she bought it for me for my thirteenth birthday. Then it was embarrassing and hopelessly out of touch. Now I appreciate the fine quality of the cotton and the delicacy of the print, in spite of, or maybe because of, being old and faded. I can see how lovely it would have looked on the girl with the soft, long hair in the photographs. I can see what she was getting at, with her pastel flowers and broderie anglaise. I would probably want to dress my daughter in this sweet, old-fashioned style that makes you think of innocence and soft-focus summer days and bare feet in the grass. I wish I had been the kind of thirteen-year-old girl who would have worn that kind of thing, who would have slipped easily into adolescence and Laura Ashley dresses both.

She is making porridge and French toast for breakfast. She thinks I'm too thin.

I sit in the rocking chair by the stove. I find myself admiring her taste as I rock gently, looking round. It is as though I've never really noticed it before, on any of my brief, dutiful visits. She has decorated the bungalow in a comfortable, higgledy-piggledy sort of way that is peculiarly stylish. It is a house that welcomes light with Mediterranean hospitality, with windows at every opportunity for it to stroll through whenever it likes. As it touches Nana's heavy dark furniture it brings out a conker sheen on the wood, so that sideboards and bookshelves no longer loom, gloomy and depressive, as they did around my chidlhood home. Mum has woven glints of her colourful patchwork and tapestry through the rooms, which give the place an artisan feel. The seaside has also seeped in — walls and floors the colour of sand and vanilla ice-cream with splashes of sea-greens and blues in the woodwork. Driftwood and pebbles and seashells collected from the beach sit comfortably amongst old china and glass ornaments on windowsills and mantelpieces. A tabby cat with markings like a rippled beach winds itself through Mum's legs as she puts the kettle on the stove to boil.

The kitchen door is open, letting in the sea air

and the sound of gulls calling as they swerve around the cliff tops in the distance. Mum has made me come for long hikes along them every day, insisting it will soon bring some colour to my pallid cheeks. She doesn't know all of what's happened, and presumes it's just the news about Vonnie that has upset me. Maybe she is right. Maybe it was the trawl through her belongings after her overdose that raked up the past and sent my mind spiralling out of control. It's been a freaky time, not knowing these past few weeks whether she would pull through and come round and be Vonnie again, or finally give up.

'I should've been more attentive,' Toby said, in the first of our long nightly chats over the phone, my mum tactfully leaving the sitting room and closing the door behind her to busy herself elsewhere. 'I know you well enough to realize the way you cope with difficult things is to disappear off somewhere inside. I should've come looking for you. I've been a self-centred arsehole. I should've known it would have affected you badly. Even though you never saw her any more, I felt you never really got over your strange connection with Vonnie.'

I feel the tears well up again. She had so much life in her, more than anyone, and it's hard to accept she would simply let go like that, without a proper Vonnie fight. I guess hers was never a spirit that was meant to grow old. It was always too big to be contained by an ageing body. I try to find comfort in the thought that her spirit is free now, forever young and wreaking havoc where it pleases.

431

Mum notices me wipe my eyes again, and pats my shoulder briskly before carrying two steaming earthenware bowls to the wrought-iron table on the patio outside the kitchen door.

'Come and sit outside, dear,' she says. 'It's going to be a lovely day.'

She is right, it is. The air is warm with the promise of sunshine, waiting for its moment to burst through happy white puffs of cloud. Beyond the vegetable plot the garden is postcard pretty, with a winding stepping-stone path that leads down the sloping lawn to the bottom between odd but perfect beds of flowers and plants, as artfully placed as impressionist brushstrokes. This place has allowed a creativity to bloom in my mother I never knew was there. But I realize now it was always there; I just never gave it any due, dismissing the unacclaimed art of the women of her generation as nothing of value. And now that I see her properly, I am amazed by her skills — able to paint with flowers, conjure food from the earth, create feasts out of leftovers, clothes out of threads, art out of scraps.

I watch her as she bustles to and fro bringing pots of golden syrup and sugar with crocheted, beaded covers. She has become a no-nonsense older woman, with no make-up and unashamedly straight grey hair in a short, easy-to-manage cut. She has taken to wearing trainers with tracksuit bottoms and fleeces — 'so warm and light to wear, so quick to dry, and no ironing!' It gives her a youthful, energetic look. She seemed older when I was growing up, in her perm and

432

knitted twin-sets. Something, whether it was the move to the sea or retirement or just age itself, seems to have liberated her. She is no longer purse-lipped.

It occurs to me that perhaps it is not having me to deal with that has sanctioned her release.

'I'm sorry about your friend, Elizabeth,' she says as I drop swirling puddles of golden syrup onto my porridge. It is the first time she has spoken of it in the three days I have been here. She seems to have just known that I couldn't speak about it before now. Maybe it's a Mum thing. 'It must be a terrible shock to you all.'

'Not a shock, really. She'd been that way for a long time. There were all the warning signs. Her family did everything they could, of course. But I didn't. I feel it was my fault.'

'Of course it wasn't. There's nothing anyone can do when someone's on that path of self-destruction.' I don't put her right about my own part in Vonnie's downfall. I would like to confess to someone one day, to unburden myself of the terrible guilt, but I know it is a secret I will carry alone to my grave. Apart from Billy. But I don't imagine Billy has been burdened with so much as a moment's thought about it for years and years.

'I assume she was an addict?' Mum goes on. She says it in a matter-of-fact, non-judgemental way. I nod. It would be ridiculous, now, to protect Vonnie from my mum, or vice versa. 'It's tragic. Those poor parents have been through a lot over that one.' It is the closest either of us have ever come to addressing the trouble Vonnie

433

and I caused as teenagers.

I watch my spoon as I mix the syrup into the porridge, daring myself to take it further. After admitting your affair to your husband, however true it wasn't, subjects somehow don't seem to be such a hard thing to broach any more. I seem to have become stronger. And the lack of accusation in her tone has stopped my defences rising.

'I know,' I agree. 'I was a bit of a nightmare too, wasn't I?' She is cautious herself, but I know she was hoping I would follow her into this conversation.

'Well. You were a teenager. Teenagers were after my time. They're like that, by all accounts.'

'I'm sorry for it, though. I was horrible to you. I feel really bad about it. I know I said and did some hurtful things.'

'You did, yes,' Mum admits. 'But I should have handled it better. I was too strict and unbending. Too humourless. I shouldn't have taken it all so seriously. Other parents laugh off how their teenagers are. I'm sure that's a much better way to deal with it.' We smile together.

'I was so pleased you'd found a best friend in Kim,' she continues. 'I was always sorry you were an only child. But you came along so late, so unexpectedly. When your father and I got married we were considered old in those days. I'd thought I'd be living out my days a spinster. And then when children didn't come along we thought we couldn't have them.' She lets out a brief laugh. 'We thought we'd missed our chance because we were in our thirties. Imagine! It's a bit different these days. I was settling into middle age when you turned up. You were a bit of a shock, to put it mildly. But such a joy, too. You were the best thing that ever happened to me.'

With a huge effort I manage to gulp down a mouthful of sticky, sweet porridge.

'It was a shame you didn't have a brother or sister. We did try, but by then I suppose it really was too late. I tried my best to make sure you mixed a lot with other children, but you were always quite introverted and shy. I worried that you were a lonely little girl. You seemed happy, though. You created whole fantasy worlds of your own to play in. You had imaginary friends to a much later age than I thought seemed normal. I nearly mentioned it to the doctor.'

'You don't say.' I grin.

'Do you remember?'

'Like it was yesterday.'

'You were so happy together, you and Kim. You were very cute, giggling away, even though I used to tell you off for it. I tried to encourage you to bring Kim round more, but you never seemed to want to. I probably shouldn't have scolded you so much together. I think you preferred being at Kim's. You could probably get away with more there. I always imagined they were quite young, fun parents, weren't they?'

My heart goes out to her, knowing all this and putting on a brave face as she tells me. It must have taken all these years to pass for her to be able to say it this way, with an offhand nonchalance, as though it's all just by the by. I can't deny it.

'I'm sorry, Mum.' She dismisses my apology with a wave of her hand.

'It can't have been easy for you. Struggling on the money I earned and your father gone. Having to take in a lodger.'

'It can't have been easy for you,' I reply, to bat the conversation away from Mr Grundy. This is hard enough. She is not used to empathy and it makes her wrestle with rising emotion.

'Maybe it was tough for both of us.' She goes to the dresser and pours the brewed tea. I like the way she still uses cups and saucers and a pot and keeps it warm with a knitted cosy.

'That's why I was hard on you,' she continues with her back to me, as though she's talking to the china. 'I didn't want you to have to struggle the way I did. You were a bright little thing. I thought if you got a good education you could train and go into a profession. I wanted you to be independent, so you didn't have to rely on getting a husband, or find yourself in the same position as me if you ever . . . lost him.'

It is too personal, and she is unable to turn back round from the dresser with the cups of tea. I am glad, for I am crying again. How did so many tears store away inside me? Will they ever finish spilling?

'I'm sorry I stuffed up,' I sniff, and she snaps herself together and brings the tea.

'Oh, come now,' she says, handing me some tissues from her pocket. 'You didn't *stuff up* forever. You've done rather well for yourself in the end, haven't you?'

I can't answer. I let her question drift into the

436

sky like a lost balloon.

It seems such an old-fashioned, Jane Austen sort of notion, that marrying a successful man is doing well for yourself. Do we still expect a man to provide us with our lives? How incredible that it could apply, in this day and age. My mother is proud, if a little shocked, that I managed to *marry well*, in spite of the kind of girl I turned out to be. Maybe my wedding was when she relaxed. She didn't have to worry about me any more.

I hide behind my teacup while I think about what she has said. Toby seems to have handled my neurotic flight as though it was all part of the service. He hasn't told me he doesn't want me any more, that it's over. But what would I have, if he did? However hard my mother tried to build a life for me that was different from hers, and however fast and far I myself ran from it, have I actually ended up in the same vulnerable position as her? With nothing to show for myself? Nothing really my own? I feel as though I have let her down, as well as myself, though I don't say it. It makes her happy to think I am still hanging on to the happy ending that she lost.

I don't know yet if my idea of a happy ending is the same as hers. I don't know what's going to happen between me and Toby. I feel as though a whirlwind picked me up from where I was, spun me wildly until I shattered, and dropped me down again in another place entirely, surrounded by all my broken bits. What can I make out of them now?

I think back over my last chat with Toby. He

had a proposition for me. He asked if I would take the studio off his hands completely, whatever happens between us. He is impressed with what I've done there, with Ady, he said. There is a role for me, if I want it, one that I love and am good at. It would be my livelihood, its success down to me. It is a scary thought. But as I think about it this morning I feel a spark inside, and I recognize it as excitement.

We'd be off to a good start. Toby's company has agreed on 'Beat Girl' as Eye Candy's second single release. Tentatively, Toby made me the offer he'd worked out for my points on the record. It sounded fair to me. I will OK it with the original Beat Girlers. Kim and Ruby could have another outing as the Bra Section — put down blasts of their gritty horns on the track. It is touch and go whether Eye Candy will break or not, but if the track makes any money I'll divide my share with the other Loose girls. There is a pleasing synchronicity about it, even though it is not quite being the guitarist in Vonnie's band.

But nothing could ever be as good as that.

'Another thing,' Toby added, in a sweet, by-the-way voice. There may also be a new signing coming the studio's way. A young singer-songwriter that the company is investing in some free studio time for. Toby thinks he could benefit from top-of-the-range micro-phones and a real string section. There is some resistance from the artist, however. He is insistent he wants to accompany himself solely with acoustic guitar and is not convinced a big company is the right one for him. Toby has told him he picked this studio in particular for the producers who are sympathetic to his musical ideals and won't smooth down his raw edge with glossy production. The artist is refusing to sign a deal until he is satisfied that the record company will give him complete artistic control.

'Good for him,' I said, and Toby and I shared a know-each-other chuckle.

'I said someone from the studio would call him to book his time,' he added. 'If that's all right with you, of course. It's entirely up to you, whatever you want to do . . . ' He waited for me to respond. I knew what he was saying.

He trusted me enough to work with Jesse.

All I could say was, 'Thank you.'

'There's no rush, anyway,' Toby carried on lightly, as if it was nothing. 'He's um . . . in the middle of moving at the moment.'

'Oh, right,' I said coolly, while my heart rate rose a few beats per minute. I waited, while Toby decided whether to say the thing he next said.

'Funnily enough he's . . . just moving into a flat in Kentish Town.'

I couldn't speak. I didn't know what it meant, but it seemed to mean something. Maybe I would work it out one day, but not now. It was too much. Toby talked on, kindly, about this and that. He really was being incredibly accepting of everything, of me. It felt quietly wondrous, somehow, that he still had faith in me and I could see all these good things in him again. Whatever happened, we would always be friends. After a while he swore he'd never ever sign another boy or girl band and we managed to laugh together. Even he hasn't failed to notice that real musicians are the thing again. There's hope for us all.

Toby said Ady and I could add songwriting to the recording/producing/engineering services we offer. And if I wanted to I could give myself a poncey title, make myself *Management* or call myself a *Creative*. It is a dream job, for a grown woman. It is me now, not my mother, who has the thankless task of trying to control the teenager in me, fantasizing wildly about running off to Nashville with nothing but a guitar on my back, determined to make it all on my own. Surely that would make a better ending? I guess it would if my life were a movie and I'd stayed nineteen forever. But here I am, having to say goodbye to my youth. Sometimes it feels like the worst goodbye of all. But maybe not the end of the world, even if it seemed like it for a while.

I realize I'm going to survive my fall back to reality. It is a bumpy landing rather than a terrible crash and I can't ask for more than that, considering.

★ ★ ★

Mum begins to clear away the breakfast things. Bless her. I suddenly feel sorry I haven't given her any grandchildren. She would have loved that. But I always felt there was something else I was meant to do with my life, even if I never knew quite what. It seems silly I suppose. But even so.

I still feel it.

It always irritated me when she used to hint gently about children. I used to wonder what had ever been so good, for her, about having a child. I'd certainly hated being one. I thought I had caused her nothing but misery, but I guess I had forgotten how much she laughed before my dad was gone.

For the first time I realize that maybe it wasn't me that made her sad after all. And now the difficult years are over and we are ageing, I see that it is a nice thing for a woman to have a daughter. And a mother. I see we are coming close to becoming close.

Mum begins to hum as she takes the dishes back through to the kitchen. I can't help but smile.

'That's better!' Mum says. 'You see?! Nana always used to say when one door closes another one opens. You just have to trust it. Things have a habit of turning out how they're meant to in the end.'

I suddenly see that it's not all over, the way I felt it was. It's not too late for a lot of things. Endings seem almost impossible to bear, but without them there would be no beginnings. Choices are appearing around me like new buds. I feel my spirits lift. A soft, clean breeze blows in from the sea and stirs my hair. I lean back in my chair and turn my face towards the new day. The sun breaks through the clouds and shines down on me, warming me through to my bones like salvation.

Epilogue

We hold a wake for Vonnie at mine and Toby's. It's the least I can do. One thing Toby and I do know how to do together is throw a party.

I put a lot of thought into it. I get Kim and Paolo to bring round Vonnie's possessions to decorate the sitting room. I stand her bass guitar and amp-speaker combo centre-stage in front of the fireplace. I plaster the walls with pictures of her and all her influences — the rock and film stars that she loved, her album covers — and all the Loose flyers and posters I can find. Kim has salvaged a bag of her clothes after all, including the leather jacket, which she has painstakingly washed and stitched back together. I hang them on mannequins and coat hangers and pose them around the room.

I burn some MP3s off her favourite scratched-up old records to play. I sort through the cassettes of our demos and live sets to play too, even the one the sound man did for us from the desk at the last gig we ever played. I've never been able to bring myself to hear it, always preferring to imagine it might not have been as bad as I thought it was. Now though, it feels right to play it, so that Vonnie gets sent off all drunken, fucked-up guns blazing.

I find a great full-length photo of her and get it blown to life size, cutting it out and sticking it on a cardboard stand, like the advertising boards you get of movie stars. She is standing defiantly in a tight red dress with her hand on her hip, pouting and sucking her cheeks in and doing a V sign to the camera. It looks as though she's saying to us all, 'So long, suckers.'

My finishing touches are dozens of red and black balloons tied with lace, leopard-print material draped over everything, and as many of my friends' stiletto shoes as I can get hold of to hang all the way around the picture rail in her honour.

Between the funeral and everybody arriving back at ours I worry I have done the wrong thing. The funeral is such a grim, depressing affair I think perhaps the grieving will be offended by the kitsch shrine I have built. But Toby squeezes my hand to reassure me.

'Come on — you know Vonnie would've loved this!' He's right. I race upstairs to change and do my hair. It is amazing how deftly I can still back-comb my roots into a Sixties bouffant, even all these years since I last did. I paint my eyelids with the thick black lines we couldn't be seen without and slip into the old white dress we found at Vonnie's, which I've soaked and scrubbed and let out as far as it would go, with a reinforced panel to hold it together down the back and a big bow to cover it up. I don't know if, even with the recent weight loss, I'm still much bigger than I was then, or if I wore things this tight in those days. However did I get around?

I wiggle downstairs to be ready to greet the carloads when they arrive. It all comes back to me, the way I felt, squeezed into this pastiche of

443

a woman. I do still feel sexy, but now I feel faintly ridiculous too. I can't remember who I was when I took it off.

Toby does a double take when he sees me. He is wearing shot suit trousers with a Ben Sherman polo shirt. It is as though we've been beamed into the shells of our past, although Toby's older frame has required a bigger waist and collar size. Inside the clothes everything boyish about him has gone. The skinny lightness of his body that gave him a quick, boy-about-town air has matured into a solid, firmly planted physique that seems to say, *Hey, I don't need to run around any more.* He has widened out around his face and neck, gone grey at the temples and grown wiry eyebrows. He has become an out-and-out man. As he looks at me his eyes quickly fill with tears. He has to look away and wait a few moments before he can say, 'You haven't changed a bit since I met you.'

It is one of the best compliments you can pay a woman, but along with being naturally flattered it makes me feel sad. Is that the best I can be — as close a resemblance as possible to myself at the height of my youth, after all these years of living?

The mourners begin to file through the front door. The only warning people have had on their invitations is that this is a party to celebrate Vonnie's life rather than a grieving for her death, and that everyone should wear something retro. As black coats and jackets and shoes come off at the door, wild splashes of colour are revealed on Fifties print shirts and Sixties dresses and handbags.

There isn't anybody who doesn't exclaim with delight and relief at the Vonnie room, even Patti and Jeff, although it makes them cry again through their smiles. I have been shocked to see them old and grey. In my head they have stayed perpetually young, trendy parents. Especially since the Seventies came back round again. I imagined Jeff still in his long sideburns and flared jeans and Patti in a kaftan.

Of course, they are in modern, sombre funeral dress with narrow lines and small lapels. They excuse themselves, however, to the downstairs loo, and come back out transformed into punk rockers. Patti has drawn an Anarchy sign on Jeff's forehead with her eye pencil and put luminous green spray through the remaining strands of his hair. He has on a ripped black shirt held together with safety pins and has pinned bondage straps to his suit trousers. Patti has spiked her hair up and put on dark lipstick and a choker. She wears a dayglo pink leopardskin T-shirt — actually one of Vonnie's first punk buys — with matching fluorescent socks under spiky shoes, a leather miniskirt and fishnets, showing the model's legs that Vonnie and Kim were so lucky to inherit.

Kim's daughter Franklin is especially thrilled at the room.

'You had the coolest auntie ever,' I say to her and she agrees as she peers through her wraparound shades and giggles at the cut-out of Vonnie signalling everyone to fuck off. Franklin is so cute, dressed like a Rude Girl in flat white shoes, black tights, white miniskirt, black jumper and white bangles, her curly hair scraped back and hidden under a pork-pie hat.

It is weird to see the band again, and wonderful, now that the subdued formality of the funeral is over. Kim has done a brilliant job of tracking people down. Through some old mutual friends, she found Ruby, who has come down from Watford on the back of her partner's motorbike. She has grown chubby over the years, but there are still vestiges of her rocking days about her in the dyed black fringe and ponytail and red lipstick that she says are not just done today for the party. In the hallway she slips into scarlet stilettos and undoes her mac to reveal a black satin bell skirt covered in poppies and a red Playtex corset with conical breasts that stick out like torpedoes.

Her bloke is *something retro* personified — an old Ted, with his hair greased back and faded indigo tattoos up his arms of music notes and sex kittens with *Man's Ruin* written beneath. Under his suit jacket he is wearing an electric-blue shirt covered in brightly coloured dice, playing cards and Las Vegas casino logos.

Nick has come up on the train from Brighton with her girlfriend Jo, whom she met when she started working for a women's building cooperative. They are a plumber and carpenter respectively, and are both dressed like James Dean.

There are other blasts from the past. Fliss, who went into graphic design and works for a swanky advertising agency, in a yellow Chanel suit, severe-square cut bob and blackrimmed designer specs. Stan, now a maintenance

446

engineer for London Transport, comes in boots and braces and a Prince Buster T-shirt. He is a natural skinhead now. Only Ava couldn't be found — an ex-boyfriend of hers thought she was living in Paris. And Billy.

But we didn't try to find Billy.

★ ★ ★

Toby tends the bar in the kitchen, making lethal cocktails. Everyone is immediately, gratefully, in a celebratory mood. I put the first compilation on. I've ordered it chronologically, starting at the beginning with the jazz tracks she learnt to dance to and the glam rock and disco singles she passed on to me as she grew out of her early years. My MP3s trace her onward journey through teenage rebellion via the Rolling Stones, the New York Dolls, and punk rock.

It turns out to be a great party. The cocktails get everybody quickly and wildly drunk. The music plays like the soundtrack to our lives, and gets everybody cheering and laughing, and dancing. Each song fills one or other of us with happy nostalgia and leads to the telling of a funny *Remember when . . . ?* Vonnie tale. The evening runs as though we're at the glitzy premiere of her infamous life story. Somehow it feels like a triumph for Vonnie.

The music crescendos up to 'Beat Girl', which stirs the band to gather round the blow-up of Vonnie and pose along with air instruments for the amusement of the other guests.

'We want Loose! We want Loose!' Fliss starts

447

up the chant as though she's our number one fan. It looks hilarious on someone so grown-up. In the end everyone is around us in a circle shouting and stomping for Loose. So I put on the recording of our last gig and we throw our arms around each other to listen. I decide the worse we are the better.

Toby cracks open the champagne.

'To our finest hour!' I toast as the noise of the cheering crowd on the tape cuts in. The crowd sounds huge and we look at each other, reliving the nerves.

'Christ! You must've been fucking terrified!' says Ruby.

'Me? Nah,' I joke and we fall against each other snorting champagne bubbles and laughter.

When the band starts up, we look at each other, impressed. We sound like a real band, not a bunch of girls. The sound we make is real, raw and energetic, a big melodious thrash. I'm amazed at how well we play. My guitaring is swift and dexterous, even though I was playing mostly rhythm. In spite of my nerves I'm brave enough to go for some cool licks. I cringe in anticipation of my puny voice coming in, but when it does, I don't recognize it. It's not God-awful, it's not great, but it sounds like a singer in a band at a live gig.

'You were so great!' Patti slurs fondly at us over her shoulder, while Jeff swings her to and fro in the jive they still remember. 'That's my girls!'

It does get worse. In the here and now we hang onto each other, bracing ourselves for the bit where it all starts to go wrong. Vonnie's bass booms out completely the wrong notes and my singing falters, but then it's over and we get it together again. We shriek with laughter now, and our friends in the room give us a heartfelt cheer. While I laugh I also hear the deep inner voice that speaks to you when you're at your drunkest say, 'There it was. *Just a moment, Beth. Not a solid thing to shape your life around forever the way you did. A fleeting moment that passed. Let it go.*'

The set does descend into a frantic mess towards the end and Vonnie's bass is all over the place and I am shouting not singing, but it is, after all, just a gig. I feel comforted now, strangely happy, when I think that it was me and Vonnie together that fucked it up. It feels right.

Our set closes and I make another toast while the sound of the crowd cheering us off stage finally fades.

'To the greatest rock and roll star that never was,' I say, turning to the cardboard statue. 'To Vonnie.'

We all raise our glasses to Vonnie and her two-finger salute.

I put on my last compilation, the collection of songs I've dedicated to Vonnie's spirit. It starts with 'Rebel Rebel', the first track I ever saw her dancing to in her teenage room, when Kim and I were just a couple of kids peering in at her from the outside. There are plenty of songs written that apply to Vonnie. Songs about women like her, desirable and untameable for mere mortal boys, and songs about freedom and life and the true heart of rock and roll. I've put the raucous ones on first: 'Wild Thing' and 'The Girl Can't Help It' and 'Wild Child', and the Sex Pistols version of 'Something Else'.

Gradually the compilation chills to wind the party down, with my favourite singer-songwriters playing their tributes to free-spirited muses with Vonnie souls.

My last dedication is a song I swore Jesse Porter wrote, 'North Star'. I thought I had gone round to his house and he'd played it to me, and I'd found some piano for it and a harmony that he made me sing. I was sure he'd told me it was what Bob Dylan called Johnny Cash. I don't know where I got that from. Maybe I dreamt it, or saw it on TV.

I still can't believe I wrote the song myself. Here at Toby's baby grand, during the limbo between Vonnie's overdose and her death, when I was too freaked out to do much of anything but clean the house and play piano and disappear into my own world. Until Toby forced me to the studio, the thing that began to unravel me and break me free of the knots, both.

I recorded it there late the other night, just me at the piano singing quietly close to the mic, the way Jesse would. Although I couldn't quite play in front of Ady, I did at least play the recording to him the next day. He showed me how to get the best out of the vocals with effects and compression. It sounded amazing when he was through with it — to me, anyway.

'It's lovely,' Ady said. 'I didn't know you wrote songs. Keep 'em coming. You never know when we'll get a new artist in here who could do with some good material.'

As it plays now, the resonance of the piano glowing in the embers of the party, I no longer fear people hearing me. Maybe I am just too drunk to. It gets to the chorus line before Kim even realizes it is my voice.

There is a ripple of quiet appreciation from the few guests still here. I am glad I put it on the playlist. It is, after all, a song for a muse. Something in the lyric fits for Vonnie. *Like the North Star, I'll steer my boat by you.* It's how it always was. I could never have got where I was going without her, whether that's a good thing or a bad thing. Right now, it feels like a good thing. She taught me all about being brave and strong and free, an individual. Though I learnt the lesson all wrong of course, and just tried to be her.

I'll be able to laugh at myself one day, for that, when it stops hurting so much and I finally get on with my own life. I bet Vonnie's laughing already. I swear I can almost hear her, making her usual dramatic exit, cackling as she leaves the last of us behind in the aftermath, the place totally trashed. It is a fitting end. She was never one to hang around once the party was over.

Now that she is released from the failings of her mind and body, the essence of her soul is what remains, forever shining in the air around us.

I zone everything else out while the song plays. It is a private moment, like a prayer. It is from me to her. It is my goodbye to Vonnie.

We do hope that you have enjoyed reading this large print book.

Did you know that all of our titles are available for purchase?

We publish a wide range of high quality large print books including:
Romances, Mysteries, Classics
General Fiction
Non Fiction and Westerns

Special interest titles available in large print are:
The Little Oxford Dictionary
Music Book
Song Book
Hymn Book
Service Book

Also available from us courtesy of Oxford University Press:
Young Readers' Dictionary
(large print edition)
Young Readers' Thesaurus
(large print edition)

For further information or a free brochure, please contact us at:
Ulverscroft Large Print Books Ltd.,
The Green, Bradgate Road, Anstey,
Leicester, LE7 7FU, England.
Tel: (00 44) 0116 236 4325
Fax: (00 44) 0116 234 0205

Other titles published by
The House of Ulverscroft:

BLACKMOOR

Edward Hogan

Bird-watching teenager Vincent Cartwright lives out a bullied, awkward existence not far from the site of Blackmoor, a mysterious Derbyshire village that no longer exists. His mother Beth had been half-blind and unknowable, and her life and death in that same village has always been a dark family secret. However, as Vincent comes of age he begins to search for the truth. His search uncovers the events that happened in Blackmoor — the destruction of an industry, the dissolution of a community, and Beth's persecution at the hands of superstitious locals. He discovers the story of a young woman whose face didn't fit, and a past that refuses to go away . . .

WILDCAT MOON

Babs Horton

The Skallies was a row of tumbledown houses built on the windlashed coast. Ten-year-old Archie Grimble, with his crippled leg and one good eye, lived a miserable existence there. Then a chance encounter with an unhappy little girl and the discovery of a locked diary set him on a mission to unravel the mystery of a boy who drowned off Skilly Point in August, 1900. But Archie's investigation was to have unexpected consequences. A shocking murder and an unexplained abduction were to shatter his world forever. Only years later, on his return to the ruined Skallies, does Archie stumble on the answer to a puzzle that has haunted him since childhood — and the extraordinary truth about the fate of Thomas Greswode is at last revealed.

BEFORE I KNEW HIM

Anna Ralph

Leo Fisch is a young man with a brilliant future ahead of him. Bright and sociable, he's on the verge of moving in with his beautiful girlfriend Kathryn. Outwardly he seems happy. Then, when a sinister discovery is made in a forest near Leo's hometown, a figure from childhood re-enters his life. David Caldwell is tough and aggressive; the opposite of the company Leo now keeps. Unlikely friends, they are bound by a shared summer — and a shared secret — they'd promised to forget. As past and present begin to close in, Leo's comfortable life starts to unravel. Their terrible truth emerges and Leo must confront the awkward, fragile boy he once was, and the events of that summer which threaten to destroy them both . . .

THE STANDING POOL

Adam Thorpe

Two Cambridge academics, the historians Nick and Sarah Mallinson, take a sabbatical with their three lively girls in a remote Languedoc farmhouse. But the farmhouse has its own histories, and the illusion of Eden begins to retreat. The couple feel the vulnerability of being among strangers, and being strangers themselves — even in their own place, and even to their own children. Sarah frets about the danger of the swimming pool and the presence of wild boar, while the local hunters' guns concern Nick. Meanwhile Jean-Luc, the gardener, lives with his invalid mother in the village, and her private world involves hammering nails into a doll, collecting arcane rubbish, and spying on Sarah's naked dips in the pool. What should the Mallinsons make of him?